DEAD SOUND

ANISE EDEN

TANGLED TREE PUBLISHING

DEAD SOUND

ANISE EDEN

TANGLED TREE PUBLISHING

For information, contact the publisher, Tangled Tree Publishing.

www.tangledtreepublishing.com

Editing: Hot Tree Editing

Cover Designer: BookSmith Design

E-book ISBN: 978-1-922359-67-4

Paperback ISBN: 978-1-922359-68-1

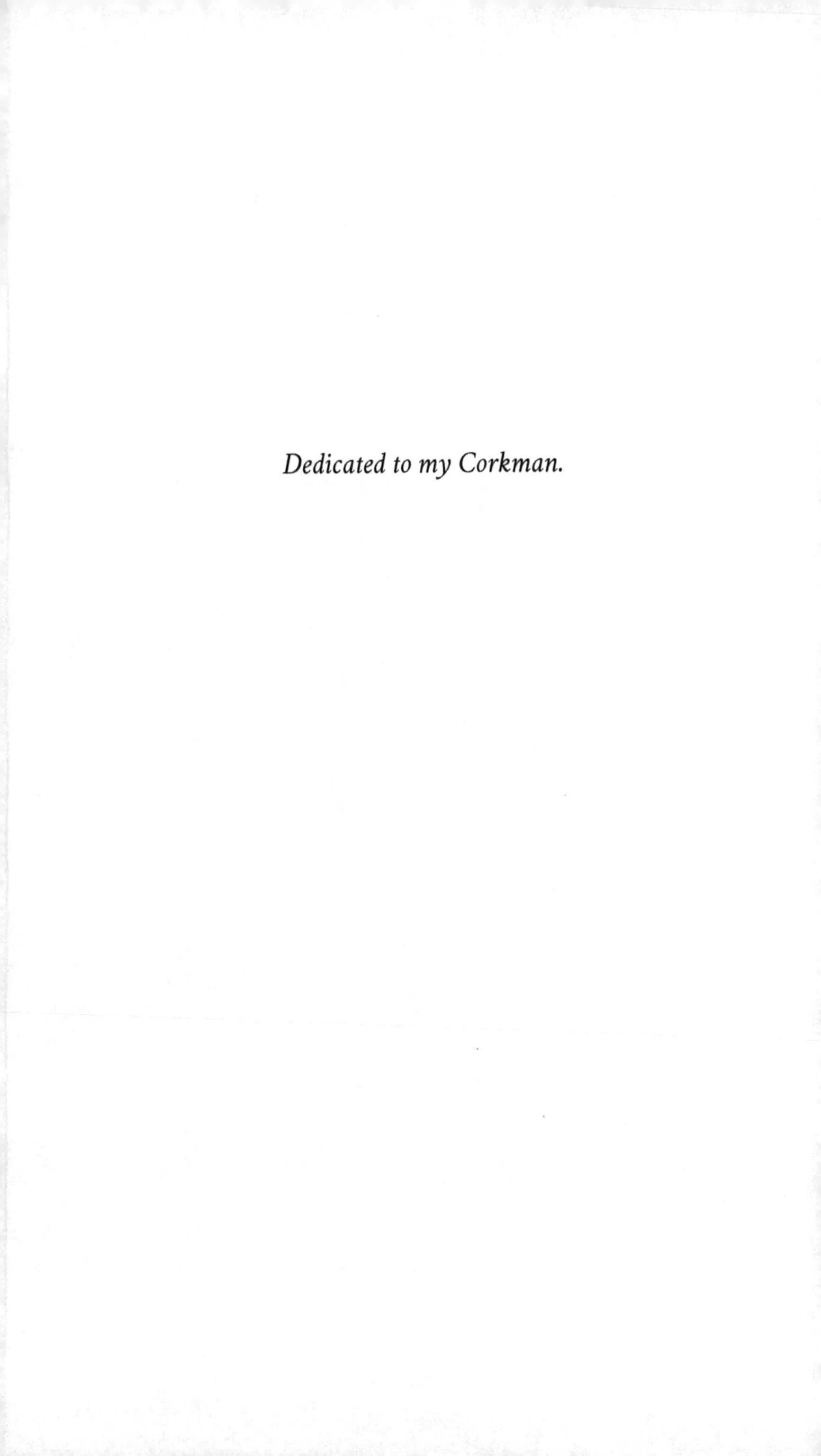

Dedicated to my Corkman.

1

NEVE

You knew this was going to be hard, I reminded myself as I stood outside the main entrance of Capitol Hill General. *Remember what you practiced. In through the nose, out through the mouth.* I took a few slow, deep breaths as the other employees bustled into the hospital. They formed a mélange of scrubs, suits, and everything in between—all people who helped other people.

Unlike me. Shame stung me like a jellyfish brushing past, a reminder of how badly I needed to get back to work and out of my head. Patting my palms dry on my peacoat, I clutched the cross-body strap of my messenger bag and forced my feet to move, one in front of the other, through the doors and into the cavernous, pristine lobby.

"Can I help you?" The security guard at the reception desk appeared pleasant but harried. Her face was new to me. I guessed a few things had changed in a month.

"Yes, hi," I said, presenting my ID card. "Neve Keane. I'm returning to work. I was told to check in here first."

"Coming back on Labor Day? That's dedication." She tapped away on her keyboard, then looked up and smiled. "You're good to go."

"Thanks." I didn't have the heart to tell her it had nothing to do with dedication. Occupational Health said I should come back on the holiday because it was likely to be a slow day, and I could ease back in. I joined the river of people heading toward the elevator bay.

Once inside the crowded space, my throat tightened as the elevator rose toward the fourth floor. When the doors opened, I pushed my shoulders back, trying to appear more confident than I felt as I walked down the hallway to Unit 4, our general inpatient psychiatry unit. Holding my ID card up to the reader, I heard a soft beep and the click of the metallic lock.

I pushed the door open and stepped into the dayroom. It was an open space, golden with autumn sunlight thanks to an entire wall of safety windows. Off in the distance, the sharp gray tip of the Washington Monument pierced the sky. A cluster of craft tables was set up near the wall. The middle of the room was cleared for exercise classes, and on the far side, a collection of armchairs and couches surrounded a large-screen TV recessed into the wall. I was greeted by the hum of fluorescent lights and the sharp scent of industrial-strength cleaning products. A few nurses were at their station, preparing morning meds. Overall, a typical morning at Capitol Hill General. The familiarity was comforting, and my anxiety began to ebb.

I did notice that more people than usual seemed to be out and about. It wasn't visiting hours yet, so I knew they must all be patients.

Maybe yoga class just ended, I thought, forcing myself to make eye contact, nod, and smile. But as I made my way across the room, some of the patients began to encircle me.

Don't be paranoid. None of their faces looked familiar, which meant they were new there and probably just curious about a stranger on the unit. I kept smiling and walked a little faster. But by the time I reached the center of the dayroom, the ring around me had tightened. I spun around and watched, bewildered, as more circles of patients formed behind the first, all facing me.

I was sure I'd fallen into some kind of horror movie dream sequence when the whole group suddenly sank to their knees, then prostrated themselves on the ground like a phalanx of worshippers.

What the hell? Slowly, I turned around, my ears filled with the *ba-boom, ba-boom* of blood pounding through my veins. *Is there something about my appearance?* But a quick scan reassured me that there weren't any religious symbols or awe-inspiring objects anywhere on my person.

This can't really be happening... can it? Was I imagining things, maybe having some sort of panic-induced hallucination?

Half of my brain felt like it was swimming in molasses, too slow-motion to process the scene. The other half was speared by white-hot terror. I was alone and surrounded. Anything could happen, as I knew all too well.

The knife scars on my abdomen began to tingle and burn. I slid my hands down to cover them, even though I knew I wouldn't have a hope of protecting myself if the crowd decided to attack. I tried to call out for help, but my mouth had gone dry.

Then the patients began to chant—a murmur at first, then more of a moan. It sounded like they were repeating something over and over, but I couldn't quite make it out. Well, I had no intention of sticking around to decipher what they were saying. I forced myself to swallow.

"Somebody!" I squawked.

Fortunately, the nurses had noticed what was happening and were already in motion. That proved I wasn't hallucinating after all—a confirmation that was both reassuring and alarming. Even as fear sent waves of heat through my body, some deeper part of me sensed that these patients didn't mean me any harm. But I'd gotten stabbed because my instincts had failed me, and I wasn't about to trust them again anytime soon.

"Hang on, Neve. Security's on their way!" Ayesha, one of the senior nurse managers, shouted as more staff came to help.

I almost collapsed with relief when I saw Mike's sizable frame barreling toward me. He hitched up the legs of his scrubs and tiptoed his way through the clot of people, miraculously avoiding stepping on anyone. As he closed in on me, he patted his shoulder. "I'll carry you out!"

I nodded, even though I had never been carried anywhere in my adult life.

Mike took one final step toward me and, in a smooth motion, leaned down and hoisted me over his shoulder. As my torso flipped upside down, my hair fell over my face like a long brown curtain. Desperate to see what was happening, I half lifted my head, gripping Mike's shirt with one hand and pushing the hair away from my eyes with the other.

He spun around and gingerly danced his way back through the throng. Visibly dismayed, the patients rose to follow. But Ayesha had already opened the partition between the dayroom and the staff wing, clearing the way for Mike to carry me through.

As the partition closed behind us, Mike carefully lowered me to the ground. Holding me by the shoulders, he looked me over. "Are you okay?"

I had no idea what "okay" meant in that context, so

I decided to go with "uninjured." "Yeah, I think so. My God, thank you." Mike looked pretty shaken himself. We were always prepared for the unexpected, but surprises on our unit usually fell into particular categories. What we'd just witnessed was way outside the norm. "How about you? Are you okay?"

Before he could answer, a group of security guards rushed down the hall toward us, barking, "Stand back!" We plastered ourselves against the wall. As the guards flowed into the dayroom, I could hear more chanting, volume rising.

We're safe, I reassured myself, but my body didn't believe it yet. Unable to get enough air into my lungs, I gasped like a fish yanked from the water.

Mike frowned down at me. "I'm good. You don't *look* okay, though. Oh, man!" His eyes widened as he glanced down at my abdomen. "I didn't hurt you, did I?"

"No," I managed. "I'm totally healed up."

Of course Mike knew about the stabbing. Everyone on Unit 4 knew. It wasn't the kind of thing that escaped one's attention—a therapist rushed to the emergency room on a gurney, her patient sedated and put in restraints.

Now that I was back at work, though, I could not fall apart. Not in front of a coworker, not while I was trying to demonstrate how fully recovered I was. To distract myself and keep the panic at bay, I focused on Mike. I reached up and patted his hands, which still held my shoulders. "I think I can stand on my own now, thanks. I feel bad, though, Mike. You always seem to get stuck handling these kinds of situations."

"My wife calls it 'the curse of the male nurse.'" He smiled as he released me, watching to be sure I was steady on my feet. "I don't mind, really. Gave me a chance to use some of my old college football moves."

I appreciated that Mike was trying to make me feel better, but I couldn't bring myself to smile back—not when shouts still penetrated the partition. We stepped over and peered through the security windows. The guards and staff were struggling to manage the situation as the patients held their hands aloft and continued to chant. To my relief, there were no sounds of real distress.

We fell into an awkward silence, and my head began to feel like the sky before a storm—dark, rumbling, and opaque. "Do you have any idea what that *was* in there?"

Mike shrugged. "No, but we're coming off a weird weekend. I mean, weirder than usual. And it wasn't even a full moon. Maybe I should walk you to your office." He pointed at my hands.

I looked down. They were shaking. I grabbed the strap of my bag and squeezed. "Yeah, maybe. Thanks. But hang on a sec." With my pulse no longer deafening me, it was easier to make out what the patients were chanting. "What are they saying?" I whispered, half afraid to hear the answer.

"Something like 'neh-vi-yah?' Ayesha said it's a brand of beauty products."

"Oh. Well, yeah." A shudder tumbled through me. "But it's also my name."

"What is?"

"Neviah. Neviah Keane."

Mike gawked, his hands dropping to his sides. "You're kidding."

"I wish I were."

"Damn. Well, if I'd known that, I would have told someone to warn you."

"Warn me?"

"I should let Rosanna explain. We have to go see her anyway." Mike shot me a sideways grin. "Welcome back, by the way."

"Yeah," I said, rolling my eyes. "Thanks."

We walked through the staff wing to our manager's office. Rosanna wasn't there, but her laptop was, as well as a mug of steaming coffee. She'd be back soon. We sat in the armchairs across from her desk and waited. The office was an organized jumble of objects accumulated over years of work, with multiple layers of folders, notebooks, and assorted papers covering every flat surface. In one corner of the room, a group of flowering plants flourished under a grow light.

Rosanna burst through the door, then started when she saw us. "*There* you are!" With her striking brown eyes, crisp black bob, and red cat's-eye glasses, she was hard to miss. Although she was five feet tall and petite, she had an imposing presence. While she could usually be found bustling around the unit with an air of relaxed efficiency, at that moment, she appeared as taut as a bowstring. "Are you both okay?"

I managed a nod.

"Neve says she is," Mike said. "I'm fine."

"Thank goodness. What happened out there?"

"Just the same thing that's been happening all weekend," Mike said, "but with a twist."

"A twist? Do I want to know?"

He hooked his thumb in my direction. "Meet Neviah."

Rosanna gaped. "The hand lotion?"

"The one and only," Mike replied.

"It's my given name," I muttered.

"What? Neve is short for… Neviah? How did I not know this?" Rosanna perched on the love seat to get a closer look at me, her expression tight with worry. "Are you sure you're okay?"

"I'm fine. Mike rescued me before anything could happen. Not that I think anything would have happened, I just…." Unsure how to finish that sentence, I shrugged.

"Yeah, it didn't look like they wanted to—" Mike stopped and cleared his throat. "I mean, it seemed more like they were worshipping her or something." He gave Rosanna a quick play-by-play.

"Good Lord," Rosanna said. "Neve, don't move. I'm

getting you some water. Mike, Ayesha might need you...."

"On my way. Glad you're okay, Neve."

"Thanks again, Mike," I called as they took off in different directions.

Once I was alone, the room began to spin. I felt like I'd swallowed a muscle relaxant and an antihistamine with a shot of tequila. The spinning slowed when Rosanna came back and pressed a cool glass into my hand. I drank deeply. "Thanks."

She squeezed my shoulder. "You're positive you're okay?"

I just nodded again, fearful that if I answered that question, my emotions would leak out.

"You look pale."

"I know you haven't seen me in a while, but I always look pale."

"I was being polite. You look like death warmed over. Are you sure you were medically cleared?"

I forced a laugh. My trauma surgeon, Dr. Mohinder, had approved my return to work, but only marginally. Physically, I was okay, but she worried about my recurring panic attacks. I'd convinced her that sitting at home was only making things worse. "You're itching to take my vitals, I can tell. Do you ever stop being a nurse?"

"Please, you know the answer to that." She smiled, but only for a second. "I'm so sorry you had to deal with all of that out there. What a 'welcome back.'"

"It's hardly your fault."

"I'm not so sure. I should have told you to stay home for another day or two at least."

"Why? What's going on out there?"

"We're still figuring it out." Rosanna slid her fingers under her glasses and rubbed her eyes. "Saturday morning, the group of people you encountered in the dayroom staged a sit-in in the emergency room, demanding admission to Unit 4. They all reported having the same delusion—apocalyptic stuff. At first, the ER docs thought maybe they'd all done drugs at the same rave or were members of a cult. But their tox screens were negative, and they claimed they'd never met each other before—adults, all different ages and backgrounds. A handful have mental health histories, but no inpatient stays."

I had seen a lot of strange things over the years, but I'd never even *heard* of anything like that happening. "Why here? Why Unit 4?"

"Apparently it's part of their shared delusion. They wanted to come to our unit and speak to someone named Neviah—you, evidently." She cocked an eyebrow at me. "As you can imagine, that part of the delusion seemed a lot more bizarre when we thought they were talking about a brand of moisturizer."

"I guess so." My brain whirred and smoked, trying to process this information. "It seems like a big group, though. How many are there?"

"Twenty-eight in total—so yes, they're taking up

almost the entire unit. We thought it best to keep them isolated from the other patients until we figure out what we're dealing with. Fortunately, with the school year beginning, the adolescent unit all but cleared out on Friday, so we were able to move our regular patients down there. It's just as well, since our unit seems to be transforming into some sort of commune-slash-conference center."

"What do you mean?"

Rosanna closed her eyes, nodding. "Not in a bad way, it's just…. There's been a lot of meditating, and they've been having discussion groups, mainly about spirituality. Not that I'm complaining. The general mood has been positive, and overall, things were pretty peaceful until you rolled in."

Avoiding her pointed gaze, I flicked an invisible piece of lint off my sleeve.

"At any rate," she continued, "they're all here voluntarily, so they can leave anytime they like, but so far, they've chosen to stay. We're certainly eager to keep them here until we figure out what's at the root of their shared delusion."

"What's it about, exactly?"

"The basic gist is they believe—" She rubbed her eyes. "—Dr. Rodwell is the incarnation of evil."

"What?" I guffawed. "Oh come on. You're sure this isn't some kind of prank?"

"No prank. And yes, I know how it sounds. Not

only that, but they believe he's going to usher in the apocalypse."

"Dr. *Rodwell*?" Our head of psychiatry was about the most harmless, non-evil person I could imagine. Mild-mannered, polite, kind…. He was a vegan, for God's sake. "Has he treated any of these people before? I mean, do they have any connection with him, some reason to be angry, hold a grudge?"

"None we can find. The whole thing is unprecedented," she said with the borderline equanimity of someone who dealt with strange situations on a regular basis. "They're not exhibiting any other psychiatric symptoms, so we don't have any formal diagnoses yet. No new meds have been ordered, just whatever they were taking when they got here. They've just persistently been requesting to speak to Neviah—you, I mean—because you are, and I quote, 'a weapon of righteousness sent by God' to stop Dr. Rodwell."

"A *what*?" That made even less sense, by my reckoning. After all, I was agnostic at best. I wrapped my arms around myself. "Why would they think the 'Neviah' they're looking for is me? I mean, I know it's not a common name, but DC is a big city, and I've always gone by Neve. How did they even recognize me when I walked in?"

"No idea. Wish I did. Don't worry, though. We'll figure this out. We always do, don't we? And at least since they think you're some sort of world savior and want your help." Rosanna shifted uncomfortably. "What I mean is I doubt they're a safety concern."

That was good to hear, and not just for the obvious reason. When I was standing in the middle of those patients, my gut had told me I was safe, and according to both Mike and Rosanna, I most likely had been. It was nice to know my instincts could still get it right sometimes.

In a decisive tone, she added, "Still, I'm not taking any chances."

I didn't like the sound of that. "Meaning what?"

"Meaning, after what happened out there, you're going to go home and stay there until we've sorted this out. Paid leave, of course."

I groaned inwardly. That was the last thing I needed —more time stuck at home, replaying the stabbing on an endless mental loop and being raked by guilt each time I relived the horror. After all, I was trained to know when clinical situations were becoming dangerous and how to defuse them. But somehow, in my last session, I had missed a red flag, some critical warning sign. Because of my mistake, I had failed my patient and myself.

More paid leave would only mean more of that mental torture, and the situation on the unit might take days to resolve, possibly longer. "Rosanna—"

"Don't 'Rosanna' me." She held her hand up like a stop sign. "If anything were to happen…. Besides, it'll agitate the patients, just knowing you're on the premises."

My pulse pounded as I slid forward to the edge of my chair. "So just tell the patients I've gone home! They'll have no way of knowing otherwise. I can use the staff entrance and stay in the office wing." I cleared my throat to suppress the desperation in my voice. "You have to admit, given the content of these patients' delusions, I'm probably the best person to help you figure out what's going on and what triggered this."

"You act like this is our first rodeo." Rosanna scowled as she stood. "We'll handle the situation. In the meantime, I'm not willing to risk your safety."

"But you said it yourself, they're here voluntarily and can leave anytime. Do you really think I'll be safer out there, living in a city where a bunch of people might be running around having unexplained delusions about me? Rosanna, please!"

I held my breath as she considered. Finally, she said, "All right, look. If it'll make you more likely to accept the inevitable no, I'll run it by Dr. Rodwell."

"You will?" Relief poured through me. "Thank you!"

"Don't thank me," she said wryly. "I'm almost certain he'll agree with me and you'll be going home."

The flap of my messenger bag emitted a loud buzzing noise.

"Go ahead, get it," Rosanna said.

I retrieved my phone. There was a new text from "Dr. Cornelius O'Brien."

Con: Latte? Whole milk?

"Please tell me that's Con and not Stephan." Rosanna knew I always got coffee with Con, our mutual friend and colleague, before work. But she also knew my newly ex-boyfriend, Stephan, had been drunk-texting me for the past six weeks, trying to get me back.

"You can relax."

"Good. Go, have your coffee. Take all the time you need, okay?"

To emphasize how ready I was to get back to work, I said, "I'll be back in time for my shift."

"That's still to be determined." She waved me out the door.

As I walked down the hall, I texted Con back.

Neve: Perfect. Thank you. I'll be there in two.

I couldn't wait to hang out with Con again at our usual haunt. It would make a nice change from his visits to my apartment after I was released from the hospital. He'd spent most of his time at my place trying to conceal how worried he was. Now, thankfully, we could get back to normal.

Normal for us, anyway. He was going to fall right off his chair when I told him about my morning.

That thought kept me smiling as I headed over to the hospital's best-kept secret: The Bean Me Café.

2

NEVE

"Jaysus!" Con's Irish brogue added punch to the exclamation. "You sure you're all right?"

"Of course I'm sure!" I was grateful for the comforting scent of coffee as we sat at our usual table, one of three set up near the beverage cart. "I'm totally fine."

Con appeared skeptical, however. He frowned as he looked me up and down, taking in every detail with doctorly precision. "And I have Mike to thank for keeping you in one piece?"

"We all agreed I was never in any real danger," I said for both our benefits. "But yes, Mike got me out of there in seconds flat. It was pretty impressive."

"Fair dues." Con's chair groaned beneath him as he leaned back. His broad, heavily muscled shoulders—a legacy of the years he'd spent on his university rugby team—were almost too much for the bijou furniture at the Bean Me to handle. Still, it was the one place in the hospital where we could get coffee in relative privacy, a staff-only space that was almost always empty. "Next time you see him, tell him I owe him a drink."

As we both paused to sip our coffees, the usual glow of attraction I felt whenever I was with Con crept in, whispering through my body and warming my heart. I did what I always did: mentally acknowledged it, then shoved it into the box in my brain marked "Repression."

It was the method I had devised to protect our friendship. I couldn't risk making things awkward between us. Con was way too important to me, and he had never shown any romantic interest. Besides, until recently, I had been with Stephan, so it had simply become a habit to push my feelings for Con into the background.

At least I could talk openly with Con about what happened on the unit. To protect patient privacy, I couldn't share details about work with anyone outside our team. Fortunately, Con was an official team member, the consulting endocrinologist to the psychiatry department, helping out with patients with issues like diabetes and thyroid problems.

Unit 4 was where we'd met two years before. Con blew into rounds one morning like a gale-force wind, his vigorous energy filling every corner of the conference room. He had just arrived at Capitol Hill General after completing his residency at a hospital across town. When Dr. Rodwell asked him to introduce himself to the team, Con came across as refreshingly straightforward and genuine. Then he took the chair next to mine, and his presence was so magnetic that it was hard work for me to keep from staring at him.

After that meeting, I couldn't remember a word he'd said, only the deep resonance of his voice and the way his accent curved around his words—including my name. Most people, me included, pronounced it with a long "e," like "Eve." But Con added an "a" sound in the middle. When he said "Ne-ave," it sounded like he was savoring a delicious chocolate.

"And what does Rosanna have to say about all this?" he asked. "Frankly, I'm surprised she didn't send you home."

"She tried to."

"Ah, but you argued."

"I made an argument," I said, tapping the table with my finger. "That's different. It was a good argument, too."

That eked a half-smile out of him. "Poor Rosanna. All right, let's hear it."

As I recounted what Rosanna had told me about the new patients, Con's reactions were satisfyingly dramatic. But when I told him I'd tried to convince her to let me stay and help, he fell silent.

"Hey, you're supposed to be on my side! Besides, my arguments—"

"Are sound. I heard you." Con reached across the

table and covered my hand with his. "But so are hers. You know I believe in erring on the side of caution. In this case, that means taking Rosanna up on her paid-leave offer. I suspect some part of you agrees with me, too, or you wouldn't be giving me such a sour look right now."

Dammit. A small, nagging voice in my head *did* agree with him, and that irritated me to no end. "Did you miss the part about me staying out of sight, hidden away in the staff wing? I think that's pretty cautious."

"Staying home would be safer," he observed. "But if you insist on working, you should at least request one of those hospital security escorts to take you to and from home until this whole thing is over."

I pulled my hand away from his. "Oh for God's sake."

"There could be more people like these patients out there, and we don't know what's going on yet—what their intentions are, their triggers. I don't mean to frighten you, but for all we know, they could be staking out the hospital right now, watching and waiting."

"Fantastic job not frightening me." I rolled my eyes as my hands tensed into fists. "These patients have given no indication that they mean me any harm. On the contrary, they seem to be... I don't know, weirdly worshipful."

His raised eyebrow told me Con didn't find that reassuring in the least. "All right," he said in a tone I suspected he used to calm anxious patients. "Let's assume you're right and they pose no threat. That doesn't change the fact that Dr. Mohinder made it clear you should be shielding yourself from unnecessary stress right now, not courting it. Look, I know you want to prove to everyone, not least yourself, that you're back to normal, or close to it—"

"Because I am!" But since we both knew better, I acknowledged, "Close to it."

"So you are." He held up his hand, silently requesting that I hear him out. "But the situation on Unit 4 isn't. At the very least, staying at work and engaging with these patients could be risky—psychologically, emotionally. And those are risks I'm sure you would counsel others to avoid, particularly if they'd nearly been killed not long ago."

I slumped back against my chair.

Nearly been killed.

Con had visited my hospital room several times a day after the stabbing. He even sat with my parents while Dr. Mohinder talked to them about my surgery and aftercare, so we both knew he was well aware of exactly how serious my injuries had been. But I was trying to move past it. Being reminded of how touch-and-go things had been didn't help.

I wanted to be irritated by Con's frank words, but I was too touched by the fact that he cared enough to try to talk sense into me—or what he saw as sense.

In my own version of a calming voice, I said, "I won't be engaging with the patients, just consulting.

Nothing more. Maybe that's not risk-free, but it's very low risk—low enough for my comfort level, anyway."

Con regarded me for a moment. He combed a hand through his unruly dark hair, which was flecked with silver and perpetually in need of a trim. I knew he had decided to give up arguing with me when he looked down at the table and muttered, "Right, so."

My stomach sank as deep lines dug their way across Con's forehead. Although my mind was made up, I didn't want him to think I was giving his advice insufficient weight. "Listen, I hear everything you're saying. I do. But this isn't just about me wanting to prove myself. I'm uniquely placed to help, not to mention I'll feel safer, and *be* safer, if I stay close enough to the situation to know what's going on. Can you imagine if they just released everyone before getting to the bottom of this whole thing? Then I really would want a security escort."

"You don't trust Rosanna and the rest of the team to handle things?"

"Of course I do. But we both know not everything is up to them," I pointed out. "These patients came here of their own accord. They can leave anytime unless they're involuntarily committed, and I doubt they meet the clinical criteria for that. I would strongly prefer to figure out what's going on before we're faced with a rash of discharges."

"All right, fair enough." Con pinched the bridge of his nose. "I blame myself for this, you know. You might've been willing to stay away from this place a bit longer if I'd found better ways to keep you entertained while you were stuck at home, recovering."

I swallowed hard, forcing my brain to stay in chaste territory. "You brought me your entire movie collection on DVD, books, art supplies, a harmonica *with* instruction booklet, and pint after pint of ice cream. Not to mention you played endless Scrabble games with me. No human being, living or dead, could have done more to entertain me."

"You do have an unhealthy obsession with Scrabble," he said with mock gravitas. "I'm saying that as a concerned medical professional."

"I'm not obsessed!" I said, smiling. "I just wanted to win one game, at least. And I would have if you hadn't kept pulling out those obscure medical terms. Plus, you were freakishly lucky with the triple word scores."

"You would belittle my brilliant Scrabble strategy by calling it luck?" His eyes flashed. "If you wanted me to let you win, Neve, you should have just said so."

I pretended to punch Con in the shoulder. He pretended to wince in pain, asking, "Is there nothing I can say to convince you to go home, take care of yourself?"

Well-meant though I knew it was, advice from Con to duck and cover rang pretty hollow. "So, as a ridiculously dedicated physician *and* a stubborn Taurus, if someone tried to force you to take paid leave due to 'psychological and emotional risks,' you're telling me you would cooperate?"

"First of all, astrology is bollocks. And *I'm* stubborn? Pot, kettle," Con said, pointing first at himself, then at me. "The difference is I can afford to be stubborn because, unlike you, I'm indestructible—so thick with scars inside and out that no further harm can come to me." Ignoring my side-eye, he continued. "As far as safety risks go, I'm a lot more dangerous than you are—physically, anyway. Don't get me wrong, I'm not denying that you're quite terrifying in other ways."

I grinned as the barista approached while absently twisting her braid around her finger. "Need a refill?"

When I shook my head, Con said, "No, thanks. We can't stay. Neve has big plans for the morning, trying to martyr herself in the pursuit of sainthood."

But years of working in the hospital had rendered the barista completely unflappable. "Okay," she said without a hint of emotion.

As she walked away, Con regarded her with awe. "One day I'll get a reaction out of her."

"She's certainly a challenge," I teased, "but you love challenges. Maybe you should ask her out."

"That would get a reaction, all right." He leaned down and knocked on the metal frame of his knee brace, covered by his pant leg. "Women can't resist my leg of steel."

"Oh please. Don't even." What I wanted to say was *With all the women who have chased after you, you're going to have to come up with a better excuse than that.* But I could never be sure whether he was just engaging in his usual self-deprecating humor or was genuinely insecure about his injury. I didn't want to risk pressing on a sore spot.

Con rarely spoke about the accident that had ended his rugby career. He'd told me he was repairing a piece of farm equipment when it collapsed on top of him, leaving his left leg "banjaxed," as he put it. He'd had multiple surgeries over the years, including a knee replacement, and he wore a knee brace for support. While Con always insisted his leg didn't give him any trouble, I knew that wasn't true. When he thought no one was watching, I had often seen him flinch while changing position or grimace when he'd been standing for too long.

Still, Con always said he'd decided early on not to let the accident stop him from doing what he wanted to in life, so it seemed inconsistent for him to blame his single status on his injury. After all, he was ruggedly handsome with large, brooding features that were more rough-hewn than chiseled. Con's six-and-a-half-foot frame stood out in any room, and his deep brown eyes gleamed with character. Some people didn't like the freedom with which he spoke his mind, but even more people admired him for the same quality, and absolutely no one could fault his work.

Con went on a couple dates a year—not because he was interested, he insisted, but to placate his friends.

He never saw the same woman twice, though. It was as though he was holding himself back from relationships, but I didn't know why. Whenever I brought it up, he just made a joke at his own expense and changed the subject. Once, I had almost confessed to him that if I'd been single when we met, I would have fallen hard for him—but only almost. I didn't want to risk saying something that might make things weird between us. Still, I sensed he was lonely, and it pained me. More than anyone, Con deserved to be happy.

I knew he wanted to see me happy, too—happier than I'd been with Stephan. Somehow, though, my now-ex had created an alternative history where our life together had been blissful, and ever since I broke up with him, he'd been waging a campaign to win me back. While *that* was never going to happen, I couldn't help wondering if I should at least give him the "chance to apologize" he kept asking for. It felt cruel not to, but the thought of being in the same room with Stephan made me cringe.

"There's that sour face again," he murmured. "What is it?"

Usually, I could talk to Con about anything. But although he'd never said a word against Stephan, he bristled slightly every time my ex came up. I didn't want him to know I was even thinking about Stephan, let alone considering seeing him.

"It's nothing," I said. "I just want to get back to the unit and find out what Dr. Rodwell decided."

"Right." His narrowed eyes told me he knew I was holding something back. "I'll be over on the unit this afternoon. If they let you stay, you can fill me in then— if you haven't gone home, that is? By any chance? Like a smart person?"

With a smirk, I replied, "If they let me stay, I'll be hiding out in my office. As we speak, Rosanna is telling the patients I've gone home. That way they won't get agitated, thinking I'm still in the building."

"Well, that's something, at least." We got up from the table. "Whatever happens, keep yourself safe, all right? For me?"

"I'll do my best."

Con grumbled, "You'll forgive me if I find that less than comforting. Tell Rosanna I tried."

I rolled my eyes, smiling. "The two of you, I swear!"

We reached the hallway, each flashing a goodbye wave. As we headed in opposite directions, a sweet ache tugged at my heart like a stitch being pulled tight. Glancing over my shoulder to watch Con turn down the adjacent hallway, I felt as I imagined the sun and moon must, morning after morning, night after night, meeting only briefly before watching one another disappear over the horizon.

3

CORNELIUS

Con cursed under his breath as he jabbed at the keyboard. He stopped when a soft voice warbled behind him.

"Dr. O'Brien, forgive me, but you seem tense this morning. Is everything all right?"

Con spun his chair around until he faced Mrs. Thorpe, the charming grandmother who was in for her regular diabetes checkup. He'd been treating her long enough that they'd grown comfortable with one another, so he wasn't surprised by the personal nature of her question, only embarrassed that he'd let his mood show.

Of course, technical problems weren't helping. "No worries. The computer's just giving me fits. One moment." He rolled his chair over to the exam room door, opened it a few inches, and barked out into the hallway, "Anne!"

Seconds later, a pleasant face appeared at the opening in the door. "You changed your password yesterday," Anne said with practiced serenity. "Added a question mark at the end, I believe."

"Oh, right," he replied, further embarrassed. "Sorry. How many is that now?"

"Four," Anne said with a grin before disappearing and closing the door behind her.

In answer to Mrs. Thorpe's puzzled look, Con said, "We have a system. I owe Anne a macchiato for each time she has to remind me of my password. It's supposed to help me remember, but as you can see...." He gave her a humble smile. "My apologies. I'll never get used to using computers for every damn thing."

"I avoid them as much as possible," Mrs. Thorpe said, waving her hand as though trying to swat a fly. "My grandson keeps up my Facepage for me."

"You have one?" Con wasn't about to correct her terminology. At ninety-two, she'd earned the right to call things whatever she wanted to. "You're way ahead of me, then."

Grateful for her understanding, he regained his composure, logged into the computer, and checked her labs from that morning. His relief was genuine when he saw the results. For the first year after her diagnosis, they'd struggled to manage her blood sugar, but it had finally stabilized, and she seemed to be maintaining.

"Well done, Mrs. Thorpe. Your numbers look brilliant. Whatever you're doing, keep on doing it. Better yet, tell me your secret."

"My secret? Having a live-in chef."

"Ah, so living with your son is working out well?"

"Beautifully. The food at the retirement community was… well, they tried. But my son is a wonderful cook. He makes sure everything I put in my mouth is off that South Pole diet. He brought me in today, in fact."

"Is that right?" Con was glad to have such a lovely soul as Mrs. Thorpe for his first patient of the day. She was brightening his mood after his worrisome conversation with Neve.

"Yes, and the whole family has made me feel welcome, even though I know it's a lot of extra work having me there."

He smiled. "I'm sure they're happy to have you. I know I would be."

"If they ever get tired of me, Dr. O'Brien, I'm going to take you up on that." Mrs. Thorpe winked. "A handsome young man like you shouldn't throw such offers around casually."

"You always know how to make my day." He stood and helped her off the exam table. "Would you like me to give your son the good report?"

"Please do," Mrs. Thorpe said. "And whatever's troubling you, don't worry. I know you'll find a way to fix it. You fixed me, didn't you?"

"You give me far too much credit." He offered her his arm and steered her toward the waiting room. He was glad his limp was almost imperceptible when he matched Mrs. Thorpe's slow pace so he could provide her with solid support. She had a cane, but she didn't use it all the time for fear that it made her look old. He admired her spirit, if not her judgment.

Con had grown confident in his ability to look after his patients' well-being. When it came to Neve, on the other hand.... Knowing her, she'd most likely been minimizing the risks of the situation on Unit 4. He would have to get more information, this time straight from the boss.

———

"CHRIST, LOLLY, IT SOUNDS LIKE A DISASTER ZONE OVER there!" Back in his office, Con sat with his elbows on the desk, holding his head in his hands. The room was his sanctuary, a leather-and-mahogany oasis in an older wing of the hospital. On a break from seeing patients, he'd retreated there to call Rosanna, whom he called Lolly. It was short for "lollygagging," the ironic nickname he'd given to his hardest-working colleague. But Rosanna's description of the events of the past few days only intensified his concern for Neve.

Con rubbed his face vigorously, then looked across the alley at the building next door, a fancy outpatient center that had opened a year before. His orthopedist kept trying to get him to go over there and try out some new treatments. Although there was nothing more they could do to repair his leg, his doctors were hopeful that they might reduce his chronic pain. He didn't share their optimism, having been on that particular merry-go-round many times before. Still, he'd promised them he would give the new treatments a try—when he found the time, that was.

"There's no need to be melodramatic." Rosanna's voice sounded tinny over the speakerphone. "We've had easier days, but you know we keep things under control."

"As much as possible. I know." Con and Rosanna sat in a lot of the same senior staff meetings, so he knew she had one of the best-managed units in the hospital. If right were right, Rosanna would be running the place. But he was starting to believe there was no such thing as "under control" where Neve was concerned. There was the stabbing, for one thing. And there was that arsehole she'd been dating….

Con was selfishly glad that Neve and Stephan's breakup had occurred well before the stabbing. With no boyfriend hanger-on, Con had been able to step in and make sure Neve was cared for properly—something he never would have trusted her ex to do. It also meant he didn't have to be in the same room as Stephan, which was fortunate, since he couldn't guarantee he wouldn't flatten the bastard—not after what he'd witnessed.

The morning after she broke up with her ex, Neve had come into work with her face puffy and distorted, like she'd been crying, and her jaw was slightly swollen on one side. Not only that, but for the first time he'd seen, she'd been wearing heavily caked-on makeup—the kind Con's sister, Una, used to cover up bruises years before when she was dating an abusive scumbag in Dublin.

When Con and his younger brother Eamonn had figured out what was going on with Una, they'd found her bastard of a boyfriend and convinced him that more than anything, he wanted to lose their sister's number and move to the other side of the country. But Neve wasn't his sister—*thank Christ*—so in her case, he had to exhibit more restraint.

If Stephan had laid a hand on her, though…. The mere thought made Con's insides boil. But when he'd asked Neve about what happened, she'd refused to talk about it, so he'd been forced to let it go. The last thing he wanted was to cause her more pain by pressing too hard. He would just have to settle for daydreaming about beating Stephan to a bloody pulp—for the moment, at least.

Neve had been through so much over the past few months. Now there was this madness on the unit. "Rodwell is really going to let her stick around and consult on these cases?"

"Yes, in spite of my best efforts," Rosanna said. "After I met with him, he wanted to talk to Neve. She made a compelling case, as you can imagine. Add in the fact that he's under a lot of pressure from some very high-up places to fix this situation ASAP… well, you know how that works. He believes Neve's input could speed things along."

"Ah, right, his usual priority list. Please the higher-ups and to hell with employee safety." Con knew it wasn't fair to blame Rodwell for Neve getting stabbed, but a part of him did anyway. After all, Rodwell was the captain of that ship, and the attack had occurred on his watch. But everyone else liked the man, and although Con thought he was a bit of a langer, it didn't matter much. For the most part, Rosanna ran the unit, and she was dead sound. "What's your take on all of this?"

"My take?" Rosanna's frustrated sigh came across as static. "Ever since Neve got hurt, I've wanted to put her in bubble wrap and stow her away in my attic. You know I love her as much as you do."

Rosanna had copped on early to how Con felt about Neve. The fact that he'd never admitted to it didn't stop her from teasing him. Still, he was grateful that Rosanna had always shared his low opinion of Stephan. It gave them both someone to vent with, although, of course, he would never let Neve know what he really thought of her ex.

At Con's first Christmas party for Unit 4 staff, Neve brought Stephan as her date. Con immediately pegged him as an arrogant gobshite. Over time, Neve had appeared increasingly unhappy, and Rosanna told Con that Stephan was the culprit—a user who took every opportunity to chip away at Neve's confidence.

Between her ex and the stabbing, Neve had been through quite enough. Con would be damned if he'd let any more trouble befall her.

"Bubble wrap would be ideal, I agree, but not doable, I'm guessing."

"Human Resources takes a dim view of that sort of thing," she replied dryly.

"And there's no talking her out of it?"

"I doubt it. She's got something to prove, and now she's got Rodwell's blessing. I tried my best, but she's already diving into case files."

"Of course she is." Con leaned back in his chair and stared at the ceiling. "You know I have complete confidence in you, Lolly—and in her. It's just…." He couldn't bring himself to finish his thought.

"I know. I couldn't bear it either if she got hurt again, which is why I'm going to make sure she doesn't. Speaking of which, Neve doesn't know this yet, but Risk Management completed their investigation into her assault."

"Oh?" *Her assault.* A lump in his throat prevented Con from saying more.

"As predicted, they concluded there was no way that Neve could have prevented the attack, nothing she should have done differently. They chalked it up to the cost of working with high-risk patients."

"Thank God we have them around to state the obvious," Con muttered, "but that's not going to stop her blaming herself."

"I know," Rosanna said, sounding defeated. "I'm just hoping that if the two of us keep working on her, she'll eventually see reason. In the meantime, we're putting some new security measures in place, and I'm keeping Neve away from patients—for the time being, at least."

Unwelcome images pulsed through Con's mind like drumbeats. Neve lying unconscious in the hospital bed, her pale skin translucent, waves of chestnut hair framing her face. ER doctors taking great care as they folded her gown up over her abdomen, exposing multiple stab wounds that looked like angry, red claw marks. Tears wetting her cheeks when she first came to and remembered what happened. Neve's voice, quiet and shaky, as she asked her first urgent question: "Is my patient okay?"

He coughed, trying to expel the emotions stirring in his chest. "You know, if you'd like me to stay on Unit 4 full-time until all this is sorted, I wouldn't object."

He could hear the smile in Rosanna's voice. "I'll make a note of it. You want me to make you Neve's personal bodyguard, as well?"

"I'd consider it an early Christmas present."

"Hah, I bet. You let me worry about unit safety. You have other things to think about."

"Such as?"

"How to snag Neve before Stephan wears her down. He hasn't given up yet, you know."

Stephan was still trying to weasel his way back in?

That news got Con's blood up. Still, he couldn't ruin his chances with her by rushing things.

Con met Neve during his first rounds on Unit 4. The room was full of people, but when he caught sight of her soft green eyes shining like two pieces of sea glass, some invisible force propelled him into the empty chair beside hers. Everything about her was refreshing, like the sky after rain. It had taken every ounce of concentration he had to follow that meeting. He'd decided then and there to get to know her better. Unfortunately, that had involved finding out she had a boyfriend. He hadn't let that stop him from trying to get closer to her, though.

The closer he got, the more his admiration for her grew. Working on cases together and watching her with the team in rounds, Con learned Neve was a whip-smart, gifted therapist who was filled not only with compassion for her patients but a fiery sense of justice on their behalf. She was dedicated and passionate, standing her ground with senior colleagues, insurance companies, hospital administration—anyone who stood in her way, really—in order to advocate for the best interests of her clients. He and Neve shared a set of values when it came to work, so they made a great team and always had each other's backs. That benefitted Con greatly, since she had a gift for diplomacy that he sometimes lacked. Her tenacity and independent spirit spoke to his soul. Between that and the physical attraction that pulled him toward her like a current, Con simply couldn't get enough of her. There was no use denying it to himself.

Besides, Con was as certain as he could be that Neve felt something for him, too. For one thing, she was the one who'd suggested their daily coffee routine. And while he doubted she was aware of it, her body always softened a bit when he drew near. When he touched her, her breath caught and her cheeks turned a shade pinker. And when he told her about his failed dates, while she expressed disappointment on his behalf, there was relief behind her eyes.

While Neve was with Stephan, Con dated periodically to keep up the façade of being "single and looking." Fortunately, once those women experienced the "work bore" persona he reserved for those occasions, they lost interest. No harm, no foul. Now, though, Neve was single again. This might be his only window of opportunity, and he was going to do things right—which meant Neve would be the first person to hear how he felt about her, not Rosanna.

"I don't know what you expect me to do about her jackass of an ex, but I wouldn't worry too much. I'm sure Neve is too smart to let that rat back into the kitchen."

"You know exactly what I expect you to do about it. And no heel dragging."

"I'm hanging up now, Lolly."

"Fine," she said, laughing.

"*Slán*," he said, using the Irish word he'd taught her for "goodbye" before hitting the Disconnect button.

Con leaned back in his chair and closed his eyes. He was dismayed, but not surprised, to hear Neve had figured out a way to get what she wanted—to stay at work with patients who were having some kind of apocalyptic delusions about her. She was already working on their cases, and there wasn't a goddamned thing he could do about it.

Christ, I need a drink.

4

———

NEVE

The chill in the night air meant October was right around the corner. I didn't care about the cold, though. I needed fresh air to invigorate me.

I popped the top off a bottle of pear cider, threw a blanket around my shoulders, and stepped out onto my balcony. It was small—just big enough for a tiny round table and two folding chairs—but it was six floors up, high enough to dampen the sounds of the city.

The only exception to that rule was the regular parade of helicopters. I lived in the Capitol Hill neighborhood, just two blocks from the hospital. The area was beautiful, and it was nice being able to walk to work, but medevacs were always flying in and out—more frequently at night, it seemed. And while my block was pretty quiet, it bordered a high-crime area, so police helicopters with searchlights added to the chaos. Helicopters taking people to the hospital; helicopters searching for people who may have just put someone in the hospital. After the sun went down, it was as though the soundtrack from a war movie was playing outside, a grim symphony.

For the moment, though, all was quiet. I closed my eyes and tried to will away the band of tension squeezing my head. I took a swig of cider. I couldn't remember when it had ever tasted quite so good, cool and smooth as it slid down my throat with the promise of relaxation just moments away.

It was a clear night, and even through the glow of the city lights, I had a good view of the constellation Orion. I had talked to the mythical hunter ever since I was a girl. I wasn't sure why. Maybe he felt real to me because his human shape was so easy to spot in the night sky. At first, I had just unloaded my problems on him, telling him about a fight with a friend or worries about grades. But when I entered my teen years, I began to ask him—pray to him, almost—to send me the man of my dreams someday. I figured that from his vantage point, he could both see everything happening on Earth and communicate with the powers that be in the heavens. Some part of me hoped he would see into my heart, know what I needed, and intercede on my behalf.

Given how badly things had turned out with Stephan, though, as far as I was concerned, Orion had a lot to answer for.

As work drew to a close, Con had texted me,

asking if I wanted to get together. I figured he wanted to check in and see how my day went since Dr. Rodwell had given me permission to stay and consult on the "apocalypse patients," the shorthand we were using behind closed doors. It was kind of Con, and while I was tempted, I was also surprised by how exhausted I felt. All I wanted to do was sit on my balcony with a cider, listen to some music, and go to bed.

Unfortunately, someone hadn't gotten the memo. There was a knock at the door, followed by a fist pounding, followed by a man's voice. "Neve? You home?"

Stephan. What's he doing here?

I was weighing whether to answer the door when I heard a key in the deadbolt. *Dammit.* I knew I should have insisted on getting my key back right away when we broke up, but I hadn't wanted to hurt his feelings even more. I stepped inside, sliding the balcony door closed behind me just as Stephan walked in.

He was wearing his usual lecturing outfit, a dark blazer and khakis. Stephan was almost as tall as Con and fit from playing in his indoor soccer league. His aristocratic good looks served him well both as a popular political science professor and a well-respected academic whose star was on the rise. His specialty was US policy in the Middle East—a complex and contentious issue that was always in the news—and he was becoming a sought-after pundit. It was also an open secret that he was considering moving into politics himself.

No wonder most people assumed it was *he* who had broken up with *me*.

"Oh!" When he saw me, Stephan took a quick step back, holding his key in one hand and a bouquet of flowers in the other. "You're home. I knocked a few times, but there was no answer."

I waved my cider through the air. "Yes, I'm home. It's my apartment. I was on the balcony."

"Of course, that's why you didn't hear me. I'm… I'm sorry," he stammered, holding the flowers out in front of him. "I thought if you weren't home, I'd just put these in some water and leave them with a note."

Not quite believing that I had to articulate the boundary, I said, "Stephan, it's not okay for you to come in here when I'm not home."

"I know, I know." He hung his head. "But I wanted to return your key. You forgot to… you know. I was going to slide it under the door after I left."

Guilt pricked at me. So he'd been trying to do something respectful, in his own clueless way. "Thanks. I'm sorry for being snippy. It's been a long day."

"Then I'm sorry for surprising you like this." Two vertical worry lines formed between his eyebrows. "Should I put these…?"

"I'll get something." I tossed my blanket onto the couch.

Stephan followed me to the kitchen as I retrieved a

vase and filled it halfway with water. He put the flowers in and began to arrange them.

Too late, it occurred to me that I'd acted without thinking. I shouldn't have accepted the flowers at all. "What are these for?"

"To apologize." He looked up from his task long enough to flash me a baleful look. "You know, for...." He touched the side of his jaw.

Reflexively, I touched the side of mine, too. It had only been tender for a couple days afterward, but I still remembered exactly where his fist had landed. "Thank you... I think." I didn't know what else to say.

"And for everything else, too." All at once, words rushed out of him, as though he was afraid I'd push him out the door before he got a chance to finish. "Everything you said, it was all true. I was a selfish boor, Neve. I didn't appreciate you like I should have, and I took so much more than I gave. I was under a lot of pressure, but that's no excuse. You deserve better. After I heard you were attacked... well, I stayed drunk most of the time, to be honest. It was the only way I could cope. I mean, from everything I heard, we almost lost you. It shook me to the core and made me realize how much I need you. That's why I've been reaching out. I wanted to say I'm sorry, Neve. I'm sorry, and I want you back."

Coldness crept through me. How quickly he'd moved from the topic of punching me in the face to how shaken up he'd been when someone *else* had attacked me. Unclenching my teeth, I said, "Look, I appreciate you saying all of that. But after everything… Stephan, no amount of talk is going to change anything between us."

He positioned the vase in the center of the table, then turned his pleading eyes on me. "Neve, what we had—what we *have*—we're so good together. This could be the great love of our lives. I know I wasn't perfect. I've acknowledged that, and I apologize. But I'm not willing to give up on us just because of one fight."

I blinked. I blinked again. "*One* fight?"

"Lots of couples fight," he continued. "Most do it a lot more than we do. Don't you think we owe it to ourselves—and to this relationship—not to give up after the first bump in the road?"

"Bump in the road?" My jaw dropped. "Stephan, you *hit* me."

He flinched. "And I'm so, so sorry. But come on, Neve. Accidents happen."

"What?" *Did he really just say…?* I stared at him. Hard. "I know you were drunk, but it was no accident."

"Of course it was! I was reaching for a book and lost my balance. You didn't really think…? My God, Neve!" He staggered backward a step. "All this time, you thought I hit you on *purpose*?"

Of course he'd hit me on purpose… hadn't he? There was no other possible way of interpreting what happened. Maybe he'd blacked out and didn't remember. But his denial seemed so adamant....

The absurdity of the situation nearly winded me. How in God's name had we gone from fairy-tale romance to *this?*

In the beginning, everything had been so magical, like a Hallmark movie. Stephan and I met over finger foods. I was attending a panel discussion on mental health care policy at the university where he worked, and at the reception afterward, he was behind me in the buffet line. He picked up on my confusion over the contents of the assortment of tiny sandwiches and helped me identify them. He was an expert, he said, because the university served the same fare at every reception. Stephan hadn't attended the panel discussion, just showed up for the free food. "You do what you have to when you're surviving on a professor's salary," he explained. I appreciated his resourcefulness. He appreciated my appreciation.

For a while, things stayed fairy-tale perfect. Stephan was clever, charming, and showed a dedication to his work that I admired. For reasons I never did fathom, his adoration for me was so complete that it almost made me wary. Over time, though, he earned my trust, and once he had that, my heart soon followed.

Stephan was entering a stage in his career when he was working hard to climb the professional ladder, so when he became irritable or drank too much, I was understanding. And when he confided in me that he'd felt unloved, rejected, and emotionally abandoned as a child, I was even more determined to look past his bad moments and become a source of unconditional love and acceptance for him.

Over time, though, the dynamic between us began to shift in subtle ways. It started with Stephan asking me to wear a particular dress or put my hair up when we went to university functions or out with his friends. I didn't mind. In fact, I was flattered that he cared enough to have preferences about such things.

But then his suggestions spread to other areas. Stephan told me I had a tendency to dominate conversations. He said I should talk less in general, "tone down" my laugh, and give brief, vague answers when people asked what I did for a living because "no one is really interested." I could tell this "feedback" came from his insecurities and fears that I might outshine him. I saw the fragile little boy inside him and became tenderly protective. I did as he asked, hoping by showing how committed I was to our relationship, I would bolster his confidence. Once he felt surer of himself, I was certain things would improve and go back to the way they'd been.

I clung to that theory even when his small requests became bigger and harder to swallow. Even when the requests turned into demands, and the demands into criticisms. Even when the criticisms transformed into drunken bouts of shouting and berating.

The hope that things would one day get better

began to slip through my fingers. But by that time, I was so worn out and hollow, I felt like a shadow of myself. I started simply doing whatever Stephan asked because it was easier than getting into an argument. I stopped pushing back when he criticized me, stopped defending myself when he accused me of things that weren't true. My strength was sapped. The only way I could think of to stop myself from disappearing completely was to break up with him, but I couldn't bring myself to hurt him, adding to his long list of wounds and betrayals.

It almost came as a perverse relief when Stephan finally hit me—not in the moment, of course, but after-ward. It was as though his fist put the emotional assaults I'd been enduring into a physical form that was undeniable, something even I couldn't excuse or explain away.

The night it happened, we were sitting on the couch at his place. Stephan was recounting the lecture he'd given his students that day about his fears that the Middle East was becoming a powder keg. After years of denying they had a nuclear weapons program, the government of Iran had recently announced that not only did they have such weapons, they were ready and willing to use them. It had thrown the whole region into chaos.

Even though Stephan's speech was slurred—a sure sign that he'd been drinking for hours—I sat there and listened.

Right up until he said that if nuclear war did break out and Washington, DC, was hit, the greatest tragedy would be that *he* would die at a defining point in history when his expertise would be sorely needed.

For some reason, at that moment, I hit some sort of an internal wall and completely lost patience with Stephan's narcissistic soliloquy. I told him that rather than argue about what constituted a "great tragedy," I was going home. But when I shifted my body in preparation to stand, he made a fist and hauled his arm back. I stopped and stared at him, wondering what he was doing. It didn't occur to me to try to move out of the way. After all, he would never—

I both heard and felt the *crack* as Stephan punched me squarely on the jaw. My head snapped to the side, and I was thrown against the back of the couch. With my skull ringing like a church bell, I was stunned into silence, unable to believe what had just happened. When I raised my head to look at him, his eyes were aflame with rage. There was no apology there, no surprise, and certainly no attempt to... reach for a *book*? Was that what he'd said he was trying to do?

"What book?"

"What?"

"You said you were reaching for a book. What book?"

Stephan shrugged. "I don't remember. I was drinking."

I pressed my fingertips against my temples. "And

your fist accidentally connected full-force with my jaw?"

"Yes, of course, accidentally," he said, incredulous. "How could you think otherwise?"

"Because I was *there!*" I started to feel like I might be losing my grip on reality, and not for the first time that day.

"Oh, Neve. This explains so much." He headed toward me, hand outstretched. "Now I understand why you were so angry, why you broke things off."

I backed away, arms folded tightly across my chest.

He paused his advance but kept talking. "Can't you see? This has all just been a terrible misunderstanding —not that you gave me a chance to explain, the way you bolted out of there that night."

So now the rift between us is my fault? No, no, no.... I hadn't been drinking that night. I had been stone-cold sober. I knew exactly what happened. I was a reliable witness, dammit.

I eyed Stephan with caution as my heart banged against my rib cage. He wouldn't hit me again, would he? No. He wouldn't dare. Then again, I hadn't been expecting the first punch either. Con's words rang in my head: *"Err on the side of caution."* "Stephan, I think you need to leave. I need to be alone for a while."

He froze in place, not moving toward me but also not moving toward the door. "Neve, you mean every-thing to me. I couldn't stand it if you spent one more second thinking I intentionally hit you. That would go against everything I stand for, everything I believe in."

He was right. It did go against everything he'd *said* he stood for and believed in—which was why it had come as such a shock.

Fat tears swelled in his eyes. "I love you, Neve. Please tell me you believe me. I'm begging you."

In a sudden moment of clarity, I realized what was going on. Stephan couldn't bear the thought that he'd hit me, so his memory had replaced the truth of what happened with a new narrative that was more acceptable. But pointing that out to him wasn't my priority at the moment. Getting him out of my apartment was.

"I believe you," I managed to whisper.

"You do?" His voice cracked, either with the desperation of hope or phantom pain from a narcissistic wound. I couldn't tell which.

Get him out. Say whatever you have to, just get him out.

"Yes," I said as calmly as I could, "but I need time to absorb all this, to sort through the implications. You understand, don't you?" He still wasn't moving toward the door, so I held out my hand. "And thank you for bringing my key back." There was no way I was going to let him leave with it, even though I knew he might have a copy of it somewhere.

"Oh, right." He fished the key out of his pocket and placed it on my palm, then wrapped his fingers around my hand, holding it for a few seconds. His face was the picture of contrition. "How much time do you think you're going to need? If you want, I can come by again tomorrow."

"No, not tomorrow. It's shaping up to be a crazy week at work. I'll probably be at the hospital late every night," I lied.

"You're still coming Saturday, though, right?"

"Saturday?"

Stephan looked like a young child whose parents had forgotten his birthday. "The White House ceremony for Lee? The National Humanities Medal?"

I tried not to show how defeated I felt by Stephan's checkmate. Months ago at a university event, his friend and fellow professor, Lee, had invited us to attend the ceremony where he was going to be honored for his work in US history. It would be horribly rude for me to miss the occasion and let Lee down after promising to be there. After all, it was a huge honor to be invited, and I was fond of Lee. It wasn't his fault Stephan and I broke up.

It would also be a terrible embarrassment for Stephan if I backed out. He could hardly find another plus-one at the last minute. It had taken weeks for us to get cleared through White House security.

Maybe I could make use of the opportunity, though. I had to end things with Stephan for good, and I had to do it in person to be certain he understood. I didn't feel safe doing it then and there, alone in my apartment. But why not on the grounds of the White House, surrounded by Secret Service agents? I could pull him aside after the event to talk. If Lee knew what had really gone on between Stephan and me, I was sure he'd have no problem with my plan.

It wasn't ideal, but it looked like the best option at the moment. Fearing I would regret it later, I nodded. "Yeah, sure. I'll be there."

That appeared to placate him. "Oh thank goodness. For a minute there, I thought you'd forgotten." Excitedly, he added, "You know, I talked to Lee last weekend, and he said we'll get our picture taken with him and the president. That'll be some souvenir, huh?"

He was trying to impress me. All I wanted to do was curl up into a tight ball.

Stephan smiled. "Neve, I'm so relieved we cleared everything up."

Trying valiantly to smile back, I walked him to the door. "I'm glad we talked."

"Take care of yourself, babe." He paused as though deciding what to do next.

Just hearing him use his old term of endearment for me made me nauseous. If he tried to kiss me….

To my great relief, he just reached over and squeezed my shoulder. I nodded and smiled until I managed to close the door behind him.

As I locked the deadbolt, a wave of self-loathing crashed over me. I was a psychotherapist, for God's sake. I was supposed to be an expert at building and maintaining healthy relationships. But somehow, with Stephan, I'd slipped into a psychological tar pit. How had I let that happen? And how could I help others with their lives if mine was such a mess?

Feeling like a turtle without a shell, I picked up the blanket again and wrapped it around my shoulders. Then I took the flowers out of the vase and threw them in the trash can, grabbed my cell phone and bottle of cider, and headed back out onto the balcony. I pulled up a search engine and typed in "24-hour locksmith capitol hill." Someone answered the third number I tried and said he'd be over within the hour.

Some deep part of me wanted to call Con. Even when we disagreed on things, he always made me feel grounded. But if I did that, he'd know instantly that something was wrong, and it wouldn't take him long to figure out that it had to do with Stephan. Con could be horribly persistent when he wanted information. Fanning the flames of his antipathy toward my ex would just create more drama, and I'd had just about enough of that for one day.

My whole body shuddered with the revulsion I'd been holding in while Stephan was here. I curled up on the chair and concentrated on trying not to cry, although I wasn't sure why I bothered. No doubt the locksmith was used to seeing emotional people in crisis.

A helicopter approached, chopping through the air on its way to the hospital. My thoughts went to the patient inside, the EMTs working hard to keep that person alive, and the crew waiting on the hospital's landing pad. "Godspeed," I whispered.

I was home, unharmed, and safe. Checking off the things I had to be thankful for helped lower my anxiety —and between Stephan's visit and the coming work week, I needed all the help I could get.

5
____

NEVE

LEANING BACK IN MY OFFICE CHAIR, I CLOSED MY EYES, taking a break from staring at the screen. It was Tuesday morning, and I had come in earlier than usual to dive back into the files on the apocalypse patients.

There was a lot at stake. I needed to do a good job on these cases and prove my involvement was helpful. If I didn't, there was a chance Dr. Rodwell would change his mind and send me home. Not only would that look bad professionally, but I'd been working hard on overcoming my anxiety symptoms. It had taken every ounce of courage I had to walk into the hospital the past two mornings, but I'd managed it. I worried another long hiatus might erode the progress I'd made.

Still, I couldn't stop thinking about the concerns Con had raised over coffee the day before. I knew my reasons for wanting to stay were valid, but he wasn't wrong either. Being involved in these cases might be stressful, and I had to figure out how I was going to manage that. If I fell apart, I'd be no good to anyone.

My office was small, quiet, and tucked away from everything else, with just enough room for my small desk and a bookshelf. I didn't need much space since I usually met with clients on the unit, and something about being tucked away in the compact room felt safe. I spent almost as much time here as I did at home, so I'd made it my own, bringing in art and knickknacks and using lamps instead of the bluish overhead lights. It was almost cozy.

My eyes rested on the painting across from my desk: three white cranes flying over the marsh. Something about the scene was calming, transporting. The painting was a gift from my parents when I was hired by the hospital. They wanted me to hang it in my office so I would remember that even when I was at work, they were only a phone call away. I only wished I could talk freely with them about my work. They gave great advice, and I could really use some.

It was because of my family that I worked in psychiatry. My father's sister, Esther, took her own life before I was a year old. Although I'd never had the chance to get to know my aunt, her absence haunted the family, and the silence about her death was deafening. Everyone seemed to avoid speaking about her, as though the intense pain of her loss, perhaps compounded by the shame and lack of understanding that swirled around suicide, was too much for my parents' generation to face. Out of respect for their sensitivities, my cousins and I didn't ask questions. It was only when I got older and took it upon myself to talk to some of my parents' friends that I learned how my aunt had died and that she had long struggled with depression. Sometimes it felt like Esther's existence had transformed into a nameless, open wound that my family had simply learned to live with, resigned to the fact that it would never heal.

In college, I took psychology classes, trying to better understand. The more I learned, the more compelled I felt by the injustice of it all. It seemed so unfair to me that our own brains—the very centers of our consciousness—could turn on us so cruelly. I wanted to help people fight their way through that twisted maze so they wouldn't go through what my aunt and my family had suffered.

Landing a job as a therapist at a prestigious hospital like Capitol Hill General was the fulfillment of my dream—or so I'd thought. In many ways, the work had been wonderful and rewarding, and my eight years at the hospital had flown by. But the knife attack had affected me much more than I would have anticipated, and I was dismayed by how long it was taking me to bounce back.

Guilt clawed at me, just as it always did when I thought about the patient who attacked me. He was such a kind man, and very gentle—no history of aggression or violence. But he was admitted to Unit 4 because, at the time, he was tormented by delusions. We later learned that he believed I'd been implanted with some kind of toxic seed. He thought he had to cut it out of me or it would grow and grow until it eventually killed me. In his mind, by attacking me, he was *saving* me. And now, because of my inadequacies as a therapist, he'd been moved from Capitol Hill General to a high-security forensic psychiatric hospital.

I closed my eyes and pressed my palms against them. If I was going to be of any help with the apocalypse patients, I needed to focus.

Gathering my energy, I returned to my reading, reviewing the clinical information that had been collected so far on our mysterious new cases. I hadn't found much out of the ordinary, which itself was odd. It was like Rosanna said: the patients represented a large cross-section of people, most of whom had no mental health history and nothing obvious connecting them.

We had discovered one anomaly, though. After the bowing and chanting incident the day before, all the apocalypse patients were administered the SRS—the Spirituality and Religiosity Scale—a questionnaire that measures spiritual beliefs, experiences, and practices. Every one of their scores topped the charts, but even that clue raised more questions than it answered. When interviewed afterward, all the patients confirmed they were highly spiritual. They came from a wide variety of religious backgrounds, though, and some didn't identify with any religion, so even that thread of connection yielded little in the way of useful information. We also had no way of knowing whether their heightened spirituality predated the onset of the collective delusion, or how the two were related. When the team tried to get more details, the patients just repeated their ongoing requests to speak to Neviah.

It wasn't long before I had to take another break. I was starting to see spots. While I rubbed my eyes, there was a light knock at the door.

"Come in."

Rosanna opened it and leaned against the frame. "Good grief, you beat me in today! Or were you here all night?"

"Wow, I must look fresh as a daisy." I pointed at the computer. "Just came in early to get a head start."

"You look exhausted, actually," she said, concern slipping into her voice. "Did you see the SRS results?"

"Yeah. Very interesting."

"But still no answers to our questions."

"Like you said, we'll get there. Hey, what's wrong?" Rosanna was wearing her "I have news—and not the good kind" look.

"Before I tell you, let me remind you that you started this. I said, 'Go home, Neve,' but you wouldn't listen—"

"I remember." Rosanna had made it clear the day before that I could change my mind and leave anytime, and that she would be overjoyed if I did. In the meantime, she was going to take every opportunity to point out that I was there against her recommendation. "Tell me."

"Okay." She pressed her fingers against her temples. "Amos Vates is in the ER, and he's going to be admitted to our unit."

"Wait a minute, don't tell me he's...?"

Rosanna nodded. "Not only is he an apocalypse patient, he claims to be their leader."

Her words made my insides crumple. Amos was one of my favorite patients—one of my favorite people, in fact. He was a talented computer programmer who'd landed in our ER after his first psychotic break. When it happened, he was eighteen years old, confused, and terrified, but he'd improved significantly over time.

Still, we saw him on Unit 4 once or twice a year thanks to a particularly diabolical characteristic of his illness: it was always trying to convince Amos that he wasn't ill. When he felt better, he would start to believe he wasn't sick after all. Eventually, he would stop taking his medications and drop out of treatment. Then his symptoms would progressively worsen until he ended up back in the ER.

Ever since his first admission, I had been Amos's inpatient therapist, and I genuinely enjoyed working with him. He was sweet and insightful, and he worked hard in treatment. But it was disappointing to hear he was back again at all, let alone as one of the mysterious apocalypse patients. During his last admission, we'd worked out what I'd thought was a robust plan to keep him out of the hospital, a strategy to ensure he would keep his appointments and stay on his medications. Clearly the plan hadn't been as foolproof as we'd thought.

"Poor Amos." I reached for the heart-shaped stress ball on my desk. "I'm so sorry to hear it. If he's in trouble, I'm glad he came in, though, instead of trying to manage on his own."

"Me, too," Rosanna said, but she looked more concerned than hopeful. "Who knows, maybe he can help us piece together this whole apocalypse puzzle."

"I hope so. I mean, it can only help that he already has a relationship with us." And with me, in particular.

My mind snapped back to the last time I'd seen him. Something strange had happened during our final session, something I hadn't thought about since. As he was leaving, Amos had turned around, grabbed my arm, and told me to be careful, that someone was going to try to hurt me. I knew warning me against some imagined threat was probably just his way of trying to express caring or gratitude, so I'd thanked him and promised him I'd be careful. But it stopped me in my tracks for a moment as I recalled his words. The knife attack had occurred just a few weeks afterward. I gave my head a shake, trying to ignore the thought that it might have been something more than a coincidence.

"Speaking of which, Dr. Rodwell wants to know—and please feel free to say no," Rosanna said. "In fact, I hope you'll say no. But he wanted me to ask if you would be willing to meet with Amos. With a security guard present, of course."

My mouth suddenly went dry. Memories of the knife attack flashed through my head. The patient becoming increasingly agitated. The tension in the room growing heavier. The knife appearing. The sudden lunge.

But this will be with Amos, I reminded myself. Amos, who I'd known for years and who wouldn't hurt a fly, let alone a person—as far as I knew, that was.

"Did the ER tell you how he's... you know... presenting?"

I must have sounded nervous, because Rosanna sighed heavily. "I knew it was too early. Forget it. I'll tell Dr. Rodwell—"

"No, Rosanna, wait." I stood up. "It's Amos. I want to help. It's just... I need to know if he's his usual self, or...."

She removed her glasses and closed her eyes. "According to them, other than the apocalyptic delusion, he's actually doing better than he usually is when he's admitted. He's calm and cooperative, sleeping fine, eating enough. He claims to be free of paranoia, hallucinations, and any *other* delusions, and according to his blood tests, he's been taking his medications. Also, his blood sugar is good."

So his diabetes was under control—a positive change. "That is better than usual."

Rosanna's eyes snapped open. "That doesn't mean you have to meet with him. Dr. Rodwell will understand completely if you say no."

Dr. Rodwell would understand what, exactly? If I couldn't meet with a patient with whom I had an excellent therapeutic relationship to help with a clinical mystery I was uniquely positioned to solve, then what use was I—to Amos, to the other patients, to the team? No use at all. Irreparably broken. A waste of space.

"Of course I'll do it," I said, doing my best to sound upbeat. "I'll be happy to meet with him."

"Oh, Neve." Rosanna pinched her nose.

"I'll be fine. You can't seriously think anything bad would happen to me with Amos, even without a security guard present."

"Ordinarily, no. But in this situation, it's not just your physical safety I'm worried about."

First Con, now Rosanna. I reached out and squeezed her arm. "Well, take my word for it. You worry too much."

"As someone who loves you, I reserve the right to worry too much." She let her head fall to one side, then the other, stretching her neck and shoulders. "All right. I'll let Dr. Rodwell know."

"It'll be fine. You'll see." I hated that the situation was making her so tense. I prayed I actually could do something to help. "If Amos really is their leader, we might have this thing sorted out in no time."

"From your lips to God's ears. He's getting transferred up here around eleven, so I'll set your session up for just after lunch. You really do look tired, by the way. Are you okay? Have you been eating?"

I tried to rub some life into my cheeks. "I'm fine, really. Not much of an appetite, though, honestly. What about you? How are you holding up?"

"Better than you. I had breakfast already." Rosanna hooked her thumb at the door. "Now go eat something, or I'll have Mike throw you over his shoulder and tote you down to the cafeteria."

I smiled. "He was a real hero yesterday. I feel like I should get him a thank-you gift, but I have no idea what he'd like."

"No need, I'm sure. He'll be dining out on that story for weeks."

"I certainly hope so."

"Go!" She opened the door and made shooing motions. "Breakfast. Now. And when you have your coffee with Con, fill him in on Amos, okay?"

"Sure thing." My body creaked from too much sitting as I pushed myself out of the chair.

Whenever Amos was on Unit 4, Con was his treating endocrinologist. No doubt he would be interested to hear that Amos might be right at the center of the apocalyptic whirlwind.

6

CORNELIUS

CON LEANED BACK IN HIS OFFICE CHAIR AND RUBBED HIS jaw. It was a good thing he had some time before he had to start seeing patients. Neve had dropped a couple major bombshells at the Bean Me that morning, and he needed a chance to absorb the impact.

Not that he had a lot of free time for contemplation. Still, he picked up his morning paper and shook it open, determined to get through his morning ritual of catching up on the affairs of the day before he had to deal with the infernal stack of files on his desk.

There were many things he loved about living in the US, but the health insurance system wasn't one of them. Every week, Con had to take hours away from patient care and spend time justifying tests he ordered and medications he prescribed. Not that he minded advocating for his patients; he was glad to do it, and he hadn't lost an appeal yet. But while he understood the need to manage limited resources and prevent fraud, he had no patience for insurance companies that gave him pushback for prescribing necessary treatments.

Arguing with insurance companies was one of those activities that always made him homesick, like reading Irish newspapers online and ordering fish and chips that never came out quite right. It had been over five years since he'd been back to Ireland—not since he'd begun his residency. To say he missed home and family didn't begin to describe the ever-present ache that was part of his life overseas. Family and friends in Cork were always asking when he was coming for a visit, and whether he planned to stay in the States long-term.

But Con had good reasons for leaving, and for staying away. Ever since his accident, his presence in the family home had been like a deep splinter that grew more painful every time he made an appearance. He tried to conceal it as best he could, but the hitch in his step was a constant reminder to his parents of what he'd been through. It was particularly hard on his father, who already suffered from chronic depression.

His parents ran a business out of their barn. His father repaired farm equipment while his mother handled the accounts. Once when Con was home on break from university, his father was going through a bad bout with his illness and wasn't up for anything, work least of all. Con's mother told him she was worried. There was a combine harvester in the yard that needed to be repaired, and the owner was growing impatient.

One morning before his parents awoke, Con decided to take a look at it. He'd helped his father for years, after all, and knew his way around the equipment. He noticed right away that the rake system needed sorting out. That involved taking off one wheel and jacking the thing up. He shouldn't have tried it on his own, but he knew if he didn't, it might never get done, and his father could start losing business. Con was on the axle stand pulling on some part or other when the machine began to shake. Too late, he realized it was coming down. He fell off the stand and landed on his tailbone just before the hub of the wheel crushed his leg.

In a matter of seconds, his world was upended. Rugby was over for him, and his offer to play professionally for Munster vanished into thin air. He was also forced to put off the final year of his university studies to focus on his recovery, which included multiple surgeries. Finally, he had to face the daunting task of learning to cope with his new physical reality.

Meanwhile, his parents each blamed themselves for the accident. His mother thought it was her fault for sharing her concerns about the business with Con. His father felt guilty for being so depressed that he couldn't work, pushing Con to feel he had to do the job himself. Con could never understand why they took the guilt on themselves, though. He was the one who had gone off half-cocked, and it had been damned foolish to try to do the work solo. His father had taught him better than that. Still, he'd never been able to convince his parents to put the blame squarely on him. Instead, they continued to shoulder the burden.

Watching them stumble under the weight of it made Con hate himself. So when the opportunity came to do his residency in Washington, DC, he grabbed it with both hands. Not only did it give him the chance to learn about his area of specialty with the best in the field, but it also offered him a way out of the emotional quagmire at home.

Endocrinology with a psychiatric specialty was a small field where word-of-mouth was powerful. Before he even finished his residency, he had several job offers around the US, but he chose Capitol Hill General. Con had always been interested in world politics, and for an avid follower of current affairs, living in Washington was brilliant. It was like living inside one of the political thrillers he read as a mental escape in his downtime. Plus, there was the attractive salary and benefits package. DC was also just a great city, with its historical sites, galleries, world-class concerts, theater…. There was always something interesting going on—if he took the time to go, that was. In truth, he spent most of his days either at work or recovering from work—and always thinking about Neve.

As he shifted around in his office chair, Con's leg began to throb. He reached into his satchel for a few anti-inflammatory tablets, pausing briefly to touch the well-oiled leather. The satchel had been a gift from his father to mark the start of his medical studies, and he'd carried it ever since. He'd caused his father enough misery; the least he could do was take good care of the satchel. It didn't have one stain, squeak, or tear yet.

Con never admitted to anyone but his doctors that pain was his constant companion. They kept offering new solutions: different classes of medications, implants, injections, patches, nerve stimulation. But with any luck, Con figured he might still have three, maybe four decades ahead of him, and he wanted to work his way as slowly as possible through the available treatments. God forbid he ever reach a point where there was nothing left to try.

His knee brace gave him both the mobility and the stability he needed, and years of practice had made him quite expert at ignoring the pain. His stomach wasn't so stoic, though, so he took another pill to keep the anti-inflammatories from giving him an ulcer. Then again, thoughts of Stephan might just burn a hole in his stomach, saving his pain meds the trouble.

Neve had thought she was giving Con good news when she told him her ex had dropped off her apartment key. But with a few casual questions, Con found out that Stephan had shown up unannounced at her place, and that something about his visit had unsettled Neve so much that she got her locks changed the very same night. Both those details had him seeing red. And when he'd asked if that was the end of Stephan, Neve had hesitated, which meant the bastard still had some hold on her. As far as Con was concerned, Stephan would be doing the world a massive favor if he just disappeared. It didn't matter where—Texas, a shallow grave, a tub of lye—as long as he never bothered Neve again.

Con was painfully aware that he himself wasn't Neve's boyfriend—though, God willing, that would soon change—but try telling that to his protective impulses. He didn't like the idea of Stephan getting anywhere near her, not unless Con was around to make sure her ex didn't step one inch out of line.

He needed a scotch. Unlike other forms of alcohol, scotch helped to clarify his thoughts. If he couldn't convince Neve to join him for dinner, he would pick up a bottle on the way home and have a solo brainstorming session. At least she'd be safe with new locks on the doors. Besides, bastard though he was, Stephan wasn't likely to show up two nights in a row; it would make him look too desperate.

That settled the matter of the coming evening. Next on Con's list of worries was Amos Vates. Unlike the news about Stephan, hearing Amos was one of the apocalypse patients had been a relief to Con. Amos had been their patient for a long time, and Con trusted him not to be a part of anything that would put Neve in danger.

The fact that Rodwell had asked Neve to meet with

Amos, and that she'd agreed, was another issue altogether. Admittedly, if Con could choose a patient for Neve's first post-stabbing therapy session, Amos would be at the top of the list. But Neve thought she was better than she was at hiding her anxiety, and by Con's assessment, it was way too soon for her to go back to working directly with patients. It wasn't like she was doing a blood draw or taking a medical history. Psychotherapy was emotionally demanding on both participants. And seeing Amos was one thing, but what if Rodwell got greedy and wanted Neve to start working with the other apocalypse patients? Con wouldn't put it past him. If Neve returned to patient care before she was ready, and something went wrong….

Con couldn't stand to think about that. Instead, he refocused his mind on his insurance calls and took comfort in the fact that he would be going over to Unit 4 later in the day for Amos's endocrinology assessment. At least then he could check out the situation in person.

Whatever else happened, one thing was certain: he would be buying the good scotch tonight.

7
___

NEVE

My leg bounced as I sat in one of three armchairs in the conference room, waiting for Amos to arrive. Rosanna had set us up in the staff wing so the other patients wouldn't get wind of the fact that I was around and grow agitated again.

My palms were sweating. I pressed them against my pants. At my request, the security guard had dragged one of the chairs into a corner, taken a seat, and put in earbuds so he could listen to a podcast while keeping watch during our session. I was glad he was there, if for no other reason than to keep my anxiety to a minimum. But Amos's space was already being invaded by a stranger; I didn't want him to feel eavesdropped upon, as well.

The door opened, and a nurse let Amos into the room. As soon as I stood to greet him, my tension melted away. His smile was warm and genuine, and his eyes were clear. He'd gathered his long dreadlocks into a black elastic band. Amos had a naturally slight frame, but he wasn't overly thin. He looked as well as I'd ever seen him, in fact, which came as both a relief and a surprise.

He approached me quickly, and I saw the security guard tense. I stepped forward, grasped Amos's hand, and shook it with enthusiasm to show the guard he was no threat. We sat down, smiling across the small distance between us.

"Amos." I shook my head. "Not that it isn't nice to see you, but I thought we had a plan in place to keep you out of here."

"Yeah, yeah, we did. It was a good plan, too. It worked, even, so don't blame any of my outpatient docs."

"Okay. Who should I blame, then?"

Amos pressed his hands together in front of his chest as though he was about to offer a prayer. Then he slid one hand up, pointing at the ceiling.

In spite of my effort to keep a neutral expression, I felt my eyebrows lift. "Sorry, do you mean… God?"

He nodded.

"Well, I guess He's to blame for everything, technically."

Amos grinned. "It's good you have a sense of humor, Neviah. You must need one in this job, and you're definitely going to need one to deal with what's coming."

I was glad he wasn't wasting any time getting to the point. "Neviah? You've always called me Neve. Why the change?"

"I don't know. Now that I know it's your given name, it just feels weird to shorten it. You know it means 'prophetess,' right?"

I'd always been told it meant "forecaster." And how he'd found out it was my given name, I didn't know. But at the moment, we had bigger fish to fry. I sat in silence, waiting. Amos started picking at the leather seam on the arm of his chair.

"I know you've been talking to my people," he said. "How much have they told you so far?"

"Hang on. Let's start there. *Your* people?"

He sighed. "I know, I know. You want me to explain everything up front so you can figure out how psychotic I am today. But can we just skip that part or leave it to someone else? Things are moving fast, and we need your help. Right now."

"Well, no, Amos, we can't skip the part where you explain what's going on." This session was going to be hard work, I could tell already. "We're here to help people, and there are an awful lot of them out there on the unit experiencing bizarre symptoms. They've been taken out of their normal lives, and we have no idea how or why. You say they're your people. I believe you after hearing about the reception you got when you arrived." There had been quite an emotional scene, with the other patients practically mobbing Amos and hailing him as their leader. Rosanna had kept him separated from the rest of the group after that. "But I need to know more. What's your relationship with these people? Why are they behaving like this? And what can we do to help them?"

He peered intently at me. "If I tell you, will you help us?"

"Help you do what, exactly? Stop the apocalypse?"

"Oh good. You already know about that." He leaned forward. The security guard leaned forward, too, but I waved him back.

"Is he going to hurt me?" Amos murmured.

"No, it's just a precaution."

"Is it because someone hurt you?"

My stomach clenched. "Why would you ask that?"

"I just… I saw it coming the last time I was with you." Worry lines creased his face. "Not the details, but shadows, intentions. Something told me you were in danger. That's why I warned you. I didn't know what it was at the time, but I can tell from the look on your face that something happened."

I tried to ignore the anxiety that was threatening to rise. "Thank you, Amos. For warning me, I mean."

"I'm just glad you're okay. You *are* okay, right?"

"Yes, I'm okay." We exchanged a look laden with emotion—his concern, my gratitude. But as often happened with Amos, our session had moved into uncharted waters. I had to try to find a way back to the subject at hand. "Is that what's happening now? You see something else coming?"

"Yes, yes. That's what this is all about." He spread his arms out in front of him, drawing a large arc. "All of this. Something big happened recently, but I'm warning you, it's going to sound weird."

"Consider me forewarned." I didn't think anything could phase me at that point. "Go ahead."

He closed his eyes for a moment, then looked up, folding his hands together in front of his chest again. "I've been called to be a messenger of God."

That caught me off guard. "Um, you mean, like... a Bible-style messenger of God?"

"Yeah, although it's not as unlikely as it sounds. There have been a lot of messengers since biblical times." Amos spoke with an unsettling calm. "The ways of God are mysterious—always have been. I mean, I've wondered myself, why would He choose someone with issues like mine to be His messenger? I mean, I already have trouble knowing if what I hear and what I think are real or not. The first time I was visited by an angel, I thought, 'Terrific. Now we can add *visual* hallucinations to my list of symptoms.'"

Poor Amos. He was having several new symptoms, then. My worries about the severity of his condition intensified. "That must have been terrifying."

"Well, yeah. Even when I figured out it really was an angel, my next thought was that God has a really messed-up sense of humor. But now I realize it's just a test of my faith. All God's servants are tested. And this particular test isn't even unique. Many of God's messengers were considered 'mad' in their time." He gave me an impish smile. "I know what you're thinking. I can see it on your face. You're thinking this is typical, right? Psychotic symptoms with a religious flavor and delusions of grandeur? I know. I've read the books."

I didn't doubt he had. Amos had dismissed his first psychotic break as the byproduct of a bad trip, since he'd been smoking synthetic marijuana at the time. But after his second hospitalization, he took the same approach to his illness as he did to his computer projects: total immersion. He'd read so many medical texts and books on psychiatric treatment that he was becoming something of an expert.

Still, it was unusual to have a patient with so much insight into their illness, particularly when their symptoms were so severe. It was a unique strength of Amos's that we could marshal to help him. "I was thinking along those lines, yes. So tell me, knowing as much as you do about your illness, why do you believe this calling from God isn't just a new symptom presenting itself?"

Amos tapped his head with his finger. "It took a while, but I've been paying super-close attention to my experiences and writing everything down. You know how when I hear voices, they're always negative? Telling me I'm no good and should kill myself?"

I nodded slowly. "That has been the pattern."

"And going to therapy, taking my medications—all that stuff makes those other voices quiet down a lot. But I'm still getting angelic visitations. The big difference with these is that they're totally loving and affirming."

"I'm glad to hear these experiences have been positive for you," I said, "but that doesn't mean this isn't a new symptom. What happens when you use your rational mind to evaluate this? You know therapy and meds can't fix everything. You have to do a lot of the work yourself, challenging thought distortions, sticking to your self-care routine—"

"I know, and I've been doing all of that, I swear." He traced an *X* over his heart. "If I could tell you everything, you would see, but there's no way I can fill you in completely in one session. There isn't enough time. Please believe me, though. I've thought a lot about this, and the only conclusion that makes sense is the one I told you: God has chosen me to be His messenger."

I looked down at the floor and took a moment to think. Amos was reporting visual hallucinations and delusions about having been called by God. At the same time, his demeanor, mood, and general presentation were completely normal, unremarkable. Meanwhile, he was the self-proclaimed leader of a group of patients suffering from a collective delusion. This was not going to be an easy knot to untie.

Tension began to work its way across my forehead.

Amos continued, "It's not like I think I'm super-special or powerful either. It's about being of service. When this angel appears, she's a being of light—in a human form, but glowing. I can hear her voice, but I can also feel her words in my head and in my heart. It's like the sound is vibrating through my cells. I'm telling you, this isn't my illness. It's something else—something divine, sacred."

It was obvious Amos had given these new experiences a great deal of thought. I had to respect the effort he'd put in, even if he had reached the wrong conclusions. "I believe you when you say you've analyzed all this, but we can both look at the phenomenon you're describing and interpret it in different ways."

"Yeah, but if you knew everything I've experienced…. Please, Neviah. We need your help. That's why all these other people are here with me, to bear witness." He pointed toward the ceiling. "God knew if it was just me in here, you wouldn't even consider the possibility that I really am His messenger, that what I have to tell you is actually true. The others came with me to get your attention, and to help me convince you to take this seriously."

It was at such moments that I wished there was some sort of all-knowing therapy fairy sitting on my shoulder who could tell me what to do. "Okay, Amos." I clasped my hands on my lap. "It still sounds to me like you're having new symptoms. And there are different treatment approaches we can try. However…."

Amos's drooping expression lit up a little. "Yes?"

"If you can tell me what's going on with these other patients and show us how to help them, once they're well enough to go home, I promise to try to put my interpretation to one side and hear you out on yours. Okay?"

"Seriously?"

"Yes," I said with a level of certainty I wished I felt. By giving Amos that kind of platform, would I be playing into his delusions, possibly making them more intractable? But my clinical sixth sense—which I used to trust, before the attack—was telling me something was different this time, that I would have to at least temporarily suspend my disbelief and get inside his head if I had any hope of figuring out what was going on with him. Good clinicians might disagree about whether that was the best strategy, but if Amos could tell us how to help the other patients, I decided it would be worth the risk.

He pushed a bit more. "You'll listen with an open mind?"

I smiled. "You drive a hard bargain, but yes. As open as I can make it, anyway."

"Thank you. That's all I need." He closed his eyes. "Well, that and one more thing."

Of course it couldn't be that easy. "What's that?"

"Before we sit down to talk about all this, I want you to read something."

"Not the Bible, I hope. I've read it already, and I have to say, it's not exactly a page-turner." *Dammit.* As a therapist, that was an inappropriate thing for me to say. Clearly I was out of practice. "I'm sorry."

"Don't be sorry. I feel the same way." He grinned. "And no, not the Bible. Just the *Book of Amos*."

"That's in the Bible. Are you testing me to see if I really read it?"

"No, I'm not testing you. And I'm not talking about the one in the Bible. My new *Book of Amos*."

"You wrote… a book?"

"Not a book. It's a file of information. I just didn't know what else to call it. But it's something I need you to read. The other patients will be fine, I swear to you. But before I help you with them, at least promise you'll read it. Please."

I had already agreed to hear him out, and other than the fact that he was making it part of the deal between us, reading something wasn't an unusual request. Patients gave me things to read all the time—journal entries, letters they were thinking of sending to family members, poems, and so forth. Maybe this *Book of Amos* was something that would give me deeper insight into his condition. "Okay, then. Once we get the other patients back to their normal selves, I'll be happy to read it."

"I can have your word? For real?"

It seemed odd that he felt the need for such a strong guarantee, but since I had every intention of following through, I didn't mind giving it. "Yes, my word. For real. Now tell me what to do to help these people."

———

Rosanna stood next to me behind the wall which, after much discussion, she had allowed me to use as cover during the big event. From there, I could see into the dayroom without being seen so I wouldn't "start another stampede," as she put it.

Scowling, Rosanna folded her arms across her chest. "I can't believe we're doing this."

All but two of our apocalypse patients were seated in the TV area. A tech assistant from the IT department was helping some of the nurses connect a laptop to the television.

"I heard it worked beautifully on the first two patients," I pointed out.

"Apparently," she conceded. "Get this—they've all made a group pact to tell everyone outside this unit that they don't remember anything of the past four days."

"They have? Why?"

"It's necessary to protect their leader, they say, and something about 'respecting the sacred nature of the mission.' Apparently 'sacred' is synonymous with 'secret' in this case."

"What are we going to tell their families, then?"

"Nothing. Nada. Even with an event this major, we can't share any patient information unless they give us permission. They haven't, and they won't. Word is the hospital higher-ups are relieved the patients are tying our hands, since we never actually nailed down a diag-nosis or found an explanation for what's going on."

"I can see that." It was something of an embarrass-ment that we still had no clue what was happening to all these people after four days of evaluation. "I bet the families aren't going to like getting the silent treatment from us, though."

She shrugged. "They'll have to take it up with the patients, then. They're all here voluntarily, and we have no reason to believe any of them are a risk to them-selves or anyone else."

"Right." Patient confidentiality was one of our core ethical principles, and as mental health patients, those on Unit 4 had even more layers of privacy protection than most.

Rosanna glared at the television screen with narrowed eyes. "I know everyone is anxious to get these folks back home as soon as possible, but still. Video therapy? Not exactly an evidence-based practice."

"You were the one who didn't want Amos to do this in person."

"I didn't want to risk a repeat of the scene he created when he first got here."

The tech asked, "Are we ready?"

A nurse gave the thumbs-up and dimmed the lights. The tech turned on the television, then hit a button on the laptop. In an instant, a video was up on the screen: a close-up of Amos smiling in front of a black background. The patients' gazes were drawn to the screen. Beatific smiles lit up their faces.

Soft piano music began to play as Video Amos pressed his palms together in front of his chest. "Peace be with you, chosen followers of the Almighty!"

"Peace," the patients responded in unison.

"This is so weird," Rosanna muttered.

"Give it a minute," I urged.

"It is I, Amos, messenger of God, and I have wonderful news," Video Amos exclaimed, sweeping his hands in an arc over his head. "Our mission has been fulfilled!"

The patients' smiles widened and there was a chorus of "ahhs" and "oohs."

"Thanks to your faithfulness and willingness to make sacrifices, our objective has been achieved. Neviah, the Weapon of God, has agreed to help us."

Some of the patients began to cry. Others clutched at their chests. Rosanna shot me a sharp look. I shrugged helplessly.

"You have played a vital role in saving the world, and today, even as I speak, you are being celebrated in heaven. You have God's eternal gratitude," Amos continued, "but now it is time for you to return home, exchanging one great miracle for the infinite small ones that grace our daily lives. If God requires you again, you will receive His call as before."

This time, Rosanna elbowed me in the ribs. "What does he mean 'again?'" she whispered fiercely.

"Amos said he had to put that in there, to tie up a loose end from his second video."

"Second video? How many were there?"

"Well, there was the first video, which he put up on one of the major video-sharing websites—a broad invitation to spiritual seekers who wanted to participate in something meaningful. It included his contact information. Then he vetted the people who responded and told whoever made it through his screening process to remain on standby. Finally, at the end of last week, he sent that group the second video, which involved some kind of spiritual guided meditation Amos said he learned during one of his 'angelic visitations.' It included instructions on how to get admitted here and find Neviah, thereby fighting the incarnation of evil, blah blah…. You know the rest."

"And have you seen these other two videos?"

"No. Amos said he deleted them after they served their purposes."

"So we're taking him at his word," she snapped. "Well, all I can say is he *better* have deleted them, because if anything like this ever happens again, I swear—"

I pointed to the screen. Rosanna turned to watch as Video Amos lit a candle and held it in front of his face.

"Focus on this light, for it is the light of God that dwells in all our souls. You followed its call, but now your work is done. God will never forget the part you played in saving this world and all the souls in it. From now on, you will never again doubt that your life has purpose. Faith will forever burn inside you. When I blow out this candle, you are released. Go in peace." He smiled, then blew out the candle with a short, intense puff. The video ended and the screen went dark.

"Good grief. Now what?" Rosanna asked.

"Just wait," I said.

For a few moments, nothing happened. Then the apocalypse patients' expressions began to transform from joyful enchantment to gentle calm. The group began to embrace one another and say their farewells. Eventually they were ushered into the conference room to wait to be given their final evaluations. Then, if all went well, they would get discharged and rejoin their loved ones.

Rosanna shook her head. "I've seen a lot in my life, but that may be the strangest thing I've ever witnessed on this unit. It would appear that Amos has fulfilled his end of the bargain, though. What did you promise to do in return, again?"

"Listen to what he has to say."

"That's it?"

"With an open mind."

"Ah. There's always a catch."

"And to read something for him."

"Well, I hope it's a hell of a good read after all this." She pulled her glasses down to the tip of her nose and shot me a stern look over the frames. "And before you listen to anything he has to say, you tell that young man

I said we're not cleaning up any more of his messes. If he wants to trigger any more mass delusions, he'll have to do it in someone else's catchment area."

With a wry smile, I said, "I'll be sure to pass that along."

Rosanna went to join the nurses.

Finally free to roam the unit, I headed down the hall toward Amos's room, anxious to let him know his "cure" appeared to have worked, and to find out how to get my hands on the *Book of Amos*.

8
___

NEVE

THERE WAS A FLURRY OF ACTIVITY IN THE HALLWAY outside Amos's room. Ayesha and Noor, one of the staff nurses, were racing in and out. I heard Con's voice call out, "Glucagon!" Noor darted past me.

I ran to the door and stuck my head inside. Amos was lying on the floor with his eyes closed. His skin had a taken on a slightly grayish pallor, and he was sweating. Con was on one knee next to Amos, leaning over him and taking his pulse. Ayesha stood behind him. Con spoke quietly, and Amos's lips moved in answer. Leaning on the bedframe for support, Con got to his feet. Then he and Ayesha helped Amos onto the bed. Tenderly but with expert efficiency, Con tucked two pillows under Amos's head. Noor returned with a syringe and administered an injection.

"I need his meal now, too. And another finger stick in fifteen," Con said.

"On it," Ayesha said as she and Noor left the room.

"Should I go, too?" I whispered.

"No. Stay." Con pointed at the chair by the small desk in the corner of the room.

My heart raced as I pulled the chair over by the bed and sat, watching Con try to coax Amos back to health. After several minutes, he stood back, satisfied that Amos was looking better.

Amos opened his eyes, saw me, and tried to whisper something. Con put his ear to Amos's lips, then said, "He wants to know if they're okay."

I shook my head in wonder. He was asking about the apocalypse patients. That was typical of Amos, worrying about other people in the middle of his own crisis. "Yes. The video worked. They appear to be fine, just like you said they would be."

Amos lifted his head and whispered loudly enough for me to hear: "You have to listen to me now."

"As soon as you're feeling better," I said. "Right now, you'd better focus on doing whatever Dr. O'Brien and the nurses tell you to do."

"He'll be all right," Con said to me, but worry lined his face. "He just needs to get his blood sugar back up. And to eat what he's given, when it's given to him," he added with a bit more volume.

"I promise, Doc," Amos whispered. "Neviah, the book I told you about. Top drawer." Weakly, he pointed to the desk.

I walked over and checked. Sure enough, in the top

desk drawer was a tiny purple thumb drive. "I'm not even going to ask how you got that in here."

He smiled and closed his eyes until Ayesha arrived with his meal.

We stayed with Amos while he ate lunch. After a while, he had another finger stick. Content enough with the results, Con murmured some instructions to the nurses and patted Amos on the shoulder. Then he stood and gestured for me to lead him out of the room.

As we walked down the hall, Con blew out a hard breath. "That young man is going to be the death of me."

"You and me both."

He pointed at the flash drive in my hand. "What's that he gave you?"

"Homework."

"Good man." He half-smiled. "The video therapy worked, did it?"

We entered the dayroom, and I pointed at the emptiness. "Perfectly. All our apocalypse patients are breezing through their final evaluations and being processed for discharge."

"Well, I'll be damned. Lolly," he said, smiling as Rosanna approached. "I *said* you should trust Neve."

Rosanna fixed him with a stare that made it clear he'd said no such thing. "How's Amos?"

"He'll be okay, but you'll have to watch him like a hawk. Any change, however slight, could be significant. Tell the team to call me anytime."

She nodded. "Consider it done. Neve, I guess your next session with him will have to wait."

"That's okay," I said. "Now that the other patients are taken care of, there's no rush. Especially if his blood sugar is out of whack, the more time he spends with us, the better, as far as I'm concerned."

"Agreed." Con rubbed his forehead. "I have to get back to my office. You'll keep me posted?"

"We will," Rosanna said.

"I'll be back later to check on him."

Rosanna turned as Ayesha called her name from the nurses' station. "Gotta run."

We waved as she dashed off. Then Con asked, "So what's your plan?"

"My plan?"

"I meant, what does the rest of your day look like? How about dinner after work, or a film?"

"A movie? On a Tuesday?"

"They do show films on Tuesdays."

He was being sweet but ridiculous. "You're worried about me."

"You say that like it's unreasonable."

"Are you afraid those discharged patients might show up at my door or something?"

His eyes widened. "I am now!"

I tilted my head. "What *were* you worried about, then?"

"Well, you've had other unexpected visitors lately," he muttered.

Is he actually concerned about...? "Stephan? Please, I can handle him," I said, but my words sounded braver than I felt. I reminded myself that the next time I saw my ex, the Secret Service would be around. That helped a little.

"Of course you can. That wasn't the reason I asked about dinner, though. I thought it might be good for us to spend some time in a less chaotic setting, going over everything that's been happening with the apocalypse cases. We might come up with some new insights that could help you with Amos, maybe prevent future mass delusions from breaking out."

The idea of discussing the case with Con was appealing, but the thought of going to a restaurant, being out in public.... I was too drained. I had the feeling I was going to want to retreat into hermit mode after work. "I don't know. I have to get started on the homework Amos gave me. Plus, I don't think I'll be in the mood to deal with random people tonight."

"I'm random?"

"You're not who I meant."

"We can get takeout, then."

I couldn't help smiling. "Why do I feel like I'm being managed?"

"The important question is are you being *well-managed?*"

"I guess that depends on what you bring over for dinner."

"Oh, I'm picking it up now, am I? And bringing it to

your place?" He smiled back. "Who's being managed now?"

"*Well*-managed," I corrected.

"Right. Thai, then?"

My absolute favorite—which he knew, of course. "Yes, please." Suddenly it occurred to me that my playful suggestion was a selfish one. Con was always accommodating me, it seemed, rarely the other way around. "Although I could just as easily bring dinner over to your place—"

"That's very brave of you, considering my bachelor pad hasn't seen a sponge or a duster since I moved in. But unless you've been vaccinated for all the rarest diseases, we'd best stick to the original plan."

I smirked. "At least let me pick up the food, then."

"The restaurant is on my way. What'll it be, lemongrass soup and chicken with red curry?"

"Wow, I'm impressed." We hadn't had Thai food in ages, but he remembered my favorite dish. Apparently he wanted to take care of everything that evening. I decided not to argue; although the week was young, it had already sapped my energy. "That would be perfect."

"Grand." He rubbed his hands together. "I'll get some pad Thai noodles, as well. No hypoglycemia for us today! I'll be leaving here around six, six thirty, so how about seven o'clock?"

"That works."

"Right, so." As he turned and headed for the door, he said over his shoulder, "And try not to stand me up

—due to having been kidnapped by recently released patients, for example."

"I'll do my best."

The apocalypse patients were heading home. Amos was going to be okay. And Con was coming over to my place for dinner. That last part made me a little nervous. He'd only seen my apartment when I was recovering from being stabbed. Under those circumstances, I could be forgiven for the place being a mess. I thought back, hoping I hadn't left it in total disarray that morning.

In spite of that small anxiety, though, I felt the tension that had gripped my body for the past couple days begin to soften. Was that due to relief or hope? Either way, I was getting lemongrass soup and red curry for dinner. In spite of its ominous beginnings, the week might not turn out to be so bad after all.

9

———————

CORNELIUS

Con stood on the threshold of Neve's apartment, wishing his hands were free so he could comb one through his hair one last time before she opened the door. Unfortunately, the Thai food take-out bag was in one hand, a paper-wrapped bouquet of flowers was in the other, and the satchel hanging off his shoulder held a chilled bottle of wine. He would just have to pray the stiff breeze outside hadn't left him comically disheveled.

Thankfully, Neve opened the door before he got the chance to become too self-conscious. He tossed her a smile. "Hungry?"

God, she was beautiful. He loved how her eyes lit up when she saw him, then closed involuntarily out of sheer pleasure when she smelled the food.

"Ahhh."

She practically moaned the word. The sound stirred

something primal in him, making him hyperaware of her physical presence. "That's a yes, so?"

"Yes, that's a yes." Neve smiled broadly as she stood back and held open the door.

Con put the food and wine on the table. Noticing an empty vase on the counter, he wondered if she'd been expecting him to bring flowers. He pointed at it. The waves of Neve's long hair bounced as she nodded. Her expressive green eyes evoked the deepest parts of the sea, and like her dark chestnut locks, they stood out against her fair complexion.

While she busied herself taking the Thai food containers out of the paper bag, Con unwrapped the flowers, arranged them in the vase, and filled the bottom half with water. Then he placed the vase on the table, the whole time struggling to watch what he was doing instead of staring at her.

Why was that so difficult tonight? When Neve had been with Stephan, Con was able to keep the intensity of his desire under wraps. She hadn't been available, and he'd respected that. Tonight was different, though. For the first time since she'd recovered from the stabbing, he was having dinner with Neve, a single woman. A single woman he'd loved, in secret and in silence, for two years. Between the intimate setting and her new availability, the lid he kept on his feelings for her was threatening to fly off.

But Con knew he had to treat the situation with delicacy and care, figuring out whether he even had a chance with Neve before he said or did anything that could damage their friendship. Besides, he sensed Neve was still healing from her breakup, not to mention the attack. If he made a move too soon or came on too strong, even if she did feel something for him, he could scare her off.

God help him, though, he couldn't take his eyes off her. Neve was so effortlessly stunning, and she appeared to have no idea of the fact. Goodness radiated from her, for starters. Just being near her filled him with warmth, and he knew he wasn't the only one who felt that way. He saw how other people reacted to her. She just made everything better, everywhere she went, without even trying.

Then there was her highly distracting physique. Tonight, she looked lovely as always, wearing a flowing pair of pants and a long tunic. But not even her loose-fitting outfit could disguise the bold geometry of her body. But unless he wanted to get slapped, Con seriously needed to get his mind off how much he would love to taste Neve's delectable curves.

Stop being a pig, he ordered himself.

But his yearning to take her into his arms stalked him the same way his little brother, Eamonn, used to whenever Con brought a girl over to their house. And just as he'd done with Eamonn, Con would have to find a way to ignore it. Maybe if he started a conversation about something completely different.

What's the least sexy thing I can think of?

That's easy. Work.

"Just think how envious those patients would be if they knew I was here, having dinner with the famous Neviah." Con smiled as Neve's eyes rolled skyward. "So Neve isn't an Anglicization of the Irish name Niamh as I'd always thought?" Mentally, he patted himself on the back. At least he'd come up with something tangentially work-related to discuss, even if it was really still about her.

"No," she said. "You know my parents are Mormons. Well, they're really into genealogy, and my mom found the name Neviah somewhere way back on the family tree. She thought it sounded pretty and liked that it was unusual. But so many people didn't know how to pronounce it, so we shortened it to Neve to make things easier."

After Neve was attacked, Con had spent a good bit of time with her parents, Jim and Leigh. They were lovely people—kind, gracious, and broad-minded. Neve was very close to them, and although her work was all-absorbing during the week, she was usually at her parents' house for Sunday dinner. He hoped to get to know them a great deal better someday.

"Any idea why this given name of yours might have been so significant to those patients?"

Neve shook her head. "All I know is it originally comes from Hebrew, and it means 'forecaster.'"

"Forecaster? Really?" Mirth tugged at the corners of his mouth. "As often as you forget your umbrella on rainy days, maybe you should claim the Irish version of the name."

He loved the way Neve narrowed her eyes at him when she knew he was slagging her. "Why, what does it mean?"

"It means 'bright'—oh, sorry. Scratch that one, too."

The laugh she gave him then was a sheer joy to hear, full and from the belly. It was the way she used to laugh, but hadn't since the knife attack. Con felt a stone lift from his heart.

Together, they arranged the food containers on the table, along with a couple plates and a bowl for Neve's soup. She sourced wineglasses and a corkscrew. Con opened the bottle and poured, hoping he'd remembered correctly that with Thai food, Neve preferred a fruity white.

They sat down, and her eyes shone as she looked at him across the table. She smiled and her shoulders visibly relaxed. "Thank you for this."

"My pleasure." If she only knew how much of a pleasure, she would toss him out the door.

He smiled back as they clinked glasses, and she moaned with delight when she tasted the wine. He'd guessed correctly, thank goodness—but once again, he needed to get his mind off carnal things. "Any updates on the apocalypse patients?"

"All good. After Amos's video, they all denied having any beliefs about me, Dr. Rodwell, or anything that brought them in. Every one of them has been discharged."

"That's good news, I suppose." They were all glad, of course, that the patients were "cured" and able to go home, but the unsolved-mystery aspect didn't sit well with anyone on the Unit 4 team. Still, Neve had probably had quite enough of work for one day. He needed another change of subject. "And how are your parents?"

"They're good. Mom says hello, by the way." She nodded toward the food as she poured soup into her bowl. "And to thank you for taking such good care of me."

"You told her I was coming over?" He was secretly pleased that he'd warranted a mention. He set about filling his plate with noodles.

"Yeah. She called earlier, just to see how my first week back was going. You made quite the impression on my parents after what happened."

He noticed that when she talked about the attack, Neve still avoided using words like "stabbing" and "knife." Emotionally, she wasn't nearly as recovered as she liked everyone to think.

"I'm glad I got to meet them," he said. "It was nice to see where their daughter came from. You're a lot like them, you know."

"They're amazing, the absolute best. I feel lucky that we're so close. I mean, we don't talk in depth about certain things—my work, politics, religion. But overall, we've come to an understanding that works for us.

That doesn't always happen when someone's kid quits the Mormon church."

"Nor the Catholic church—not in Ireland, at least." Their shared "black sheep" status had been a topic of conversation between them in the past.

"So you and your family…?"

"They never ask about such things," he said breezily. "That way they can keep on believing I go to mass every day and twice on Sundays."

"Hah!" Grinning, she raised a fork into the air. "I doubt that's what they believe, given they've met you."

"If ever they do ask, I can tell them honestly that I have no need of a priest. I confess all my sins to you over morning coffee."

She dipped her gaze, and Con could have sworn he saw her blush. Or was it the spices from the soup? He decided to probe. "And you don't need church because you have no sins to confess, I'm guessing?"

He was certain she was blushing this time. Her cheeks turned a deep red. Con heard her breath catch on an inhale. *What could she be thinking about?* Neve reached for her wineglass, and after a couple of sips, she appeared to recover her composure—much to his dismay.

"Not only do I sin, but I plan it ahead of time," she said. "For example, tonight I fully intent to commit the cardinal sin of gluttony."

"Premeditated gluttony?" Con pretended to count

on his fingers. "That's at least three hundred years in purgatory."

"Mormons don't believe in purgatory."

"Well, I hope they're wrong. I've been looking forward to spending quite a bit of time with you in the next life before we're judged at the final judgment and you float up to heaven while I plunge into hell."

He was rewarded with another beautiful laugh. "You, in hell? For what? Working too much?"

"Oh, dear Neve, you have no idea the depths of my depravity. If I ever truly did confess all my sins to you over coffee, you'd run away at high speed."

She shot him an accusing look. "Is this about not dusting your bachelor pad?"

Before he could come up with a witty reply, his mobile phone jangled loudly with his "old-fashioned telephone" ringtone. "Feck. Sorry, I forgot to put it on vibrate." He pulled it out of his pocket, saw who was calling, and with an apologetic wave to Neve, he answered. "Faraz, hello."

His friend and fellow endocrinologist Dr. Faraz Kamali was covering the unit that evening, and he sounded tense. "Hey. Sorry to bother you, but I knew you'd want to know. I'm with your patient, Amos Vates. He's in the ICU."

Con pushed himself to his feet. "Christ, I just saw him a few hours ago. What happened?"

"No one's sure. The nurses on Unit 4 said he'd stabilized, so they were monitoring him every half hour. They don't know why his blood sugar plummeted, or exactly when. The maximum amount of time he could have been in this state is thirty minutes."

"What state? What's his status?"

"He's in a coma. We've been able to keep his glucose in normal range, but he's dehydrated, and urine is positive for ketones. We're doing a full blood workup and an ABG analysis."

Suddenly off balance, Con grabbed his chair. "I'll be right over."

"No need," Faraz said. "I'm on it, don't worry. I have your notes from earlier today, so we know he was hypoglycemic several hours ago. Did he mention taking any medications that aren't on our list?"

"You're thinking about SGLT-2 inhibitors? No, he hasn't taken anything like that, not to my knowledge. We could check with his outpatient doc."

"Okay, I will. Just trying to put the pieces together. There's nothing for you to do, Con. I only called because I knew you'd want to know what was going on."

"Right." Con tried to talk himself down. Of course there was no need for him to race over. Amos was a patient, not a family member; Faraz had called as a professional courtesy. He'd take just as good care of Amos as Con would, if not better, since Faraz had more experience with this type of crisis management. "Thanks for letting me know. Don't hesitate to call back if you need anything—more history, anything at all."

"We're good. Your notes are in the system. But I'll call you if anything comes up."

"If he does come around, tell him I'll be over to see him first thing in the morning."

"Will do."

"Thanks again."

"No problem." Faraz hung up, and there was a deafening silence on the line.

Con settled back down into his chair. He must have looked shaken, because Neve reached over and placed her hand on his arm. "What happened?"

He closed his eyes, hating to tell her but knowing he had to. "Amos is in a coma. Faraz is with him in the ICU." Con looked up as shock flitted across Neve's face.

"Oh my God. What…? How…?"

"They're not sure. It's not straightforward. They're running tests now." But he knew Faraz was ruling out euglycemic diabetic ketoacidosis, a rare problem and a cumbersome one to treat.

Con felt the beginnings of rage stirring inside him. Had he missed something earlier, some sign or symptom? He'd told Rosanna's staff to keep a close eye on Amos. Did this happen because someone on Unit 4 hadn't been doing their job properly?

But neither possibility was a problem he could address at the moment. He swallowed his anger down.

Tomorrow, he would focus his energy on getting Amos better.

"You're not going over there?"

"No, and neither are you," he said, heading her off at the pass. It was tempting, since the hospital was so close by. But he knew Neve in particular had to be careful about letting her concern about cases interfere with crucial aspects of her self-care, such as eating and sleeping. "The best thing we can do for him tonight is to make sure we're rested and nourished for tomorrow."

Looking ashen, she slumped back into her chair. "If you say so."

"I do. He's in good hands with Faraz." Con pointed at her soup bowl and spoon. "Come on, let's eat."

With a heavy sigh, she pulled the bowl closer to her, leaned forward, and took a spoonful. "I want to call Unit 4."

"Tomorrow," he insisted. "He's not even there anymore."

Her internal struggled played out on her face. "You're right. Okay."

Neve resumed eating, but with no apparent enjoyment. Not wanting to be a hypocrite, Con joined her, even though he felt sick about Amos's condition. He was also disappointed that she wasn't going to get the peaceful evening she so badly needed.

They finished their meals and cleaned up in a relative silence that was broken only by the sounds of Neve loading the dishwasher and her occasional medical questions about diabetic comas.

When Con went to throw away the empty food containers, he spotted a bouquet of what appeared to be fresh flowers in the bin. He must have stood and stared at them longer than he intended to, because Neve noticed.

"From Stephan," she said without emotion.

"Ah. Should I…?" He pointed at the food containers, while at the same time mentally constructing a likely sequence of events that would explain both the trashed flowers and the vase Neve had out when Con arrived. That gowl Stephan had brought flowers along on his surprise visit. She'd no doubt put them in a vase to be polite, then tossed them after he left.

That meant Stephan still wanted her, but she didn't want him. But it also meant she didn't want to upset Stephan. Why? Compassion or pity would make sense —and would fit with her personality. He couldn't stand the thought that she might be placating Stephan because he made her fearful or uncomfortable.

"Yes, it's fine," Neve said. "They're in the trash for a reason."

Con nodded, feeling more satisfied than he should have as he pushed the food containers into the bin, flattening the flowers.

"Besides, I have these now."

Neve smiled as she stroked the petals of one of the flowers Con brought. After agonizing much too long over what would be appropriate, he had opted for a mix of fall colors to fit the season.

"They're beautiful, by the way," she said. "Thank you."

"Not a bother."

"I'm having coffee. Would you like some? Or tea?"

"Do you have herbal?"

"Mandarin Orange Spice okay?"

"Perfect," he said. "Any chance you'll join me in that instead of pumping caffeine into your veins at this hour?"

Neve rolled her eyes at him as she put the kettle on. "I need to stay awake if we're going to go over the apocalypse cases."

"I know that was the plan"—he took two mugs out of the cupboard—"but there's no urgency about it at this point. You're not going to be working with Amos for several days, at least. Once he leaves the ICU, he'll be moved over to endocrinology for observation." Con had noticed the dark circles under Neve's eyes growing darker over the past couple days. She was pushing herself too hard. "Maybe tonight would be a good opportunity to catch up on sleep."

"Yes, Doctor," she said in a saccharine voice as she retrieved the box of tea bags. "Fine. Mandarin Orange Spice for me, too."

"Good girl. Have a seat in the living room and I'll bring it out."

The news about Amos had smashed the mood to

smithereens. At times like this, Con reflected, the best one could do was rely on creature comforts. With the tea made, they sat in silence, getting what pleasure they could from the scent of cloves and citrus.

Eventually, Neve's eyes started closing for much longer than a blink. When she nodded off for a moment, Con added their mugs to the load in the dishwasher.

"Sorry," she called after him. "I think I fell asleep for a minute there."

"Don't apologize," he said. "Sleeping is exactly what you should be doing. I'll leave you to it."

She smiled wearily. "Thank you for dinner. I'm sorry we didn't get more accomplished."

"I take full blame for that."

Neve handed him his satchel and walked him to the door. Furrows creased her forehead, and Con was certain he had a matching set. "I'll check on Amos first thing and have an update for you over coffee. Okay?"

"Okay. Although you might see me in the ICU if I can't stay away."

"Understood." He put his hands on her shoulders and squeezed lightly. "Get some rest."

She nodded. "I don't think I'll be able to help it."

"Good. Tomorrow, then."

"Tomorrow. 'Night."

"Good night."

Although Neve closed the door with a smile on her face, Con's spirits fell the second it clicked shut. He hoped to God the day would come when saying, "Good night," to Neve would be accompanied by rolling over in bed and turning off the light. Every step of his journey home, he battled dueling desires: to stand guard outside her door and to go to the hospital and check on Amos.

10

———

NEVE

THERE WAS NO GETTING AROUND IT.

I couldn't sleep.

I nodded off while Con was here, but after he left, my mind lit up with thoughts about Amos. Maybe being in my bedroom would help. The small room was taken up almost entirely by the queen-sized bed where I loved to sprawl out. To make the space feel peaceful and soothing, my mom had helped me decorate it in shades of dove gray and sky blue. I climbed into the bed and lay there for a while, staring at the ceiling and counting sheep, meditating, listening to soothing music —basically trying everything I could think of—but nothing worked. The more I tried to shut my brain off, the more it fought to stay alert.

Finally I gave up and decided it was time to at least take a look at the *Book of Amos*. It would help me feel connected to him, and besides, I'd promised. Also, if it was anything like the Bible, there was a good chance it would knock me out.

With my laptop and Amos's thumb drive, I went back out to the couch and got comfortable. But when I plugged in the drive, I could hear something wasn't right. The computer made that "cha-chunk, cha-chunk" sound it made when it was trying and failing to read something. The welcome screen came up, but after a few more "cha-chunks," a black square with a white skull and crossbones symbol popped up in the middle of the screen.

This can't be good. There was a button at the bottom of the square. I clicked on it, and a scrollable text box appeared. I almost had to put my nose up against the screen to read the tiny type.

Hi, Neviah. Don't worry, your computer is fine. But FYI, the *Book of Amos* contains highly sensitive and confidential documents related to a plot that will trigger the apocalypse. To protect it, I had to make it hard to read, so it's encrypted. I'm sorry to make more work for you, but you're going to have to get help decrypting this. Find someone you trust, and tell them I used the Dead Parrot Protocol. Again, I apologize for the trouble, but this is about saving the world, so I figured you'd understand if I used an extra layer of caution. I hope this piques your interest instead of killing it. We're all in your hands now.

If anything happens to me, don't feel bad. I've done what I was put on this Earth to do. How many people can say that? Thank you for everything, Neve. Peace out. Amos.

"Jesus, Amos," I said aloud, thinking of him lying in the ICU.

What did he mean, "if anything happens to me"? Had God—or something—warned him in advance about his diabetic coma, just as Amos had warned me that someone was going to try to hurt me? My stomach quaked. I clutched it, flopping backward onto the couch and staring at the ceiling.

"We're all in your hands now," he had written. What in the hell had he meant by that? And how on earth was I supposed to find… what did I need? A hacker?

Maybe I could ask Con if he knew any potential candidates. With the exception of computer gaming, he hated everything about the digital age, so he'd culti-vated some tech-savvy connections to help him cope with life in modernity. Once I explained to him why I needed such help, I knew he would understand and not judge. Plus, he usually didn't have any qualms about working outside the lines when necessary.

There was nothing left to do before morning, though. I couldn't read the *Book of Amos*, and it was too late at night to bother Con about the hacker. It would all have to wait.

With that decision made, I put my laptop on the

coffee table and went back to bed. This time, I was asleep moments after my head hit the pillow.

———

WEDNESDAY MORNING, I DIDN'T HAVE TO ASK ANYONE for help finding the right room in the ICU—Con was already there, hovering in the doorway, watching whatever was going on inside and peppering someone with questions. As I approached, I saw the subject of his interrogation was the nurse who was taking Amos's vitals. She exhibited saintlike patience as Con asked about insulin dosage and glucose levels. I gave her a grateful smile as she slipped out the door.

The depth of Con's gloom became clear when he greeted me with a nod and a grunt. We stepped as quietly as we could into Amos's room and stood by the bed, surrounded by the bracing scents of laundry detergent, hand sanitizer, and various antiseptics. Amos seemed so out of place, a flesh-and-blood person in a sea of cloth, plastic, and metal. His body looked like it was being swallowed by the bed, and numerous tubes and wires connected him to monitors and an IV drip. At least he appeared comfortable enough, not perspiring or in any visible pain. I wanted to believe he was just sleeping, but Con's face looked like a dried riverbed with worry lines forming a network of cracks and crevices.

"Something's wrong," Con muttered. "He has

euglycemic diabetic ketoacidosis—euDKA. It's very rare, and we have no idea what caused it. Also, with the treatment he's been getting, he should be awake by now."

"What do you think the problem is?" I asked, realizing he'd just answered that question but not knowing what else to say.

"I don't know." His words were heavy with self-reproach. "We've missed something, but for the life of me, I can't figure out what. Neither can Faraz. But something is definitely off." He raked his fingers through his hair, and I saw his eyes were rimmed with red.

"How long have you been here?" I asked.

"Not long."

"Did you sleep at all?"

"A bit. You?"

"A bit," I repeated, knowing that for both of us, it was a generous assessment. "Is there anything left to do here? Anyone you need to talk to?"

Defeated, Con shook his head. Then he cocked an eyebrow at me. "You're about to try to take care of me, aren't you? I can feel it in my bones."

Mustering a smile, I said, "You poor thing, saddled with people who care about you."

That turned the corners of his mouth up slightly.

Since neither of us had to be at work for another hour, I considered suggesting we grab a bite at the diner around the corner. But given Amos's situation, I didn't want to be that far away from him, and I knew Con wouldn't either. "Anyway, you took care of me last night—don't even try to deny it—so turnabout is fair play. Bean Me? My treat?"

"Fair play, is it?" He addressed our unconscious friend. "Amos, she's trying to shame me with moral arguments. I'd better go. Please be awake and hypnotizing the staff by the time we get back. You've given us a scare. The least you can do now is give us a laugh."

Con turned to me and gave me a heartbreaking smile. He was clearly gutted by grief but fighting hard to hide it. He swept his hand out, inviting me to lead the way. After one last look at Amos, I swallowed down a wave of emotion and headed toward the café.

———

THE RICH AROMAS OF ROASTED COFFEE BEANS AND steamed milk stood in welcome contrast to the sharp smells of the ICU. *What a way to start the morning.* Something had unraveled inside me, seeing Amos lying unconscious on that bed, as helpless and out of place as a starfish stranded on a dry beach. And I'd never seen Con so uncertain about the reasons behind a patient's clinical presentation. Frankly, it scared me. After all, he was a leading expert and knew Amos's case well. If he couldn't figure out what was going on, what hope did anyone else have?

Ruminating about it would do no good, however. I

forced myself to focus not on the things that were out of my control but on what I could do—specifically, what I could do for Amos. It was time to stick my neck out. I cleared my throat and leaned in close to Con.

"Do you know any hackers?" I whispered the last word, not wanting to be overheard by the barista. She didn't seem like the gossiping type, but I didn't want to take any chances.

Con's head snapped up. "What?"

"Hackers," I hissed. "Do you know any?"

As his eyebrows rose, he leaned back against his chair. The wood made a sharp cracking sound, but it held. "Why on earth would I know a hacker?"

"I don't know. Maybe you don't. But you seem to know a lot of computer people, and I didn't know who else to ask."

"Ah, Jaysus." His expression darkened. "You're not being harassed online, are you?"

"No. Why would you think that?"

"Then what kind of trouble are you in?"

I shook my head. "I'm not in any trouble."

"What in hell's name do you need a hacker for, then?"

"It's not for me."

"Ah, well." His expression flattened into a perfect poker face. "In that case, I don't know any hackers."

"Oh for God's sake." I wrapped my hands around my mug and stared down at the table. "Fine. Forget I asked. I'll just figure out how to get on the dark web and hire one myself."

I could feel Con's eyes drilling a hole in the top of my head. "Oh no you won't."

"Oh yes I will." I raised my gaze to meet his. "It's for Amos."

Rarely had I seen Con so taken by surprise. "What?"

"The homework he gave me. It's encrypted, and I need someone to un-encrypt it."

"You mean decrypt it."

"Yeah, okay. That."

"Even unconscious, Amos can't stop making trouble, can he?" he asked with a mix of affection and frustration. "What's this homework?"

"He called it the *Book of Amos*, but it's really a computer file on that thumb drive he gave me. I promised him I'd read it if he helped us with the apocalypse patients. He did his part, so now…."

I didn't even want to think about "now" when it came to Amos.

"I see. You want to finish your homework before he gets back to Unit 4."

"Yeah. So I guess I'm off to the dark web."

Eyeing me warily, Con took a long sip of coffee. I casually slid one hand under the table and crossed my fingers. Finally, he muttered, "Give me the thumb drive. I'll see what I can do."

"Oh no, not a chance." I knew Amos trusted Con, but he'd given this task to me. I was reluctant to let the thumb drive out of my sight. Plus, the idea of partnering with Con in a clandestine operation held an irresistible appeal. "I have to give it to the hacker myself."

"What? Why?"

"Amos gave me very specific instructions about the decryption," I said, which was technically true, although the instructions were also on the drive itself for anyone to read. "Plus, I'm not passing up an opportunity to meet a real live hacker."

Con folded his arms across his chest. "You say that like you're expecting some kind of James Bond character."

"Oh come on." I threw my hands up. "You're the one who's always saying I do nothing but work. You know how boring my life is. You can't deny me this."

"'Boring' is not the word I would use."

Breakup. Stabbing. Patient mob. I had to concede he had a point. "Okay, but this would be a fun adventure, instead of… you know, the other kind. Come on, Con."

I felt a little guilty when I saw how much my pleading tone affected him. I was about to relent when he spoke.

"All right, fine. I know someone. If you like, I'll ask if he'll meet you. I can't make any promises, though."

"Thank you." I tried not to bounce in my chair. Not only were we going to unlock the secret to Amos's files, but I also might get to meet one of the shadowy antiheroes of the Information Age. "And you can tell him I'm a therapist, so I know all about confidentiality and being discreet."

"I'm sure that will impress him."

With a smirk, I asked, "How do you know a hacker, anyway?"

"If he agrees to help you, you'll figure it out." The shine in Con's eyes told me he was starting to enjoy the idea.

"Deal."

After the morning we'd had, the prospect of a secret adventure was giving us both a much-needed boost. As we departed the Bean Me, I decided to spend the rest of the morning hiding out in my office, trying to focus on work while waiting for Con to call, hopefully with good news about either Amos or the hacker.

———

I spent the next few hours immersed in apocalypse patient files. No matter how many times I went through them, though, I couldn't find anything new or helpful. Hopefully the *Book of Amos* would give us some answers.

My phone buzzed in my pocket, jolting me out of my state of concentration. It was a text from Con.

Con: Free for lunch?

I froze. If he wanted to meet in person, he must have important news.

Neve: Absolutely.

Con: I'll come by your office. 1:00?

That only gave me five minutes, but I didn't need any more time than that to get ready.

Neve: Perfect.

Con: Bring the "book" in a plain envelope.

My heart skipped. It was hacker time.

Neve: Got it.

I closed all my files, logged out of my computer, consulted my compact mirror, and tucked Amos's thumb drive into an envelope. I couldn't believe I was on my way to meet one of the dark lords of the digital underworld.

11

NEVE

CON WAS VERY TIGHT-LIPPED ABOUT WHAT THE LUNCH hour held as we picked up not two but three take-out meals from the Indian restaurant on the corner. Back at the hospital, we took a freight elevator to the subbasement that housed the labs and large diagnostic equipment. I'd been down there many times with Con to visit his friend Eric, who worked in the hematology lab. I assumed Con wanted to talk to him about Amos's blood tests, so we weren't meeting the hacker—at least not yet.

As part of the same orientation group when they started work at the hospital, Con and Eric had bonded over their love of computer gaming. They'd spent most of their first day playing *Death Dealers: Annihilation* together on their laptops while pretending to take notes on the presentations. As far as I could tell, Eric was one of the few people Con spent time with outside work. Con seemed to favor a few close friendships over a large social circle.

I shielded my eyes as we arrived at the hematology lab. It always took a minute for my vision to adjust to the bright space. Nearly every surface was white, and strong fluorescent lights hummed in tune with various machines sitting on rows of long counters with cabinets beneath. Presumably because it was lunchtime, there were only a couple people there, bent over plastic honeycomb test tube holders and other pieces of complex-looking equipment I couldn't begin to identify.

In the back of the lab, a small kitchenette was partitioned off by a glass wall. Eric was in there, waving for us to join him.

"Yesssss!" he said with a fist pump as we walked through the door. "Korma, baby."

"As requested." Con put the take-out bag on the table, opened the top, and waved the scented air in Eric's direction.

"You rock, big guy. Hey, Neve," Eric said with a grin. He had an open, intelligent expression and wore his light brown hair in a buzz cut. While Eric always looked conservative in his work uniform of khaki pants and a plain button-up shirt, Con had told me that on the weekends, Eric played in a blues and rock band, and that his back and shoulders were completely covered by an elaborate tattoo of a Fender Sunburst guitar.

"Hi, Eric. How's it going?"

"Oh, you know. Bloody hell—literally," he said, gesturing toward the lab.

"You're trying to ruin our appetites before we've even started," Con complained.

Eric held his hands up defensively. "Hey, I'm married to a minister. I consider hell to be light mealtime conversation."

"Oh please. We've met her, remember?" I smiled as we sorted the paper plates and plastic utensils the restaurant had packed, figured out who got which containers, and passed out the soda cans. Eric's wife, Katie, who was indeed a minister, had joined us for lunch a few times, and she always struck me as being kind to a fault. It was hard to imagine her even saying the word "hell," let alone raising the topic over dinner. "She's hardly the fire-and-brimstone type."

Eric smiled, a dreamy expression on his face. "You're right. She's more the saintly type."

"Now you're trying to sicken us," Con exclaimed. "Not that Katie isn't a saint. She most certainly is, which raises the question of why she's with you, my profane friend."

"A fair question," Eric conceded, "and one I ask myself daily. *Mangia!*"

We spooned our aromatic dishes onto the plates and dug in. As I expected, Con and Eric talked shop for a while about Amos's blood tests and some special markers Con wanted investigated.

Then the conversation moved on to their computer gaming hobby. They recounted the tale of an epic battle they'd lost in spectacular fashion to some guys in Slovakia the previous week. The most advanced video game I'd played was one of those arcade games where you sit in a console and pretend to drive a race car, so I didn't understand much of what they said, but I caught enough to share in their enjoyment. When they talked about gaming, it took ten years off them both.

While we ate our fill, I wondered to myself if we were going to meet the hacker after lunch. I didn't have to wait long to find out. As we put leftovers into containers and trash into the take-out bag, Con said, "Neve, do you have the envelope?"

I looked from Con to Eric, then back to Con. "Um… yes. You want it… now?"

"Just hand it to me without any ceremony," Eric said with a subtle glance at the small black box affixed to the ceiling in the corner of the room. Those CCTV cameras were ubiquitous in the hospital, covering most spaces, especially places like the lab where multiple people worked and sensitive information was handled. "Then you can tell me what you need to tell me about the file."

Eric is the hacker? I couldn't believe it. Yet he and Con were both looking at me expectantly, even intensely, while maintaining relaxed body language— for the benefit of the cameras, no doubt. I felt like we really were in a spy movie.

With a nervous laugh, I asked, "Con, care to explain?"

"I didn't tell you earlier because you were a little bit too excited about meeting—what did you call him?—a 'real live hacker,'" Con said. "I was afraid you'd act strange during lunch and raise suspicions, so please don't start now." He nodded in Eric's direction. "Prepare yourself. Not only is this Eric, this is Erik the Viking."

"Sorry, who? Wait, wasn't that a movie?"

"Yes, and I'm impressed you know it! It's a modern-day classic," Eric said, grinning. "Which is why I borrowed the title for my screen name. I mean, my 'real live hacker' screen name. Eric but with a *k*."

"Oh for goodness' sake." I grinned back, then toned it down, trying to act natural. "Seriously? Does Katie know?"

"That *would* be your first question," Con remarked.

"Of course she knows," Eric said. "Luckily for me, there were no such things as computers in biblical times, so there are no specific prohibitions against hacking in the Good Book." He winked playfully. "Plus I'm a white hat, so she figures God would approve."

"A white hat? What's that?"

"Well, hacking is pretty much a gray area by definition," Eric explained, "but some of us use our powers for good, some for evil, and some for whoever is the highest bidder. In a nutshell, that is. I could go into all the variations and nuances, but Con would die of boredom before I finished, and he's the only doctor here, so I'm pretty sure we wouldn't be able to revive him."

"How thoughtful of you," Con said dryly. "Erik the Viking is known across the globe as a talented white hat. A lot of people would be very envious to know he's agreed to help you with this file of yours."

"Oh, right, the file." Well, Eric was certainly someone I trusted, so I knew Amos would approve. As casually as possible, I removed the envelope from my pocket and slid it across the table.

Eric pocketed it quickly. "What is it?"

"A file. A collection of documents," I said. "I don't know what kind or what's in them. I'm kind of clueless in general, to be honest."

"Con said you have to give me some kind of specific instructions to open it?"

"Right." I nodded, casting a quick glance at Con. "The instructions will pop up on the screen when you plug in the thumb drive. But the gist is that it was encrypted using the Dead Parrot Protocol."

"Dead Parrot Protocol. Got it."

I was stunned that Eric appeared to grasp the meaning of that information right away. "You know what that means?"

"Of course! It won't be a problem."

I felt my shoulders relax for the first time in ages. "Oh my gosh, Eric, that's so great to hear. Thank you so much. I gave him my word that I'd read this."

"Don't worry, Neve," Eric said, smiling broadly. "I won't make a liar out of you."

Meanwhile, Con turned toward me, his facial muscles twitching with the effort it was taking to look undisturbed. "That's it?"

In the hopes of looking innocent, I bit my lip and looked back at him with wide eyes. "Hmm?"

"That's the reason you needed to meet the hacker in person? The reason I asked Erik the Viking to unmask himself?" he probed. "To give him instructions he's going to see anyway when he plugs in the drive?"

Busted. I opened my mouth to speak, but no words came out. After a few awkward moments, I managed, "I wanted an adventure, remember?"

Eric grinned. "Then I'm sorry. This must have been pretty disappointing for you. But as I told Con, I don't mind you knowing about my Viking identity. I trust you. To be honest, I can't wait to get home and get started on this. The Dead Parrot Protocol is challenging, but it's fun. I get to watch that Monty Python sketch over and over again, for one thing, as part of the decryption process."

"Well, I'm glad someone's enjoying this." Con pushed his chair away from the table. "We'd better go. I have to reorder those tests on Amos, then put in a few hours at the clinic."

"Eric, thank you so much for helping us," I said, resisting the impulse to hug him in case it might look suspicious to whoever monitored the cameras. "It means a great deal."

"For you? No problem." Eric winked. "Con, I'll text you when I have something, and you can tell Neve?" He walked me to the door, murmuring, "Better you and I not have direct contact for a while after this."

"Okay," I agreed, "but don't you think you guys are a little paranoid? I mean, aren't we being a bit too cloak-and-daggery about all this?"

Eric closed his eyes and groaned. "Oh, Neve. Poor, naïve Neve."

Con quickly ushered me through the doorway. "Christ, Eric, don't give her your 'Big Brother is watching' speech. She'll have nightmares for weeks."

"It's important for her to know what's going on in the world," Eric said. "Important for everyone!"

"I don't disagree," Con called back as he steered me down the hallway. "Another time, though."

"I'll hold you to that," Eric called after us.

I smiled and waved over my shoulder as we turned a corner and left Eric's line of sight.

"Don't get me wrong," Con said. "I'm sure everything he has to say about the surveillance state is valid. But believe me, it's far better to take in his treatise over a long evening, with a good meal and several bottles of wine to hand."

"Noted." We paused, waiting for the elevator. "Listen, I'm sorry. I shouldn't have pretended that I had to deliver that Dead Parrot message in person. If I'd known it was just Eric—"

"'Just Eric'?" Con chuckled. "Please call him that the next time you see him, as a personal favor to me. In truth, though, I would have preferred not to involve you directly. Eric has to guard his identity closely, and the only way to do that is to keep the circle of people who know who he is as small as possible. It's not that he believes his friends would reveal him on purpose, but we all make mistakes. Sometimes things slip out. So the fewer people who know about Eric, the safer he is. And you would have been safer, as well, not knowing who he is."

"Safer? What do you mean? What is he into, exactly?"

The elevator arrived. We stood back while a health aide wheeled out a patient on a gurney. Once we stepped inside and the doors closed, Con said, "I can't tell you. I don't even understand most of it. But he assures me it's nothing his wife wouldn't approve of."

"That's comforting, I guess."

"The safety issue is more about the powerful interests he annoys, and to a certain extent, the company he keeps—online, that is. He's told me tales about the hacker world that made my hair stand on end. If you really want to know more, I'm sure he'll tell you himself sometime."

The weight of the responsibility and trust that had been given to me started to sink in. "I get it, Con. I won't tell anyone, ever. I swear. No mistakes, no letting things slip."

"Of course not. I know that. So does Eric, which is why he agreed to bring you into his inner circle." He smiled, and although I could tell he was trying to be reassuring, I still felt a bit spooked.

"I'll text you when I have news," Con said when we reached his floor. "A change in Amos's status, information about your homework...."

"Thank you," I said as he stepped out. He shot me a thumbs-up as he walked off down the corridor.

I sighed heavily as the elevator doors closed. Now all I could do was go back to my office, ponder a whole new set of worries, and wait.

12

NEVE

A FUCHSIA STICKY NOTE ON MY COMPUTER SCREEN greeted me.

CALL ME AS SOON AS YOU GET BACK. -R

Rosanna didn't usually write in all caps, so I assumed there was some kind of emergency. My heart fluttered as I picked up the phone and dialed her extension.

"Neve, hi. Can you come over to my office?"

She sounded mildly annoyed, not worried. Still, I asked, "Is everything okay? The patients? Is Amos…?"

"Everything's fine. Patients are fine," Rosanna said in the super-neutral tone she used when she was leading meetings. She must not have been alone. "No word on Amos, no change. We just need to talk. Are you free?"

"Yes, of course," I said. "On my way."

"Thanks." *Click.*

That was unusually abrupt. Something was up. I turned back out the door and headed to Rosanna's office.

As I approached, I saw the door was open. A calm, deep voice drifted into the hallway: Dr. Rodwell's. I hadn't met with him since before we used Amos's video cure on the apocalypse patients. Maybe he just wanted to debrief.

I caught Rosanna's eye when I reached the doorway. Before I could even knock, she was ushering me inside and closing the door behind me. "Neve, thanks for coming so quickly."

"Yes, thank you. Our very own 'weapon of right-eousness'!" Dr. Rodwell smiled broadly and offered me a seat. He was a tall, lanky man with refined features that made him look more like a TV doctor than a real one. He wore his white coat like he was born to it, with a white shirt, blue tie, and gray suit pants underneath. We always knew when he was coming down the hallway because his highly polished dress shoes clapped against the tile floor when he walked—and walking, like everything else, was something he did with confidence.

I rolled my eyes at his ribbing. "No problem."

They sat down, and Dr. Rodwell's tone changed from amused to concerned. "How are things?"

"Good," I replied, happy to be able to reassure him.

"All the apocalypse patients are back home and doing well—as far as I know, anyway. Is that… still accurate, Rosanna?" I asked just in case something had changed in the past hour.

"Yes."

I nodded. "And I started my work with Amos, but as I'm sure you also know, he had a health crisis and is in ICU. I went to see him this morning, but he's… well, he can't talk."

"I heard." Dr. Rodwell bowed his head. "In a diabetic coma, is that right?"

I nodded. "Con said they're still not sure what happened."

"Unfortunately, Amos has always been medically fragile." Dr. Rodwell rested his hand on the arm of my chair. "I'm sorry, Neve. You've worked with Amos for a long time. This must be very difficult for you."

"It's not easy. But it helps to know he's in good hands."

"Yes, we're lucky to have Con." Dr. Rodwell nodded. "Still, I understand that even in the best-case scenario, it'll be a while before we get Amos back. Which is why I asked to meet with you and Rosanna. If she can spare you, I'd like you to take the rest of this week and next week off—paid leave, of course. It's our way of thanking you for your help with the apocalypse patients."

"What?" I glanced over at Rosanna, who wore a

resigned expression. "I mean, I appreciate the gesture, but I was just doing my job."

"Just doing your job?" He glanced at Rosanna. "I'd say you're understating things quite a bit there, Neve. You saved our bacon, not to mention the patients. And you showed tremendous commitment, agreeing to meet with Amos—at my request, let's not forget—which returned you to direct care earlier than was recommended. All of that, you did on a case where you were being targeted in a very personal way. What you did was heroic."

Heroic? That was a wild exaggeration, but beyond that, "heroic" wasn't a word we used to describe one another's work at the hospital. Going above and beyond was part of the job description.

That was unless Dr. Rodwell still saw me as somehow impaired after the stabbing.

Good God, not this again. Am I always going to be seen as "poor Neve"?

I cleared my throat and gave him a tight smile. "I appreciate the compliment, but people do heroic things here all the time—present company included."

"Your modesty is admirable." He smiled back. "But these instructions come from higher up. One of the apocalypse patients is a relative of a VIP who sits on the board of the hospital, someone who's determined to show their appreciation. Budgets being as they are, a bonus wasn't an option, but I think extra vacation time is more appropriate anyway. I know no one here likes to admit to being human, but after the last couple days, on top of what you went through last month, I'm ordering you some more time off to rest and recover. I won't take no for an answer."

Cold tendrils of despair snaked their way up my neck. *A week and a half? No morning coffee with Con, no Rosanna, no work to keep me busy and distracted?* "But I promised Amos—"

This time, Rosanna spoke. "I know what you're going to say. You promised Amos you'd hear him out, and you will. But for starters, it'll be a while before we get him back on our unit. And given the current state of his health, both mental and physical, I'm sure he'll still be here when you get back."

Dammit. "But don't you need me to keep reviewing the apocalypse patient files? And what about other work? I don't want my absence to be a burden on the staff—"

Dr. Rodwell stood and held his hand up. "We'll work it out," he said firmly. "Like I said, I won't take no for an answer. I'll leave it to you and Rosanna to wrap things up, but when I get back from my next meeting, you'd better be gone—and I mean that in the nicest way possible."

Even though he was usually flexible and fair, once Dr. Rodwell made a decision, it was the end of the discussion. I'd already pushed back more than I should have.

I stood as well. "Thank you, Dr. Rodwell. It's very kind of you."

"It's the least we can do." He shook my hand, then saluted Rosanna as he headed for the door. "See you after the meeting?"

"Right-o," she said.

Once he'd gone, we sat back down and looked at one another across the desk. There wasn't much else to say. "I'm sorry," she ventured. "I tried to convince him to at least make it optional, but his mind was set."

"Thanks for trying." My heart sank. "Can I at least get updates on how Amos is doing?"

"Of course. I'll call you as soon as I hear anything. I'll ask Con to call you, too, if something changes."

"Okay." At least that was something. "I hate this, Rosanna."

"I know." She looked genuinely sympathetic. "Don't worry about us, though. People don't mind picking up the slack. Besides, you did us all a huge service, resolving the situation with the apocalypse patients. Take advantage of the time off. I'm sure your parents would love to see more of you, right?"

"I'm sure they would, but I'll probably just stick to our usual Sunday dinners. If they know I'm taking more time off work, they'll just get worried and ask me questions I can't answer. Then they'll restart their campaign to convince me that I should quit and take a nice, safe teaching job."

"Oh that's right. I remember. Because teachers never get attacked, right?"

"Right." I smirked. "So Dr. Rodwell really wants me out of here this afternoon, huh?"

"Before his meeting ends in an hour, in fact, so you'd better get to it. Just put in any notes you haven't entered yet and make sure everything's up-to-date in the system case management-wise. We'll take it from there."

"Okay." My body felt leaden as I rose from the chair.

"Oh stop sulking," Rosanna chided. "I'd kill for a week and a half off."

"Please. You love working so much, you volunteer at the homeless clinic in your free time," I said pointedly. "You may live to regret this, you know. I might like being off so much, I'll decide not to come back."

"Bite your tongue," she called after me as I left the room.

I knew Rosanna wanted me to focus on the positive, but I just couldn't. I suspected I was being sent home because someone had told this VIP board member that given recent events, I might be too fragile to handle everything that had happened. The hospital was probably afraid I'd have a nervous breakdown and drop a worker's compensation claim in their laps. So much for my efforts to overcome my anxieties and convince my coworkers that I was fully recovered and back to normal.

At least I would be getting updates from Rosanna and Con. I just prayed Eric would crack the *Book of Amos* soon so I'd have something interesting to read before boredom drove me mad.

13

———————

CORNELIUS

It was early Thursday morning, and although he had yet to see any patients, Con was already worn out. His elbows were planted on the desk, hands cradling his aching head. Eric was in his office describing how he'd employed the Dead Parrot Protocol to decrypt Amos's file, and while Con was listening attentively, he just couldn't share Eric's excitement about the code-cracking process.

Eric paused, then leaned in and twisted his head to make eye contact with Con. "Hey, aren't you listening? This is epic stuff I'm talking about here."

"No doubt. It's a bit over my head, that's all."

"Well, I have to tell somebody. Neve is more tech-savvy than you are, right? Maybe she'll have a greater appreciation for this."

"No!" Con's gaze snapped up to meet Eric's. "Don't tell her about any of this."

"Wait, what?" Eric gave Con a quizzical look. "I thought this was *for* her?"

"Sorry. That came out harsher than intended." Con raked a hand through his hair. "I just don't want to get her involved until I understand what all this is about."

"Oh, I get it," Eric said, nodding slowly. "There's more going on here than I know about, right? I suspected as much."

"A bit." Con wished he could fill Eric in on everything that had happened with the apocalypse patients on the unit, as well as Dr. Mohinder's directive to Neve that she avoid unnecessary stress. At least he knew his friend understood the need to keep information siloed at times.

"So, if I run into Neve or she contacts me or something, what do you want me to say? I mean, Amos is her patient; he did give the drive to her. Plus, she's kind of… what's the word?"

"Stubborn? Relentless? Bloody-minded? Bent on achieving her own destruction?"

Eric's cheeks puffed as he blew out a slow breath. "I was going to go with dedicated, or maybe loyal."

"Too loyal, sometimes." Stephan came to mind, further darkening Con's mood. "I doubt she'll contact you, but for the moment, if she does, just say you're still working on it. Once I make up my mind whether to show her the file and talk to her about it, I'll let you know."

"So you want me to lie."

"For now, yes. Sorry." Con knew that while Eric had somewhat flexible ethics when it came to hacking, he was scrupulously honest in his personal relationships. However, he also knew that when push came to shove, Eric would have his back—and that he had a deep appreciation for fine whiskey. "If it helps, there's a bottle of Redbreast 21 in it for you."

Eric gave a low whistle. "*Those* are the wages of sin? Must be important." His expression brightened. "Okay, your secret's safe with me. You are aware, though, that if you keep this from her and she finds out, she's going to be royally pissed."

"Sure, don't I know?" The truth was the thought of keeping the *Book of Amos* from Neve weighed heavily on Con, but he'd be damned if he was going to smooth the road for her to get involved in anything that might cause her additional strain. Lately, he'd spent much more time than he would have preferred worrying about Neve—not to mention sitting by her hospital bedside, watching her eyelids for the merest flutter, holding her icy hand, wondering if she would live or die. She'd asked for his help with the *Book of Amos*, and he would give it to her—just not in the way she'd antic-ipated. "Let me worry about that."

"Better you than me." Eric returned to examining the printouts. "I have to give Amos credit. He used the Dead Parrot Protocol brilliantly. It took me all night to break the code. He threw a few clever wrenches into the works. And how he pieced together all this information…. All I can say is he's either working with somebody on the inside over there, or he's a genius. Just for fun, I poked around the firewall at the Brickhaven Foundation—"

"The think tank?"

"Right, and I couldn't find any chinks in the armor at all. I mean, given more time… but if some of this stuff really is from their internal servers, Amos must have mad hacking skills."

"And piss-poor judgment, messing around with them. Some heavy hitters, there." Con didn't know what this Brickhaven crowd did exactly, but he knew it wasn't a knitting circle.

"True. At least they seem to have good intentions, though."

"The same good intentions that pave the road to hell, you mean?" Con pointed at one of the documents on Brickhaven letterhead. "Look at their motto: *Alea iacta est.* 'The die is cast.' That doesn't exactly smack of altruism."

"Maybe those prep school kids just love a good game of backgammon." Eric grinned. "Since you're Mr. Glass Half-Empty, I feel obligated to throw a little balance into the conversation."

"Noted." Con tried to rub the tension from his forehead. "I can't thank you enough for doing this—and for bringing the results to me first."

"Well, that was the plan." Eric flopped back in his chair. "Here's what I don't get, though. Even if you decide to hide all this from Neve, won't she just find out what's on the drive eventually? From Amos, I mean?"

Neve hearing all about it in the controlled environment of a therapy session didn't worry Con nearly as much as the thought of her diving in and trying to make sense of the documents on her own—and becoming obsessed with the task, no doubt, now that she was off work and stuck at home. "Most likely. But I should have a better handle on all this, and on Amos, by the time he makes it back up to her unit."

"Oh, yeah. Sorry, man." Eric shook his head. "I forgot about the coma."

Con's heart constricted in his chest as he remembered the latest update on their patient: no sign of change, no improvement. In fact, judging from Amos's lab reports, it was shocking that he was still alive. "Well, hopefully he'll wake up soon. And when he does, I'll do my best to convince him to drop the whole thing before he makes some dangerous enemies. If he insists on talking to someone about it, I'll persuade him to confide in me instead and leave Neve out of it."

"He might just take that deal. I mean, if he thinks Brickhaven's up to something so shady that he hacked in there and went to the trouble of encrypting what he found, I don't know why he went to Neve for help in the first place instead of someone like you."

"Someone like me?"

"You know," Eric said, grinning. "Bulky. Resource-ful. With a mean streak."

"Hah!" Con thought he should send that description to Human Resources. They'd been pestering him for something to put on his employee profile for the hospital website. "Fair point."

Eric waved his hand over the file folder and print-outs. "Okay, well, when you need my help figuring all this out, just let me know."

"Thanks, but I've troubled you enough."

"That's never stopped you before. Besides, you know I love a mystery."

"It certainly is that." Con eyed the strange assort-ment of documents. "Although, to be honest, I doubt I'll touch any of this again until I get a chance to talk to Amos about it."

"Yeah, that totally sounds like you." Eric reached for his wallet. "Twenty bucks says you'll be calling me for more help within forty-eight hours."

Con knew Eric might be right—a fact which made him even more irritable. "Put away your cursed Viking gold and get out of here!"

"Whatever you say, big guy," Eric said as he headed for the door. Just before it banged shut, Con heard him call from the hallway, "I'll clear my schedule!"

Con glanced down at the open file folder. "Fecking hell," he muttered, unable to resist the lure. He started from the beginning once again.

The first page had a typed note with a quote from the Bible in big letters and a note from Amos.

FORGIVE THEM, FOR THEY KNOW NOT WHAT THEY DO.

With thanks, Amos. P.S. Focus on the dates.

What that meant, Con had yet to figure out. There were several news articles about Iran's newly revealed nuclear weapon capabilities and the recent worsening of tensions in the Middle East; printouts of papers Rodwell had published in psychiatric journals; and for reasons Con had yet to ascertain, copies of Rodwell's personal calendar for the past several months. Amos must have hacked directly into Rodwell's phone or computer to get that information. Then there were pages that looked like they came from the White House outlining the president's itinerary, also for the past few months. It wasn't too detailed, though, so Con figured it could have been public information from the Press Office. He hoped that was the case, at least, and that Amos hadn't been reckless enough to hack into the White House.

The rest was a mishmash of internal documents from the Brickhaven Foundation, as well as a couple web pages Eric had printed out— Brickhaven's site and public information listed about the organization. Brickhaven's minimalist website described it as an "innovative think tank." Apparently it was registered as a not-for-profit organization in the education sector.

For a think tank, Brickhaven didn't seem to Con to

be very productive. According to their website, they only published one piece of writing per year, an annual report written for presentation at a global economic conference. Amos had managed to get a copy of the most recent report. It was wide-ranging, with analysis and predictions on everything from international trade and US foreign policy to tech-enabled finance and artificial intelligence. An interesting document, yes, but Con had read similar things in magazine think pieces. It didn't contain anything particularly unique or groundbreaking.

Brickhaven also didn't appear to have a specific political affiliation, instead siding with whoever was doing the most to promote free enterprise at any given point in time. In fact, the whole organization seemed pretty unremarkable—until Con got to a multipage document on Brickhaven letterhead that he and Eric had glanced over. It was divided into two columns, with the first column labelled "Member Name" and the second, "Project." That was where things got interesting, and where that gobsheen Rodwell entered the Brickhaven picture: he was listed as a member.

Zzzt, zzzt. Con flinched as the sound of his phone vibrating in the desk drawer pulled him out of his thoughts. He retrieved the phone, frowning. A text from Neve—usually the person he most wanted to hear from. At the moment, though, he wasn't ready to talk to her.

Neve: Dying of boredom—literally. Emailing you my self-authored obituary now.

Con chuckled. Off work less than a day, and Neve already had cabin fever. It had been hard enough to convince her to stay home from work when she was recovering from multiple stab wounds. Now he could picture her sitting at home, mindlessly ambling around the apartment, flitting from one task to the next with an adorably disgruntled look on her face.

The more he pictured it, the more he thought about how much he'd love to kiss the frown from her lips and replace it with an entirely different expression....

Forcing himself to focus, he texted her back.

Con: Do you want it published online only, or also in the Post & the Times?

Neve: Newspapers, too, of course. Some of the people who would want to know about my demise aren't digital natives.

He should end the conversation before Neve could ask for an update on Eric's progress. Con needed time to decide what he was going to tell her.

Con: How about this: survive today, and I'll treat you to dinner.

There was a pause, and he wondered if he was pushing his luck. Finally she replied.

Neve: Deal.

Seeing that one little word on his screen made him far happier than it had any right to.

Con: Grand. I have to go. Work beckons.

Of course, he didn't specify what kind of work.

Neve: Have fun. See you tonight. :)

A smiley face emoji. At least he'd cheered her up a little. And he had another dinner date with Neve—two in one week. If he and God were on more than nodding terms, Con might think he was being blessed for his patience. Of course, he shouldn't get carried away. Neve most likely didn't think of these as *dates* at all, merely more dinners out with a friend from work. A man could dream, though.

He frowned down at the sheet in front of him. So Rodwell was a member of a think tank. Nothing so odd about that. This was Washington, after all. The few years he'd been living in the city had taught Con that whatever their professions, many people came there hoping to cut off a piece of the massive DC pie. Think tanks, nonprofits, and other foundations were some of the vehicles used to gain access to influence, power, and money.

According to their site, this particular think tank was named after Brickhaven Academy, a posh DC prep school of which all the members were alums. But that wasn't so odd either. People often formed organizations with those they'd known for a long time, or with whom they had a common bond. There could be comfort in familiarity, and trust borne of a shared history.

He looked again at the list of member names and projects. In addition to Rodwell, the member list

included Orson Taul, whom Con and Eric had immediately recognized as the US attorney general. There
were also several other familiar names—businessmen
and government officials important enough to merit
occasional mention in the papers.

As for the project list, some had titles only, while
others included brief notes. Still, what little information there was suggested lofty ambitions. For example,
there were names of some major federal spending
bills, big defense contractors, and well-known
international treaties. It wasn't clear whether the list
was identifying these as areas of research, subjects
Brickhaven sought to influence, or something else
entirely.

The project next to Rodwell's name had no notes,
just a title: "*Magnum Concilium: Curia Regis.*" It had been
a long time since Con had sat in Latin class, so he
opened a web browser on his computer and pulled out
a pen and notepad. He discovered that "Magnum
Concilium" referred to a meeting between influential
people and the king in historic England, with the last
such council occurring in 1640. "Curia Regis," meanwhile, meant "King's Council," a name given to groups
of advisors who served the early kings of France and
England.

He flipped through the membership list again, spot-
ting two other projects that started with "Magnum
Concilium." One appeared next to the name of
Attorney General Orson Taul. He typed the rest of

Taul's project name into the translation site: "*Non ducor, duco.*" It meant "I am not led, I lead."

Con had to admit, he was curious as to what kind of project Rodwell could be working on with his fellow prep school alum the attorney general—not that it was any of his business what Rodwell did in his downtime, he reminded himself.

He scanned the rest of the names and found one more person, Riggs Sanderson, working on "Magnum Concilium." He knew he'd seen that name somewhere before. Sure enough, an online search quickly revealed several news articles naming Sanderson as a retired US Army Green Beret and founder of Primehook Security Services, a private military company. Two years before, Primehook operatives were accused of destroying a village in Afghanistan, killing multiple innocent civilians. They claimed it was a result of bad intelligence, that they'd been told the village was home only to a terrorist cell. But there were also accusations that the contractors involved in the operation were part of an illegal opium trade ring and that they destroyed the village as revenge for a drug deal that had gone bad. As yet, there hadn't been a formal investigation or any arrests made—a fact that had generated quite a bit of outrage, both in the US and internationally.

"Jaysus," Con muttered to himself. He couldn't help wondering if Sanderson's Brickhaven brother, the attorney general, was shielding Primehook from prosecution somehow.

Con translated the second part of Sanderson's project name, "*Sic semper tyrannis.*" The phrase, which meant "Thus always to tyrants," was apparently connected to the assassinations of both Julius Caesar and Abraham Lincoln. Less ominously, it was also the motto of a couple places in the US and some military naval vessels.

Con's frown deepened as he looked over the notes he'd jotted down. So Rodwell was working on something with the attorney general and a former Green Beret-turned-military contractor who was currently under a murderous cloud. That was all he needed to know. Whatever Amos's initial reasons for hacking into Brickhaven, he may well have stumbled onto something real and potentially dodgy involving some very high-level players. Between that and the likely illegal hacking involved, whatever was going on between Amos and Brickhaven, there was no way Con was letting Neve anywhere near it.

Through his work with Neve and the rest of the team on Unit 4, Con had learned the fiendish methods by which mental illness sometimes insinuated itself. He could imagine how it might have begun this time for Amos. Perhaps he'd learned some piece of information about Brickhaven that activated his symptoms of paranoia, leading him to construct an apocalyptic conspiracy theory with the think tank at the center. Now Amos wanted to convince Neve of whatever wild ideas he was having on one level because, in his mind, he needed her help to prevent this apocalypse. But on a deeper level, if Amos could get Neve to believe him, it would validate his delusions. Then he could finally embrace the compelling lie his illness was always trying to sell him: that he wasn't ill, after all.

No doubt Amos intended to try to pull the threads together and make his case to Neve at their next therapy session. Fortunately, since she was off work for the next week and a half, even if Amos woke up in the next five minutes, that session wouldn't be happening anytime soon.

If Amos woke up, that was.

Con leaned his chair back, closed his eyes, and pressed the heels of his palms into his eyelids. On top of the usual weighty sense of responsibility he felt toward his patients, over time, he'd developed a deep fondness for Amos. Con didn't think he could bear to lose him. But if being a doctor had taught him anything, it was that what he could or could not bear was of no consequence.

Before he'd realized that God would do whatever He wanted regardless, Con might have said a prayer for the lad. Physicians and God were in related businesses, after all—saving lives, saving souls. But over the course of his career, while he'd seen some patient recoveries that could be considered miraculous, Con had also signed hospice admission papers for a three-year-old girl and saved the life of a man who went on to murder his wife. If that was all part of a greater plan, he didn't want to know the Planner.

At any rate, it wasn't God's intervention but Rodwell's for which he was grateful that morning. Rodwell didn't know it, but he'd actually helped Con by sending Neve home for a while. The last thing she needed was more stress in her life, and no matter what was going on with Amos, Brickhaven, and the apocalypse patients, it would definitely put her under more stress, not less.

He pushed the papers back into the file folder and stuffed it into his satchel. Then he tore the paper from his notepad and folded it around the thumb drive, tucking them both into his shirt pocket. At least he had the rest of the afternoon to figure out what he was going to say to Neve, and how to ease her inevitable disappointment.

14

NEVE

After a day of climbing the walls at home, I couldn't wait to hear the latest updates from Con. I was glad to be back at Catch 22, one of our favorite haunts. The diner was decorated to look like it was on a beach boardwalk, with crab pots and fishing nets strategically placed, driftwood detailing, and vintage brass nautical lanterns for lighting. They had great standard diner fare, but they also had an impressive selection of seafood and a dessert case filled with gorgeous temptations from a nearby French patisserie. The speakers played soft crooner-type tunes from the thirties and forties, giving the place a charming warmth.

But Con appeared a bit dejected, and I began to fear the news wasn't good. "Please don't keep me in suspense. What's going on?"

He looked down at his hands. "I'm sorry, Neve. Eric

did his best, but I'm afraid I don't have anything to show you."

"What? Are you serious?" Eric had sounded so confident about being able to decrypt the drive with the Dead Parrot Protocol, it hadn't even occurred to me to doubt him. "But he seemed so certain...."

"I know. I'm sorry. I don't know what else to say."

I slumped against the padded vinyl booth. The one and only thing I could do for Amos while he was out of commission was read the file he'd given me. Now I couldn't even do that—and after I'd promised. I felt like a deflated balloon, empty and purposeless.

But Con looked like he felt guilty, which was ridiculous. It wasn't his fault, and the last thing I wanted to do was make him feel worse. "Hey, it's okay. We tried, right? Unless you have another hacker in your back pocket?"

He shook his head. "I'm afraid not."

"Then we'll just have to wait for *our friend* to wake up and explain it to us," I said, using the phrase to protect Amos's privacy since we were in public. "Not the end of the world—so to speak." I forced myself to smile as I slid out of the booth. "Stop looking so glum, okay? I'm going to the ladies' room. Back in a minute."

"If the waiter comes back?"

"My usual."

Con nodded.

I tried to look upbeat, but once inside the restroom,

I closed myself into a stall and let the mask fall. My eyes stung with the threat of tears, but I reminded myself that decrypting the thumb drive would only have given me the illusion of doing something positive. It wouldn't have actually helped Amos, not in his current condition.

I stepped out and spoke to my reflection in the mirror. "So it didn't work. Get over it. Being upset helps no one." Reminding myself that I was not only helpless but useless didn't really make me feel any better, but it did drive home how silly it was to get emotional about something as trivial as a thumb drive when Amos was clinging to life. I straightened up and walked back to the table, determined to convince Con that there was no reason to feel bad about the situation.

He was still frowning when I returned.

"See? I'm good." I pointed to the fake-bright expression on my face as I sat back into the booth.

"That's a fine acting job. Right, so. If it helps, I'll pretend to believe you." He waved in the direction of the kitchen. "Food's been ordered."

"Wonderful. Thank you." On cue, my mouth started to water. Chicken breast stuffed with crab was only minutes away. At least I was going to get some top-notch comfort food. "If you really want to make me feel better, help me think of a way to keep myself busy for the next week and a half. Otherwise, I'm afraid I'll end up doing something drastic."

He cocked an eyebrow. "Such as?"

Because I knew his opinion on the matter, and because I desperately needed entertainment, I said, "I don't know, maybe get a full-sleeve tattoo?"

Predictably, he groaned.

Smiling, I needled on. "I've always wanted one, you know."

"You already have that one on your shoulder, which you've told me you regret. Plus, a tattoo you can only cover with long sleeves isn't practical when you live in a city that's hot as Hades half the year and work in a hospital that requires you to cover all body art."

"I never said I regretted the one on my shoulder. It was just... you know...." I searched for words. "Not very well-executed." The slightly mushy pair of butterflies had been a graduation gift from my high school boyfriend, who broke up with me a week afterward, but I wasn't about to tell Con the real reason for my regret. "I'll research artists more thoroughly this time. And you can cover tattoos with makeup, you know."

"Makeup that will come off when you perspire—or in your case, when you inevitably spill a drink on your arm."

I grinned. "Admit it, you just don't like tattoos. You think they're trashy."

He scowled at me as a few heads swiveled in our direction. "That's not—" Con stared at the ceiling and spoke haltingly. "I never said—"

"You're friends with Eric," I pointed out. "He's more inked than I am."

"I don't care what Eric does to his body!" Con declared. When a few more people looked his way, he lowered his voice. "Look, I'm a doctor. I have more respect for the epidermis than to puncture it without reason. And with skin as exquisite as yours, it would be absolutely criminal. There are multiple risks of infection, not to mention the heavy metals in the ink, and the fact that you could be obscuring the site of a future melanoma—"

Unable to hold back anymore, I started to laugh. "Con, stop. Please. I'm not getting a tattoo, okay? I was joking."

His glare just made it harder for me to stop laughing. "You were winding me up?"

I grinned. "Yes, and I'm giving myself an A-plus for that one."

"A-plus indeed. Well done."

My heart lightened as he smiled for the first time since our conversation about the thumb drive. Then heat crept into my cheeks as one of his comments sank in. "And please, there's no need to exaggerate. My skin is just skin. It's entirely ordinary, not 'exquisite.'"

"Ah, now, I beg to differ. In fact, I'd say 'exquisite' is a small word." Con leaned forward and rested his elbows on the table. He caught my gaze and said in a low rumble, "Surely you know everything about you is stunning."

Something in his eyes made my breath catch. I couldn't remember him ever looking at me quite like that before. There was a sharp longing, almost a hunger. I mean, he probably *was* hungry, but this was different. Con looked hungry for *me*.

Was he… could he possibly be *flirting* with me? The blush crept down my neck. No, certainly not. I must have been imagining things. Waving the idea away, I said lightly, "You only think that because you've never seen me first thing in the morning."

"Yes I have."

"You have?" I thought back, then remembered that yes, he had—both in the hospital after the attack and when he'd visited me at home during my recovery. "Okay, well, maybe you have, but that's not the point."

Con leaned forward, bringing his brown-eyed gaze that much closer to mine. In a voice as devilish and dry as whiskey, he said, "My mistake." The corners of his mouth twitched upward. "What *was* the point, then?"

Fighting the sudden and inexplicable urge to look at his lips, I swallowed hard. "My point," I replied, "was that it's obvious you just said that to be kind—the 'stunning' part, I mean. So thank you. For being kind, I mean. And for saying that, even though it's not true." I heard myself rambling, but I couldn't seem to help it. In those few moments, something small but significant had shifted between Con and me—something that, while exciting, also made me nervous.

If he knew what effect our conversation was having on me, then he was merciless, because he kept staring at me like I was an oasis he'd discovered while wandering the desert. With pure solemnity, he said, "When it comes to you, Neve, I always speak the truth. And you are, hands down, the most stunningly beautiful woman, both inside and out, I've ever had the good fortune to know."

My eyes locked onto his. An intense current of energy flowed between us. I didn't want to move, or even breathe, for fear of disturbing the moment.

What is happening? I'd suppressed my attraction to Con for two years—mainly because of Stephan, but also because I knew Con didn't feel the same way about me. It had been very hard work at times, but I'd done it. But now he was… what *was* he doing? Joking around with me? Or just being nice? I shouldn't read too much into it, should I? After all, if I misread him, it could make things awkward between us. Whatever else, I didn't want that to happen.

I coughed out an awkward laugh. "Well, um, thank you, I guess." Gathering my courage, I decided to test the waters a little. I looked down and twisted my napkin tightly around my finger. "You're not so bad yourself, you know."

"Is that so?" Now it was Con's turn to look surprised. "Or are *you* just saying *that* to be kind? Because if you are, that's grand. But if you genuinely think I'm 'not so bad,' well, that's more than I could ever dare hope for."

His tone was teasing but intimate. There was no mistaking it now: attraction crackled in the air between us. It was open and frank from his side of the table. From mine, it was tentative but undeniably present. The coals I'd so meticulously banked were glowing, and the heat literally had me squirming in my seat.

Con must have been either oblivious to my discomfort or enjoying it somehow, because he didn't look away, or even say something to lighten the moment and let me off the hook. That was when I realized he was testing the waters, too.

Oh my God, was it possible? Could he really have feelings for me? And if so, what was I supposed to do with that information after all this time?

The electricity in the booth had built to the point where it felt like the air itself might combust. The ball was in my court. I had to say something. Something honest but not too forward. Something that would leave me wiggle room in case I'd misinterpreted what was going on.

Finally I settled on "You can go ahead and hope, then."

He blinked, and it pleased me on a deep level that my response had left him speechless—for a second, at least. "Really?"

"Mm-hmm."

"How about dare?"

"Yeah," I replied, giving my hair a playful toss in an effort to hide my nerves. "You can do both those things."

The energy shifted yet again as Con leaned forward, suddenly serious and with a new intensity in his eyes. "Neve, there's something I've been wanting to say to you—"

"Crab-stuffed chicken breast?"

The waiter's voice made me jump. Con closed his eyes and slowly leaned back, disappointment written across his face.

"That's me," I said, clearing some space for the large plate.

"And fish and chips." The waiter set the pile of fried cod and french fries in front of Con, who normally lit up at the sight. Fish and chips was one of his favorite meals, and Con said Catch 22 was the only place in DC that made it like they did back in Ireland. But he didn't even appear to see the food. With clear effort, he smiled and thanked the waiter.

"Yes, thank you," I said as adrenaline ran riot through my body. I was grateful the food had arrived, because it was going to take some time for me to adjust to whatever was happening between Con and me. I pointed at his plate. "You should probably eat that before it gets cold. I know how much you hate cold fish and chips."

"Cold fish and chips isn't my main concern at the

moment." His eyes flashed with anticipation. "After dinner, what do you say we finish that conversation, pick up where we left off? Somewhere private?"

Well, that settled it. I hadn't misread a damned thing. My heart thumped so loudly I was certain he could hear it. "Sure, okay," I replied, my voice wavering.

As we started in on our respective dishes, a new warm glow of energy surrounded us. We kept stealing glances at each other like teenagers on a first date, cautiously curious and trying to guess whether something would develop. It was so strange but also exhilarating, uncomfortable yet thrilling. I didn't know what to think.

Whatever is happening here, he's still Con, I reminded myself, trying not to freak out. I ate my food on autopilot as my rational mind worked overtime trying to convince me that we would figure things out, no matter the outcome. Con had shown me time and again that looking out for me, and for us, was his top priority. And since it was mine too, we would be okay.

In what seemed like no time, both our plates were empty and the waiter was standing by the table again, asking if we wanted dessert. We both rushed to say no, that we didn't have any room left—not our usual response. It was obvious that we were both anxious to get out of there and go, as Con had said, "somewhere private." The waiter dropped the check on the table and left with our empty dishes.

Con picked up the check. "I've got this. No arguments. This was my idea."

"Who's arguing?" I was more than ready to get to the next part of the evening.

We exchanged smiles as he went to stand in the long line behind the front counter, where it appeared a new employee was being trained on the cash register.

Con's departure left a vacuum of energy in the booth. Taking a deep breath, I tried to cool myself down in every respect. My eyes darted around, searching for a distraction, finally coming to rest on Con's satchel. It was crafted from supple leather that had taken on many shades of brown after years of use and tender care. To me, it was symbolic of his personality. He took excellent care of the things he valued; neither objects nor relationships were disposable to him.

I knew he always carried a book in there, one of those political thrillers he liked. A few minutes of reading might help me calm down a bit. I reached across the table, grabbed the satchel by the strap, and lifted it over onto the seat next to me. Opening the flap, I saw a thick hardback by one of his favorite authors tucked against a bunch of patient files. I honestly didn't mean to snoop, but one file folder caught my eye. On the tab was scrawled, "DEAD PARROT."

Since the writing wasn't Con's, it must have been Eric's. I assumed the folder was either empty or had documentation of Eric's failed attempts to decrypt the thumb drive. I was tempted to steal a look.

The wrongness of looking at Con's files without his permission was obvious. On the other hand, the file was about the *Book of Amos*, something I'd passed on to Con in the first place. It was my file, then, really. He was just carrying it for me.

I glanced over at the cashier's line. There were still three people in front of Con. A potent combination of impatience and curiosity overruled my moral qualms. I eased the file out and slid it onto the table. It was a lot thicker than I'd anticipated. Then again, I imagined computer coding documents could be lengthy. I closed Con's satchel, put it back on his seat, and turned my attention to the file.

The first thing I saw when I opened it was a... note from Amos?

FORGIVE THEM, FOR THEY KNOW NOT WHAT THEY DO.

With thanks, Amos. P.S. Focus on the dates.

Was that some kind of cover sheet Eric had managed to print out without decrypting the rest of the file? Well, that was more than I'd managed, at least. I'd have to ask Amos what it meant.

I flipped to the next page. It was a printout of someone's electronic calendar. Upon closer inspection, I realized it was Dr. Rodwell's personal calendar. There were notes about errands he planned to run, personal training sessions, his wife's birthday.... *How did that get in here?*

I kept flipping. Some of Dr. Rodwell's publications. A series of news articles about the Middle East. Printouts from something called the Brickhaven Foundation. Several pages on White House stationery that outlined a rough itinerary for President Duran—the president of the United States.

Everything inside me stilled.

"What are you doing?" Con asked quietly. He was standing next to the table.

I just stared at the pile of documents, both wanting and not wanting to make sense of what I was seeing. The inevitable conclusion hurtled toward me like a speeding train while I was tied to the tracks, unable to move.

"Neve."

An overhead light glowed behind Con's head, hiding his expression in shadow. Squinting up at him, I asked, "Is this...?"

He nodded.

A cold feeling of dread slammed into the pit of my stomach. "But you said...."

Con sat in the booth across from me. His expression was wary, as though he sensed a storm coming. "I know. I had my reasons."

Tears sprang into the corners of my eyes. I blinked them back. "What the fuck, Con?"

Peering at me intently, he said, "Look, I've read that file. Whatever our friend has gotten himself into, while it may have started in his imagination, now it looks like it could be real trouble. And you've dealt with more than your share of trouble lately. I thought it best—"

"You thought it best to lie to me? To my face? About *this*?" Con, whom I trusted and counted on. Con, whom I clung to as my center of gravity. Con, who, more than anyone, knew how important it was for me to keep my promise to Amos.

He slid his hand across the table toward me, palm up. I sat back, folding my arms tightly across my chest.

"I know how much you care about our friend," he said, "and I know how much you want to do something for him right now, so I knew if I gave you the file, you'd be like a dog with a bone. You'd dive in and do research, or whatever you feel you need to do to try and understand his symptoms, his behavior. But unlike you, I've read what's in the file, and I can tell you for certain it's not going to help you understand anything. In fact, it'll only confuse things further. It's nothing but a quagmire, and you'd do well to stay away from it."

I heard Con's voice speaking words, but none of them registered. I just kept flashing back to his lips moving and the words coming out: *"Eric did his best, but I'm afraid I don't have anything to show you."*

"So you just decided to lie to me?" I squawked as my throat tightened. "You didn't even blink." *What* else *did he lie to me about? Oh God, what if he was just flirting with me to distract me, to keep me from getting suspicious and draw my attention away from the* Book of Amos? *Well, bravo—it worked.*

Fueled by the fresh humiliation of that possibility, my thoughts began to spin even faster. *Did I really allow myself to get snowed like that—and so soon after finding out how badly I misjudged Stephan? Am I just an idiot, or is no one who I thought they were?* Suddenly it became hard to breathe.

"It wasn't easy at all," Con said, sounding pained. "Lying to you was the last thing I wanted to do. But it's not wise for you to get mixed up in this. Trust me."

His outstretched hand took the shape of a pincher claw, as though he expected me to give him back the file.

Gaping at him, I quickly stuffed the papers back into the folder and shoved it into my messenger bag. "Trust you? Are you serious right now?"

Con pinched the bridge of his nose. "Ah, come now."

My face and palms dampened with cold perspiration. "Were you ever going to tell me the truth?"

He raked a hand through his hair, silently weighing his response. Finally he said, "I hadn't decided yet."

"Jesus, Con!" A surge of outrage propelled me up and out of the booth. I slung the strap of my bag over my head.

"Calm down, please, and listen to me." Con pushed himself to his feet. "You've already taken on more than you should have this week. In any case, the file is incomplete, a puzzle with too many missing pieces. No one will be able to make any sense of it until our friend wakes up." He held out his hand again. "Once he does, I'll talk to him, I promise, and I'll deal with it."

I shoved his hand to the side. "Are you listening to yourself? There is no way I'm going to trust you or anyone else with this. Our friend asked for my help, and I'm damn sure not going to let you push me away from my own patient!"

"I'm not the one who sent you off work," he said sharply, then softened his tone. "Look, there's nothing you can do from home anyway. Leave this with me, all right? Let me help."

His words stung. Reflexively, I lashed out. "If this is what help from you looks like, you can keep it," I snapped as my hands began to tremble. "I gave our friend my word that I would read the file. My *word*, Con. Keeping that promise is the one and only thing I can do for him right now, so you can be damned sure I'm going to follow through whether I'm officially off work or not!"

Worry lines shot across his face. "Neve, don't let yourself get worked up. I know you're concerned about our friend. I am, too. But we both know the only meaningful things that can be done for him right now are being done in the ICU. It's frustrating, but there's nothing you can do to help, least of all reading that fecking file!"

"You're right!" I could hear the pitch of my voice rising, but I was unable to control it. "I can't do anything to help him medically. But when he wakes up, it will matter to him that I've kept my promise. Maybe you don't believe maintaining integrity in relationships is 'meaningful,' but I do, and I'm willing to bet our friend does, too."

Con rubbed his forehead so hard that his fingers left behind white streaks. "You know that's not what I meant."

"How am I supposed to know what you meant?" It felt like my heart was ricocheting around inside my chest. "Seconds after you just lied to my face, you said that when it comes to me, you always speak the truth. What did you mean *then*?"

Con glanced heavenward, as though hoping for divine intervention. Then he pinned me with a hard look. "When it comes to you, I always *do* speak the truth. But the contents of that thumb drive have nothing to do with you."

"How do I know when I haven't even read the file? It's not like I can take your word for it!" The tears that had been threatening began to slide in rivulets down my cheeks. "I don't get it, Con! After everything… why are you trying to stand in my way now, instead of helping me?"

"Why?" A vein in his neck began to throb. "Why am I not helping you get yourself mixed up in some shady business, you mean? Have you forgotten how close you were to death's door? Can you not see that the same knife that cut you cut the people who love you, as well? We're all still bleeding, but you're primed to go on another mad tear, chasing trouble," he bellowed. "Could you not spare a thought for the rest of us? Everyone else's wounds don't heal as fast as yours!"

Con's words felt like a kick to the chest, knocking the wind out of me.

I'd had no idea that my stabbing had affected him so deeply, hurt him so much. Or maybe I had known, deep down, but didn't want to think about it. Rosanna never minced words, so I knew how upset she'd been. But when it came to Con's feelings, evidently he'd only shown me the tip of the iceberg.

What about my parents? Had they been putting on a brave face as well?

Shame scalded me from the inside out. Was I a terrible daughter, and a worse friend? I had never talked to Con or my parents about how the stabbing had affected them. I was a therapist, for God's sake. It should have occurred to me to invite them to talk to me about their feelings, to get whatever concerns they had off their chests—if for no other reason than I could have put their minds at ease.

Con stood in front of me, red-faced and radiating pain. Part of me wanted to reach out and comfort him. The other part wanted to run away and escape the echo chamber of suffering. Either way, I had to do something to break the deafening silence that pounded against my ears.

Wait a minute. Silence? In a busy diner?

Tentatively, I glanced around us. Everyone had stopped talking, stopped moving. They were either openly staring at us or working hard not to.

I managed to suck in a few shallow breaths as our waiter gingerly made his way toward us. When he was just over arm's length away, he stage-whispered, "Um, you know we never like to rush people out of here, but, uh, it is very busy right now, and there are people waiting for tables, so unless you want something else…."

Con looked from the waiter to me and nodded slightly, as though to indicate the decision was mine.

Mortified and moved by compassion for our poor waiter, I rooted around in my bag, found my wallet, and handed him a twenty-dollar bill. "We're going," I whispered. "Sorry for the trouble."

The waiter fake-smiled at me. "Thanks," he said as we headed toward the door. "Enjoy your night!"

Yeah, like that's going to happen.

I darted out of the diner, wrapping my hands around my throat in an attempt to stop the cold fingers of panic creeping up my neck.

The bells on the door jingled. I heard Con's footfalls as he walked up behind me. "I'm sorry. I shouldn't have said those things."

I spun around to face him and stepped back. My

whole body was trembling now. "No, you *should* have said those things," I cried out. "You should have told me how you felt a long time ago, in fact. But that's not what you should be apologizing for!"

His expression darkened. "If you're waiting for me to apologize for trying to keep you out of whatever nonsense Amos is mixed up in, I can tell you right now that's going to be quite a long wait."

"Ahh!" I cradled my head in my hands. All at once, everything felt like too much. The desire to flee the scene was becoming overwhelming.

Con laid his hand on my arm. "Neve."

The physical contact jolted me, a reminder of the newly unleashed attraction between us that I now wanted to forget. I shrugged him off. "Don't touch me!"

"All right," he said, "but you don't look well. Let me walk you home."

Of course I wasn't well. The sense of panic that had been building since I discovered Con's lie was peaking. But he was the problem, not the cure. The acute need to get away from him screeched through me like bats fleeing a cave. I couldn't bear to be around him, not for another second.

"Leave me alone!" I shouted, bolting down the street like a gazelle with a lion on its tail.

I heard Con calling after me, but I was consumed by the need to run, to pound the pavement and feel my steps jolting through my body, to force air into my lungs, and to get to a safe place where I could fall apart in private.

Once I reached home, I threw my bag on the kitchen table, flopped onto the couch, and allowed the gasping sobs to take me. How long they would continue, I didn't know. But given how I was feeling, they might last for a long, long time.

15

———

NEVE

I awoke to a faint beeping. Rather, I tried not to wake, but the beeping was persistent. As I left the fog of sleep behind, I recognized the sound. It was my phone, telling me someone had left a voice mail.

I cursed myself for failing to put my phone on silent mode before going to bed. Clothes tugged at me, and I tried and failed to stretch my legs out straight.

Cracking one eyelid open, I saw I was lying on my couch. *Wait, why am I not in my bed?* Judging by the quality of the light coming in through the window, it was midmorning. *What day is it? Thursday?* And I was on forced leave. At least I didn't have to worry about being late for work.

I tried to open my eyes fully, but they felt swollen. *Oh.*

All at once and with devastating clarity, I remembered. My head ached as the events of the previous night smacked into my brain. I rubbed my eyes, which were itching. I had cried myself to sleep and straight into dehydration.

And now I had to listen to my voice mail. It could be something important.

Maybe Amos had woken up. That thought propelled me into a sitting position. I waited for the phone to beep again. Guided by some kind of sleep-fog sonar, I determined it was on the kitchen table. I was up and moving.

Let's see.... Approximately a hundred texts from Con. I flipped through them quickly, even though scanning them made my chest feel as sore as a fresh bruise. Things like "I'm sorry, let's talk, please pick up, I'm worried," etc. Nothing about Amos. I checked my voice mail. Again, approximately a hundred messages from Con, but none of them were any more recent than his texts, so I could conclude they had nothing to do with Amos either. There had only been one call that morning, and it was from Stephan.

Oh for God's sake. I flopped back down on the sofa and listened to Stephan sounding nervous, yet hopeful on his voice mail message.

"Hi, babe. The weekend is getting closer. I hope you're as excited as I am about Saturday. I was thinking I'd pick you up around eleven. How does that sound? Just give me a buzz, okay? Don't forget, White House photo op, so you'll want to wear some-thing... you know, nice. So you'll want to go shopping. It's on me. I guess that's it. Call me when you get this."

It was fortunate I hadn't eaten breakfast yet, because if I had, I would have retched. I knew Stephan well enough to infer what he really meant: in his opinion, none of the clothing I already owned would make me appropriately impressive arm candy for him in our picture with Lee and the president. Well, he could forget it; I wasn't going dress shopping. And there was no way I was going to let him drive me to the White House. I would feel awkward enough being there with him, knowing I was going to tell him afterward for the third and final time that things between us were over for good. I didn't need to spend time stuck in a car alone with him as well.

I sent Stephan a quick text, telling him I was busy Saturday morning and would meet him at the event, and asking him to email me the details of when and where to arrive.

As for Con....

My throat tightened as I remembered the raw agony in his voice when he told me how the knife that cut me had cut him, too. In spite of all that had happened the night before, I knew his fear that I'd get hurt again was real and that his desire to protect me came from a genuine place.

Then there was the fact that he'd included himself in the list of people who loved me.

Loved?

And he'd said there was something he'd been wanting to say to me....

I desperately needed some water.

I went to the sink and stood over it, filling a glass and focusing on deep breathing. I took a sip of water and closed my eyes as the cool liquid soothed my raw throat. The ache in my chest softened just a bit, enough that I could bear it, at least.

At the diner, my emotions had been all over the place. First, disappointment that Eric couldn't crack the code. Then disbelief, excitement, nervousness, and an almost painful sense of hope—all inspired by Con's flirtation, which had almost taken a serious turn. Finally, shock at the discovery that he'd outright lied to me—about Amos, of all things—followed by outrage. Hurt. Guilt. Humiliation. The list went on.

In hindsight, I knew Con hadn't faked romantic interest in me to distract me from his deception. He would never do something that hurtful. In fact, that idea was so ridiculous, it smacked of irrational fear— irrational like running away into the night like a maniac.

Never had thinking about Con inspired anything but warmth in me. But now the warmth had been replaced by extremes of heat and cold, and worse, pain at being away from him, and pain at the thought of seeing him again. Hurt by his betrayal and hurt by the thought that things might never be the same between us. My heart felt like a garment torn in the throes of grief.

How had everything managed to get so screwed up in less than twenty-four hours? And what had possessed him?

All right, I was curious. I wanted to know what could possibly have inspired Con to lie to me, and the answers had to be in the *Book of Amos*. I would figure out what it was he thought I needed protection from, and if there was something that required handling, I would handle it. Alone. No more drama, no more scenes, and no more "help" from Con or anyone.

A solid breakfast, coffee, a hot shower. That was what I needed.

Afterward, I would look over the file and try to figure out what Amos had gotten himself into. Then I would call Con and start trying to stitch the torn pieces of our friendship back together.

16

CORNELIUS

Con hated his leg.

He knew that wasn't a reasonable thing to feel. The leg wasn't to blame for the accident and its aftermath. Usually he was able to tamp down the waves of ill feeling toward the broken parts of his body, waves that sometimes crested inside him.

That particular morning, though.... As he sat at his office desk and massaged a knotted muscle in his thigh, the underlying current of his resentment exploded into full-blown, black-hearted hatred.

Because of his leg, when Neve had run away from him outside the diner the night before, he hadn't been able to give chase. He'd had no hope of catching up to her—not before she got home, locked the door, and erected a wall around her heart. The moment of possibility had passed.

If he'd been able to catch her, he could have walked her home, comforted her, and asked for her forgiveness —something he realized he needed to do after playing their conversation over in his head all night. He'd been a colossal arse, and there were an infinite number of ways in which he could have handled the situation better.

Also, they could have talked about *them*, about the feelings they had for one another that were finally coming out into the light of day. He could have confessed to Neve that she held his heart entirely in her hands.

All that might have happened if it hadn't been for his damned leg.

Of course, it could have gone the other way, too. If he had chased her, it might have just made her angrier and driven more of a wedge between them. But he would never know now.

Con tried to latch on to something his first physical therapist had told him after the accident—to think of his leg as a friend, a partner, and to treat it with compassion. He had taken that approach, and by all measures, he'd done much better than his original doctors predicted. In truth, his leg's recovery was quite remarkable. He should have been regarding it with admiration.

Definitely not hatred.

And yet….

Neve hadn't answered any of his texts or messages,

not that he'd expected her to. He'd forced himself to stop trying to reach her after a couple hours. The only thing he could do now without acting like a stalker was wait for her to contact him.

Wait. Helplessly. Just like with Amos. An infuriating pattern was forming.

At least having read the *Book of Amos*, Con knew the file didn't make enough sense for Neve to do anything with it. Before she could dig much deeper, she would need Amos to connect some dots for her—if, indeed, there were any to connect in the realm of reality. And since Amos wasn't available for the moment, at least, Neve would just have to remain as confused and stuck as Con had been after reading the file. Stuck was exactly how he wanted her—stuck and away from the hospital, unable to do anything reckless.

Meanwhile, Eric would be pleased to learn he wouldn't have to lie to Neve after all. Con shot off a text to let him know. After responding to a return text that yes, Eric would still be getting his bottle of Redbreast 21, Con's mobile phone buzzed, this time with an incoming call.

The screen showed a photo of his brother, Eamonn. Not Neve, then—and unexpected. He and his siblings usually communicated by text, and whenever they did call each other, it was on the weekend.

Con answered with his usual lighthearted greeting. "Eamonn! Who's dead?"

He was relieved to hear his brother's laughter on

the other end of the line. "Sorry to disappoint you, but we're all still alive and kicking."

"Thank Christ for that. You've never called me at work before. I didn't know what to think."

"If I'm honest, I thought I'd be leaving a message."

"Well, lucky you," Con said, "you got me. How's the *craic*?"

"Ah, you know. Same as always."

"Still enjoying the glamorous life of a brewmaster?" Eamonn had recently been promoted to supervisor at Calfwood Brewery, a craft beer enterprise in Cork.

Eamonn chuckled. "Nonstop excitement—or it would be if I wasn't up at the crack of dawn every day. I have to be the first one in now."

"I told you, you should have become a doctor."

"Right, the easy life. I know you're just arsing around over there, *Tarbh*."

Con squeezed his eyes shut. It did him no good to hear his old rugby nickname, the Irish word for "bull." His days of sport felt like a lifetime ago, but reminders could still bring feelings of grief and disappointment rushing back to the surface. He knew Eamonn meant no harm, though, and the moniker had stuck to him long after he stopped playing—due to his tendency toward bloody-mindedness, he'd been told.

Con cleared his throat and changed the subject. "How are the folks? Una?"

"Sure, you know yourself," Eamonn said, the cheer

drained from his voice. "Da's working away. Ma keeps asking when you're coming for a visit. As for Una, you know as much as I do. Far as I know, she's grand, away in Dublin."

A brief summary, but it spoke volumes to Con, who knew how to read between the lines. So Una was fine, it sounded like. And their parents were still running their farm equipment repair business, but their father was struggling with his depression. If their mother was asking for Con, it meant she felt under pressure and thought a visit from him might lift their father's mood —or just give her some needed encouragement, perhaps.

Con certainly wanted to be of support to his mother, but he knew visiting wasn't the way. Watching him limp around the place wouldn't help either of his parents. He would give her a call at the weekend.

Not much had changed at home, in other words. Eamonn had recently become engaged. Hopefully there weren't problems there. "Have you set a date yet?"

"No, not yet."

"I'm surprised Ma's not putting the pressure on. She wants grandchildren, and you know she doesn't like to be kept waiting."

Eamonn scoffed. "You're the oldest! What are you rushing me for?"

"I believe I've made myself clear. That chore is for you and Una." Con's family knew he didn't want children. He'd always felt uncomfortable around them. For one thing, he never knew what to say to children outside of a doctor-patient scenario. Then there was the fact that he knew he had a powerful temper when driven to it, and he would never want to inflict that on a small one. Plus, since the accident, taking care of himself required extra time and effort. He'd happily add taking care of Neve to his list, but a child as well? He'd have to say farewell to relaxing evenings with a bottle of scotch for the next eighteen years at least.

That said, if things worked out the way Con hoped they would with Neve, and *she* wanted children, he would agree to it. To secure her happiness, he was hard-pressed to think of anything he wouldn't do. But he was getting ahead of himself—very far ahead. "And how's Ciara?"

Eamonn exhaled through his teeth with a hiss. "Well, you remember when we had to put manners on that abusive prick Una was seeing?"

"Christ's sake, don't tell me he's back."

"Nah. Rumor is we scared him so badly he fecked off to Australia," Eamonn said. "It's Ciara. She's got an ex kind of like that over in Galway, and he keeps messing with her head."

"Jaysus. Sorry to hear that." That must be terrible for Ciara, and he could only imagine how his brother was feeling. Con wasn't clear why Eamonn was calling him about it, though. There wasn't much he could do from three thousand miles away.

"The strange part is they were broken up before we met, and they hadn't seen or talked to each other since —until we got engaged, that is. Seems that news got his knickers in a twist. The whole situation's fecked."

"Sounds like."

"Anyhow, she started having some physical problems recently—nothing really serious, just strange. We don't know for sure what's going on yet, but Ciara is convinced the stress of the situation with this ex of hers is affecting her somehow."

Now Con understood why Eamonn had called. "Has she been to the doctor?"

"A whole stable of them. They don't know what's wrong yet. They're running a slew of tests at the moment."

"Sounds like a good start."

"I suppose. But you know you're the only doctor I trust."

Con knew it was likely there was nothing he could do for Ciara that her doctors weren't already doing, but if he could help put Eamonn's mind at ease, he would. "What can I do to help?"

"If they email some of her records to you, could you look them over?" Eamonn asked, sounding a bit more hopeful. "Only if you're not too busy, of course. I'd just feel better if you were involved. You might see something they haven't."

Con was tempted to ask more details about her condition, but if Eamonn wasn't offering them up, he must have his reasons. Con would find out once he got the records, anyway. "Of course. I'd be happy to consult."

"Right, consult. That's the word I was looking for." Eamonn sounded relieved. "Thanks a million, Con."

"No bother." Con would do anything for either of his siblings. They'd grown up with a father whose depression often manifested as anger and a mother who was always preoccupied with trying to keep the peace. With only each other to lean on, they'd forged close bonds.

"I'll have them send the records, then."

"I'll keep an eye out."

"Brilliant." There was a pause before Eamonn continued. "And how are you getting on?"

Con appreciated his brother asking, even though it had been an afterthought. "Let's get Ciara sorted first. Then I'll share my spellbinding tales."

"Hah! Fair enough. Grand. Thanks, Con. Talk soon."

"Right, so. Talk soon." He shook his head as he hit Disconnect. He hated that Ciara was unwell, but he knew if anyone could help her handle the situation, it was his brother.

Meanwhile, he was done waiting helplessly for things to happen. At least he could do something for his own patient. Amos wasn't awake yet, but he'd improved enough that they'd transferred him from the ICU to Con's unit. He would visit and review the chart again, see if there had been any changes overnight.

The knot in his leg was somewhat improved. Still, he took a couple pain pills for good measure. Then he pulled himself out of his chair, picked up his tablet computer, and headed to Endocrinology.

———

Con might have been imagining things, but he thought Amos looked a little better. He sat on the rolling stool at the computer monitor and checked the chart. The blood levels that had been out of whack for days had normalized the night before and were stabilizing. Some good news at last. So why wasn't Amos awake?

He rolled the stool over to the side of the bed. "Amos, wake up," he murmured, as though that would have any impact. Moved by a wave of affection, he reached down and squeezed Amos's hand. "Just wake—Jaysus!" he shouted as Amos opened his eyes.

"Ow, my hand!"

"Sorry." Con's grip had tightened in surprise. He released Amos's hand. "Christ, you had us worried."

Amos blinked and looked around the room, confused. "What happened?" he asked in a croaky voice. "Where am I?"

Con's shoulders dropped, releasing some of the tension they'd been holding. "You've been unconscious for a couple days. You're on the endocrinology unit."

"Days? No wonder I'm so hungry. And thirsty."

"Hang on."

Con stepped out to the nurses' station and told them the good news. Several nurses rushed into Amos's room. Con stood back and watched them work, taking vitals, checking the chart, drawing blood from the IV, and talking Amos through his breakfast options. Once the nurses had cleared the room, Con sat down next to the bed while Amos sipped on the cup of ice water that had magically appeared.

"If you were trying to get our attention, well done," Con scolded, trying to cover the intensity of his happiness. He didn't want Amos to know just how serious the situation had been, at least not until he was stronger. "How are you feeling?"

Amos smiled apologetically. "Weak, kinda tired. But okay, I guess."

"I'll take it." Con said a silent prayer of thanks. "We'll talk after you eat and rest a bit more."

Amos raised himself up on his elbows. "When am I going back to Unit 4?"

"That's your first question?" He wondered how much Amos remembered from before the coma but didn't want to press him right away. "Don't you like our unit here?"

"Oh yeah, it's great. Nothing personal. I just have unfinished business over there."

"Ah, I see." So Amos hadn't forgotten about Neve and the thumb drive. "I'm sorry to say it's going to have to stay unfinished for a while. Neve is off work."

"Oh." Amos squinted up at him. "Is she okay?"

"Yes, she's fine."

"Not sick?"

"No."

"When does she get back?"

"In a while. You'll be staying here for several days, at least. We have to make sure you're stable before we send you back. I'd also like to figure out what triggered your bit of a crisis there so we can prevent a recurrence."

"Yeah. I'm sorry, Doc, I don't remember much after you came to my room on Unit 4. My blood sugar dropped, right?"

"That's right."

"But then I just remember going to sleep, and nothing else after that until you woke me up a few minutes ago."

"It's all right," Con reassured. The conversation was clearly a strain on Amos; it was beginning to show on his face. "We'll figure it out. You just rest. Soon you'll be right as rain."

"Wait, Doc. You're friends with Neviah, right? I mean, outside work."

Con saw no reason to deny it. "Yes."

"Do you know if she did that favor for me?"

Since he'd already planned to talk with Amos about Brickhaven, Con took the opportunity to reveal that he was in the know. "You mean, reading the *Book of Amos*?"

Amos laid back in the bed and smiled. "Oh good.

I'm so glad she told you. That makes things easier. Wait, are you a hacker?"

Con smiled as excitement lit up Amos's face. "No, I just… have friends."

"Cool, so we're all, like, a team now. Can you call her for me? Maybe put her on speaker?"

I could if she were taking my calls, Con thought ruefully. "There will be ample opportunity to talk about all these things later. But allow me to remind you that you just woke up after being out of it for two entire days. Eat. Rest. Then talk. That's the order in which we're going to do things. Understood?"

"Yeah, okay." Amos's eyelids half closed. "Actually, I am kind of tired."

"Then rest. Breakfast will be here soon."

"Mm-hmm." Amos was already drifting off again, this time into what appeared to be an ordinary cat nap.

Con poked him on the shoulder, and he roused instantly. "Just checking."

Amos smiled, then closed his eyes again. "Thanks, Doc."

Con's relief would have been complete if it weren't run through by a vein of annoyance. Amos's first priority upon waking was to drag Neve into whatever he imagined was going on at Brickhaven. No doubt he also planned to continue pulling at threads with dangerous people on the other end. Fortunately, as Amos's doctor, Con had control over who had access to his patient. He would make an order of no visitors until he'd had a chance to convince Amos that Neve couldn't be of any help to him with Brickhaven and that he should confide in Con instead. Then he could share what he learned with the psychiatry department and get Amos the treatment he needed.

If he remained medically stable, Amos would almost certainly return to Unit 4 before Neve returned and start seeing a different therapist. Problem solved—temporarily, at least, and maybe permanently if Con could convince Rosanna to transfer the case to someone else for good. If Neve found out he'd intervened to keep her away from Amos, then so be it. He didn't think she could get any angrier at him than she already was.

Unless he didn't let her know Amos was awake, of course. Neve had specifically asked him to keep her updated on that. He could text her, at least.

On the other hand, she hadn't responded to any of his other texts. She might have blocked him at this stage. The surest way to make certain she got the message would be to tell Lolly and let her give Neve the news. Not until later that afternoon, though—after he'd had a chance to straighten the lad out on the topic of Brickhaven.

Con had a conversation with the nurses before he left, instructing them to put the "no visitors" protocol in place. Having received reassurance that someone would call him if there was any deterioration in Amos's condition, he headed back to his office to work and wait.

17

NEVE

I was on coffee number three and reading the *Book of Amos.* While I didn't have a full grasp on what it meant yet, it was clear that Con had been right: everything in the file pointed to a potential quagmire—one of Amos's creation. Clearly he'd hacked into places he shouldn't, which could get him into serious trouble.

That didn't absolve Con for lying to me, of course, but at least now I understood why he'd done it—not that I intended to "leave it with him." Con had said he knew if he gave me the file, I'd be like a dog with a bone, and I wasn't going to disappoint him.

Amos had gotten ahold of Dr. Rodwell's personal calendar, which was bad enough, but he also had a bunch of documents marked "private" and "confidential" from a think tank called the Brickhaven Foundation. The first one I picked up was a list of members and their projects. Dr. Rodwell's name was on there with a project title that appeared to be in Latin: "*Magnum Concilium: Curia Regis.*" As I continued to skim the list, I saw the name Orson Taul, at which point I dropped the list like it bit me, then immediately took all the papers with Brickhaven's name on them and stuffed them back into the file folder. I wasn't keen on violating anyone's privacy, especially not the attorney general's.

Finding out that Dr. Rodwell was a member of Brickhaven had surprised me. From the printouts of their public website, it didn't seem like a secret society or anything, but for some reason, he'd kept it off his list of affiliations. Why, I had no idea. Everyone in DC seemed to be a member of a think tank, and it was generally considered something to crow about, not keep hidden.

Quite apart from all that, though, the collection of articles about the situation in the Middle East was quite concerning. Since Stephan and I broke up, I'd been kind of avoiding any political news. It was silly, I knew, but it reminded me of him. Apparently, though, Stephan had been right; the region was becoming a powder keg, and there was good evidence that with Iran's revelation that it was now a nuclear state, multiple countries were rattling their sabers. At least according to some news outlets, President Duran, a self-described foreign policy "dove," might be making real inroads in facilitating peace negotiations.

For a brief moment, I thought about calling Stephan

to get his latest insights, but I discarded that idea quickly. Any such phone call from me would be taken as a sign of hope that our romance could be rekindled.

Meanwhile, it appeared that Amos thought there was some connection between Dr. Rodwell, Brickhaven, and the situation in the Middle East—not to mention the apocalypse. I was starting to get a sense of the expansive nature of his new delusion.

My cell phone started playing "That's Amore," the ringtone Rosanna had chosen for herself. I dropped the phone twice in my rush to pick it up. "Hey, Rosanna."

"Good morning. And how are you coping, living in the hellscape of paid time off?"

I smirked. "Don't ask. Seriously. But what's up? Is there news?"

"Yes, and it's good. I just heard through the nurse grapevine that they transferred Amos from the ICU to Endocrinology yesterday, and he woke up this morning. Now he's up to his usual tricks."

I stifled a cry of relief. *Thank God.* "Charming all the nurses, I'm guessing?"

"Oh yeah, he's got them raiding the gift shop for him, bringing him newspapers and crossword puzzles. I wouldn't be surprised if he's getting umbrellas in his drinks."

"Oh, Rosanna." My eyes moistened. "Thank you for letting me know."

"Of course, hon. But this happened hours ago. I'm surprised I'm the first to give you the news."

A geyser of irritation erupted inside me. It had been hours? Why hadn't Con called me? He knew I would want to hear this, even after everything....

Then again, after I ran away from him the night before, maybe he'd concluded that I was too difficult, not worth the trouble. That thought put an icy chill on my internal temper tantrum.

Earlier that morning, sometime after coffee number one, I realized that the night before, I'd probably over-reacted. As good friends as we were, I should have given Con the benefit of the doubt. He was a thoughtful person, not a claw hammer like Stephan. My ex believed his reasoning was always right simply because it was his, but Con would have weighed things carefully before deciding to keep the *Book of Amos* file from me. Being angry that he lied to me was justified, but the intensity of my reaction was over the top.

In other words, Con had pushed my anxiety buttons, but he wasn't responsible for installing them. I had the stabbing to thank for that.

It was embarrassing that I hadn't gotten a better handle on my panic symptoms since the attack. Con and Dr. Mohinder had agreed that I should seek professional help, but I wanted to try working on it myself first. I was a therapist, after all. And I had made some progress, but it was taking much longer than I'd hoped. The fact that I'd been overwhelmed by the compulsion to flee from my best friend the night before only underscored that fact.

Had my overreaction soured things with Con? At the very least, it had poured ice water all over our first potentially romantic interaction. Of course, we'd have to hash out the whole "lying to me without breaking a sweat" issue before that went any further.

If he was still interested, that was. The thought that he might not be chilled me from the inside out.

I couldn't deal with any of that at the moment, though. There was no time. I had to snap myself out of it and focus. Amos was awake, and while I understood why Con might be avoiding me, I couldn't understand why he hadn't at least called Rosanna personally to give her the news.

"I'm sure he's just busy," I said. Who knew? Maybe it was even true. "I'll swing by and see Amos this afternoon. Maybe—"

"Hold it right there, missy. You're off work, remember? Do you understand that concept, or do you need me to explain it to you again?"

"Oh come on. This is different."

"It is not even in the least bit different. Dr. Rodwell said he doesn't want to see you in the hospital for the next week and a half unless you're here as a patient."

I was starting to revise my previously favorable opinion of Dr. Rodwell. "Surely he didn't mean I couldn't visit Amos."

"I think that's one of the things he specifically meant, yes. Amos is your patient, Neve. By definition, visiting him is a work thing. And you're off work. Do you need me to send you a diagram?"

"Goddammit," I muttered under my breath.

"What was that?"

"You're serious about this? What if I come in wearing a wig and big sunglasses?"

The burst of static on the line sounded like an exasperated sigh. "I'm going to pretend I didn't hear that. Besides, word on the street is that Con hasn't even cleared Amos for visitors yet. Stay home, or not. Go out and enjoy the many wonderful sights and amenities DC has to offer. Take a nap. Become a beauty vlogger. Adopt an alpaca. I don't care what you do, just do something other than work. I promise I'll call you with any further updates. Understood?"

Oh hell. I was going to have to sneak in.

I had to see Amos. I'd promised to read the file and listen to him, and after all the trouble he'd taken to get my attention specifically, I doubted he'd open up to anyone else. I needed to assess his current symptoms so I could figure out exactly what was happening in that head of his, and what kind of help he needed. Otherwise, despite what Rosanna had said, Amos could potentially convince the team that he was stable enough to be discharged before I returned to work. He could be pretty compelling when he wanted to be, and if he was released before he was ready, God only knew what might happen next—or more to the point, where he might hack into next, possibly landing himself in jail.

There was no question. I had to go in and see him.

When Rosanna eventually found out, she would just have to forgive me. For now, though, she had to think I was being compliant. "Well, I was thinking of getting a full-sleeve tattoo."

"Excellent. See if you can incorporate my name in there, with a heart around it, of course."

At that, I laughed. "Of course. Okay. I'll wait to hear from you. How are you, by the way? How is your day going?"

"Other than the fact that Doug woke up this morning and told me he wants us to take up rock climbing, I'm spiffy."

"Rosanna, how cool!" Her husband was the outdoorsy type, forever pulling her out of her climate-controlled comfort zone to take on new adventures. She was always resistant at first but inevitably ended up enjoying herself. "You know he's good for you, right?"

"Tell me that when I come to work in a wrist cast and I make you type all my notes. Speaking of which, I'm sorry, but I have to run."

"Sure, of course. Thank you for calling. If Amos asks—"

"I'll tell him you send hugs and kisses."

"Maybe just hugs. Professional boundaries and all."

"Consider it done. You know I love you, right?"

If only she knew how much it meant to me to hear those words just then. "I love you, too. Now hang up. I have a tattoo to design."

"Enjoy!" And with that, she was gone.

Well, that phone call had set my agenda for the afternoon, and it was going to be more of a challenge than I'd imagined.

With my mind full of what I'd been reading, I tucked the *Book of Amos* pages back into their file folder and tried to think through the steps I'd need to take to get onto the endocrinology unit without being found out. The fact that Amos hadn't been cleared for visitors complicated things. Con must have thought he was still pretty fragile from a medical perspective.

Con. The mere thought of him made my chest ache. Two years of suppressed longing. Countless meaningful moments we'd shared. Last night's betrayal mixed in with the promise of possibilities. If I had any hope of being able to concentrate enough to make and execute a plan to visit Amos, I had to take at least one step toward making things right with Con first.

I didn't want to have an actual conversation, though. I wasn't ready. Plus, we'd end up talking about Amos, and that topic was a landmine between us that I still had no idea how to defuse. The longer communications between Con and me remained in a deep freeze, the more I feared irreversible harm was being done, and no matter how angry I was, I couldn't bear that. I just couldn't.

A text, then.

I chewed off the tips of two fingernails while trying to think of just the right formula of words. Then I sat down on the couch, touched Con's name on my messenger app, and typed.

Neve: I'm sorry I ran off last night.

I drummed my remaining fingernails on my leg as I waited. A minute passed. Two. *He's probably with a patient,* I told myself as my pulse quickened. Three minutes. Four.

If I sat around waiting, I wasn't going to have any nails left. Just as I resolved to go take a shower, the phone vibrated. When I saw Con's name, the hit of relief was intense.

Con: Are you all right?

Neve: Yes, I'm fine. Really.

Con: Good. I'm glad. I was worried.

Guilt pricked at me as I recalled his numerous texts and phone calls—all of which I had ignored. He'd been worried, and I'd left him hanging. I could at least try to explain.

Neve: Sorry. I think... I mean, there's a strong chance that I may possibly have had an almost-panic attack.

Con: You don't say? ;)

Oh my God, what was that? Is he actually goading me? I can't believe—

Before I could get up a full head of steam, the phone vibrated again.

Con: Sorry, I pushed RETURN too early. I meant to add that you have nothing at all to apologize for. I, on the other hand....

Ah, okay. That sounded more like Con. So we were both sorry, at least in general terms. But I couldn't just leave it there. I had to know where we stood on the *other* thing. I bit my lip hard and typed.

Neve: Yes, you, on the other hand, do owe me an apology—but not for saying you think I'm stunning. That was nice.

I held my breath until his reply popped up.

Con: I'm glad you still feel that way. And thank you for giving me permission to hope—and dare.

Upon reading his words, my body was awash in a prickly heat. Could I be having a hot flash? Was thirty-three too young?

Before I could even think of a reply, he texted again.

Con: Any chance we could talk tonight?

Just talk, he'd said, not specifying whether in person or on the phone. He was giving me the prerogative, which I appreciated. I thought I should make sure he knew what he was getting into, though, especially since he'd failed to tell me Amos was awake. Our upcoming conversation wasn't going to be all hearts and flowers.

Neve: I'm still really angry with you.

He replied right away.

Con: I understand.

Okay, that was promising. I thought I'd better give him fair warning of my expectations.

Neve: I plan to extract vows of unconditional honesty from you, complete with a list of gruesome medieval consequences if you break them.

Con: I would expect no less. You know, we can do more than talk.

My heart skipped a beat. *Is he suggesting...?*

Con: You can also yell, scream, and throw things at me if you like.

Grinning, I shook my head.

Neve: You're only saying that because you know how highly unlikely it is that I would engage in such behavior.

Con: On the contrary. I'm wide open to histrionics if they would make you feel better.

I scowled. Now he was teasing me. Although, in fairness, I had opened that door. It was too soon for lightheartedness between us, though. There was too much to sort out.

Neve: Tonight, then. Text me when you get off work.

I waited to see if he would mention Amos's awakening before the conversation ended.

Con: I will. Around six most likely. Thank you for this.

An expression of gratitude, which was nice, but no mention of our mutual patient whatsoever. So Con was still opting to keep secrets. Irritation buzzed loudly in my head. "There may well be histrionics tonight after all," I muttered as I typed one last message.

Neve: Okay, talk then.

Then I turned off the phone, giving him no chance to reply. It might be good to let him stew over my terse final message, now that we'd smoothed out the important things. He knew I wasn't a pushover, but given his ongoing silence about Amos, it couldn't hurt to remind him.

18

NEVE

I decided that my best chance of getting to Amos was not to disguise myself at all but to look as normal as possible, like I belonged at the hospital with everyone else. I knew that when employees were put on involuntary leave, the magnetic strips on their ID badges were typically disabled. Since I wasn't sure how my "paid time off" had been entered in the system, I couldn't count on my badge working. But I had another idea. There was one spot on hospital grounds where smoking was still allowed. Yellow paint delineated a small square near a staff entrance, and at certain times of the day, it was populated by a clot of employees puffing away. I arrived at roughly 3:00 p.m., a common time for afternoon breaks.

To look as professional and inconspicuous as possible, I'd put work into my hair and makeup, donned a black shift dress and pumps, and retrieved my never-before-worn hospital lab coat from the back of my closet. While lab coats had been distributed to all the therapists, we wore regular clothes on the unit so our patients could readily distinguish us from the doctors and nurses. Then I tucked the *Book of Amos* file, a notebook and pen, the essential contents of my messenger bag, and my ID badge into my travel laptop case.

I stood around the corner from the smokers' spot and watched them congregate. Just as a few put out their cigarettes and headed inside, I joined them on their walk to the door. My plan if confronted was to claim that I'd forgotten my ID badge, but as we entered the building, no one batted an eyelash. So much for hospital security—or maybe I was benefiting from smoker solidarity. Either way, I was in.

I stuck close to two women in colorful scrubs who were walking in the direction of the main building's east wing, home to the endocrinology unit. I didn't recognize them, and I assumed they didn't know me either, but my lab coat had the desired effect. They swiped in and held the door for me.

Capitol Hill General was such a large, busy complex that I doubted I'd run into anyone from Unit 4. I was in a completely different part of the hospital, for one thing. I didn't see any familiar faces on the elevator, and upon reaching the third floor, I headed straight to the ladies' room, shutting myself inside a stall. I needed to calm down before the final leg of my journey. I locked the stall door, leaned back against the cool metal wall, and closed my eyes. *Almost there.*

I knew most of the nurses on the endocrinology unit by sight, since we often had patients in common. They all knew I worked with Con, too, which might help me massage my way in. I'd checked with his outpatient clinic and confirmed that Con was seeing patients there all afternoon, as was usual for a Thursday, so I wouldn't have to worry about running into him on the unit. Even if I saw him, though, what of it? What was he going to say? There we would all be, with Amos wide awake. Caught keeping secrets for a second time, Con would hardly be in a position to pick a fight with me.

The only remaining hurdle was to get past the nurses. With a "no visitors" order in place, my best chance was to make myself as inconspicuous as possible and just sneak into his room. If I timed it right, it shouldn't be impossible to do. If I was discovered, I would just have to wing it and hope for the best.

There was no point waiting any longer. Trying to look smooth, I strolled out of the ladies' room and paused at the entrance to the endocrinology unit. I had called Patient Information to get Amos's new room number. I had a rough idea of where his room was, but I took a moment to confirm it on the unit map by the entryway.

Six rooms down on the left. I had his door in my sights. I chose a moment when there were very few staff in the corridor and all were absorbed in their work. I stepped onto the unit and tried to glide down the hall with a neutral expression on my face. It felt like ages before I reached Amos's door, although it must have taken less than ten seconds for me to get from point A to point B. Gingerly, I pushed on the door handle and slid inside, holding it so it closed slowly and clicked shut quietly.

The room was dark, with the overhead lights dimmed and the blinds closed. It took my eyes a moment to adjust. Like most of the newer hospital rooms, it was private. The bed was to my right, a splash of white and blue surrounded by a halo of lit machines that beeped at regular intervals. I could make out Amos's form beneath the blankets and sheets, the dark shadow of his hair against the pillow, but there was no motion or sound. Sleeping, I guessed.

To my left was a sink surrounded by cabinets, a wipe board on the wall listing the names of Amos's medical team, and the door to the bathroom. On the far side of the bed was a rolling tray table, a large recliner, and two small chairs. On the table sat a huge floral arrangement and a teddy bear with "GET WELL SOON" helium balloons tied to its wrist. The lilacs from the bouquet scented the air.

If Con wasn't allowing Amos visitors, he must have medical reasons. There hadn't been any sign on the door requiring infection precautions, but just to be safe, I used the hand sanitizer and took a surgical mask and gloves from the cabinet. The last thing I wanted to do was give Amos some germ I'd picked up on the way in. Lord knew he had enough to deal with.

I looked at the card attached to the bear. It was from Con. The flowers were from Unit 4. It gladdened me to see that Amos was getting so much love. I hoped the nurses would leave him alone for a while to sleep. I would just have to pull up a chair, wait, and hope we got at least a few minutes to talk before someone asked me to leave.

I had just gotten comfortable and was going through the *Book of Amos* file folder again when I heard a soft voice. "Neviah?"

Never had I heard so welcome a sound. "Amos!" I slid toward him and gripped the bedrail. "Boy, am I glad to hear your voice."

"Why are you wearing a mask? Are you okay?" His large eyes shone with curiosity.

"I'm absolutely fine. It's to protect you, just in case I tracked some germ in here."

"Please take it off." He grabbed the controller for his bed and adjusted it until he was sitting upright. "No one else has been wearing masks. It's weird not to be able to see your face."

"If you insist. I'm going to sit back, though, just to be safe." I slid my chair back and removed the mask.

He grinned. "Wow, you're all dressed up!"

I smiled back. "It's not every day my favorite patient comes out of a coma."

"Yeah, the coma thing, that pretty much sucked. I think Con was really worried—which means you probably were, too, right? I'm sorry."

"Good grief, don't apologize. It's not like it was your fault. And we worry because we care about you." I pointed at the stuffed bear and flowers. "A lot of people around here do."

A noise outside the door made me jump.

He tilted his head. "You sure you're okay?"

"Yes, I'm fine," I reassured him. "It's just that, technically, I'm not supposed to be here. I kind of snuck in. Con hasn't cleared you for visitors." I saw no point in sharing the other reason.

"Yeah, but you're not a visitor. You're part of my team."

I didn't have to look to know that my name wasn't on his wipe board. "Not at the moment. Not until you're back on Unit 4."

"I don't mean *that* team, I mean our *other* team," he said, eyes sparkling. "Our 'Save The World' team. You, me, and Con—and whatever hacker he knows, I guess."

"Oh, *that* team." I forced myself to smile, even though I was steaming. Not only had Con kept Amos's recovery from me, he had also already talked to Amos about hacking the thumb drive.

He raised himself up on his elbow and looked at the stack of papers on the tray table. "Is that the *Book of Amos?*"

His single-mindedness was impressive, that was for

sure. "Yes it is." I rolled the tray over so we could both look at the papers.

"Oh, cool." Amos's expression brightened as he flipped through the file. "Looks like somebody did extra research."

"Did they?"

"Yeah, there's a few extra pages in here. Whoever it was, tell them I said thanks."

I didn't know whether Con or Eric should get the credit. "I'll pass along the message."

"Have you read it?"

"Almost all of it. I read the articles, the *public* information about Brickhaven," I said pointedly, "and I looked at the calendars. Amos, you really shouldn't have a lot of this stuff, including Dr. Rodwell's calendar. You know that, right?"

He rolled his eyes. "*You* used a hacker!"

"Yes, well, unlike you, I didn't know I was opening something I shouldn't have access to," I pointed out. "And please tell me the president's itinerary was in the public domain."

"It was, I swear." He smiled and shook his head.

"That's no laughing matter."

"I know, it's just that you're worried about all the wrong things."

Was he serious? Hacking into the White House would have been a federal offence. I tried to sound stern. "Amos—"

"It's public domain, I swear. It's on the White House

website. You can check it out yourself if you want to." With his finger, he drew a cross over his heart. "What parts haven't you read yet?"

"I only glanced at Brickhaven's list of members and projects, but then, for ethical reasons, I decided not to read the rest of their *private and confidential* documents," I said firmly. "I also only skimmed Dr. Rodwell's publications about treatment-resistant depression, but I'm pretty familiar with those."

"Okay, cool." Amos closed his eyes and massaged his temple.

A bolt of worry slid through me. "Are you all right?"

"Yeah, I'm fine. It's just this headache. They tell me it's a side effect from the coma. It'll go away."

"I can leave—" I began to stand.

"No, no," he pleaded. "This can't wait. I don't have much energy, though. If you tell me what you've figured out, I'll fill in the blanks."

"If you're sure."

He nodded, then laid his head back and closed his eyes.

All at once, I noticed how drained he looked. Second thoughts needled me. Maybe this had been a bad idea. I waited a moment to see if he would fall back asleep.

"Neviah, you promised, remember?"

"All right, okay." The last thing I wanted to do was upset him. I decided to speak in my soothing-therapist tone. If he fell asleep, that would prove he wasn't up to talking, and I'd slip out the door. "So Brickhaven is a think tank based in DC, and Dr. Rodwell is a member, along with a bunch of other people who went to his prep school. They produce an annual report that gets presented at a global economic conference."

"Mm-hmm."

"Also, according to the articles in here, it sounds like the brinkmanship in the Middle East is rising, and people are worried about nuclear conflict, but the US is trying to broker peace in the region right now."

"Right." His voice was still soft but clear as a bell. At least he appeared calmer. I kept going.

"As for your instruction to focus on the dates, I have to admit, it took me a while to figure that out. Luckily for you, I'm good at puzzles."

Amos smiled. "You found the relationship?"

"I don't know if it's what you had in mind, and frankly, I'm uncomfortable talking with you about Dr. Rodwell's personal calendar," I said pointedly, "but I did notice that the title of Dr. Rodwell's project with Brickhaven, Curia Regis, has the initials CR, and on all the dates when the notation CR appears on his calendar, the president's itinerary said he was in DC. That's the only connection I found, though."

"Wow, you *are* good at puzzles!" Amos opened his eyes and smiled. "Okay, so, did you know Dr. Rodwell sees patients outside the hospital?"

I suddenly felt defensive on Dr. Rodwell's behalf. Where was Amos going with this? "No, but it's not unusual for doctors here to maintain some kind of private practice."

"Well, President Duran is one of Dr. Rodwell's private patients."

Oh no. A murky sense of sorrow seeped through me. Here it came: the delusions, the conspiracy theories. Amos's mental health was in even worse shape than I'd thought.

I closed my eyes to buffer myself against the barrage of distorted thoughts I knew I was about to hear.

19

NEVE

"It's true, I swear," Amos half whispered, like he was worried about being overheard. "President Duran has depression, and it's been getting worse ever since he took office. Brickhaven is always looking for ways to get more influence, so when Duran started looking for a psychiatrist, they found a way to push Dr. Rodwell's name to the top of the list. Getting one of their members so close to the president was too awesome an opportunity to pass up. And now it's become a part of this plot."

My heart sank. Amos was gone, well and truly gone. Could I find a way to bring him back, at least part of the way? "Amos, we've been working together a long time, right?"

"Yes, which is why I know what you're thinking. But I can prove it to you."

It was clear that, for the moment at least, I had lost

him to his illness. I knew I should just get up, walk out, and tell the nurses to check on Amos because he was exhibiting signs of confusion. But the truth was, although the content of his thoughts was irrational, his thought processes were logical enough, and he still appeared calm. I decided to play along for a few minutes and try to assess how entrenched his delusions were. "Prove what, exactly?"

He closed his eyes and mouthed, "Thank you," as though in prayer. Then he propped himself up again, leaned toward me, and said, "Okay, so in a lockbox in his office on Unit 4, Dr. Rodwell keeps his private patient files, including Duran's. The CR dates from Rodwell's calendar match the dates he had treatment sessions with Duran. If you check the lockbox, you'll see."

"I see. And what do the initials CR have to do with the president?"

"'Curia Regis' means 'King's Council,' which is what Dr. Rodwell is right now, if you see the president as the king. It's a code."

A plot. A code. I should have seen all this coming. The realization landed on my heart with a cold thud: Amos's delusions were more intractable than ever. "So all this—the encrypted thumb drive, the patients you hypnotized—it was… what? Designed to convince me to sneak a look at Dr. Rodwell's office so I can see that the president is one of his private patients?"

"No, that's not it! The president is one of Rodwell's

private patients so Brickhaven can *influence* him. It's all part of the plot. Neviah." Amos grabbed the bedrail. "You're not listening. You promised to listen."

He was starting to get upset. I decided to stop challenging his delusions; there would be plenty of time for that back on Unit 4. At the moment, he needed support and gentle care. I had hoped that one of the benefits of my meeting with Amos would be that it would allow him to get some things off his chest and ease his psychological tension, but instead he was getting agitated. It was time to bring the conversation to a close. "I am listening, but I think you need to rest. And I hope you'll rest easier knowing I've read the *Book of Amos* and you've told me what you wanted to. We can talk more about this later, okay?"

Amos looked over at the sink and seemed to be focused on something, his brow wrinkling with concentration. *Is he hallucinating?* I was about to call the nurse when he lay back against the bed, turned to face me, and said, "Your boyfriend hit you."

I froze. *Did he just say...?*

"Right in the jaw," Amos whispered, aghast. "Steven, right? No, Stephan. Sorry, your ex-boyfriend. Wow, Neviah, I'm glad you left him."

My mind reeled. It was no secret that I had dated Stephan, or that we had broken up. Amos could have found that out somehow. But the fact that Stephan had hit me? I hadn't told a soul, and Stephan certainly wouldn't. Had it been that obvious, and I just didn't realize? Maybe someone noticed and there had been gossip. "Why would you say that?"

As though something in my reaction bolstered his confidence, Amos appeared to be infused with a new energy. "I said it because it's true. And I know it happened because the angel just told me. She's over there by the sink."

I knew it was ridiculous, but I couldn't help checking. Without moving my head, I looked at the sink out of the corner of my eye and saw... a sink. "There's no one there, Amos."

"You're not meant to see her. I'm God's messenger. Only I can see her."

"Okay." I took a deep breath and released it slowly as I tried to think. In our earlier session, Amos had mentioned having visual hallucinations, his "angelic visitations." But for him to have such an experience while I was in the room—that was new clinical territory for us. I needed to reassess his symptoms. "Did she just now appear?"

"No, she's been here the whole time. I'm sorry, I should have told you we weren't alone." He looked over at the sink again. "Now she's telling me... oh no." He turned back to me, eyes wide. "You were stabbed? By a patient? He thought you had something toxic inside you, and he was trying to cut it out to save your life. But instead you almost died. That's the danger I warned you about, isn't it? I'm so sorry, Neviah. That's horrible."

How in the hell...? Once I pulled my jaw off the floor, I cleared my throat and said, "I appreciate your sympathy, Amos, but I'm fine now." I didn't want him to waste his limited energy feeling bad for me. "I think we should be focusing instead on the fact that you hacked into Unit 4's patient records—"

"I didn't, I swear! I would never do that. The angel is telling me this!"

"All right, look—"

"No, wait!" He paused to peer at the sink, listening intently. Then he spoke as though repeating what he was hearing. "She says God told me to warn you before it happened, but only so that now you would have one more piece of evidence that I'm His messenger. God knew the attack would happen whether I warned you or not, but it was also necessary as part of a larger plan to help you." He blinked in surprise, then added, "If you'd never been attacked, they wouldn't have found that tumor—what's that?" He regarded the sink again, then looked back to me and pointed to my head. "She says if you hadn't been stabbed, they wouldn't have found your ovarian tumor until long after the brain swelling had started."

Well, I knew for sure that I didn't have an ovarian tumor or brain swelling. How Amos knew what he knew about everything else, I had no idea, but it was clear his grip on reality was slipping even further. "Amos—"

He continued, "Your patient is better now, right?

Sorry, you probably can't answer that. It's okay, the angel says he's better, and he's going to make a full recovery."

He was right. The patient who stabbed me *was* doing much better—which was the only reason I could sleep at night—*and* I couldn't talk to Amos about it. But those were both reasonable guesses, not proof of an angelic presence.

Then Amos's eyes softened. He smiled and cooed, "And you and Con? That's awesome! You two are perfect for each other. But you had a fight last night?"

Jolted, I jumped to my feet. "Okay, Amos, stop right there." How would he know about that? Con would never have told him about us, or about our fight... would he?

"I'm sorry. I'm not trying to freak you out, I swear," he said, appearing genuinely remorseful. "I just need to show you that this messenger of God thing is real. I'm not even that good a hacker. I wouldn't have been able to break into Brickhaven's servers if the angel hadn't talked me through it. She's giving me all this stuff to tell you because we need you to listen to what I have to say about Brickhaven and the president. The future of the world depends on it."

My head was spinning. I had no idea what to do with the fact that Amos was sitting in front of me, spilling my secrets. Urgently, I tried to sort through the things he'd said and figure out which ones he could have discovered by hacking into the hospital or my phone, or by bugging my office. How long had he been watching, listening?

I rubbed my cheeks briskly. Now my own thoughts were taking on a paranoid flavor. Maybe it was contagious. I needed to pull myself together and focus on Amos, get to the bottom of his delusions. "The future of the world depends on it? Why? Because Dr. Rodwell is the incarnation of evil, and I'm a weapon of God sent to prevent him from causing the apocalypse?"

To my complete surprise, Amos laughed.

"Amos, if this is some kind of joke, you need to let me in on it. Right now."

"No, no, it's not a joke." He took a deep breath and got himself under control. "I was laughing because the angel told me what you were thinking, about my paranoia being contagious. And I swear I never hacked the hospital or your phone, and I didn't bug your office or anything. I would never stalk you like that."

I hadn't said any of those things aloud… had I? Was I the one losing my grip on reality?

Very slowly, I turned my head toward the sink.

"And no," Amos continued, "Dr. Rodwell hasn't become the full incarnation of evil yet, but he will soon if he's not stopped. You read my note, right? 'Forgive them, for they know not what they do?'"

Stunned into silence, I nodded.

"The people at Brickhaven, Dr. Rodwell—even though they use totally unethical methods at times, they really believe they're doing good. The problem is they're totally wrong about that. Like right now, they're trying to force the president out of office. That's the plot I've been trying to tell you about. I'm not sure how they're going to do it exactly, but they want him out of the way, for sure."

Just in case I needed more proof that Amos was imagining things…. Everybody liked President Duran. He was the most popular president we'd had in decades. He'd managed to get the two major political parties working together again, and Congress was getting things done that had been in limbo for years. He even had broad support from other world leaders. "Why on earth would anyone want President Duran out of the way? And out of the way of what?"

"Vice President Rabec," Amos said. "With Duran out, Rabec will be in. He went to Brickhaven Academy, too. You won't find his name on the foundation's membership list, but he's heavily involved. Rabec is a real foreign policy hawk, and Brickhaven thinks that's what we need right now—especially in the Middle East."

I squeezed my eyes shut and tried to recall the articles he'd given me. "So Brickhaven doesn't like what President Duran is doing, trying to negotiate peace?"

"Exactly!" Amos pounded his fist into the air. "Brickhaven has their hands in everything over there— weapons sales, intelligence sharing, and a lot of other profitable stuff they don't want to give up. Right now it's like the Wild West, and they want to keep it wild. If there's peace, that means stability, which means Brickhaven and their buddies can't take advantage of the chaos anymore. Stability might also mean the end of super-cheap oil, which would suck for the US economy. That's their so-called 'patriotic' reason for opposing peace talks."

Thanks to the many hours I'd spent listening to Stephan talk about his work, I had some idea of what Amos was talking about. "But a lot of different interests are always competing for influence in the Middle East," I pointed out, trying to be the calming voice of reason. "That's not a new situation."

"No, but what *is* new is that President Duran is actually starting to make progress, even though Iran has nukes now. This isn't public knowledge yet, but he's managed to get all the leaders in the region to agree to come to a summit at Camp David—all of them, sitting down at one table. That hasn't happened in, well, ever."

I hadn't seen anything about a peace summit in the news, which meant either he was right and it hadn't been made public yet, or Amos was inventing it.

"If that's true," I said cautiously, "it's a very hopeful sign."

"It *is* true." He inclined his head toward the sink, but I forced myself not to look. "Look, Brickhaven is blinded by arrogance," he continued. "They think Rabec can keep the Middle East in just enough chaos to serve US interests—and Brickhaven's—without the region tipping over into war. But the angel says this is a pivotal moment in history. If President Duran holds his summit, they *will* make peace. If he doesn't, though...." Amos pressed his fists together, then extended his fingers and pulled his hands apart quickly, as though mimicking an explosion. "Before long, war will break out, and it'll spread quickly. It'll get really, really bad. Like Armageddon bad."

It took me a second to realize he was referring to *actual* Armageddon, not the movie.

"Oh, come on! *Armageddon* was a *great* movie," Amos objected. "The plot was a little out there, but it was awesome entertainment."

How did he know I was thinking that? I knew for sure I hadn't said that out loud. I blinked hard. It was wrong, I knew, and clinically inappropriate, but I couldn't help it: I was starting to believe that Amos had some kind of paranormal access to information—about me, at least. About the rest of it, I had no idea. I'd never believed in telepathy before, but maybe it was real after all, and maybe Amos had that gift.

"I'm not a telepath."

I narrowed my eyes at him. "Saying that right after I thought it in no way disproves my theory."

"Okay, fair enough," he conceded. "But listen, here's the thing. I don't know what's in them exactly, but the angel told me the documents needed to stop Brick-haven and prevent Armageddon are in Dr. Rodwell's private files on the president. That's why we need you to go to his office and find the lockbox."

"I see." Finally we were reaching the crux of his delusion. "Look, Amos. I don't know whether there's an angel in here with us right now or not, but either way, you've created serious trouble for a lot of innocent people recently. You explained to me before why you involved the other patients—to get my attention, to make me take you seriously. But if you believe there's a conspiracy against the president, why did you go to all that trouble instead of just warning the president directly?"

"Yeah, I thought of that, but the angel told me how that would go." Amos held an imaginary phone up to his ear. "'Hey, President Duran, there's a guy on the phone for you who says he's a messenger of God. He wants to tell you about a conspiracy against you, but he has no evidence. Oh, and he's getting his information from an angel *only he* can see and hear.'" Amos dropped his imaginary phone and gave me a half smile. "Even leaving that last bit out, there's zero chance of me getting past the call screeners. And if I called the cops, we'd have even more fun. They'd either arrest me for hacking or take me back to Unit 4. Probably both."

Part of me couldn't believe I was actually engaging in such an absurd conversation, but I couldn't seem to stop myself from asking more questions. "And you didn't just ask one of your followers to do that part for you because…?"

"I would never do that to them! The police would want to know how they got their information, especially after they confirmed that the conspiracy is real. I might get off lightly for hacking because I'm 'ill,' but the fallout for my followers would be much more serious."

"And what about the fallout for *me?*" If, theoretically, I accepted that everything Amos was saying was true, that question remained. "If I do what you're asking me to do and go snooping around in Dr. Rodwell's office, the most likely outcome is that I'll get arrested and/or fired."

Amos folded his hands in his lap and looked down at them. "I'm sorry, I don't know what the outcome will be. The angel won't show me anything more than I need to know for right now."

God had put his so-called messenger on a need-to-know basis? Typical divinity. "You can see, can't you, why this whole situation makes me feel manipulated? And why ask me for help with something like breaking and entering, anyway? It's not exactly in my wheelhouse."

"I'm sorry. I really am." Amos cast a pleading gaze in the direction of the sink. "The angel just keeps repeating what she told me before."

"Which is?"

"That you're the key. For one thing, she says you were the only person who would listen to me long enough to let me convince you that it wasn't my illness talking this time."

I nodded. "Okay, it may be true that I've listened longer than most people would, but you haven't convinced me of any such thing."

Amos was unfazed. "She also says God chose you to help us because He has faith in you. And I don't know how, but the angel insists you can find a way to get the evidence to the president." In response to my incredulous expression, Amos threw his hands in the air. "I have no idea, that's just what she said."

"Because President Duran and I are such close personal friends?" I smirked at our invisible visitor by the sink.

"She says you'll find a way... on Saturday?" He shrugged.

Saturday. *Oh God.* My heart tumbled like it was rolling down a hill.

"Oh wow." His eyes widened. "You know what she's talking about, don't you? I can see it on your face!"

My White House date with Stephan. How in God's name had Amos found out about that? I dropped my head into my hands.

"I'm so sorry I ever doubted you," Amos whispered. "Please forgive me."

I looked up to respond, but he'd been addressing his apology to the sink.

I had let this conversation go on far too long.

Things were getting out of control. I needed to reel it back in, pronto.

"Look, Amos," I said carefully, "I believe there's something happening here that is beyond my understanding. But what you're saying about Dr. Rodwell, the Middle East, Brickhaven—we'll have to revisit all that when you're back on Unit 4. In the meantime, I cannot and will not do what you're asking of me. You understand that, right?"

Tears began to slide down his cheeks.

"I'm sorry. Are you in pain? Do you need me to get help?"

"No, no help." He sniffled. "And yes, I'm in pain, but it's not physical."

"Oh, Amos." I took the tissue box from the table and put it on his lap. "I'm sorry if you're disappointed."

"It's not that." His shoulders rose and fell with a heavy sigh. "I know you'll end up doing what I'm asking you to. But the angel is telling me it won't be as simple or easy as I thought it would be. She says you'll have to be brave." He opened his eyes and looked at me, tears flowing freely. "She never told me that before. I don't like how that sounds."

I pulled out some tissues and pressed them into his hands. "I'm not going to break into Dr. Rodwell's office, and I'm not going to give anything to the president. So there will be no need for bravery on my part, and there's nothing for you to worry about. Okay?"

As he dried his eyes, Amos looked toward the door.

"Someone's coming. I have to tell you one last thing. The combination to Dr. Rodwell's lockbox is a six-digit date, the date Brickhaven Academy was founded."

Now I felt like crying, too. He wasn't hearing me. "Amos, please—"

The door swung open, and one of the nurses from the unit stepped in. "Hey," she called as she flipped on the bright lights, then jumped when she saw me.

"Hey," Amos called back.

I cleared my throat and tried to act casual. "Hi there."

"Oh, hello." The nurse cocked her head to one side. "You work with Dr. O'Brien, right?"

"Yes. Neve Keane. Amos is our mutual patient."

"Okay, got it. Amos isn't supposed to have any visitors, though."

"Oh, really?" I did my best to look surprised. "Dr. O'Brien didn't say anything to me about that."

Amos shrugged. "I didn't know either."

The nurse appeared to buy our innocent act. "I apologize. I don't mean to interrupt you two, but Dr. O'Brien is at the nurses' station asking for clinical updates. Miss Keane, I'm afraid we'll need some privacy."

Oh hell. Con is at the nurses' station? "I thought Dr. O'Brien was in clinic this afternoon."

"Me, too. He must have snuck away. He's been keeping close tabs on this guy here." She winked at Amos.

Con's voice floated in from the hallway. Amos and I exchanged grave looks. "It's okay, go ahead," he said, forcing a smile. "I've said everything I needed to say for now. Like you said, we can talk more later. Thanks a lot for coming over."

"No problem." So Amos was done with me. I felt guilty for feeling so relieved. Hurriedly, I collected the *Book of Amos* papers into their file folder and stood, turning around to retrieve my laptop case.

"Neve?"

I froze in mid-reach, thankful that at the angle I was standing, no one in the room could see me wince. With a deep breath, I turned around and smiled brightly. "Oh hi, Con."

I thought it was an Oscar-worthy performance. The nurse seemed to buy it, anyway. Amos just sat looking down at his hands.

Con's broad frame filled the doorway, his expression a confused mixture of shock, happiness, and disapproval. "I wasn't expecting to see you," he said, his tone completely neutral.

I cleared my throat. "I thought I'd stop by." With my laptop case in one hand and the file folder in the other, I took a step toward the door. "I was just leaving. Why didn't you *tell* me Amos wasn't supposed to have any visitors?" *Or tell me he was awake at all?*

A cloud of guilt passed across Con's face as he understood my unspoken question. "A regrettable oversight on my part."

"Yes, regrettable," I agreed.

"In my defense, I thought you were off work today." He lifted an accusing eyebrow.

The nurse started to look uncomfortable, as though she was beginning to pick up on the tension in the room. "Um, Dr. O'Brien, do you still want me to take that blood draw now? Because I can come back—"

"No, please. Take it now. Miss Keane is leaving." He opened the door wide.

I gave Amos what I hoped was an encouraging smile before turning to Con and lifting my chin toward the hallway. "A word?"

"Certainly."

"Bye," Amos said with a weak wave.

"Bye." I waved back—using, as it turned out, the hand that was holding the file folder.

Con glanced at the folder as I slid it into my laptop case. He then laid his hand lightly on the small of my back and steered me through the doorway.

Once we were in the hallway, Con shut the door behind us and gave me a dark look. "Enjoying your vacation, I see."

I glared back at him. "Don't even start," I hissed in a stage whisper, whipping off my gloves and shoving them into my pocket. "I cannot *believe* you didn't tell me he was awake!"

As he folded his arms across his chest, Con appeared to double in size. "Would telling you have prevented you from coming to work when you're supposed to be off and violating my 'no visitors' order?"

His eyes smoldered, but I had just as much right to be angry as he did, dammit. Evening up the score wasn't the priority, though. I had to fill him in on Amos's symptoms. "Look, I didn't ask to have a word with you so we could argue. While I was in there, Amos…." The words caught in my throat.

Con unfolded his arms and murmured, "Neve, what is it?"

Pull it together. I cleared my throat and met his gaze. "Amos is actively delusional."

"About the same things, or something new?"

"The same themes, just very elaborate and entrenched," I said, glad he'd grasped my meaning. "And he's having visual and auditory hallucinations. He said his angel was visiting while I was there, and he was carrying on a conversation with her. Did you take him off his meds?"

"No, we continued them," Con said, frowning. "I'll order a psych consult right away and keep an eye on him myself, as well. Anything else I should know?"

There were so many things, but none that were quite as urgent. And since we were short on time, the rest would have to wait. "That's it for now. His mood seemed fine, and he wasn't unduly agitated." With my message delivered, I suddenly felt useless, like a spare part that wasn't needed. "I'd put a note in the system, but—"

"You're not supposed to be here." Con nodded. "Don't worry, I'll take care of it. You should go, though. I doubt whoever they send for the psych consult will share my sense of discretion."

"Right." In that moment, I was so grateful for Con. Whatever else, I knew I could count on him to take care of Amos. "You'll text me later?"

"The moment I'm off work."

"Okay." I looked down at my feet, which for some reason were reluctant to leave.

"Go home," he said quietly. "I've got this."

Glancing up, I saw he looked as worried as I felt—but he also meant business. "Okay. Thanks." With effort, I turned and tried to look nonchalant as I walked down the corridor toward the exit.

I ducked into the same ladies' room as before, again shutting myself into a stall. I collapsed with my back against the door. As embarrassed as I was at getting caught, I tried to focus on the positives. I'd seen Amos, and we'd managed to have the session I'd promised him. It would take me a good bit of time to sort out everything that had happened, but at least most of my questions had been answered, and Amos had essentially released me at the end, apparently satisfied with our conversation. I hoped he would feel more at peace now, at least until that damned meddling angel of his—imaginary or otherwise—gave him another harebrained conspiracy theory to obsess over.

Even Con's unexpected appearance had been a

blessing, since it gave me the opportunity to tell him about Amos's symptoms. And during our interaction, if only for a moment, Con and I had shifted back into our usual space: caring about patients and each other. Things between us didn't feel back to normal yet, but they were better than they had been. One step at a time —and the next step was to wait for his text after work.

20

———

NEVE

FOR A WHILE, I JUST STAYED IN THE BATHROOM STALL, giving myself time to breathe. Unfortunately, the ladies' room smelled like chemical air freshener—not nearly as pleasant as the fresh lilacs in Amos's room. Still, I was reluctant to leave. Maybe because I'd worked so hard to sneak into the hospital, or because I felt that by rights, I belonged there, not sitting at home twiddling my thumbs. I just wanted to be in my office on Unit 4, where I could clear my head and think.

A vague plan began to form in my head. If I could wait until five thirty or so, Dr. Rodwell and the rest of the daytime staff would be gone. Even Rosanna would leave on time; Thursday was the day she volunteered after work at the homeless clinic. If I could get onto the unit, I could probably slip into my office without drawing too much attention. If anyone challenged me,

I could say I'd come in to pick up something I'd forgotten.

The more I thought about the idea, the more it appealed to me. Even if I just spent an hour in my office, I could take my time and make sure I'd dotted all the i's and crossed all the t's on my case notes, instead of doing it in rush like I'd been forced to on Tuesday. That would make me feel better about staying home for the remaining days of my time-off sentence.

Besides, my office was the best place for me to concentrate without distractions, and I needed to put my thoughts in order after that mind-boggling meeting with Amos. I could review his case notes, including any new ones that had been entered. With the new information I had, I could also go over the apocalypse patient files one more time and see if there was anything I'd missed that could be helpful in Amos's treatment.

Well, that settled it. I would be going to Unit 4 after hours. But I still had an hour and a half to kill. Fortunately, I knew a place I could hide out without a chance of running into any coworkers.

I stepped out of the stall, washed my hands out of sheer force of habit, and made my way to the hospital chapel.

As expected, it was empty, which suited me perfectly. The chapel was a beautiful space, so peaceful and visually distinct from the rest of the hospital that once inside, it felt like I was somewhere else entirely.

The soundproofed interior was constructed from wood, with a tall ceiling that formed a pointed arch. There were rows of padded pews, and the front of the room was lined with tables covered with tealight candles in red glass holders. Being a multi-faith space, there were no religious symbols, just a backlit stained glass window at the front of the room featuring a floral design.

I walked down the back pew and took a seat next to the wall, resting my head against the smooth wood paneling. It was the first time I could ever remember being alone in a place of worship, just me and the divine, with no service or sermon going on. I looked around, wondering if Amos's angel had followed me, then laughed at how ridiculous that thought was.

Nonetheless, if I was honest with myself, my meeting with Amos had stirred something inside me that had been dormant for over a decade. I had lost interest in religion during my first year of college. In Philosophy 101, I learned about confirmation bias and all the ways in which we favor information that supports what we already believe. Then, in Introduction to Psychology, we read studies on cognitive dissonance, and I learned that when we're confronted with conflicting beliefs, we just alter one to achieve consistency and restore balance. Those two concepts opened crucial doors in my mind, leading me to the conclusion that the powerful experiences I'd always attributed to my religious faith hadn't come from God at all. They were just products of my own brain. I had tricked myself into believing, truth be damned.

I valued my integrity too much to keep pretending, though. So after I had my epiphanies, I left the Mormon fold and went off-script. For a while, I rejected all things spiritual, not trusting myself to make good judgments on the subject. But then, slowly, I cobbled together my own version of a spiritual life, and after concluding that it was unfair to blame the divine for all our human foolishness, I called a truce. Over time, I had opened a frank but respectful channel of communication with God, even though I didn't have a clear idea anymore who or what that was.

After the bombshells Amos had just dropped on me, I felt like God and I needed to talk. Unfortunately, I didn't have an angel like Amos claimed he had, so I knew I couldn't expect any answers. At least I could express my concerns, though.

"Hi," I said softly to the empty chapel. There was no echo, and the sound of my voice was swallowed by the room. "It's me, but I guess you know that. It's been a while. I hope you're well."

I knew that sounded ridiculous, but I figured God could handle it.

"Amos tells me you sent him an angel. I don't know anything about angels, but as you know, he told me a lot of stuff that only I know, and you, probably, and I just…."

I shrugged. No doubt God already knew. Still, it might feel good to say it.

"I just don't know what to make of it. I mean, I teach other people all the time how to tell what's real from what's not, but this has me stumped. I can't think of any way he could have known a lot of the things he told me. But an angel? I don't know. If not that, then what, though? Was he tapping into some type of energy that physics just hasn't discovered yet?"

I looked at the front of the chapel, hoping for some kind of sign—what, I didn't know. But the silence remained perfect, and the flames of the candles burned straight and unmoving, without a breath of wind to disturb them.

"Okay, well." I sighed. What had I been hoping for? "If I could just ask one thing. If this *is* you—on the off chance that you did send Amos an angel, and if there is something you need me to do—then please give me some guidance, because I'm at a complete loss. I don't know, leave a few bread crumbs for me or something. I'm pretty sure none of this is coming from you, but if it is, and if it's important, I wouldn't want to screw it up."

Oh good grief. What am I saying? I rubbed my face. "Of course, if I'm right and it's *not* you, then just help us to help Amos, please, because I really care about him, and I think we both know that at this point, you've put way more on his plate than is fair. All right? Thank you. Amen."

If anyone had overheard my prayer, they would surely have laughed. The thought made me smile to myself. Well, I'd said what I needed to say. I decided to empty my mind before I uttered any more absurdities. Closing my eyes, I tried to meditate, focusing on my breath as it flowed in and out, in and out.

———

"Oh, I'm sorry." A bright female voice jolted me awake. "I didn't realize there was anyone in here. I'll come back later."

It took me a few seconds to orient myself. *Oh, right, the chapel.* I had fallen asleep. I looked over and saw a member of the cleaning staff hauling an industrial-sized vacuum cleaner behind her.

"No, come in. I don't mind."

"It's no bother—"

"Really, it's fine. Do you happen to know what time it is, though?" I rubbed the side of my head, which had grown sore from pressing against the hard wall.

"About six thirty, I think?"

With a bit of trepidation, I asked, "In the evening, right?"

She smiled kindly. "Yes. I guess you were pretty out of it, huh?"

"I guess I was. I'm leaving now, though. You've got the place to yourself."

"Okay, then. Have a good night."

"You, too."

I heard the drone of the vacuum as I walked down the hallway. I'd slept longer than intended, but at least I could be certain by now that Rosanna was gone for the day.

I went to the back door of Unit 4 to at least try my ID badge before resorting to banging on the front door of the unit and asking someone to let me in. *Beep, click.* It worked! God bless Dr. Rodwell. He must have entered my leave as "voluntary." Of course, it probably was pretty unusual for anyone to come to work when they didn't have to.

The staff hallway was empty. I walked right to my office door and slipped inside without being noticed.

It felt so good to be back in my own workspace. I turned on the desk lamp and settled into my chair. The red light on my phone was blinking rapidly, indicating that calls were being forwarded to my out-of-office voice mail message. Anyone who had called knew I wasn't in, so any messages that had been left could wait until I officially returned.

I powered on my computer. The desktop program started up, and as usual, there was a notification on the screen that I had new emails. They could wait. First, I wanted to check the latest notes on Amos.

I opened the electronic medical records program and navigated to his chart. There was a note Con put in that afternoon saying "a visitor" had told him Amos was experiencing delusions and hallucinations, so he'd ordered a psych consult. The consult note was also in the system. Unsurprisingly, Amos had denied everything, telling the psychiatrist who examined him that he wasn't experiencing anything out of the ordinary. His mental status was determined to be "within normal limits." At least I knew Con would be keeping an eye on him.

I was stunned by how many emails had accumulated in the day and a half I'd been gone. Most were routine patient reports I'd been CC'd on, but there was one email flagged "Important," addressed directly to me. It was from Dr. Mohinder. That was strange. Her office usually contacted me by phone, and only to confirm appointments. She'd sent the email at eight thirty that morning. The subject read "Test results." I didn't have any outstanding tests that I knew of. She may have sent something to me in error that was intended for another patient. I decided I'd better open it, find out, and let her know right away, since someone else might be waiting for important news.

Hi Neve,

I'm sorry to email you like this, but I tried your office phone with no luck, and I wanted to speak with you as soon as possible. There's nothing to worry about, but I received a new flag on your CT scan from the ER. When you were in emergency, we were so focused on the injuries from your attack that it seems we missed something. I'd like

to discuss it with you. Again, don't be concerned, but do call me when you get a chance. Thanks.

   - Aanya Mohinder, MD

I stared at the screen. *A new flag? On my old CT scan? What on earth could they have missed?*

"Nothing to worry about," she'd written. "Don't be concerned." Had she forgotten that she was addressing someone with serious anxiety issues?

After everything else that had happened over the past few days, I didn't think I could handle waiting until she was back in the office the next day to find out what was going on. Worrying about other people, I could handle. But if something was wrong with me, with my body—if I had to sit with that possibility for fourteen hours, a panic attack would be inevitable. I could already feel my heart rate rising.

One of the first things they'd hammered into us at employee orientation was that under no circumstances were we allowed to access our own charts on the electronic medical records system. If we wanted to see our records, we had to put in a request with the records department just like everyone else. In all my time at the hospital, I had never been tempted to break that rule— not until that moment.

It would be going too far, though, to snoop around in Dr. Mohinder's records. She'd be able to see who last opened them, first of all, but it also just seemed like a violation of trust. However, I knew from working with our own patients that ER records, including test results, were stored in their own section of the program. I could access my CT scan results that way, and the chances were slim to none that anyone would ever notice. Even if they did, I would be willing to bet that under the circumstances, an official reprimand in my Human Resources file was the worst that would happen. That was a risk I was willing to take.

In minutes, I had located my test results. Steeling myself, I opened the file. The flag was immediately visible, so I clicked on it. A popup window appeared.

Evaluate tumor on left ovary. Appears benign. Possible teratoma.

With lightning speed, I hit Alt+F4, quickly closing the program. My hand flew down to cover the left side of my abdomen, as though I could somehow shield it from harm.

Tumor.

It was the second time I'd heard that word in one day—the first time, from Amos.

Thankfully, the terror that would normally accompany the sight of those words in one's medical record was softened by the word "benign," which I knew meant Dr. Mohinder was right. In all likelihood, there was nothing to worry about.

In all likelihood.

Of course, that didn't stop me from going straight

to an internet search. It turned out that teratomas were a bit of a medical oddity. They were tumors made up of things like hair and bone growing in parts of the body where you wouldn't normally find those types of tissues—the ovaries, for example.

Fortunately, everything I discovered seemed to confirm that there was probably no reason for concern.

Probably.

I kept searching, reading, trying to find some solid, reassuring information I could hang on to, but the opposite happened. In an online encyclopedia article on teratomas, I saw something that stopped me in my tracks. If undiscovered and untreated, in rare circumstances, ovarian teratomas could cause a serious complication: encephalitis.

Encephalitis. Inflammation of the brain tissue. Or, as Amos had put it, "brain swelling."

"No way," I whispered in awe to the empty room.

The question flashed through my mind: Did the patient who attacked me have some kind of sixth sense? Because it turned out he could be right. I might have a sort of toxic seed in my abdomen. Was Amos right, too, that the attack really had been God looking out for me, making sure they found the tumor before there were any negative side effects?

Just the thought of that possibility made my head feel like it might explode. If that were true, I would have to rethink everything. Everything about the attack, God—and the possibility that Amos wasn't hallucinating after all.

Every last thing Amos had said about *me* was turning out to be true. But that didn't mean *everything* he said—about Brickhaven, for example—came from a divine source. That whole story sounded too much like a typical product of paranoia and delusional tendencies. The whole conspiracy theory must have been something Amos ran across, probably online, and his illness had simply grabbed hold of it.

Just to satisfy my curiosity, I did another internet search, this time for Vice President Rabec. His official bio confirmed that he was, in fact, a Brickhaven Academy alumnus.

All right, another point for Amos, but it wasn't proof of anything. There was no way to verify any of it.

Except there *was* a way.

Amos had even told me how to find Dr. Rodwell's lockbox combination—allegedly.

Damn it all to hell. The encephalitis must have already been kicking in, because I began to wonder how I would feel if, in the near future, I saw headlines like "President Duran Steps Aside" and "Vice President Rabec Sworn In." Could I live with the suspicion that Brickhaven had won and I hadn't lifted a finger to stop them?

All I had to do was check the lockbox.

What else was it Amos had said to me? That I would end up doing what he'd asked?

Well, whether or not he was divinely inspired, Amos must have been able to predict the future at least, because there I was, sitting in my chair, actually considering breaking into Dr. Rodwell's office.

For a few seconds, I entertained the thought of calling Con, but I already knew what he would say. He would try to talk me out of it, and if that didn't work, he would interfere. I would have to make this decision on my own.

And I was leaning more toward breaking and entering by the minute.

———

Breaking into the office was surprisingly easy, if guilt-inducing. Custodial staff were cleaning the office wing. While they were busy working, I snagged one of their badges from the cart in the corridor. Although shaking and slick with cold perspiration, my hands didn't fail me, and I was able to open Dr. Rodwell's door, return the badge, and close myself into his office without being seen.

Finding the lockbox was another matter. I didn't dare turn on the lights for fear of revealing myself, so I searched for a good half hour using the tiny flashlight on my keychain.

Eventually I focused on the small rug under the desk. It was intricately designed, a beautiful combination of duck egg blue, wine red, and shades of beige. I had admired it the first time I visited his office. Dr. Rodwell said it was a one-of-a kind hand-knotted wool Persian carpet from an importer in northern Virginia. Looking at it again, I wondered why anyone would bring such a rug into a hospital, where it could potentially meet with all manner of hazards. It just struck me as an odd choice. On impulse, I lifted one corner.

The industrial gray carpet beneath the rug had been sliced through.

I pulled the rug up farther and saw that the gray carpet had been cut in a four-foot square. A sense of urgency gripped me. Searching the desk for a tool, I came across a letter opener. It looked like an antique, with a thick, elaborate brass handle. I used it as a lever to lift the edge of the gray carpet. It came up easily, as though it was removed often.

There was a small door built into the floor beneath. Breathlessly, I ran my hands over it until I felt the beveled edge of a handle. *Gotcha.* I gripped the edge and pulled upward.

The door opened without a problem, and sure enough, inside was a metal box, just the right size for storing files, with a round combination lock. It was a bit heavy, so instead of trying to pull the box out, I reached down and entered the combination. I had found the date of Brickhaven Academy's founding online. When the last pair of numbers landed on the arrow, I heard a low click.

It's working, I marveled, pausing to rock back on my

heels before proceeding. I had already broken several rules, not to mention laws. But now I was about to violate a principle that, ordinarily, I protected with passion: patient confidentiality.

What am I doing? I pinched the bridge of my nose and tried to think. It wasn't too late to just stop, close everything up, and go home.

I pictured myself doing just that. Turning around, going home, relaxing on the couch with a glass of wine, binge-watching something absorbing on TV. Except I was supposed to talk to Con after work. I felt another pang of guilt. He'd probably been trying to reach me.

I pulled my phone out of my pocket. I'd forgotten that I'd left it turned off. Covering the glow of the screen with my hand, I powered it up and quickly put it on silent mode. Good grief. It was eight thirty already. Sure enough, there were several texts from Con, plus four missed calls, three from him and one from Rosanna. The thought that Con might be waiting for me to call him back squeezed my heart.

Whatever I was going to do, I needed to do it quickly. Turning back wasn't an option. The conversation I'd had with Amos that afternoon had been too compelling, and I was still convinced by the reasoning that had led me down the path I was currently on. I was there to find out for sure: either the Brickhaven conspiracy might be real, or not. All I had to do was look. I didn't have to steal anything, or even tell anyone, just look inside the lockbox and see if there was a file for President Duran. If there was such a file, I could peek inside just far enough to see whether the dates checked out and if there was any hint of Brickhaven's involvement. I had no intention of reading the session notes. If Dr. Rodwell was indeed treating the president, the details were none of my business.

I was doing a horrible job of rationalizing something I knew perfectly well was wrong. It went against everything I believed in, everything I stood for. But with each moment that passed, it became clearer that I had to either act, or leave.

Oh for God's sake. I knew I'd never forgive myself, but that was going to be true no matter what I did. So I steeled myself, swallowed hard, and opened the door to the lockbox, shining my flashlight inside.

Neatly arranged files, alphabetized by initials. None with the president's initials, JD. But there was a file marked "CR."

Hating myself more by the second, I slid the file out of the box and pulled down one corner. There was the patient's name on the corner of the sheet: Jefferey Duran.

My hands started to shake. The file fell from my grasp, and papers fanned out across the floor. I tried to stand but hit my head on the underside of the desk. Much whispered cursing ensued. Crouching on the balls of my feet, I lay my flashlight on the floor pointing toward the papers as I tried to tap them back into a pile while keeping the pages in something close to their original order. As I slid them together, I saw that some pages were white and others were blue. The blue pages were handwritten while the white pages were typed on what appeared to be some kind of letterhead.

Once I had reassembled the pile, I found myself face-to-face with the top page—one white sheet of paper with the Brickhaven logo on it. Within seconds, I took in the first two lines.

URGENT / September 2 / Confidential Memo to Brickhaven Board / RE: Magnum Concilium - Curia Regis Project / POTUS Update / EMERGENCY INTERVENTION REQUIRED.

I shuddered as something inside me went very cold. I read on.

In our treatment session today, POTUS confirmed he is still planning to host the Middle East Peace Summit at Camp David in two weeks' time. I employed the usual therapeutic techniques to encourage him to doubt his judgment. For example, I pointed out that a cooperative plan, regardless of its wisdom or lack thereof, would seem unnaturally attractive to him because it eased subconscious anxieties formed during those childhood years when his parents were in a period of high conflict. I also pushed him to explore how his depressive symptoms and the weaker aspects of his personality might be making it difficult for him to adhere to a more hardline strategy. These interventions were somewhat effective in that, by the end of the session, he did express increased doubt and anxiety. However, as of this writing, he remains determined to hold the Camp David Summit.

Two new medications were prescribed which will further impair his sleep and increase agitation and mood swings. It is my hope that these developments will cause POTUS to question his own fitness and delegate decision-making about important topics such as the Summit to VP Rabec. I will encourage this line of thinking in our session a week from Monday. In the meantime, I request an emergency meeting of the board this Friday to review our strategy.

RE: Contingency Plan A: It remains my opinion that having POTUS declared unfit would require more clinical evidence than we can convincingly produce. It would also require corroboration by psychiatrists known and trusted by the family, which would be very difficult to obtain, if not impossible. Even if my therapeutic efforts succeed over the next several days and POTUS hands the reins to the VP, he could still change his mind and take back control at any time. There is also the time factor to consider, which, in my opinion, pushes us to Contingency Plan B.

RE: Contingency Plan B: The board can rest assured that at this stage, I have documented enough clinical evidence that should his apparent suicide need to be arranged, the death of POTUS will be regarded by all reasonable people as a tragedy that could not have been prevented or predicted. I am assured that "Sic Semper Tyrannis" is ready to be executed, after which "Non Ducor, Duco" will be put into motion to ensure the investigation moves in the desired direction. Should any doubts be raised about the clinical documentation, they will be confined to questions about my professional competence, a potential burden which I am, of course, willing to bear if needed to ensure a successful outcome for our project.

Signed, Frank Rodwell, MD

I squeezed my eyes shut, but it didn't work. I couldn't unsee what I had just read. The memo crashed through the window of my brain like a Molotov cocktail. It had launched me into a new reality, and it was inescapable.

Not only had Amos had been right about Brickhaven's conspiracy to push the president aside, but it was even more diabolical than he'd imagined, and Dr. Rodwell was... well, evil. There was no other word for it. Not that I could claim to be a paragon of moral virtue at that moment. But while I didn't understand all the details, it was clear that Dr. Rodwell was playing a key role in a conspiracy to assassinate the president and make it look like a suicide.

Even if the plot never came to fruition, Dr. Rodwell had already horribly violated President Duran's trust,

using intimate knowledge gained through his privi-
leged position as a psychiatrist to manipulate his
patient in the service of a political goal. He'd even gone
so far as to drug the president of United States to
worsen his symptoms and make him more malleable.
Then he had composed a memo—no, memos, I could
see—disclosing the private contents of their sessions to
the Brickhaven board. Dr. Rodwell wasn't treating
President Duran. He was using him and abusing him to
serve the foundation's agenda and setting the scene for
a potential murder.

A wave of nausea hit me hard. I tilted my head back
and tried to breathe. If I lost my lunch on Dr. Rodwell's
Persian carpet, there would be no hiding the fact that
there had been an intruder.

Thankfully, adrenaline began to pump through my
system, just enough to help me focus. I had to get what
I needed and get the hell out of there. A quick glance at
the papers told me the blue sheets were Dr. Rodwell's
actual session notes—I wouldn't even look at those—
and the white ones were Brickhaven memos. I could
take pictures of at least a few of those, including the
latest one. If Amos was right and I was supposed to
show President Duran evidence of what Dr. Rodwell
and Brickhaven were up to, those documents should be
sufficient.

As I crouched on the floor, my heart pounded in my
ears like war drums. I held the flashlight between my
teeth as I went to work. I photographed the memos,

afraid that using the flash on my phone could attract attention. I was only able to snap pictures of three memos before my flashlight died.

Whispering another elaborate string of curses, I shook it hard, clicking the power button off and on a few times and tapping it against the floor, but no luck. I didn't want to use the flashlight on my phone, either, because the beam was so bright it would definitely be noticed by passersby.

Maybe there was a flashlight app I could download that would focus the beam? I opened the app store and typed "flashlight beam" into the search bar.

BOOM!

I fell backward as the door of the office burst open.

"Stay where you are! Don't move!"

"Okay," I half whispered. There was no question of moving. I was frozen in shock.

From where I was sitting, I could see over the desk to the top half of the door. Two hospital security guards rushed in and ran toward me.

"Don't move!"

"I'm not, I'm not!"

"It's her," one of them called toward the door. "It's Neve Keane."

Two of the nurses from our unit entered the room cautiously, as though they were expecting me to jump them. It was a petite woman and a brawny man. We worked different shifts, so I knew them by sight but not by name. "It's just me," I called to them. "Everything's okay."

"Miss Keane?" The female nurse peered down at me over the desk. "I'm going to need you to come with us, okay?" She was talking with exaggerated calm, as though I was a stray dog she was trying to coax out of an alley.

"Yes, of course I'll come with you." I looked up at the security guards. "Can I move now?"

"I'm going to need to put these on you first," said the guard to my left. He held out a pair of padded wrist cuffs, the kind we used to restrain patients who were behaving violently.

"What?" Confusion addled me. "Why?"

The nurse sounded apologetic. "Just do as they ask, okay, Miss Keane? Then you can come with us and we'll talk, all right?"

Alarm bells rang loudly in my head. I had no idea what was going on, but it wasn't good. I felt an overwhelming urge to bolt, but there were four trained professionals between me and the door. My odds of getting past them were nonexistent.

I looked up at the nurse. Nervousness rippled beneath her forced smile. Because of me? That didn't make any sense. Still, I knew how much the nurses had to deal with on a daily basis, and I didn't want to add to her burden. I'd been caught, and I had to face the consequences. There was no need to ruin anyone else's day because of the choices I'd made.

"Okay, fine." Making a quick calculation in my head, I slid the cell phone on top of the letter opener where it lay on the floor as I moved my hands. Then I held my wrists out in front of me. "I might need some help putting those on."

"Sure," said the guard on my left.

I swallowed down a feeling of rising panic as he put on the wrist cuffs, closed the buckles, and locked them shut. They were snug. I wasn't getting out of them until someone let me out.

"Some help getting up?"

The guards moved in closer and reached for my elbows. "Just take it easy, lady. No sudden moves."

Who did they think I was, some kind of secret agent? I let them lift me. Once I was almost standing, I pretended to slip. Before they could figure out what was happening, I took the opportunity to stomp down several times as hard as I could on my cell phone. With the letter opener beneath it, the screen made a satisfying crunching sound. Shards of plastic flew everywhere.

"Hey, what did I just say?" one of the guards shouted. The nurse jumped backward, gaping at me. The guards jerked me to the side, then dragged me around the desk and out the door before I could find my footing again.

"Stop, wait. I'll walk."

The guards stopped and glared at me. "No you won't. Don't move. Miriam?"

The nurse, Miriam, ran down the corridor away from us.

"Wasn't I supposed to go with her?" I asked. "What the hell is going on?"

But the guards pretended they couldn't hear me. A moment later, Miriam reappeared with a wheelchair.

"Oh come on." I rolled my eyes. "I told you I'll walk."

"Sit," the guard said gruffly, rotating me around and pushing me into the chair. While Miriam stood back at a safe distance, the guards put cuffs around my ankles and secured my legs to the footrests. Then they separated the handcuffs, which came apart in the middle, and attached my wrists to the armrests. While this absurdity was going on, it took every bit of self-control I had not to resist, but I'd already startled them once. I didn't want to turn them against me entirely, lest I lose my independence for a moment longer than necessary.

The brawny nurse reappeared carrying a small metal tray. He and Miriam nodded at one another. The guards positioned themselves behind the wheelchair, their hands on my shoulders as though they were trying to prevent me from thrashing about.

Miriam looked a little less scared but still worried as she took an alcohol wipe and a syringe from the metal tray.

My eyes widened. "Miriam? What are you doing?"

"It's okay, Miss Keane," she said. "This is just something to relax you."

"Relax me?" My pulse jump-started. "Look, I know I

wasn't supposed to be in Dr. Rodwell's office, but I assure you, I'm not a harm risk. I swear."

"You harmed that cell phone pretty bad," one of the guards pointed out.

"That was an inanimate object," I countered, "and one which belonged to me, might I add. Miriam, please." She'd pulled out a pair of safety scissors and begun cutting open the sleeve of my lab coat from cuff to shoulder. "What on earth are you doing? Please call Rosanna. Just call her before you do something you can't undo. Miriam, please, listen to me. I am not a patient. I work here."

But if Miriam was listening, my words were not penetrating. Before I knew it, she was wiping my upper arm with the alcohol swab. "Just relax, Miss Keane. You'll feel better in a minute."

"Ow ow ow!" Miriam had a gentle touch, but that didn't stop the injection from stinging like hell. I was going to have a painful knot there, I could already tell. "I can't believe you just did that! Would you please call Rosanna? I'm begging you. This is outrageous. What is going on? On whose orders...? What...?" Words became more difficult to form as my head started to swim. "My God, what was *in* that?" My speech was already slurring, and my vision began to blur. I felt the muscles in my neck relax so much that they could hardly hold my head up. It lolled to one side.

The guards released their grip on my shoulders.

Another figure approached, this one wearing a white lab coat like mine and large brown shoes. A man.

"Don't worry," the man's voice said. "It's just the usual cocktail. As you know, it works quickly, but it wears off quickly, too. You'll wake up shortly after we get you settled."

I knew that voice. Who was it? I tried to say, "Settled where?" but I wasn't sure how it came out.

"You're clearly a harm risk—to others, if not to yourself—so for everyone's safety, Neve, I'm committing you. You'll be in one of the seclusion rooms tonight. We'll do everything we can to make you comfortable. Then, in the morning, we'll talk."

Oh God. He's getting me out of the way, taking me out of the equation. I tried to shout, "I'm not a harm risk. You can't commit me!" but only "I'm not" came out before the words slurred horribly.

Miriam leaned down and met my blurred gaze. She seemed kind, even concerned. "Don't worry, Miss Keane. We'll take good care of you." Then she stood up again, saying, "Which room, Dr. Rodwell?"

Terror speared through me like a poisoned arrow in the remaining seconds before I lost consciousness.

21

———

NEVE

THERE WAS A TUGGING AT MY WRISTS. THEN AT MY ankles.

Was I dreaming? Having a nightmare, more like.

Wake up, I ordered myself. My mind began to sharpen, and the tugging sensations went away. I felt half asleep, but I wasn't in my bed—the mattress felt too firm and too thin.

Wait a minute. There were voices. A woman, a man. Talking low. I inhaled the dull scent of old vinyl, but I couldn't move. Maybe it was one of those dreams where your mind woke up before your body. Either way, it was creepy, and I wanted out.

With great effort, I pushed my eyelids open a crack.

Fluorescent lights, lots of blue. There were people standing near what looked like an open door that let more light in. I strained to hear what the voices were saying. At first, it sounded like we were all underwater, but soon the sounds became more distinct. I could make out the woman's voice first.

"You're sure you don't want me to call Rosanna?"

The nurse, Miriam. Recent memories poured into me like water gushing through a sluice.

"Absolutely not. There's nothing she can do right now. No point worrying her."

The man. Dr. Rodwell. The incarnation of evil.

"Okay. I think she's waking up."

"Oh good. You can go. I'll sit with her for a while in case she's disoriented. I don't want her to...."

"To be scared. I know." I saw Miriam standing close to the bed. She put something cool and hard into my hand and closed my fingers around it. "The nurses' call handset. It's one of the new wireless, voice-activated models we're trying out with patients who have... limited mobility."

That was one way of putting it. I knew she meant well, but I couldn't help smirking.

"Just say 'nurse alert' if you need anything, Miss Keane," she added before stepping away. "Don't worry, Dr. Rodwell, I'll tell everyone what you said. VIP treatment."

"Thanks, Miriam. Close the door on your way out?"

"Of course." The beam of light disappeared as Miriam pulled the door shut behind her.

I heard the rasp of chair legs against the floor and saw Dr. Rodwell sit down next to my bed. It had rails. Definitely a hospital bed. There was a draft, and something felt scratchy against my skin. They must have taken my clothes and put me in a paper hospital gown and ankle socks.

A frenzy of fear raced through my veins. I made an effort to move but felt resistance at my wrists, ankles, and across my waist. I must have been in five-point restraints. I'd read about those in grad school but never seen them used. In any case, I was truly a captive audience.

I rolled my head to the side and looked at Dr. Rodwell. He was smiling down at me with his usual confident, reassuring expression. "You've noticed, I'm sure, that I had Miriam change your clothes. Just standard procedure, as you know. I'm sorry about this, Neve."

I looked around and realized we were in Seclusion Room 3. The walls were covered with blue safety pads, with the exception of one window, which was sealed shut. I also knew the door was bolted from the outside. Even if I managed to break out of my restraints, there was no way to escape the room.

That meant the only tool I had at my disposal was conversation. I didn't know how much Dr. Rodwell knew about what I knew, so I decided to play dumb until I had a better idea. "What's going on?" At least my speech wasn't slurred anymore.

"Quite a bit, apparently," he said, consulting the tablet computer balanced on his knee. "Let's see. For starters, against direct instructions from me, you snuck into the hospital this afternoon and went to see your patient, Amos Vates, in violation of the no-visitors protocol Dr. O'Brien had put in place."

How on earth did he find out about that, and so quickly?

Dr. Rodwell must have seen the confusion on my face. "The nurses' grapevine is a powerful thing, Neve. You can't get anything past them. You should know that by now. It wasn't long after you left Endocrinology that Rosanna was alerted to your visit. She was pretty irate, I can tell you."

So that was why she'd called me. I really, really needed to start listening to my voice mails in a timelier fashion.

"That's when I asked security to put a silent alert on your ID badge. If you had just gone home and stayed there…. But when you swiped into the unit and sent me those threatening emails from your office computer, it became clear that something had to be done."

My stomach clenched. "What emails?"

"Well, let's see." He looked down and read from his tablet. "'Dr. Rodwell, I'm coming to kill you tonight, I'll find a way, you're not safe anywhere, I know you're Satan, you must be sacrificed for the good of the world,' etc. etc. Sound familiar?"

He's framing me. In despair, I screwed my eyes shut.

"No, I imagine not, since you're hearing these for the first time."

Now, having rendered me unable to warn anyone

about him, Dr. Rodwell was showing me his true face at last. Cold with terror, I grasped at the nurses' call handset.

"Don't bother calling for help," he said. "The nurses know I'm in here with you, and they've all been briefed on your mental state. Speaking of which, I must thank you. You played right into my narrative when you broke into my office and hid in there with the lights off. And smashing your phone? I'm not sure what possessed you to do that, but it added a memorable element of drama to your erratic behavior. Then they found my letter opener on the floor, looking very much like a potential weapon." He clucked disapprovingly. "Not a good scene, Neve. Thank goodness we got to you before you could hurt anyone."

So the silent alert had told him I was on the unit. But how had he known I was in his office? "I don't understand...."

"I know you don't," he said indulgently, patting the back of my hand. "There are some things I don't understand, as well. I'm hoping you and Amos can fill in some of the blanks for us tomorrow."

Amos. My heart lurched as though trying to escape my chest. "If you hurt him, I swear to God...."

"What are you talking about?" Dr. Rodwell feigned offense. "Hurt one of our patients? Never. You know better than anyone how dedicated I am to the well-being of everyone in our care."

I glared at him and tugged at my restraints.

"Please try to relax. You'll get the best possible treatment, just like all our patients. As for Amos, it's very sad that he's so ill right now, but we're very familiar with his case. We know what he needs, and we'll take good care of him."

Clearly Dr. Rodwell knew *something* of what I'd been up to. He'd felt threatened enough to frame me, and to immobilize me. But what did he know exactly, and how? I decided to keep probing. "Why are you doing this to me?"

"I didn't want to, believe me. But you forced my hand." He leaned back and shook his head. "Ever since the Brickhaven servers were hacked a few weeks ago, we've been on high alert. While the miscreant covered his tracks well, we could at least tell which files had been accessed. Since none of them contained any truly sensitive information, we were more curious than concerned. Then the apocalypse patients started showing up, and Amos as their leader, saying I was— what was it, again—the incarnation of evil? We weren't sure what that meant at first, but we suspected it might not be a coincidence. Then Amos placed *you* at the center of everything. That part took a while to figure out. Actually, I owe you an apology."

I raised my eyebrows at him. "Just one?"

He held up one finger and smiled. "I used you, I admit. Maybe it wasn't the best thing for your well-being to let you near the apocalypse patients' cases, but I felt like we needed to let the situation play out the way Amos wanted it to until we could get to the bottom of things. We knew he had that thumb drive hidden in his room, for example, but I told the nurses not to confiscate it. I wanted to see what he'd do with it. When he passed it off to you, I figured out that he was trying to recruit you to his cause—whatever that may be. I'm unclear on the details. I know Amos wants to sabotage Brickhaven's work with the president by undermining my influence, but I don't understand all the ins and outs."

"Brickhaven's *work?*"

He looked down and shook his head. "I don't know what misapprehension Amos is under, but the fact is we're the good guys, Neve. Over the years, Brickhaven has done more to serve the world than you can even imagine." Dr. Rodwell rested his hand lightly on my shoulder. "Honestly, after the knife attack you suffered, you were the last person I thought would get sucked in by a patient's delusions. In the end, I guess Amos knew you better than any of us, didn't he?"

I squirmed in disgust. To my relief, he removed his hand from mine.

"Rosanna will have me out of here first thing in the morning."

He gave me a pitying look. "I wouldn't be so sure about that. You're very fortunate, as you do have good friends, but tonight you threatened my life and broke into my office. Then, somehow, you broke into my lockbox—which was put there specifically to protect the confidentiality of high-profile patients, by the way. These are not the actions of the Neve we all know and love. Frankly, attributing your behavior to a psychiatric breakdown is the most forgiving interpretation available, and the one I believe your friends will be most likely to embrace. After all, we all know how much you've been through lately, with the attack...."

He couldn't be right... could he? Surely Rosanna and Con would listen to me. But as I tried to imagine what I was going to say to them, hopelessness crept in. They were both complete skeptics when it came to paranormal phenomenon. Amos and I were the only witnesses to what had transpired during our visit that afternoon, and I had already given Con my assessment that Amos was delusional and hallucinating. Not to mention that I couldn't produce any evidence of Dr. Rodwell's plot against President Duran while strapped to a bed in Seclusion Room 3. Dr. Rodwell had done a damn fine job of framing me, and he was right—my actions had only strengthened his case. How was I going to explain myself?

"It's distressing, I know," he said, and I hated myself for letting my emotions show on my face. "It's obvious that we overestimated your capacity to handle stress. Then again, you did a very good job of convincing Rosanna and me that you'd recovered enough from the attack to help with apocalypse patients. I should have listened to Rosanna, though. She said you weren't ready. And here you are, suffering a breakdown. This is on me. I can see now that I made the wrong call, and I take full responsibility."

So that was how he was going to spin it. I flinched as he patted my ankle restraint.

"Don't worry, we'll take good care of you," he said as he stood and headed for the door.

He was going to leave me alone in there. Desperation clawed at me. "You're a murderer!" I blurted.

When he glanced back at me, I saw a flash of the real Dr. Rodwell—a man who imagined himself to be one of the untouchable masters of the universe. "Don't worry. No one would bother killing you, Neve. You're not important enough—unlike the president."

Without waiting for a reply, he left, closing the door behind him. I heard the click of the handle, then metal sliding against metal as he locked the safety bolt.

After his footsteps faded down the hall, it grew so quiet in the room that my ears began to ache. I felt the tickle of a tear as it ran from the corner of my eye down my temple and into my hairline.

Pull yourself together. If I gave in to despair, Dr. Rodwell would have already won. I needed to tap into emotions that were energizing—outrage, for example. There was plenty of outrage at my disposal. I closed my eyes and focused on stoking it.

I needed a plan. I had the nurses' call handset. I could ask them for a bathroom break. They would take me out in restraints, but at least I'd be off the bed and out of the room.

Then what? Make a scene? Try to run? These nurses were experienced, and I was far from the cleverest patient they'd ever dealt with. If I were, I never would have ended up in this mess. Even if I managed to escape from the unit, security would be put on full alert, and there was no chance I'd make it out of the hospital.

I could do something drastic like take a hostage, but I would never inflict that kind of trauma on anyone. And even if I could bring myself to do something like that, it would only feed into Dr. Rodwell's story about my psychiatric state. No, an escape attempt wasn't feasible. I would just end up right back where I was—probably with another jab in my arm. I couldn't let that happen either. I needed my head to be as clear as possible.

What else could I do? Protocol meant I could ask the staff to inform my emergency contact that I'd been admitted. In my case, that was my parents, and they might insist on talking to me, in which case I could ask them to call Con or Rosanna.

But that still didn't solve the main problem. Whoever made the call to my parents would give them Dr. Rodwell's version of events before I got a chance to tell my side of the story. Frankly, "Neve had a breakdown" didn't even sound that unbelievable to *my* ears, and since the stabbing, everyone had worried that returning to work might prove to be too much of a strain. The onus would be on me to convince them that the staff of the hospital where I worked—the staff about whose excellence I had bragged many times—was unwittingly part of a conspiracy on the part of our medical director to kidnap me and hold me against my will.

Frustration was beginning to smother my outrage. I was lying there, helpless. No way out, no way to get help. With nothing left to do, I whispered a brief prayer. "I'm sorry, God. If Amos is right and you wanted me to help him, I guess you put your faith in the wrong girl."

A wash of tears soaked both sides of my face as my last bit of hope was snuffed out.

22

CORNELIUS

It was after nine o'clock at night. Con knew he should have left the office hours ago, but he was on tenterhooks waiting for Neve to call or text him back.

She hadn't seemed quite as angry at him after their conversation outside Amos's room that afternoon. On the other hand, she might have just been behaving professionally, while inside, she was outraged that Con hadn't called to tell her Amos was awake. Still, she'd reaffirmed their plan to connect after work, and regardless of how angry she might be, it was unlike Neve to make a plan and then back out without even getting in touch. Con couldn't remember it ever happening before, in fact, and he was starting to get worried.

All his calls went straight to her voice mail. Her phone was either turned off or she'd forgotten to charge it, which would also be unusual for her.

He couldn't just sit around any longer. He would go by her place on the way home and check on her. What was the worst that could happen? She could yell at him for being presumptuous enough to come by unannounced and tell him to bugger off. At least then he would know she was all right. He could fix the rest later.

Con was gathering his things to leave when the office phone beeped. Someone was paging him. He hit the speakerphone button. "Yes?"

"Dr. O'Brien, I'm glad you're still here. It's your patient, Amos Vates. We can't find any medical reason for it, but he's acting extremely agitated. He asked to see you, but we told him we thought you were gone for the night. Would you like us to call Psychiatry again?"

"No need. I'll be right there." He quickly hung up the phone, grabbed his tablet computer, and headed to the unit.

Con could hear voices coming from Amos's room even before he reached the nurses' station. Amos was shouting, and the nurse who'd paged Con was trying to calm him down.

"Amos!" he called down the dimmed hallway, hoping the sound of his voice would have an impact. It worked. There was silence until he reached the room.

Amos was standing next to the bed, holding onto the bedrail for balance. Tense and wild-eyed, he looked terrified, his eyes red and wet with tears.

The nurse gave Con a grateful look as he walked in and said, "You can go. I've got this."

"All his numbers are okay," the nurse whispered to him on her way out the door.

"Thank you." Con turned his attention to Amos. "Back in the bed with you. Now."

"But it's Neve! She's in danger!"

Something about the intensity of Amos's proclamation triggered a primal reaction in Con. He wanted to grab the lad, shake him, and ask him what he meant. But Neve had told him Amos was delusional, and his patient's well-being took priority over his own emotions. "If that's the case, I'll take care of it. But you can't help anyone by making yourself sick." He pointed at the bed. "In."

Con could see from Amos's expression that his words were sinking in. "Okay," Amos said as he sat down on the edge of the mattress.

Con helped him back into the bed and pulled the sheet and blankets over him. Then he handed Amos a cup of water from the rolling tray and pulled a chair over to the bedside. "I'm here, as you requested. Now what are you on about?"

Amos sipped the water with his eyes closed, as though recovering from his outburst. After a few moments, he lifted himself up on one elbow. His voice raw with urgency, Amos said, "Neve is in serious trouble, Doc. I know this is going to sound crazy, but you have to believe me."

If Con hadn't already been worried about Neve, it would have been easier for him to dismiss Amos's concern as paranoia. Under the circumstances, though, he would at least hear him out. "I'll be the judge of 'crazy.' Tell me about this trouble."

"It's about the *Book of Amos*. I asked her to do something for me, something kind of… well, I knew it might get her in trouble with her boss or something, but I had no idea it might be dangerous!"

Con didn't want to believe what he was hearing, but his instincts were whispering to him that Amos was telling the truth—as he saw it, at least. "Dangerous how?"

"I asked her to get something from Dr. Rodwell's office, and please don't ask me how I know this, but I'm pretty sure he caught her and he's locked her up on Unit 4."

"What?" That made no sense at all. Why would Neve have done the bidding of someone who, just a few hours earlier, she'd said was delusional, hallucinating, and in need of a psych consult? Amos couldn't be right.

So why did it feel like Con's heart was constricting?

"There's no time to explain." Amos tried to pull himself out of the bed again, but Con guided him back down. "You have to go to her now, Doc! This'll be your only chance." Amos folded his arms across his chest and turned away. "That's all I'm going to say. Otherwise, you're going to stay here asking me questions instead of rescuing her."

Fecking hell. It took every ounce of self-control he had to remain calm. "You are a very frustrating young man, Amos, do you know that?"

But Amos didn't answer, just kept looking away from him.

"You disrupt the unit, defy your nurses, call me down here, and now you won't tell me any more about what's going on? Is that it?" Con got to his feet. "If I leave here to check out what you're saying, first of all, it had better not be true. Neve had better be safe at home, having a nice cup of tea. Either way, you are to stay in the bed and follow your nurse's orders to the absolute letter from this moment until I'm cold in the ground. Do we understand each other?"

Still silent, Amos met Con's gaze and nodded.

"All right, then. Sit. Stay." He pointed a commanding finger at Amos. "I'll be checking in on you."

"Hurry, Doc," he heard Amos call as he left the room and went to the nurses' station. The nurse who'd paged him was there.

"He's calm, but if he gives you one more ounce of trouble tonight, I want you to call me on my mobile right away."

"Thank you, Doctor." The poor nurse's eyes were ringed with circles of exhaustion. Amos was driving them all spare.

He would check out Amos's story. If it was all part

of a delusion, as Con suspected, at least he could reassure the boy. "Can you do me a favor? Check on the computer to see if Psychiatry Unit 4 has admitted anyone tonight."

"Of course." A few moments of typing and clicking later, she said, "One admission tonight. Caucasian female, age thirty-three. The name is in private mode."

Con felt a chill, as though a ghost walked right through him. "Does it say where the patient came from?"

"This is kind of strange. It says she was a walk-in—to the unit, not even to the ER. But that's an inpatient unit. Do they even allow walk-ins?"

"Not that I know of." The chill deepened. "Who's the admitting physician?"

"Dr. Rodwell. Well, since he's head of the department, I guess he could have brought a patient in himself. That explains the walk-in part." The nurse appeared satisfied. "Do you need anything else?"

It was Neve. Somehow, in his bones, he knew it. "No, nothing else. Thank you for paging me. And feel free to sit on Amos if he tries to move."

She smiled. "I'll make a note in the chart."

What kind of madness were Neve and Amos perpetrating? Con tried to conceal his sense of urgency as he left his unit and went straight to Psychiatry, collecting his thoughts on the way over. If a rescue was indeed what was needed, he'd better work fast and sound like he knew what he was doing. Once he reached Unit 4, he swiped his badge and opened the main doors, holding out his tablet computer so he'd look like he was reading something important as he strode toward the nurses' station.

"I need to see Neve Keane immediately," he barked. "Take me to her."

The nurse at the station jumped. "Dr. O'Brien?"

"Where is she?"

"Um…." The nurse looked around. "I'm not sure I can—"

"It's all right, I know Dr. Rodwell admitted her." He glanced down at his tablet. "I have reason to believe she could be having a medical emergency. I need to examine her right away."

He didn't like playing the domineering physician ordering people around, but at least he didn't have to fabricate how imperative he felt the situation was.

"Oh my goodness, I had no idea. I'll take you to her." The nurse made a quick phone call. After a moment, one of her colleagues appeared at the desk. "Take over for a minute?"

Con took note of their path as he followed her down a series of corridors. He decided it would be wise to get her on side, in case he needed her later. "I'm sorry for being so gruff. You understand."

"Yes, of course," she said, sounding concerned. "I had no idea Miss Keane had a medical problem."

"No one did until a few hours ago," he said. "That's why I'm here. And please, call me Con. You are…?"

"Miriam," she said, stopping in front of one of the seclusion rooms with the number 3 on the door. "She's in here."

Amos had said he thought Neve was "locked up on Unit 4," but Con hadn't realized he meant it so literally. How on earth Amos had known, Con had no idea, but at the moment, he was too busy forcing himself to keep his emotions in check to think about solving mysteries. "Thanks, Miriam. I'll take it from here."

She bobbed her head back and forth. "Um, might you need my help? Examining her, I mean. She has to stay in five-point restraints. Dr. Rodwell's orders."

Jaysus. He'd always known Rodwell was a prick, but this? "Surely not all night?"

Miriam looked at the floor. They both knew it went against protocol to keep patients in seclusion once a crisis had passed, let alone in restraints. "Well, she's been asleep. We're supposed to offer her a choice when she wakes up."

Con's stomach roiled. "You mean restraints or sedation?"

Miriam nodded. "I know that sounds extreme, but between her violent behavior and her threats to kill Dr. Rodwell…."

Con nodded knowingly, trying to hide his surprise at these details. Still, he knew "violent behavior" could mean a whole range of things, some of which he would likely engage in himself if someone tried to lock him in seclusion. And, of course, Miriam had no way of knowing that Con considered a threat to kill Dr. Rodwell to be a sign of robust mental health. He would be fascinated to hear all about the day's events from the horse's mouth—once he got the horse safely out of the barn, that was.

Miriam continued, "We gave her one injection when she was first admitted, nothing since. No standing medication orders yet."

"Understood," Con said, taking care to maintain a neutral tone as he imagined squashing Rodwell's head like a grape. "You can go. I'll manage. Just leave the door ajar for me."

"Okay." She unlocked the door and let him inside.

What he saw was like a scene from a nightmare too unthinkable for his mind to dream up. There, amid blue walls that appeared harsh and cold under the fluorescent ceiling lights, lay Neve. She was either asleep or faking sleep on a hospital bed in socks and a paper gown, without even a blanket to keep her warm. Cuffs on her ankles and wrists were attached to the bedframe, along with a strap across her waist holding her down.

The impulse to race over, rip off the restraints, and carry her out of there was almost too strong to resist. But if he was going to get Neve out of that room and the hospital before any alarms were raised, he had to stay in control. Some clever acting would be required.

There was one chair in the room. He moved it next to the bed and sat. Con's heart cracked like a dropped glass as he reached out and touched the back of her hand. "Neve?"

She began to rouse. So she had been asleep. He was glad of it. Every moment of this ordeal that she missed was to be considered a blessing.

But as she woke, Neve tried to move, and the tug of her restraints seemed to jolt her back into an awareness of the situation. She clenched her fists and turned her head to face him, wild-eyed.

"It's me," he said softly, mindful that someone walking by the door might overhear. "It's Con."

Her expression morphed instantly from one of agony to relief, and her eyes swelled with tears. "Con! How did you find me?"

"Shh." He held his index finger up to his mouth and pointed at the door, which stood open a crack. "Softly. I'll explain later. Right now, I'm getting you out of here."

Her eyes glued to his, Neve began to cry in earnest. Con stroked her hand. "It's all right. I told them you were having a medical emergency. I just need to think up one that will sound convincing enough that they'll release you into my care." He smoothed away the hair that perspiration had plastered to her forehead. "Can you tell me anything that might help? What are they saying your symptoms are?"

"Oh God." She pressed her eyes closed as more tears fell. "I can't believe you're really here."

"Well, I am, and I wish we could have a nice long

chat. But time is of the essence. At some point, it's going to occur to Nurse Miriam that she should call Rodwell, and I want to have you well away from here before he makes an appearance."

"Okay. Okay." He could see her struggling to focus. Then her face lit up. "What about encephalitis?"

He squinted down at her. "You have encephalitis?"

"No. Not yet, anyway," she said, "but I have an ovarian tumor. Possibly a teratoma. I got an email tonight from Dr. Mohinder."

"Oh." Con took a deep breath and focused on remaining calm for Neve. A teratoma, probably nothing to worry about.

"It's okay. They think it's benign," she continued. "They just found it on my old CT scan from the ER. It's not confirmed yet, but I did an internet search, and it said that left untreated, it could trigger swelling of the brain or something. Is that really a thing?"

"One second." Con was already doing a search on his tablet. It wasn't his area of expertise, but he thought he remembered learning something about ovarian tumors triggering autoimmune reactions…. Ah. There it was. "Anti-NMDA receptor encephalitis?"

"That sounds right. Wait, why are you asking me? Aren't you the doctor?"

He sighed with relief. Neve was coming back to herself. "No, I'm telling you. And Dr. Mohinder did, in fact, contact you about this tumor today? That's a true story?"

"Of course it's true. You think I'm making this up?"

"No, it's not that." He was glad to see she was getting angry at him. She would need that energy. "I just need to make sure I have my story straight in case someone double-checks it. The fewer suspicions we raise, the more time we'll buy for ourselves."

"Oh. Okay, that makes sense."

"Right, so. I'll make a big scene. I should tell them about the ovarian tumor. They can verify that, and it could conceivably connect with Endocrinology, which would explain my involvement. Is that okay with you?"

She nodded.

"It would be easiest to wheel you out of here as you are. Miriam seemed pretty nervous about taking off the restraints, and her cooperation would be helpful." But as Neve's face began to fall, he said, "Forget it. I'll ask for a wheelchair—"

"No, you're right. We shouldn't take any risks. Leave the restraints on."

It just about broke him to watch her lie there, helpless and clearly suffering for it, yet still determined to rally her courage. "Good girl, you are. All right." He stood up and moved the nurses' call handset to the chair. Then, with his foot, he released the brakes on the bed's wheels. "You should probably act sick."

"Sick how?"

"Can you fake a seizure? No, wait. They might call someone else in for that. How about unsteady breathing, dizziness, agitation?"

"Yeah, I can do that." She closed her eyes, and he could see she was preparing. "Okay, I'm ready when you are."

Con pushed the door open wide, then went back and positioned himself at the top of the bed. As Neve looked up at him with wide eyes, he gave her as reassuring a smile as he could muster. "Onward we go, and well. Start acting."

Neve started to take fast, shallow breaths and move her head from side to side. Con rolled the bed into the hallway and backtracked to the nurses' station. Miriam was sitting there along with two other nurses. As soon as she spotted them, Miriam stood, a shocked expression on her face.

"Miriam, I'm taking her to the ER," Con bellowed, turning the bed toward the main entrance.

"Dr. O'Brien, wait!" Miriam ran out from behind the desk. "I talked to Dr. Rodwell. He's on his way, and he said not to let Neve off the unit under any circumstances until he gets here."

Neve rolled her eyes back and began to moan and twist. She made it look as though only the restraints were keeping her from falling to the floor.

Playing off Neve's impressive performance, Con turned to face Miriam. In spite of feeling instantly guilty about it, he positioned himself to look as large and intimidating as possible and shouted, "Under *any* circumstances? And did you tell him that the circumstances are potentially life-threatening symptoms of late-stage anti-NMDA receptor encephalitis secondary to an ovarian teratoma—the condition that has clearly caused Neve's erratic behavior? No, you did not, because you didn't know about the tumor, and neither does Dr. Rodwell. No one knew until Dr. Mohinder received the test results today. We can only thank Christ it was found in time." He stepped back and made pointed eye contact with each of the nurses in turn. "I'm taking her to the ER, and I'll take full responsibility. Once you explain the situation to Dr. Rodwell, I'm sure he'll thank you for not standing between me and saving Neve's life."

After exchanging anxious glances, the nurses appeared to reach the unspoken conclusion that it would be unwise to stand between Con and anything. Miriam jogged ahead of the bed and held open the unit doors. "One of us can go with you—"

"Not necessary," Con snapped, pushing Neve through the doors. "Once I've written my note, I'll forward it to you so you can give it to Dr. Rodwell."

Neve's moaning and twisting intensified. Internally, Con beamed with admiration at her commitment to the role.

"Good luck," he heard Miriam call after them as he steered Neve around the corner toward the elevator bay.

"Okay, we're in the clear," he whispered, and Neve's "symptoms" stopped instantly. "Just pretend to be asleep for a few minutes."

Neve closed her eyes. Once they were alone in an elevator, he continued, "I want to rip these restraints off you, but that might look odd to anyone else who gets on."

"I understand," she whispered. The resignation in her tone raked at him.

"Just a few minutes more. Our clinic has closed for the night, so I'll take you there. We'll get you some scrubs. Then we'll get the hell out of here."

Her lids fluttered open, and she stared up at him. Though her expression was pained, her eyes appeared lit from within. Then, to his complete and utter amazement, she whispered, "I love you."

Con gripped the bed, afraid his legs might buckle beneath him. Fecking hell, how long had he been waiting to hear those words? How many times had he fantasized about Neve's lips forming each syllable of that phrase? His heart swelled until it felt like his lungs were being pushed aside. More than anything in the world, he wanted to lean down and take her mouth….

But she was tied down, for Christ's sake, and besides, these were hardly the ideal circumstances for serious declarations. Neve was emotional, terrified. He couldn't take anything she said right then as a fully rational utterance.

Pushing himself hard to be responsible, he smiled down at her. "My dear Neve, if I could be sure that wasn't the encephalitis talking, you would have just made me the happiest man on earth."

She smiled back, and he would have been content to die in that moment, satisfied that his life had been well-lived.

The elevator bounced, pulling their attention away from one another as they reached their floor. As quickly as possible, Con rolled Neve the short distance to his clinic. All the lights were off, which meant their timing was good and they'd missed the cleaning crew. He pushed her into an exam room and immediately set about releasing her restraints. Once freed, she practically flew off the bed and flung herself at him, hugging him so tightly that he had to work to breathe. His arms wound around her as well, and he buried his face in her hair, his mouth next to ear, murmuring, "It's okay, I've got you. I've got you."

He held her as she wept, trying not to crush her with the strength of his embrace. Light sobs shook her body, and with every soft mewl that emanated from her throat, he felt a new surge of murderous intent toward Rodwell.

Eventually she began to quiet and pulled away from him. After handing her a box of tissues, Con watched as Neve worked hard to get her emotions under control. She tugged at the corner of her paper gown and cleared her throat. "Scrubs?"

"Right." He wasn't sure what size she wore, so he took a pair of every size from the storage room and brought the whole pile to her. That produced the most delectable sound he'd ever heard: Neve's giggle.

For her continued amusement, he feigned indignation. "I know how women are with clothes. I wanted to make sure you had plenty of choices."

She picked up a top and held it against her, illustrating that three of her could fit inside. "This'll work."

He couldn't believe that just two teasing words from Neve could make him love her even more. "Right, so. I'll leave you to it, then."

"It might take me a while. You know how women are with clothes," she said, still grinning as she shut the door behind him.

In his office, Con picked up the things he'd left behind when he rushed off to see Amos: overcoat, satchel, mobile, car keys. By the time he got back to Neve, she was dressed in scrubs and tying a bow in the drawstring of her pants. Only then did he notice she didn't have shoes, only the ankle socks she'd been wearing when he found her on Unit 4.

Her gaze followed his.

He scowled. "Wear mine."

"Your shoes are twice as big as my feet," she pointed out. "That would look weirder. Plus, they'd keep falling off."

"I could carry you."

"Even weirder."

There were no satisfactory options, in other words. "We don't have far to walk. Just watch where you're stepping. And put on my overcoat."

She nodded and slipped the coat on. It reached her

ankles and wrapped around her twice. "See? This coat is so huge on me, no one will notice my feet."

"You could be right. Okay, then. Let's go."

Trying not to look suspicious, they moved as efficiently as possible through the least-traveled hospital corridors until they reached the parking garage. Con made a mental note of all the security cameras they were passing. If anyone chose to go looking for it, there would be plenty of evidence to hang them both. He hoped Neve could tell him something, anything, that he could give to Rosanna—some explanation or excuse Lolly could use to keep the dogs at bay while he took Neve somewhere safe to regroup.

On his department head's recommendation, Con had recently replaced his old car with a sports utility vehicle. Apparently he hadn't been projecting the right image for the hospital, driving around in his "ancient, clapped-out hatchback." Not wishing to drive a monstrosity, he'd opted for a midsize model. It was an improvement, certainly—big enough for him to sit in comfortably, with enough room up front to straighten out his banjaxed leg if he wanted to. At the moment, though, its most valuable feature was that black SUVs were thick on the ground in the DC area, so he and Neve would blend in on the roads.

Con only relaxed a notch once he'd bundled Neve into the car and shut the door behind her. But it wasn't until he'd swiped out of the garage, driven down the driveway, and turned onto the public road that he let himself breathe a true sigh of relief. What would happen next, he had no idea. But Neve was safe and within his reach, and he was determined to keep it that way.

Neve sat quietly and stared out the window, not even asking where they were going. He didn't know either, but he'd decided to take I-395 South, the fastest way out of the District from where they were.

As the adrenaline that had been pumping through his system began to wear off, his leg began to throb, and there was a new, sharp pain shooting down his back and into his hip. Ever since he'd received the page about Amos, he'd been focusing more on speed than form, abandoning the usual care he took with his physical movements. Con knew from experience that he'd be feeling the effects for days, but if that was the price he had to pay to see Neve safe, he'd do it a thousand times over.

He fished around in his satchel and grabbed his pill bottle, but as he tried to open it one-handed, it jumped from his grasp and flew onto the floor between Neve's feet.

She picked up the bottle and opened it for him. "How many?"

He hated himself in that moment, not for needing the painkillers but for letting Neve find out that he needed them. "Two," he said, even though he could have used three or four.

Neve tapped two pills into his open hand, then closed the bottle and tucked it back into his satchel.

"Thanks." He could see both the concern on her face and her effort to conceal it. No doubt she wasn't asking questions because she didn't want to embarrass him, but that made him feel even worse somehow.

Eventually she went back to staring out the window. Con hated to imagine what Neve might be thinking about, what horrors she might be recalling.

"Are you all right?" he asked gently. He didn't want her to feel pressured to talk, but he wanted to give her the opening.

"Yeah," she murmured. "Just looking at the stars."

Her answer pained his heart. After being subjected to so much ugliness, she must have been seeking comfort in beauty.

Con felt a strong urge to just keep driving. Maybe go to the airport and get on a plane. Or stay on the road and go west, where the highways were endless. He knew it wasn't practical yet, but the minute they sorted out this mess, he wanted to take Neve away somewhere far away from all the pain and chaos—somewhere she would find as soothing as a sky full of stars.

It was a real option. His department kept asking him to take some of the vacation time he'd accumulated before it buggered up their accounting. In truth, it would be difficult for Con to be away from his patients, but his colleague Faraz went away often enough and managed to keep his hand in between phone calls, emails, and those in-office video chats they had now—"virtual office visits," they were called. It would be awkward, but Con could adjust. For Neve, he could do anything.

He glanced back over, surprised to find her still awake. It was as good a time as any for him to answer the one question she'd asked that he hadn't answered yet: how he'd known where to find her.

"It was your man Amos, by the way," Con said. "He told me where you were."

She looked surprised, but only for a moment. "Oh, okay."

No follow-up questions? Con certainly had plenty. For example, why had Neve told him Amos was delusional one minute, then recklessly followed his instructions the next? But he was hardly going to interrogate her after what she'd been through. "I wish I could let him know you're okay, but I don't think it would be wise for me to call the hospital right now. Too many potential questions I won't be able to answer."

Neve reached over and rested her hand on his arm. "It's okay. I'm pretty sure he knows."

She sounded quite confident, so Con just nodded. First, a safe place. Then shoes. Then food. Then rest. Then, and only then, questions.

And Neve definitely needed rest. She'd pulled his coat up to form a makeshift pillow between her head and the window. Her eyes were closing gradually, as though she was trying not to fall asleep, but sleep was winning.

Suddenly, she forced her eyes open and peered at him. "Con?"

"Yes?"

"Why did you save me?"

He took his eyes off the road just long enough to look at her like she'd lost her senses.

"No, really," she said. "I was afraid you would believe—"

"I will always save you." The words were out of his mouth before he could even think, uttered with a conviction as deep and unchanging as the sea.

There was a pause as his words hung there, filling the air, holding their own. Just as Neve's eyes drifted closed, he heard her say, "Thank you."

Con had never felt prouder in his life than he did hearing those words from her, knowing everything that was behind them.

He waited until he was sure she was asleep before putting his mobile phone earpiece in and calling the one person he could think of who understood enough about what was going on to be of help to them. It was well after eleven o'clock, but Con knew Eric was a night owl.

"Conman the Barbarian!" As expected, Eric sounded wide awake.

"Eric, how's the *craic*?" Con asked, having taught Eric the common Irish greeting.

"Not bad. I'm deep into a medieval quest with a badass group of Texans."

Gaming, as usual. That explained the heavy metal music playing in the background. "I hope my call didn't wake Katie."

"Oh no. She's at a silent retreat with their sister church in Portland until next Tuesday."

Which explained why the music was playing so loudly that Eric was practically yelling to make himself heard. "Lucky girl, that one."

"Yeah, well, you know she loves that stuff."

"I think she loves getting away from *you* for a few days."

"Who could blame her? So what's going on? You never call me at home this late."

"I need your help. I have a situation."

"Hold on a second." The sound of heavy metal disappeared. "What do you need?"

Con thought for a moment, choosing his words carefully. Eric was convinced that all phone calls were monitored and recorded, so sensitive subjects should only be discussed either in code or in person. He needed to be vague and clear at the same time. "I need a place to lie low for a few days."

"Oh." The mirth left Eric's voice. "That serious?"

"I'm afraid so."

"Well, you can always come here. I mean, there's room."

"I'm not sure that's a good idea. We're avoiding certain people, and you're a known acquaintance."

"Wait a minute, 'we'? Are you talking about who I think you're talking about?"

"Unfortunately, yes."

"Oh, man, I'm sorry to hear that." He paused a moment. "Hang on a second. I have an idea, but I have to check something."

"Okay." Con sat drumming his fingers on the steering wheel while he listened to the sound of footsteps, followed by drawers opening and closing and objects rustling.

Eric sounded victorious when he returned. "I know a place."

Con heard jingling keys. "Already?"

"Yeah. One of Katie's buildings is empty until close to Thanksgiving."

"Katie's buildings?" He must have meant a church facility. "It's not exactly yours to offer, then, is it?"

"Well, Katie could offer it, and if she knew the situation, she would. So as her spouse, I'm acting as her agent and offering you *sanctuary*, if you catch my meaning."

Con smiled. Eric sounded extremely pleased with his impromptu code for "church." "I just don't want to get anyone in trouble."

"Okay, how's this? If you destroy the property or break your leg on the stairs or something, I'll pretend I knew nothing and suggest you and your co-conspirator broke in to enjoy a kinky weekend."

"That makes me feel much better."

"Excellent. Remember the place where we bought the malt liquor?"

"I never forget the locations of my worst lapses in judgment."

"Are you anywhere near it?"

"Forty-five minutes away, I'd say."

"Great. I'll meet you there."

"Thanks. I can't tell you how much I appreciate this."

"No problem. Do you need any supplies?"

"We can take care of that when we get there. But my companion could use some clothes, and a pair of shoes. Would Katie have anything to spare?"

"She has some workout stuff that might do, and like twelve pairs of sneakers. She's a shoe hoarder."

"I had no idea. I guess everyone has their vices. Bring whatever you think is best."

"Sure, no problem. Oh, and you guys should turn your phones off now. Like, off-off, not airplane mode. See you soon."

"Right, thanks. See you."

Con pressed and held the power button on his phone, and as the screen went dark, he felt his shoulders relax for the first time in ages. He didn't have to worry about Neve's phone, of course, since she'd had nothing on her but a paper gown when they escaped

Unit 4. At least they had a place to go for the moment, anyway. And thank Christ for Eric. He was as sound as they came.

As they rolled down the highway, Con was almost as surprised to hear Neve's voice as he was by the words she spoke.

"Conman the Barbarian?"

He looked at her sharply. "You heard that?"

"He was kind of shouting." Her eyes sparkled with amusement. "Is that your gaming handle or something?"

"I plead the Fifth."

"It is? That's awesome! Does Rosanna know?"

"I take back what I said," he muttered. "I'm not saving you anymore."

Neve smiled broadly as she closed her eyes again. "I think I'll sleep for a few minutes. Good night, Conman."

"I have to think of an embarrassing nickname for you now, you realize."

"Do your worst, Barbarian."

As he merged into traffic, Con smiled to himself. He couldn't help marveling at his brilliant good luck.

Neve had said she loved him. Under duress, of course, and she might not have meant it the way he hoped she did, but still. He'd heard her say the words, and they'd been a balm to his soul.

He still had no idea what in the hell was going on between Neve and Amos. Given what Rodwell had done, though, he knew there was a possibility she could still be in danger. And since he broke her out under false pretenses, they might both get fired, or even face legal charges. Worst of all, when she woke up again, Neve might remember why she'd been mad at Con the night before and resume that argument.

But none of that mattered. Neve had said she loved him, and as long as he had the memory of that, he had everything.

23

———

NEVE

I was touched by Eric's generosity, letting us stay in Katie's church's building. Watching the road signs, I figured out we were in Virginia somewhere near Woodbridge. We arrived at a huge gray house in the woods, situated at the end of its own road. Eric said it was a youth center in the summer, and the church either used it themselves or rented it out for conferences and retreats the rest of the year. He showed us around the ground floor, which had a living room, a meeting room, and a big eat-in kitchen with a bathroom toward the back. Upstairs were dormitory-style bedrooms.

We made the kitchen our headquarters. Eric was glad Con had asked him to bring me some clothes. He pointed out that if anyone was searching for us, we didn't want to make it any easier for them. My scrubs not only looked conspicuous, but they also had our hospital's logo printed on them.

Eric had brought a whole pile of clothes from Katie's wardrobe. She was two sizes smaller than I was, but I found a stretchy pair of black yoga pants I could squeeze into, along with a bright pink T-shirt that was probably baggy on her and only a bit tight on me. We wore almost the same shoe size, though, and I found a pair of sneakers that were pretty comfortable. Thankfully Eric had thought to bring socks, because the pair I was wearing were filthy. No undergarments, but that was just as well. I would have felt weird wearing someone else's intimates. I could shop for those in the morning.

Having checked myself out in the bathroom mirror, I knew in my new outfit, I looked like someone who was going to the gym for the express purpose of displaying their assets to attract a mate—the polar opposite of my usual style. But it met our needs, so I decided not to focus on how self-conscious I felt.

The look of frank admiration that flashed across Con's face when I came out of the bathroom didn't help. Heat spread steadily across my cheeks and down my neck.

"Glad you found something that works," Eric said as I handed him the bag of unused clothes.

"Yes, well done," Con added but quickly looked at the floor when I shot him a warning glance.

I balled up my scrubs and put them on the kitchen

counter. "Someone please burn those. I don't know what kind of detergent they use at the hospital, but my skin is itching."

Con turned serious in an instant. "Any rash?"

"No, Doctor," I said rolling my eyes.

"I'm asking," he said pointedly, "because they injected you with something earlier. You could be having an allergic reaction. May I take a look?"

"Injected you with something?" Eric asked as I acquiesced and approached Con. "Who?"

"A well-meaning nurse," I said as Con examined my face, followed by my wrist and the underside of my arm.

"Yeah, okay," Eric said, but he was openly skeptical. "Are you going to tell me what the hell is going on now?"

"You'll live, but you should take an antihistamine," Con said, releasing my wrist.

"There might be something here." Eric retrieved a first aid kit from the cabinet under the kitchen sink and started looking through it. "Here," he said, holding a small pill bottle.

Con took the bottle before I got a chance and read the label. "One to stop the itching, two to block out the world." He handed me the bottle. "Hang on to that in case the itching continues."

"Thanks." I sourced a glass of water and took one pill; I wanted to stay awake and alert for as long as possible. Then we all sat down at the large, round kitchen table.

"Let's talk," Con began. "Eric, you're a lifesaver, as always. This week in particular, you've gone way above and beyond the call. I'm in your debt."

"We both are," I added.

"Stop talking to me like you're about to send me away," Eric replied. "If this has something to do with that thumb drive—and I'm willing to bet a whole lot of money that it does—you're going to need my help."

Con shook his head. "I don't even know what we're dealing with yet, not fully, but I can tell you it has already become a dangerous situation. As of this moment, nothing you've done for us has broken any laws—"

"No major ones," Eric corrected.

"The point is you haven't done anything to put yourself in the crosshairs. If you help us any more, you might. And if you get into any trouble because of me or, God forbid, get hurt, Katie will flay me alive."

Eric nodded. "Maybe. But if you guys get hurt because I could have helped you and didn't, she'll flay *me* alive. And I can tell you for sure, she'd torture me a lot worse than she would you. It would hurt more, she'd make it last longer…."

It was impossible for me to imagine Katie even raising her voice, let alone hurting anyone. Then again, maybe she didn't shy away from fire and brimstone after all if she felt the situation called for it. Just one more thing to like about her, in my book.

"I mean it, Eric." Con's expression grew grim. "You've done more than enough. We'll be gone in the morning."

"We will?" I asked hesitantly. I was grateful Con hadn't asked me too many questions yet—I had needed time to recover after the ordeal at the hospital—but I was confused as to why he was making plans when he didn't even know half of what was going on.

"I mean it, too," Eric said, equally somber. "What the hell are friends for if not to help each other at times like this? You'd do the same for me."

The two men sat silently, glowering across the table at one another, neither one having a clue what they were volunteering for. I held up my finger. "Guys, this whole mess started because a patient asked for my help. It's my fault that both of you are involved."

Con turned his eyes on me, his face a dark cloud. "Your point being?"

"My point being that both of you can, and should, walk away right now," I said.

"Bollocks!" Con thundered. "I've been in love with you since the day we met. If anything happens to you, I'll lose my will to live. So no, I can't walk away."

I sat, stunned, eyes wide. "You... you've *what?*"

"What?" Con squinted in confusion for a moment, then realized what I was asking. "Sure, you knew that!"

In response to my continued look of shock, he clarified, "I told you. At the diner."

What the hell? "No you did not!" I covered my throat with my hand in an effort to conceal the hot blush climbing up my neck. "We never even finished that conversation!"

With visible effort, Con managed to lower his voice. "I'm sorry," he said with quiet intensity. "I thought I made my feelings clear. And after what *you* said—"

My heart ricocheted around in my chest. "In the elevator?"

"No!" Con reached out and captured my hand. "Not when you were… under duress," he said softly. "I meant after what you said at the *diner*, I gathered…."

"Oh, *that*." I pulled my hand away. The onslaught of feelings I was experiencing was powerful enough without adding his touch to the mix.

Flustered, I cast a glance at Eric, who could hear every word we were saying but was pretending to be fascinated by the kitchen cabinets. I had no desire to talk through how Con and I felt about one another in front of an audience, but I was also so bowled over, I had no idea what to say next. Twisting my fingers together, I murmured, "So… um…."

With both Eric and me at a loss for words, Con grabbed the conversational baton, abandoning any pretense of calm in the process. "Right, so. Now that you dumped that eejit you were seeing, you and I can finally get on with things. But only if you don't get yourself killed first!"

"I knew it!" Eric exclaimed, pumping his fist in the air as my jaw dropped. "You two are a thing!" Grinning, he added, "Katie owes me twenty bucks. Not that it matters much, since we have a joint bank account, but still."

"Congratulations," Con said, his voice a bit softer but still thick with emotion. Not for a second did he take his eyes off me.

I swallowed hard. When I'd told Con I loved him in the elevator, he'd chosen to lighten the moment with a joke. I didn't know what to make of that at the time. I'd guessed it meant that either he didn't feel the same or he wasn't ready to make any such declarations. Clearly I'd been dead wrong.

And now there we were, with Con's cards on the table and all eyes on me. As his words began to sink in, the love I felt for him, so long buried, rose like the sun, warming me from the inside. Tears stung my eyes, but I didn't let them fall. I couldn't allow myself to be overwhelmed by emotion, not if Con and Eric really were determined to stand with me against Brickhaven. I was the only one who knew how dangerous the situation really was, and I had to fill them in before another moment passed. After all, if we ended up in prison or dead, being in love would be a moot point.

"Yeah. So, speaking of getting killed...." The last word came out as a dry whisper. I cleared my throat and tried again. "You guys should know that Brick-haven is planning to kill President Duran."

"Wait, what? President of the United *States* Duran?" Eric gaped.

Con also looked so astonished that I immediately doubted my choice of an opener. Trying to walk it back a bit, I said, "I just mean that if you both are considering sticking around, you should probably know that's the kind of thing we're dealing with."

Eric and Con exchanged a pointed look.

"The *kind* of thing," Con asked, "or the *actual* thing?"

Stapling my gaze to the ceiling, I muttered, "The actual thing."

"Aw, hell." Eric slapped his hands on the table. "You're definitely going to need Erik the Viking's skill set, then. I don't know what this guy's going to do, though." He pointed a thumb in Con's direction. "Maybe patch me up if I catch a bullet?"

"Don't even joke about that," I said, horrified.

"Okay, okay, sorry." Then Eric's face fell. "Wait, you're serious, aren't you?"

I nodded.

Con reached his hand across the table to me. I took it, and he squeezed, speaking gently. "Maybe now would be a good time to tell us what happened today—if you're not too tired, that is."

"I'm fine." I smiled at the absurdity of his thoughtfulness—as though my fatigue could be more important than filling them in on a plan to assassinate the president. "Where should I start?"

"Well," Con asked, "when exactly did you decide to sneak in and visit Amos?"

I started with Rosanna's morning phone call and went from there. I didn't go into every detail of my conversation with Amos. It had been too bizarre, like a cognitive blender, and I was still trying to process it. Besides, if I told them that I suspected Amos might have paranormal gifts, Con and Eric might conclude that either Amos had succeeded in hypnotizing me or that Con should have left me in the seclusion room on Unit 4 after all.

However, I did share a couple examples of Amos's uncanny knowledge about things that had happened to me, just to give them some understanding of how and why he'd captured my attention. That I was attacked by a patient was easy enough information to come by, so I also told them Amos knew Stephan had hit me.

As soon as the words were out of my mouth, though, I regretted them.

"Oh, man, Neve," Eric said. "I'm really sorry."

"Don't worry," I replied. "I dumped him immediately."

Meanwhile, Con's face had transformed into a mask of barely contained rage. He was so angry, I could tell he didn't even trust himself to speak.

I moved on quickly, explaining that initially, I'd thought Amos's claims about talking to an angel were merely symptoms of his illness, as I'd told Con. But later, when it turned out his statements about my tumor were correct, I began to question myself. Angel or no angel, if Amos was right about that, what else might he be right about? That was why I'd broken into Dr. Rodwell's files—to find out once and for all if there was any truth to Amos's suspicions about Brickhaven. If Con and Eric thought I was a complete idiot for taking that course of action, they had the good grace not to show it.

When I got to the part where Dr. Rodwell caught me and locked me up, Con's eyes went so cold that it made me nervous. Eric asked me to recall my conversation with Dr. Rodwell as precisely as I could. He also wanted a detailed description of the nurses' call handset. Why that was of interest, I had no idea, but I decided to trust his process and did the best I could to recall exactly what the handset looked like and how it worked.

From there, Con took over, telling us how Amos had warned him I was in danger and explaining to Eric how we'd escaped. Once all additional questions had been asked and answered, Con and Eric were convinced that regardless of how Amos knew what he knew, what I'd read in Dr. Rodwell's memos was credible evidence of a plot to assassinate the president, and that was reason enough to act.

When I mentioned that, coincidentally, I had a date with Stephan at the White House on Saturday and we would be getting our picture taken with the president, both men's eyebrows shot up. I quickly clarified that I'd only agreed to go because Lee was a friend, and it would be extremely bad grace to let him down—and that I planned to take the opportunity to tell Stephan once and for all that we were through so he'd stop trying to win me back. At least Eric nodded in understanding.

Then Con mentioned that Rosanna had called him earlier that afternoon when she heard from the nurses on the endocrinology unit that I'd visited Amos. She'd wanted to know if he knew I'd been planning to come visit. He assured her that he had not. Rosanna was "spitting mad" at me, he said, but also worried.

Guilt drenched me. Rosanna was going to be frantic when she heard about Dr. Rodwell having me committed, and my subsequent escape. "I should call her," I said.

"Not from your phone," Eric said. "Not now."

"Not ever, actually," I corrected him. "I stomped it to smithereens."

"You what?" Con asked.

"Oh, yeah." I'd forgotten to tell them the most important part. "When they caught me in Rodwell's office, I smashed it so he wouldn't know I'd taken pictures of the memos."

Eric nodded. "That was good thinking, although it sure would've been nice if you had those pictures to show the president on Saturday."

"We haven't decided who's going where yet, or when," Con objected.

"Regardless," I said, shooting him a curious look, "we do have the pictures of the memos, or we should, at least. Right before I took them, I logged onto my personal email through my phone. After I snapped each photo, I emailed them to myself, just to be safe. You know, in case I got interrupted."

Eric jumped up and did a jig around his chair. "Neve, that's brilliant! You're a genius."

Still scowling, Con said, "Fair dues."

"This is awesome," Eric said, suddenly full of energy. "I'll be right back."

He rushed out of the house, leaving the front door hanging open. Outside, we could hear car doors opening and closing. When Eric returned, he was carrying a large canvas bag, which he set on the kitchen table. He unzipped it and began pulling things out. "Okay, here we go. Laptops, chargers, burner phones." He rummaged through the rest of the bag. "And a few other bits and pieces."

I gawked as he sorted the equipment into piles. Everything was brand-new, still in its packaging. "Where did you get all this stuff at this hour of the night?"

"My garage," he said with a note of pride. "I have a stash."

"But why did you bring it?"

He shrugged. "It's my version of an emergency kit, and Con sounded pretty squirrely on the phone."

Con shook his head. "You were never going to take 'go home' for an answer, were you?"

"Nope." Eric sat down and powered up one of the laptops. "Okay, Neve, we've got to grab those image files from your email before it occurs to one of those Brickhaven goons to check your private accounts. And we're up. What's your email service?"

"SecureMail.net."

"Cool, old-school. Username?"

I froze.

Eric gave me a strange look, then started to turn the laptop screen toward me. "Sorry, Neve. I just got excited. If you want to type it in yourself, I totally get it."

Oh God. He thought I didn't trust him with my username. I couldn't let him believe that, not after all the help he was giving us. "No, you do it. It's just…. It's a very old account. I've had it since middle school."

Con's interest was piqued. "Have you now? By all means, tell us."

"ShadowKeane," I muttered. "All one word, cap *S*, cap *K*."

"Sweet!" Eric grinned. "Like Shadow King from the X-Men, right? So you're a comic book geek. I knew there was something I liked about you."

"Thanks," I said dryly.

Con's eyes shone with amusement. "Who or what is Shadow King?"

"He's a kick-ass telepath and psi-warfare supervillain from the Marvel Comics universe. You wouldn't know anything about it." Eric rolled his eyes in Con's direction. "He grew up reading real books and stuff."

The look on Con's face told me he'd see to it that the newly discovered nickname stuck to me forever. "That was then," he said. "I think I could get into reading comic books now."

Mercifully, Eric cut in. "Password?"

Are all of my humiliating secrets destined to be revealed in the course of one night? "Um, actually, I just changed it recently. I got one of those identity theft security warnings, so I used the first thing that came to mind, you know? We'd probably just had coffee…."

Eric's fingers hovered over the keyboard as he squinted at me, perplexed.

Rip off the bandage, I ordered myself. "It's all lower-case, 'conobrien,' without the apostrophe, but the *O*s are zeros, and the *I* is a one."

I couldn't see their reactions because I covered my face with my hands.

"Don't be embarrassed," Eric said. "I'm sure all Con's passwords are variations on 'I love Neve, Neve rocks, Neve is hot,' smiley faces, hearts, etc."

"He's not wrong," Con said, "but I've been using the Irish spelling all this time. I have to change everything now."

I couldn't believe it. Con had succeeded in making me smile. His expression was so soft with affection that I wanted to crawl into his lap, wrap myself around him, and stay there for hours.

"Bingo!" Eric cried out, pulling us back down to earth. "Found the pictures. Okay, I'm going to save these to this hard drive and back them up on a secure off-site server." He typed so fast it sounded like water rushing. "Done."

"Let's have a look," Con said.

Reflexively, I objected, "But they're the president's private… medical…."

I stopped talking when I saw the "You can't be serious" expressions on Con's and Eric's faces.

"No, you're right," I admitted. We all knew how to be discreet, and besides that, we had way bigger concerns at the moment. "Have at it."

Eric slid the laptop over so both he and Con could see the screen. They stared intently, alternating control of the trackpad as they clicked and scrolled. I expected their looks of surprise and disgust, but after several minutes, Con emitted a low moan and leaned back against his chair.

"What is it?" I asked as he rubbed his hands vigorously over his face.

"Bloody hell." Con blew out a hard breath, then pointed to the screen. "In the memo, there. 'Sic semper tyrannis.' It means 'Thus always to tyrants.' That's Riggs Sanderson's project."

"Where have I heard that name?" Eric asked.

"Military contractor," Con said, "and Brickhaven member."

"Oh hell no!" Eric's eyes widened. "That shady guy whose drug-dealing employees flattened that village and got away with it?"

Con nodded slowly. "And 'Non ducor, duco—'I am not led, I lead'—that's Orson Taul's project."

My brain struggled to process what Con was saying. "Where did you get that from?"

"Those were the project titles next to their names on the Brickhaven membership list," Con said. "Rodwell, Sanderson, Taul—all had different parts of this project called 'Magnum Concilium,' the 'great council.'"

"That was all on the list?" Eric smacked his forehead. "Why didn't I put that together?"

"You were a bit busy decrypting the damn thing," Con pointed out.

I got up and stood behind them so we could all see the screen. I pointed at the memo. "So there's the project name 'Magnum Concilium' right at the top—"

"Oh yeah," Eric said, awestruck. "And 'Sic Semper Tyrannis' is ready to go—so Sanderson and his guys already have a plan in place for the assassination."

Con pointed at the next phrase. "And 'Non ducor, duco' means Taul is ready to step in and redirect the investigation, should someone suspect anything other than suicide."

There were a few beats of silence in the room as the weight of those words sank in.

"Man, they've got all their bases covered." Eric stood and began to pace the room.

Con asked, "Eric, did you keep a copy of the *Book of Amos* file?"

"Yeah," he said, visibly shaken. "Wouldn't be much of a hacker if I hadn't, would I?" He tried to smile. "I'll get the list of members and project names to put with these memos Neve found so she can give everything to the president. Then his people can put the pieces together."

"Slow down, there. Can't we just email copies to the White House, the police, the FBI? Everyone?" Con asked.

"That would be a no," Eric replied. "If we just send this stuff to the authorities—or even take them in person to law enforcement—*we're* going to look like the threat. Think about it. Why would we have documents about a presidential assassination plot? We'd get charged with domestic terrorism and who knows what else. By the time officials investigate us and verify the documents—which might *never* happen if Brickhaven interfered, and you know they would—the assassination plot would probably already have been executed, so to speak. Also, by then, Brickhaven would have had plenty of time to frame us the way Rodwell tried to frame Neve. Game, set, and match to the bad guys."

Con frowned. "All right, I see what you're saying,

but what if we get the files to them anonymously somehow?"

"Send them from a new email account?" I suggested. "Or maybe just drop off printouts at the police station and walk away?"

"Yeah, we could do that," Eric said, "but odds are the president would still end up dead. He gets so many threats every day, the one we're trying to expose would never rise to the top of the priority list in time. Any half-decent graphic designer could have mocked up these documents. It would be too easy for them to write the threat off as a hoax if the documents just showed up out of nowhere, or if we make an anonymous phone call or something. Odds are Duran would never even hear about it."

"Fair point." Con appeared disappointed but convinced. "But why even consider taking the documents to the White House, then? Won't we just run into the same problem there?"

"There's always a chance, yes," Eric conceded, "but not until after Neve speaks directly to the president. Real-time, direct, firsthand access, where she can explain what's going on to the one man who will understand instantly what she's talking about. After all, I'm assuming he was the only other person in those psychiatry sessions with Rodwell. He'll also be the person most motivated to listen to you, Neve, since he has the most to lose."

"That makes sense," I conceded, if reluctantly. The

whole idea of taking this information to the president myself made my stomach churn.

Con must have sensed that I was sliding into a state of heightened anxiety. "I see the merits in what you're saying, Eric, but that doesn't mean it has to be Neve who does this."

I slid my hand into the air. "Um, it kind of does, since I'm the only one of us with an invitation to the White House."

As I watched Con brood over that piece of information, Eric continued. "I know it sucks, but since she's getting her photo taken with the president, Neve will have a few moments with him, at least. She'll have to grab his attention, and we'll have to plan exactly what she's going to say—something that will make the president hear her out before she gets carted off by the Secret Service."

"Whoa, whoa." Con held up his hands. "Nobody's getting carted off by anyone. We have all day tomorrow to develop our plan."

"Right, of course." Eric nodded. "Sorry, I talk while I think, but my first ideas are rarely my best. Of course we'll figure something out."

That was good to hear. I liked to think of myself as brave, but my sweaty palms and rapid heartbeat told a different story. I closed my eyes and focused on steadying my breathing.

I felt Con's hand on my shoulder. "Are you okay?"

"I'm fine," I said, "I just need a minute to myself."

"You got it." Con and Eric went to the far corner of the room and spoke in low tones. Part of me wanted to know what they were saying, but another part wanted to take three or four more antihistamines and check out for a few hours.

That wasn't an option, though. Amos had involved *me*, asked for *my* help. I was also the one who had a date at the White House coming up just in time to save the president. I would have to see the situation through —not Con, and not Eric, although I knew they'd help as much as they could. But there was also no way I was going to let the two of them take any risks that I wasn't taking myself.

After a few minutes, my anxiety began to ebb. "Guys? I'm okay now. Thank you. What's next on the agenda?"

As they returned to the table, Con said, "I was just thinking you were right. We should contact Lolly before much longer. She could be putting out fires at the hospital and buying us some time so no serious alarms get raised until Monday, at least. I know it's the middle of the night, but we should try her soon and at least leave a message. We just have to figure out what to tell her. The same goes for Faraz and my department."

"You're right, that should be our first priority." I picked up one of the burner phone boxes. "Hopefully no one has told her yet what happened with me on

Unit 4. Can we check our voice mails remotely from these, Eric?"

"Yeah," he said, sitting down at the laptop. "I'll look up the access numbers. By the way, there's an email in your inbox from Stephan, subject line 'White House.' No content, just an attachment. I'm assuming I should download that, too?"

"Yes, please," I muttered, avoiding Con's gaze.

"By the way, I'm glad at least one of you is tech-savvy," Eric said. "That'll make this whole thing much easier."

"Indeed," Con said, "we're very lucky to have Shadow Keane on our side. Ow!" He laughed as I playfully pinched his arm. "Supervillain indeed."

24

CORNELIUS

The mood was tense as Con sat with Neve at the kitchen table, preparing to call Rosanna. Eric had gone home, not wanting any raised eyebrows from his nosy neighbors for staying out all night while Katie was away, so they were on their own.

They had planned out what they were going to say, but they knew only so much brainstorming was help-ful. It was impossible to predict what Rosanna might ask or what twists and turns the conversation might take. They had to be on their toes and ready to improvise.

Con insisted he should initiate the call, not Neve. He argued that if Rosanna was upset, he might be able to calm her down more quickly. In reality, though, he wanted to absorb the worst of Rosanna's worry and anger before Neve joined the conversation. He wanted to protect her from any undue stress, knowing her state of mind might be quite fragile.

Anyone would be traumatized after what Neve had been through, especially the latest episode with Rodwell. But although she hadn't said it outright, it seemed like Neve might actually believe Amos was talking to angels. There was a mystery at hand, certainly, and Con didn't claim to know all the answers. But when the truth came out, Amos's "angels" would no doubt turn out to be some combination of eavesdropping technology and an accomplice inside the hospital. Meanwhile, it was extremely out of character for Neve to abandon rational explanations in favor of preposterous ones. It was a sign that the strain was getting to her. Con wondered how much more pressure she could take and what might happen when she reached her limit. He certainly didn't want to find out.

"Ready when you are." Neve bit her lip and crossed her fingers.

"All right." Con dialed and held the phone up to his ear. "Here goes." He winced when Rosanna picked up on the first ring.

"Hello? Who is this?"

She hadn't been asleep, then. That didn't bode well. "It's Con. Sorry, I'm not calling from my own phone."

There was a long pause. "You had better be calling from a *coffin* phone, then, because if you're not already dead, I'm going to strangle the life out of you."

His first instinct was to ask why anyone would put a phone in a coffin, but he restrained himself. "Fair enough, Lolly. Thanks for picking up."

"Don't 'Lolly' me. Is she okay? Is she with you?"

So either Unit 4 or Rodwell had already called Rosanna. She must have been terrified for Neve. "Yes, and yes. That's what I called to tell you."

"At what, two in the morning?" The pitch of her voice rose at least an octave. "It's been hours since you scared the living daylights out of my nurses and stole Neve from the hospital. Start talking, Con. Now."

"Neve is 100 percent safe and healthy," he began. "Rodwell lied about her condition to get her committed, so I had to lie to get her out of there. But at no point was there anything wrong with her, I promise."

"Let me talk to her."

At least the emotional boil had been lanced and Rosanna reassured. Laying the phone on the kitchen table, he put it on speaker and gestured for Neve to speak.

She leaned in. "I'm so sorry you were worried, Rosanna. I'm okay, really."

Con and Neve exchanged remorseful looks as a cry of relief emitted from the phone. "Neve, thank God! I thought you were… well, I didn't know what to think. What the hell is going on? What happened between you and Dr. Rodwell? And what does Con mean, he lied to get you committed?"

"It's a long story," Neve said. "Rosanna, I know this

is going to sound absurd, but just listen to me for a second. Today I learned that Dr. Rodwell has been engaged in some unethical behavior, and I thought it might involve an imminent risk to patient safety. I went into his office because he keeps personal files there. I was looking through them and trying to investigate when he caught me."

"Dr. Rodwell?" Rosanna sounded utterly confused. "You went into his personal files? I don't understand. Neve, I've worked with Frank for ages, and he's never been anything but professional. What patient safety risk? What kind of unethical behavior?"

Neve looked at Con, who gave her a reassuring nod. "First of all, it turns out there was no patient safety risk, so don't worry. I only had partial information, and I got my wires crossed. As for what he's been up to, I'll tell you, but I'm warning you, it's going to sound crazy."

An exasperated sigh. "Out with it!"

"Okay, look. He's having an affair with another senior staff member who is married." Neve and Con shrugged at one another. It was the best they'd been able to come up with on short notice.

"Oh for God's sake." Con could almost hear the wheels turning as Rosanna went through the list of senior staff members in her head. "You're trying to tell me that Dr. Rodwell had you sedated and put in seclusion because you found out that he's a hound dog?"

"Yes?" Neve gave Con a desperate look.

Rosanna wasn't buying it. They would have to take their plan to Phase Two. "Not just any senior staff member," Con chimed in. "Someone whose spouse has close ties to a major pharmaceutical company."

Neve quickly added, "There's corruption involved, and kickbacks. It's a huge scandal. It even goes beyond Capitol Hill General."

"My God! Are you serious? Who is it?" Rosanna demanded.

"I can't tell you," Neve said, "not until I share everything I know with the FBI."

Con gave her a thumbs-up. "That's what we're doing later today."

"Holy...." Rosanna was silent for a few moments. "You're going to the FBI together?"

"Yes," Con said. He and Neve exchanged a knowing look, aware of the irony that they were using an agency that reported to the traitorous attorney general as a cover.

"And that's why you—what are we calling it—'broke out' of Unit 4?"

"Yes, exactly."

"But the nurses told me it looked like Neve was having some kind of fit."

Cringing, Neve said, "I was faking it."

"You were *faking it*?"

"I had to do something! Dr. Rodwell convinced the nurses and the security guards that I was having a breakdown. He was trying to discredit me before I could tell anyone what I found out."

"I coached her on how to fake acute encephalitis," Con said, trying to shield Neve from blame as much as he could. "It was my idea entirely. Neve was willing to stay until morning when she could talk to you, but given the extreme lengths Rodwell had already gone to, I thought it unwise."

"Of course it was your idea," Rosanna said wryly. "This whole thing has Con written all over it. But, Neve, when you didn't show up at the ER, the staff checked the test results Con mentioned to Miriam, and—"

"I know, the ovarian tumor," Neve said. "That part was real. But the tumor is benign, and it hasn't caused any problems yet. I swear I'm okay. I'll have it removed before anything bad can happen, I promise."

"I read the results myself," Con lied. "It's nothing to worry about."

"Oh, boy." Another heavy sigh. "You two are pretty clever."

"You don't sound surprised," Con said, trying to lighten the mood.

"I'm not. I'm just commenting."

"I'm so sorry we worried you," Neve said.

"But you're the first person we called." Con had actually called Faraz first to get Amos sorted, but Rosanna didn't have to know that.

"It's the first chance we've had," Neve added.

"The important thing is you're both okay." Rosanna blew out a breath. "Good Lord, Neve. What a nightmare."

Con sat back while Rosanna got all the details of Neve's confinement from her firsthand, starting with the moment she was caught by Dr. Rodwell and ending with their dramatic escape. Of course, Neve changed the story where necessary to support their "affair and corruption" accusations. By the time she finished, both women were tearful.

When Rosanna offered to come with them to the FBI for moral support, Con shut down the idea. "No way, Lolly. You've got to stay at work, act normal, and cover for us. If Rodwell suspects the word is out, he'll try to cover his tracks, and that would impede the investigation." He was pulling from his memory of TV police procedurals. He prayed he sounded convincing.

"I guess that makes sense. But how do I cover for you two? Even the police are looking for you now. Can't you have the FBI call them off?"

"If we did that, it would tip off Rodwell," Con said, winging it. "Tell everyone that after we left the unit, Neve stabilized enough for me to have her taken by private ambulance to another hospital I felt was better equipped to treat her condition."

"Con, you're asking me to lie to the hospital. The one we work for. About a patient."

"Well, technically," Neve ventured, "I was a prisoner, not a patient."

"Oh, Neve." Rosanna sounded pained. "I still can't believe that happened to you, and on our unit. I feel sick just thinking about it. I'm also wondering how I'm going to keep myself from strangling Frank the next time I see him."

Neve smiled. "I appreciate the impulse, believe me. But the best thing you can do to help us is to act normal and convince everybody that everything is okay."

"I'm going to have to call in sick, then, because I'm not that good an actress. I'll call the hospital and plant your lie from home."

"Whatever you need to do," Con said, pleased Rosanna was on side. "It's a solid story, though. No one can dispute it, even if they call every hospital in the city. Neve could easily have requested that her name be kept private upon check-in, and the rest is her personal medical information."

"But surely we'll all come clean after the scandal breaks… right?"

Neve waved Con into silence. "We'll have to get the FBI to advise us on that, but either way, no one is going to blame you for telling a harmless lie to aid a federal investigation."

"That's right," Con said. "Think of it this way: you're an undercover agent for the day. You're the hero of this story, Lolly, not the villain."

That seemed to comfort her a bit. "It sounds to me like Neve is the real hero here."

"Indeed," Con agreed.

"I don't know, Con's been pretty heroic," Neve said.

"Maybe," Rosanna said. "I'm still angry with him, though. I'm not sure why exactly, but it'll come to me. Speaking of which, Con, I heard you had Amos Vates transferred out from under us."

"That's true." Neither Con nor Neve had felt comfortable leaving Amos in the same vicinity as Rodwell. "The condition that put Amos in a coma is very unusual, and a colleague of Faraz's is a specialist. He told her about the case, and she asked us to send Amos to Baltimore for observation. They're going to run some tests. Don't worry, as soon as they're done and Amos is feeling strong enough, he'll be back on Unit 4." Con was relieved to be able to tell Rosanna the truth about something, at least.

"Well, I'm glad he's in good hands," she said. "Neve, I'll read you the riot act later for sneaking in to see Amos yesterday. Right now, though, I should call the hospital and give them your story before anyone wastes any more time and resources looking for you—not to mention worrying about you."

Neve grimaced. "Again, I'm so sorry."

"I'm the one who's sorry to hear about everything you went through today. Good grief. You'll keep me updated? Let me know if I can do anything else?"

"Of course. Thanks, Rosanna." Neve closed her eyes and leaned back in her chair.

"Con, call me when you have some free time so I

can yell at you," Rosanna added. "Between the encephalitis scare and the disappearing act, you took ten years off my life."

"I'll happily do whatever penance you have in mind for me."

"Smooth talker. Just take care of our girl."

"You know I will."

"And try not to get into any more trouble, okay?"

Con and Neve exchanged a knowing look. More trouble was definitely coming.

"Okay," Neve said brightly. "Thanks for everything, Rosanna, seriously. I appreciate it so much."

"Yes, thank you," Con added with genuine feeling. "We owe you."

"That you do. Good night."

"Good night," Con and Neve said in unison.

He powered the phone off and rubbed his forehead. That conversation had been even more grueling than he'd expected, and the way Neve was slumped in her chair, he could see it had taken a toll on her, too.

They sat in the silence of the kitchen for a few moments. The church building was in a remote enough area that they couldn't even hear the sounds of nearby traffic. It almost felt peaceful. Almost.

Then Neve spoke. "That was awful, Con. I hate lying to her."

"I know. I have to say, though, you were brilliant—nimble, creative, quick on your feet."

"Just following your lead. I feel so guilty, though."

"Lolly loves you, Neve. She'll forgive you anything. Me, on the other hand…."

"I don't mean about Rosanna—although of course I feel guilty about lying to her. I meant about Amos."

"Why in God's name would you feel guilty about Amos?" Con asked, unable to conceal his disbelief. "You went to hell and back for him tonight!"

"I know, but it's looking like he was right this whole time, and I doubted him. I chalked everything up to his illness instead of…."

"Instead of what?" He ducked down so he could look straight into her eyes. "Instead of believing everything he told you hook, line, and sinker from day one? Amos came to you at your place of work in a professional capacity. You're a social worker, not a priest, for Christ's sake. He knew that, and he knew that was the context in which you'd evaluate his claims. I'm sure he expected you to require a very high standard of proof before you'd believe him. That's why he came prepared with his group of minions and his accursed thumb drive." As much as Con cared about Amos, he was exasperated with the lad, not least for causing Neve to doubt herself.

"I guess you're right," she said softly.

He was gratified that she appeared at least partially convinced, but she was also fighting to keep her eyes open.

"We've done all we can for tonight," he said. "Eric is

bringing breakfast in a few hours. We should sleep while we can."

"I don't think I have much of a choice," Neve conceded. "I'm about to fall over."

"It's been a long day, to say the least. And you may still have some sedatives in your bloodstream. Head upstairs, pick a room, and go to bed. I'll lock up down here after I take care of a couple things."

In truth, Con had no intention of going to sleep himself. He couldn't be sure Neve was safe unless someone was standing watch. He would ask Eric to take a shift sometime tomorrow so he could catch a few hours of shut-eye.

Neve stood and stretched. Con exerted consider-able effort not to stare at her exquisite form, so perfectly outlined by Katie's gym clothes. Still, she caught him stealing a glance.

"You better lock the door to your bedroom tonight," she teased.

His heart jolted in his chest. "And why is that?"

"If she weren't so exhausted," she said coyly, "some woman might come in and try to have her way with you."

There it was—Neve's devilish side. She usually kept that part of herself well hidden, making it all the more thrilling when it made an appearance.

Squinting up at her, Con rubbed his chin. "That would be a terrible, terrible thing indeed."

She rewarded him with a smile, but it faded quickly.

"Listen, with everything we could be facing—Dr. Rodwell, Brickhaven, military contractors, the freaking attorney general—I don't know. What you said earlier, about our conversation at the diner… there's so much I want to say to you, but I'm so tired right now. I'm afraid if I start talking, I'll say it all wrong."

He stood up, ignoring the renewed throbbing in his leg. "Look, I have a novel's worth to say to you as well, but don't worry. Once we're through this mess, we'll have plenty of time to talk." Stepping over to her, Con placed his hand lightly on the small of her back. "I want to apologize, by the way. I didn't mean to shock you earlier with what I said."

"It's okay." Her cheeks flushed bright pink. "You did kind of shock me. But I'm really glad to know… I mean, I'm glad you said what you said."

"Good." They exchanged smiles once more. Neve appeared as reluctant to part as he was, but everything about her telegraphed exhaustion. Con walked over to the stairs and she followed alongside, responding to the gentle pressure of his touch.

"I'd kiss you goodnight," she said with a sigh, "but I'm afraid I wouldn't be able to stop."

For future reference, Con made a mental note that the sleepier Neve got, the less she censored herself. "Believe me, I share your conundrum," he said, fighting the delicious urge to let his hand wander. "In fact, you'd better get up those stairs before something scandalous happens."

"Promises, promises," she said dreamily. "Good night."

"Good night." He stood at the foot of the stairs until she reached the top and turned in to the first room on the right. He heard the rustling of linens, then the light thud of a body hitting a mattress. Soon after, silence.

"Thank Christ," he muttered to himself. Although Neve leaving the room caused a sharp, sweet pain in the middle of his chest, he was relieved that she was finally getting some much-needed rest. Eric had promised to come in quietly the next day so as not to wake her. Con wished she'd sleep all the way through to Sunday, although he didn't think his luck was that good.

He went back to the kitchen and found a mug, a kettle, and some tea. His night was planned out. Con would sit in the front room with one eye on the door, figuring out how he was going to keep Neve far, far away from Stephan, Rodwell, and a US president with a target on his back.

25

NEVE

Thank goodness I'd gone with the well-lined, short-sleeved dress.

Given that I was drenched in perspiration, dark circles would have already appeared under the armholes of the sleeveless version of my burgundy shift. And I hadn't even gotten out of the car yet.

I couldn't believe it was already Saturday and we were actually in one of the White House parking garages, getting ready to execute a plan to confront the president of the United States. The only thing keeping me from fainting from anxiety was the fact that Con was there with me. Posing as my driver, he sat in the front seat of his car while I was in the back. My breath had been snatched away when I first saw him in his new "uniform," a black suit with a white shirt and a classy gray tie. Eric had wanted to put him in a chauffeur hat, but Con argued that it might fall into his eyes and interfere while he was "beating the hell out of Stephan"—a possibility Con had so far refused to rule out.

According to the instructions Stephan had emailed, per White House security, we couldn't carry much of anything with us into the West Wing. Car keys and most items of jewelry were the only non-prohibited items Con and I could bring or wear without raising eyebrows. I couldn't even take a purse.

I did have to bring photo ID, however, so I'd chosen a dress with pockets. I checked them for the umpteenth time, and it was still there: my new, official-looking driver's license. That was courtesy of Shane, an old high school buddy of Eric's who made fake IDs in the back of his computer repair shop. My real license had been confiscated when I was on Unit 4, and since I couldn't exactly walk into the Department of Motor Vehicles while the police might still be looking for me, a fake was the best solution we could come up with.

Manifesting my new nervous habit, I fingered the pendant that hung just below my collarbone on a silver box chain. Eric had sourced it the day before. It was a thick, silver-colored heart covered in pavé-set white crystals. Although it was only a little over an inch in diameter, it held a compact USB drive the size of my thumbnail, which now had the documents for the president stored on it. The USB drive was accessed by pulling apart the two halves of the heart, but thanks to the pendant's design, the seam was as good as invisible.

Eric said the heart was made of a tungsten alloy that would conceal the hidden chamber from any security scanners. When I asked where on earth he'd found such a unique item, and so quickly, he just shrugged and said, "I'm a hacker who lives near Langley. Erik the Viking at your service."

Con had frowned when he saw the necklace but said nothing. If he was concerned about what Stephan might read into the fact that I was wearing a piece of heart-shaped jewelry to our meeting, he wasn't the only one.

I closed my eyes, took a deep breath, and wiped my damp palms on my dress. It was almost time.

———

FRIDAY HAD FLOWN BY. ERIC CAME OVER EARLY, AND THE smell of coffee and bagels lured me out of bed.

Then we got to work. We brainstormed a lot of possible alternatives for stopping Brickhaven and Rodwell. Con was determined to come up with a risk-free idea, but we kept returning to the original plan. It was the only one with a reasonable chance of working. I would go to the White House ceremony, then use our photo op to warn the president about Rodwell and Brickhaven.

By early afternoon, Eric and I got Con to acquiesce —with the caveat that he would accompany me. Figuring out how to make that work took a bit more brainstorming, but once Eric's friend Shane agreed to stay up all night producing the necessary materials for us, the pieces began to click into place.

It was Eric who had the idea to buy our outfits online. We were hopeful that Rosanna's story had convinced the police to stop looking for us, but we couldn't be certain. Being seen in public or caught on a security camera wouldn't be wise. Fortunately, the website of a local high-end department store had an in-store pickup option, so our new White House wardrobes were bought, paid for, and picked up by Eric before the end of the day.

When he wasn't out running errands, Eric was working away on the computer. He managed to get Con White House security clearance as a chauffeur—a much faster process than obtaining clearance for a guest who was going to be in the same room as the president. After we finished the pizza he'd picked up for dinner, Eric returned to his laptop only to curse a blue streak. "Neve, they got to you!"

"What? Who got to me?"

Eric turned the screen to face me. His web browser was opened to my email website, SecureMail.net, but there was an error message. "It must have been Brick-haven. They disabled your Shadow Keane account and most likely any other ones you have. Don't worry, though. I scrubbed the memos and any trace of them from your account last night. There's no way they can know what you have, so we're still one step ahead."

The idea that Brickhaven had me in their crosshairs gave me chills. I decided to check my voice mail again to see if there were any other surprises. Sure enough, there were several frantic messages from my parents saying the police had called them, along with a "private investigator"—someone from Brickhaven, we guessed —who told them I'd had a nervous breakdown and was missing. Fortunately, their most recent message said they'd spoken to Rosanna. She hadn't told them much, though, only that I was with Con and being taken care of, so they were still worried.

Outraged that Brickhaven had brought my parents into the mix, I called them from another burner phone and tried to sound calm as I reassured them that yes, I was fine, and yes, I was with Con. He sat with me on the couch for moral support as I answered all their questions. I felt sicker inside with each lie I was forced to tell. In the end, they believed I'd developed a new allergy to mollusks, and that after having escargot at dinner, my violent physical reaction had been misdiagnosed at the hospital. I explained that Con had been quick and level-headed enough to administer an antihistamine injection and that I was now fully recovered and resting. I also told them that in all the confusion, I had lost my phone, and having no idea I'd been listed as missing, it didn't occur to me that they would be worried or that I should check my messages until just then.

My parents wanted to come over and see me, but I

told them I was staying at Con's place so he could keep an eye on me. I put him on the phone to reassure them. Fortunately, that worked like a charm. When they were sufficiently calm, they let me go, but only after inviting Con to Sunday dinner so they could thank him for his help. He eagerly accepted their invitation.

After the call, I felt exhausted again. I let my head fall onto Con's shoulder. "Thanks for that."

"No worries." He patted my leg, leaving his hand resting on my thigh. "I'm getting a homecooked meal, am I not?"

Tearing my focus away from those several square inches where his touch warmed my leg, I cleared my throat. "Just so you know, it's kind of a big deal that my parents invited you over for Sunday dinner. It's usually a family-only thing. Stephan was only ever invited twice."

"Huh." Con grunted his displeasure at the mention of my ex. "What about friends? Lolly?"

I thought back, then shook my head. "As far as I remember, they've only ever invited family, and... well, people I was dating, I guess."

"Well, that's encouraging." The corners of his mouth twitched upward as he gave my thigh a gentle squeeze.

Con's flirtation sent a comforting wave of warmth through me. Ever since he declared his feelings the night before, my insecurities had started bubbling to the surface. I'd begun to wonder whether the week's back-to-back crises might have artificially intensified his emotions, creating exaggerated feelings of affection for a brief moment in time. I knew those thoughts were probably just a product of my heightened anxiety, but a small, terrified part of me still needed reassurance.

Gathering my courage, I poked the back of his hand on my thigh. "You sound pretty confident for a guy who hasn't even asked me on a date yet, let alone kissed me."

As soon as the word "kissed" passed my lips, Con's head swiveled around. I straightened up as his eyes flashed, locking on to mine.

"Fair point." He tilted his head to the side, considering. "At the moment, I believe we have too much to do before tomorrow to add planning a date to the mix. Rest assured, though, as soon as this is over, it's at the top of my agenda."

"Ah," I whispered, failing to sound nonchalant. "Good to know."

Con's gaze radiated heat. He lifted his free hand, stroking a line down my jaw with his fingertip. Then, taking my chin gently between his thumb and forefinger, he continued, "As for the latter oversight, there's nothing I'd like more than to correct that immediately. However, what did we agree upon last night?" He leaned in close, placing his mouth next to my ear so I could feel his breath against my neck. "If we start, we might not be able to stop. And I'd hate to scandalize Eric, especially in a virtual house of God."

My breathing became ragged. I felt like I was trembling from the inside out. Con was right, of course; we didn't have the house to ourselves. But my skin felt like it was humming, and his lips were so close. If I just turned my head slightly….

Clomp, clomp, clomp! Eric strode in from the kitchen, approaching the couch from behind.

I snapped away from Con as though he'd stung me. He sat back, too, but his eyes remained laser-focused on mine.

"You done with that?" Eric asked, pointing at my burner phone.

He sounded totally normal. *Maybe Eric didn't see…?*

I let out the breath I was holding. "Yeah, done."

"Okay," he said. "We should destroy it, just to be safe."

"Good man," Con muttered. "You're grand at destroying things." He looked like he wanted to grab Eric and throw him bodily out of the room. I tried to suppress a laugh, but it came out as an awkward snort.

"You guys know there are empty rooms upstairs, right?" Eric asked lightly as he took the phone from my outstretched hand. "In case you want to *get a room* or something."

Con muttered a string of curses as Eric retreated to the kitchen, grinning. Then Con turned to me with a gleam in his eye. "The next time I get you alone…."

"Promises, promises," I said, making my own reference to our conversation the night before.

"That's one you can count on." Con swept his finger down my jawline again, as though to seal the vow, and my breath caught as our eyes met once more. I realized my doubts about Con's feelings had melted away—for the time being, at least.

With substantial effort, we turned away from one another and went back to planning the next day's activities.

Later that afternoon, Con slept for a few hours while Eric "kept watch." When I offered to keep watch, Con informed me that I was the person they needed to watch over. That seemed utterly ridiculous to me, but they both seemed to think it made perfect sense. With the accumulated exhaustion of the past couple days hitting me hard, I didn't have the energy to argue.

Eric and I made a small bonfire in the backyard, destroying Amos's thumb drive and everything else we wouldn't want anyone to find in the event that we got arrested. We didn't want to leave behind anything that could be used against Amos, or further incriminate us. When Con awoke, I went upstairs for what I knew would be a night of restless sleep and troubled dreams.

By the time I woke up Saturday morning, Eric had already picked up what he needed from Shane, and he and Con were putting replacement tags and fake chauffeur company stickers on the SUV. Quickly but methodically, we ate, showered, dressed, reviewed the plan a few more times, and put our gear together.

Before I knew what happened, it was early afternoon and our two-car caravan was underway.

The ride to DC was fairly quiet, with both Con and me engaged in our own methods of preparation. For me, that meant imagining possible worst-case scenarios and breathing through them in the hopes of staving off a panic attack should they occur. The plan was pretty simple, and we knew it backward and forward. It was the potential for the unknown or unexpected that made me nervous. In truth, we were flying by the seats of our pants, with my secret spy necklace and the element of surprise our only solid advantages.

Coming up with a contingency plan had proven to be a challenge. Cell phones were another item on the West Wing's "prohibited" list. In addition, Eric did some digging and found out that all unofficial communication signals in and out of the West Wing were jammed, which meant we had no way to keep in touch with Eric if things went sideways. The best solution we could come up with was for Eric to wait for us, parked a short distance away. We guessed that the president would want to keep me for a while to answer questions after I presented him with the documents. But if we didn't emerge by nightfall, we figured Eric could assume something had gone wrong and try to get us some help. After all, if we disappeared somehow, Eric would be the only person on the outside who knew where we were and why.

I had driven past the White House many times

before, so I knew it wasn't as large and imposing as they made it appear on TV. Still, the symbolism and meaning of the stately building put a lump in my throat when we first spotted it. I couldn't take my eyes off it as we drove past the lawns, drawing ever closer.

It was 1:40 p.m.—right on time. Following Stephan's directions, we turned in just beside the Eisenhower Executive Office Building. Con stopped at a gated checkpoint and gave our IDs to one of the guards. *One point for Shane,* I thought as they waved us through.

We were instructed to turn left down another drive, where we reached another checkpoint. Once again, we got through without incident and were directed to enter an underground parking garage. Everywhere we looked there were White House police in black uniforms and baseball caps, carrying hefty-looking sidearms. They pointed out where we should turn, then waved us into a parking spot. Con pulled in and turned off the engine.

Now, having double-checked my ID, fiddled with my pendant, and wiped off my sweaty palms, there was nothing else I could do to prepare. We had officially reached the point of no return. I sat, heart pounding, trying to siphon some extra courage off Con as I readied myself to crash a party at the White House.

"Neve, remember, you can abort the plan at any moment."

"I know," I said, then took a slow, deep breath. "If I

feel like something's not right, I just go through the motions and attend the ceremony and reception as planned."

"Right. It's entirely up to you, but whatever happens, I'm there. I've got you."

"Okay." My mind flashed back to the moments in the room of Con's outpatient clinic after he rescued me from Unit 4, when I was bawling like a baby. He'd said "I've got you" then, too—and he had. That gave me the spark of courage I needed.

Con smiled at me in the rearview mirror. "Just let me know when you're ready and I'll come open your door for you, like a proper chauffeur."

"Rosanna was right. You are a smooth talker," I said, smiling back as best I could. "Okay, I'm ready."

Two of the uniformed officers were waiting outside the car for us. They led us to an elevator, up one floor, and into the ground-floor lobby of what we were told was the West Wing. In spite of the tense situation we were in, I had a moment of feeling starstruck as I recognized the elegantly appointed room, which as far as I could see had been faithfully duplicated in Hollywood depictions. It was a long, narrow space lined with wingback chairs and sofas. I recognized some of the famous paintings on the walls and had to force myself not to gawk.

An officer instructed us to empty our pockets into bins to be put through the security scanner. Con only had his car keys on him at that stage, but I was asked to put my necklace through, as well. I tried not to show my nerves as I walked through the metal detector first. When my necklace was returned to me without incident, my respect for Eric's cloak-and-dagger skills ticked up several notches. Con's replacement knee set off the metal detector when he went through, but after a wand scan of his leg, he was cleared. Then we were both searched by hand. The officer must have noticed how tense I was, because she reassured me it was standard protocol. I forced a smile and pushed myself to breathe.

Once we were through security, a perfectly coiffed woman in a silk pantsuit checked our names off two separate lists—one for guests, one for drivers—and guided us through a few doors and hallways.

We reached a set of french doors. On the other side, I could see the open columned walkway leading out to the famous Rose Garden, home to so many televised White House events.

It suddenly hit me where we were, and why. I began to feel small, insignificant, and completely ridiculous. Who was I to enter such an important place with plans to create chaos?

On the other hand, who was Dr. Rodwell to plan something so much worse?

Remembering the gravity of our task, I steeled myself for the next step.

Pantsuit Lady stopped us just before we reached the french doors and showed us to a doorway on our left.

She asked Con to take another left turn into a room where he would be allowed to wait with the other drivers, while I would be in the Press Briefing Room on the right. She explained that the ceremony itself would be short. Then I would have my picture taken with my honoree and the president. Afterward, President Duran would have other business to attend to, but I would be taken to the Executive Residence, where the guests and honorees would attend a reception. Then the guests would be brought back to the West Wing to reunite with our drivers and exit the same way we'd come.

Con smiled agreeably at her but shot me a weighty look as we parted. I gave him a quick nod to let him know I was ready. Then, on my own, I entered the Press Briefing Room.

It was smaller than I'd imagined, with a wooden pedestal in the front, white walls, and fixed rows of blue seats. The back of the room was filled with filming equipment. A throng of people had already gathered. Everyone was standing and mingling.

"Neve!" Stephan called from behind me, sounding jubilant. "So glad to see you. You look, uh, good." His smile dimmed a little, and I could tell he was disappointed. Evidently my outfit wasn't quite glamorous enough for his taste. "I was starting to worry that you wouldn't make it. Did you drive?"

"I hired a driver," I said, "and I'm pretty sure I'm exactly on time."

"Oh, yeah, I guess you're right," he said, checking his

watch as he took me by the elbow. I involuntarily flinched at his touch. Stephan didn't appear to notice as he led me over to one of the windows looking out onto the Rose Garden. "Isn't it beautiful out there?"

"It really is," I said sincerely. It was a bright, clear day. Sunlight beamed through the window, warming us.

The eager look on Stephan's face gave me a sharp twinge of guilt. It was clear that by bringing me to this event, he was trying to show me that if I came back to him, I would spend my life rubbing shoulders with people of status and power. But the fact that he thought that would impress me just proved he didn't know me at all.

Stephan's smile widened when my pendant caught his eye. "I like your necklace. Is that heart for me?"

Not knowing what to say, I tried to smile, suddenly anxious for the ceremony to begin. I just wanted to do what I came to do and get it over with. I glanced around the room. No one was sitting down yet. "Where's Lee?"

"Oh, he's in some room getting his nose powdered. His mom and other friends are here already," he said, waving at someone across the room. "This whole thing is going to be filmed, and then there's the photos. We'll all get a copy of the picture. That'll be a nice souvenir, huh?"

"Sure." I kept my smile pasted on.

Stephan's eyes softened with emotion, and I fought

the urge to turn around and run. I didn't want to spend another moment with him. On the other hand, I didn't want to be cruel. I was about to ruin his day as it was, along with Lee's and everyone else's.

"Neve," he began, "I'm so glad we straightened out that misunderstanding we had. You know I would never intentionally hurt you."

There was nothing I could say in response that wouldn't start an argument. I gritted my teeth and forced myself to remain silent.

"I know we still have a lot to talk about, but together, we have such bright future," Stephan continued. "You're so supportive of my work, and—"

Bang! We both jumped as something smacked into the window next to us. Was it a bird? We turned to look.

No, not a bird. I gasped. Just on the other side of the glass stood Dr. Rodwell. His face was red with fury, and he was pointing at me and shouting to the two uniformed officers standing beside him.

Everything about me froze—my body, my heart, my breath. Petrified in every sense of the word, not even my thoughts were moving.

Stephan looked at Dr. Rodwell like he was a strange animal on display in a zoo. Pointing, he said, "There's something going on out there."

I just stood there, unable to do anything but watch as Dr. Rodwell and the officers rushed from the window to the french doors and into the West Wing.

They gathered at the door to the Press Briefing Room. The officers were looking at me, and they appeared ready for action.

Even though I knew what was going to happen next, I felt powerless to stop it. I heard Dr. Rodwell's voice shouting from the hallway. "There she is! That's her! In the red dress! Neve Keane!"

Stephan gripped my shoulder. "Neve, who is that? What's going on?" he asked, but before he could get another word out, the officers were on either side of me.

"Please come with us, ma'am," one of them said gruffly as they ushered me to the door.

"Hey, what are you doing?" Stephan yelled, following us. "That's my girlfriend!" But one of the officers ordered him to stay put, offering no further explanation. "Neve!" I heard him call one last time as I was dragged out into the hallway.

26

NEVE

IN THE NEXT FEW SECONDS, SEVERAL THINGS HAPPENED at once.

Dr. Rodwell stood in the hallway just inside the french doors, still shouting and pointing at me. Con must have heard Dr. Rodwell yelling my name, because he barreled out of the chauffeurs' waiting room. Once he spotted me, Con began to argue with the officers who were holding on to me, shouting and pointing at Dr. Rodwell. More officers appeared, seemingly out of nowhere, and gathered around us.

Through the doors, I saw a cloud of people in dark suits walking toward us from the Rose Garden. President Duran was in the middle, a head taller than the rest of the group. They stopped when they spotted us in the hallway, and one of the officers flanking me spoke into his walkie-talkie. I saw President Duran lean down, talking to the people in suits—Secret

Service agents, I guessed—then glancing over at Dr. Rodwell and me. Even though it was only seconds long, that moment seemed suspended in time.

As Dr. Rodwell grew more outraged and Con's voice rose, my brain began to click back into action. Where had Dr. Rodwell come from? As far as I remembered from his memo in President Duran's file, their next session wasn't until the coming Monday. What was he doing there?

The cloud of suits outside restarted their journey toward us. The french doors opened, and seconds later, I was in the presence of the president.

President Duran possessed an effortless yet undeniable air of authority. Upon his arrival, everyone went silent—everyone but Con, that was, who continued ordering the officer holding my arm to let go of me and grab Dr. Rodwell.

President Duran spoke to one of the officers. "Take all three of them to the Fish Room and get Liu. I'll deal with this."

Was the president referring to Brent Liu, his chief of staff? Black uniforms closed in and shuttled us down the hallway. I could hear Dr. Rodwell still shouting somewhere in front of me, as well as Con behind me telling the officers he was going wherever I was going.

Seconds later, Dr. Rodwell, Con, and I were herded into a gold-toned room with a long, gleaming wooden table surrounded by brown leather chairs. There was a fireplace at one end. Hanging above it was a large portrait of Theodore Roosevelt astride a rearing horse. The Roosevelt Conference Room; I recognized it from TV, which made everything even more surreal.

Con and Dr. Rodwell were politely asked to sit at opposite ends of the table. Someone must have been convinced I was a threat, though, because my wrists were tied together in front of me with a zip tie and I was unceremoniously pushed down into a chair in the middle.

It felt like 90 percent of my brain was encased in ice. The working 10 percent was split between relief that I was with Con, confusion about where Dr. Rodwell had come from, and the thought, *Well, this isn't going as planned.*

While we waited for President Duran, Dr. Rodwell and Con fell into a staring match. It was clear they were both having murderous thoughts, though they had the sense not to articulate them in front of the officers.

Minutes later, the wait was over. Into the room strode Chief of Staff Liu, followed by four Secret Service agents and President Duran. The president took a seat in the middle of the conference table directly across from me. Liu stood behind him.

President Duran nodded a greeting to Dr. Rodwell and gave Con a once-over before turning to me. I hoped the zip tie cuffs hadn't ruined my chances of making a positive first impression.

"All right," President Duran said, clearly irritated

but controlling it well. "There are forty people in the Press Briefing Room right now waiting for me to honor some very deserving individuals. Dr. Rodwell, you raised the alarm. Can you explain to me why, instead of being there, I'm here with the three of you?"

I was surprised that the president wasn't speaking to Dr. Rodwell more respectfully, but it also made me a little hopeful. Maybe he already had mixed feelings about his psychiatrist.

Dr. Rodwell sighed heavily. "I sincerely regret disturbing your schedule, Mr. President," he began, "but I was genuinely concerned for your safety. This young woman"—he stabbed the air with his index finger, pointing at me—"is a psychiatric patient who I had hospitalized after she made an attempt on my life. She was broken out of our secure unit Thursday night by this man." He moved his accusing finger toward Con. "He is a doctor at our hospital, but he has developed a friendship with this woman which has clearly clouded his judgment and allowed him to be manipulated by her. The police have been searching for them with no luck, so you can imagine my shock when, on my way to the Executive Residence to prepare for our session later today, I saw this woman through a window, standing in the Press Briefing Room." He spread his hands out in front of him, palms up, as though presenting an irrefutable conclusion. "I have no idea what she's doing here, but given her violent behavior and bizarre delusions—some of which have focused on you, Mr. President—I feared she might attempt to harm you. In fact, one of the reasons I requested that you and I move our appointment up to today was so I could alert you to this potential threat. Had I realized she might be diabolical and resourceful enough to actually gain entrance to the White House, I would have warned you earlier. My sincere apologies for failing to do so."

Dr. Rodwell leaned back in his chair and folded his arms. The fake expression of concern he was wearing provided only thin cover for the smug self-satisfaction emanating from him.

"I see," President Duran said. "Thank you, Dr. Rodwell." Liu, who was watching all of us with the intensity of a starving hawk eyeing a group of rabbits, leaned down and murmured something in the president's ear. "Yes, I agree. Let's hear from the other doctor in the room. Not a chauffeur, I take it? Your name is?"

"Cornelius O'Brien, and no. Not a chauffeur." Remarkably, in spite of the content of Dr. Rodwell's preposterous speech, Con seemed to have his anger under control. He spoke calmly. "It's a pleasure to meet you, Mr. President, although I wish it were under different circumstances."

Dr. Rodwell's lips pursed like he was sucking on a lemon. It looked like he was struggling to keep himself from jumping in but was trying to defer to the president.

"Indeed," President Duran said. "You're from Ireland, I take it?"

"County Cork."

"A beautiful part of the world. And you work at Capitol Hill General?"

"Yes. I'm an endocrinologist."

"So tell me, why would an endocrinologist break this, uh, violent and delusional patient out of a hospital psychiatry unit?" I was gratified to hear him pause before "violent and delusional." Perhaps he wasn't yet convinced.

"Because she is not, and never has been, either violent or delusional," Con said. "Neve is a mental health social worker on Rodwell's unit. She was never a patient there, only the victim of unlawful confinement by Rodwell, about whom she had discovered damning information that she was about to expose. He sought to prevent the release of this evidence by having her committed."

The president's eyebrows rose. "That's quite a story."

Unable to hold back any longer, Dr. Rodwell broke in. "Mr. President, if I may—"

"Patience, Dr. Rodwell," President Duran replied. "You're the one who told me studies have shown that individuals with depression see reality with greater accuracy than other people. If that's true, then I am uniquely well-equipped to get to the bottom of this situation." Dr. Rodwell looked sufficiently chastened as the president continued, "Liu, what do you think? Should we hear from the violent and delusional woman?"

"If you wish, sir," Liu said, sounding completely neutral on the subject.

When the president turned his attention to me, I steeled myself for a panic attack, but it didn't come. Instead, I just felt admiration for the man, compassion for the difficulty of his situation, and an urgent desire to give him the information he needed to protect his life.

"And you are?" he asked.

"Neve Keane, sir."

"And you also work at the hospital?"

"Yes, sir. Like Dr. O'Brien said, I am a mental health social worker on Dr. Rodwell's unit."

President Duran nodded to one of the Secret Service agents, who left the room, presumably to check out the information Con and I had given him so far. "And what brings you to the White House today?"

"Well, initially I came because I was invited by an honoree to be a guest at the Humanities Medal ceremony."

"Initially? But now you have another reason?"

"Yes, sir, I do. I'm so sorry to have to tell you this, but Dr. Rodwell is part of a plot to take your life and make it look like a suicide."

At the words "take your life," every Secret Service

agent and uniformed officer in the room tensed. Some of their hands moved to their sidearms.

"Is that so?" The president lifted one eyebrow. "For what possible reason?"

I swallowed hard. "So Vice President Rabec can be installed in your place and stop the Middle East Peace Summit from happening at Camp David."

Suddenly, the air in the room became heavy and pressurized, as though we were sitting in a hyperbaric chamber. I forced myself to pull in a breath as the president's gaze bored into mine like a steel-tipped drill bit.

"Jeffrey," Dr. Rodwell broke in, "this is what I'm talking about. Wild delusions. Have mercy on this poor woman. She needs proper care. She needs to be in the hospital."

"I heard you the first time, Dr. Rodwell," President Duran said, but he kept looking at me. Now both of his eyebrows were raised. "Ms. Keane, while you do not appear to me to be violent or threatening, you must admit, your assertions do have a delusional flair. I also find myself wondering how you came upon the information you claim to have."

Clearly the mention of the secret Camp David talks had succeeded in getting his attention. Now I had to present the evidence. My nerves were so jangled, I was grateful we'd rehearsed the plan over and over. "Sir, at your last session with Dr. Rodwell, he prescribed two new medications," I said. "Whatever he told you they were for, they were actually prescribed to induce insomnia, mood swings, agitation—"

"Please, Jeffrey," Dr. Rodwell interjected, "I'm begging you. Take this woman out of here and put her in an ambulance before she makes a sudden move. She tried to kill me!"

But something I said must have given the president pause. "Did you try to kill him?"

"No," I replied flatly. "It was a lie he told to justify my confinement."

"You deny that you were found hiding in my office with a letter opener?" Rodwell frothed.

"Yes, I was in your office getting copies of the memos you wrote to the board of the Brickhaven Foundation describing the content of your treatment sessions with President Duran—memos which are now stored in my necklace." I reached up and, after a moment of struggling with my pendant, managed to pull off the half that held the USB drive. "There is also a document on there showing that Brickhaven members Orson Taul and Riggs Sanderson are involved in the plot, as well."

"Attorney General Taul?" Liu asked, incredulous.

I nodded as Dr. Rodwell's jaw dropped. At least the element of surprise bought us one moment of silence from him.

President Duran gestured to the officer standing next to me. He plucked the USB drive from my bound hands, walked around the table, and handed it to Liu.

One of the Secret Service agents produced a computer tablet, which Liu took, inserting my USB drive. After tapping the screen a few times, Liu passed the tablet to the president.

As President Duran began to read, Dr. Rodwell could no longer contain himself. "She's lying," he blurted. "She doesn't know reality from fantasy. It's part of her illness. Whatever you're looking at there, she made it up. Anyone can forge anything these days. If you let her continue with this charade, you'll be strengthening her delusion, and it will be harder for us to treat her, to bring her back to reality. Jeffrey, listen to me—"

"Dr. Rodwell." President Duran's voice, though soft, had enough gravitas to command silence.

As he slid his finger along the tablet screen, scrolling through the documents, the tension in the room thickened. Dr. Rodwell sat with his eyes screwed shut, hands clenched together, knuckles whitening on top of the table. Con was attentively observing the president, but his expression was inscrutable. I knew we'd reached the moment of truth. I just prayed it wouldn't end with me returning to Unit 4 strapped to a gurney.

President Duran passed the tablet over his shoulder to Liu. The Secret Service agent who'd gone out earlier came back and murmured something indecipherable to the president.

"Fascinating, Ms. Keane," President Duran said.

"However, you must know how far-fetched your accusations sound, and I've just been told that you entered my house using a fake ID. This warrants investigation."

Dr. Rodwell gave an audible sigh of relief.

"That will take some time, of course," the president continued. "While we investigate you and check out these files of yours, you and our esteemed guest from Ireland, who is also here under false pretenses, will not be going anywhere. Take them to detention."

"Mr. President." Everyone was so surprised to hear Con speak that the whole room seemed to jump. "I don't wish to alarm anyone, but at this point, in order to provide you with all the relevant information, I must retrieve my car keys from my trouser pocket."

President Duran and Liu exchanged a concerned glance. Without waiting for permission, Con slowly rose to his feet.

"What's this, O'Brien?" Dr. Rodwell said sharply. "What are you playing at?"

"Freeze!" a Secret Service agent shouted as Con put his hand in his pocket. Two officers pounced on him, slamming his torso down on the table and wrenching his arms behind his back. Con winced but didn't try to resist.

"Stop!" I shouted. "Leave him alone!" I leapt to my feet, but my contingent of officers had me sitting back in my chair in a second flat.

One of the officers holding him down reached into Con's pocket and took out his car keys. He carefully examined the keys and the black oval-shaped fob with two buttons on it. "It's just keys and an electronic fob. There's no weapon," he declared.

One of the Secret Service agents took the keys and looked them over. Then he nodded to the president and said, "I don't see anything unusual."

Like everyone else in the room, I was utterly confused. I had no idea what Con was doing, or why he'd put himself in that position. It tied my insides in knots to see him being held down by the officers, even though, given his size and bulk relative to theirs, it looked like he could throw them off if he wanted to. Still, there were many more of them, and they had guns, so I hoped to God he wouldn't try.

"Dr. O'Brien, please tell us," President Duran said dryly, "what information can your car keys provide?"

"If I could have them back, I would be glad to demonstrate," Con said with the side of his head pressed against the table.

Everyone in the room tensed at this odd-sounding proposition, except for President Duran, who appeared curious. He nodded to the Secret Service agent holding the keys. "Give the man his car keys. You can let him up now, officers."

The men holding Con released him but only stepped back a few inches. Con rose from the table slowly, presumably not wanting to startle anyone. With a nod, he took his keys from the Secret Service agent.

Con held up his key fob and addressed the president. "You see, if you press both the gray and red buttons simultaneously…."

He demonstrated, and we all jumped as my voice suddenly came out of the fob. *"Why are you doing this to me?"*

The volume was low, but the sound was clear enough as it played Rodwell's voice. *"I didn't want to, believe me. But you forced my hand. Ever since the Brickhaven servers were hacked a few weeks ago, we've been on high alert. While the miscreant covered his tracks well, we could at least tell which files had been accessed. Since none of them contained any truly sensitive information, we were more curious than concerned."*

My mouth fell open as I recognized the conversation between Dr. Rodwell and me in Seclusion Room 3. How had Con managed to get a recording? And why hadn't I known about it?

Dr. Rodwell shot to his feet. "What is this?" he shouted as the recording continued to play in the background. "This is preposterous. Turn that thing off."

"Silence!" President Duran held up his hand, and everything in the room stilled.

Dr. Rodwell's eyes darted around frantically as the recording continued to play his words. *"Then Amos placed you at the center of everything. That part took a while to figure out. Actually, I owe you an apology."*

"Just one?"

"I used you, I admit. Maybe it wasn't the best thing for your well-being to let you near the apocalypse patients' cases,

but I felt like we needed to let the situation play out the way Amos wanted it to until we could get to the bottom of things. We knew he had that thumb drive hidden in his room, for example, but I told the nurses not to confiscate it. I wanted to see what he'd do with it. When he passed it off to you, I figured out that he was trying to recruit you to his cause—whatever that may be. I'm unclear on the details. I know Amos wants to sabotage Brickhaven's work with the president by undermining my influence, but I don't understand all the ins and outs."

President Duran stood and slammed his fist on the table. "I've heard enough. Detain all of them—and give me those keys."

The officers moved swiftly. One of them grabbed Con's keys and handed them to the president, who kept listening as the recording played on.

The other officers zip-tied Con's and Dr. Rodwell's wrists behind their backs. Dr. Rodwell screamed his objections.

"Dr. Rodwell," the president commanded, "you will be silent, and you will stay here until I have sorted this out. Is that understood?

"Jeffrey, I don't know what you think you're hearing—"

"I don't either," President Duran replied, "but I know it's not good."

As though to underline that point, in the silence that followed, my accusation rang out from the key fob. *"You're a murderer!"*

Then came Dr. Rodwell's chilling reply. *"Don't worry. No one would bother killing you, Neve. You're not important enough—unlike the president."*

The recording stopped as abruptly as it had begun.

Everyone in the room froze. President Duran turned a cold eye on Dr. Rodwell. Then he flicked a finger, and all three of us were escorted from the room.

The officers took us down a set of stairs to the lower level of the West Wing, presumably to wherever "detention" was. Just as they were about to separate us, Con and I managed to make eye contact. He gave me a subtle wink, and I understood his silent message. From his perspective, our plan had gone off well, and when all was said and done, hopefully it would be game, set, and match to the good guys.

27

———

NEVE

THE NIGHT IN WHITE HOUSE DETENTION WASN'T THE most comfortable I'd ever spent, but it could have been worse. The West Wing's basement had what could only be described as posh holding cells. We were locked in, but they removed my zip tie cuffs. My cell was like a small college dorm room, with a twin-sized bed, a desk, and a chair. There was also a tiny bathroom with a folding door that provided some privacy, along with a desk lamp and a blank notebook and pen—maybe placed there so I could write out my confession. Staff members kept checking in to see if I needed anything, and they brought sandwiches for lunch and dinner.

I couldn't see or hear Con or Dr. Rodwell, but I assumed they were in similar accommodations. I started having uncomfortable flashbacks to Seclusion Room 3 as the minutes, then hours, ticked by, so it was something of a relief when a Secret Service agent knocked on the door. She took me to another room that looked like a police interrogation room. It was small and painted steely gray, with a metal table in the middle, three chairs, and a huge mirror on the wall which I assumed was two-way. The agent was joined by a uniformed officer, and they asked me a slew of questions while keeping the tone conversational.

I gave them the story we'd come up with to explain how I knew about Rodwell's plot without either involving poor Amos or making me sound like a loon. As a favor to him, I explained, Dr. Rodwell had asked me to retrieve some of his private patient files from the safe in his office. (He would deny that part, of course, but once they figured out that Dr. Rodwell was plotting to kill the president, we figured his credibility would be shot.) I told them I had picked up the president's file by accident. The latest memo had fallen out, and without meaning to, I glimpsed a few worrisome phrases. In the interest of patient safety, I'd read on. I claimed the Brickhaven membership and project list had been in the file as well, and that it caught my eye because it was on different letterhead. Once I figured out what I was looking at, I took pictures of a few of the documents and emailed them to myself before Dr. Rodwell caught me and had me committed to hide his nefarious plan. Fortunately, Con got worried when I didn't contact him as promised and came looking for me on the unit. After he succeeded in getting me out, I asked him for help warning the president, making use of my entirely coincidental invitation to the White House. At least that last part was both true and verifiable. I also confirmed for them that Con's recording was indeed of a conversation I'd had with Dr. Rodwell while he had me confined on the unit, though I could honestly say I had no idea how Con had obtained it.

Maybe Con was right and I was a good liar, because they appeared to believe me. I felt nauseated the whole time, and probably looked awful, but maybe they thought it was appropriate for me to be a ball of nerves under the circumstances.

There was another interrogation session a few hours later. This time, they asked about Amos and the apocalypse patients. I guessed Rodwell had mentioned them in a desperate attempt to absolve himself somehow, but I knew he couldn't prove there was any connection. After all, he'd told me himself that Brickhaven was unable to track whoever hacked into their servers, and that he'd told the nurses not to confiscate Amos's thumb drive at the hospital. Even if he had stolen a look at the thumb drive, I doubted Rodwell knew the Dead Parrot Protocol. Again, I gave the officers our rehearsed answer: Amos was a longtime patient with religious delusions and enough charisma to establish a dedicated online following, but their cases were unrelated to the Rodwell-Brickhaven saga or our trip to the White House.

On the way back to my cell after the second bout of questioning, the agent told me that Lee and Stephan had been raising quite a stink, demanding to know what happened to me. They had been told I was fine, just helping with an investigation into a security matter. She asked if I wanted her to relay any additional message. I thanked her for giving them that cover story and asked her to tell them I said not to worry, and that I'd call Stephan when we were finished.

By evening, the flashbacks to my confinement on Unit 4 had faded a bit. We were safe for the time being, I knew Con must be somewhere nearby, and we'd done our best to warn the president. We were hours late to meet Eric, so he was no doubt already in the process of getting us some help. Knowing all that gave me some sense of calm, and I fell into a patchy sleep.

I was already awake when another agent arrived in the morning with some travel-sized toiletries so I could freshen up. My presence was being requested at a debriefing, she said, after which I would be released. I asked if Con was being released as well, but she didn't answer. My heart lurched sideways as I quickly got ready.

A few minutes later, the agent took me upstairs. I was heartened by the fact that no other guards were with us; they must have decided I wasn't a threat after all. She led me into what appeared to be a small conference room, with a long table, chairs, and a coffee station set up in the far corner. Tears sprang into my eyes at the sight of Con standing in the back, looking rumpled but otherwise unharmed.

His face looked like a rough ocean with waves of competing emotions crashing into each other. But when he caught sight of me, intense relief and pure happiness washed the rest away. I threw myself into his arms and held on like he was the mast of a boat sailing through a hurricane.

As Con wrapped his arms around me, I was shocked to hear Eric's voice. "Neve!" he cried out, hugging me from behind.

I spun around. "Eric, what are you doing here?"

He shrugged, grinning broadly. "What can I say? When you guys didn't show up, I just couldn't bring myself to stay away and let you have all the fun. Don't worry, I called my lawyer first and gave him the low-down."

I smiled back, shaking my head. "You have a lawyer? Like, on standby?"

"Me? No. But Erik the Viking...."

"Ah, right," I said as he double-tapped the side of his nose. Risk being an unavoidable part of hacker life, I should have known Eric would be prepared for any eventuality.

Con planted a firm, lingering kiss on top of my head. "You all right?" he murmured.

His lips ignited a warm glow that filled my whole being. I decided then and there that there was nothing better in the entire universe than hearing Con's voice and being in his arms. "Yeah. You?"

He pulled away and looked down at me, as though

to verify for himself that I was, in fact, okay. "Grand." His forehead wrinkled with concern. "You look tired."

Before I could state the obvious—that the circumstances hadn't exactly been ideal for a solid night's sleep—another agent swept into the room, closely followed by Chief of Staff Liu. "Good morning, everyone," Liu said, his tone businesslike. "Have a seat and we'll get you out of here as quickly as possible."

Smiling broadly, I released Con. They were letting us out—all of us! We sat at the table, the three of us on one side and the three of them on the other.

Liu laid a thick file folder of papers on the table and opened it. "As you know, you're being released. The president extends his thanks for your cooperation and says he hopes your accommodations were comfortable," he said, though he didn't look up to see our response. "The documents and the sound recording you provided have been verified. Although you're guilty of several legal infractions, both minor and major"—Liu gave Eric a stern look—"we now know they were committed for the purpose of protecting the president. Therefore, no charges will be filed against you. However, due to the sensitive nature of the information you obtained, we must request your complete discretion and ask you to sign nondisclosure agreements. Agent Banai?"

The agent who'd accompanied Liu gave us the forms, along with three pens. Agent Banai reviewed the agreements with us quickly but comprehensively, making it clear that if we ever breathed a word to anyone about what happened or about what we knew of Brickhaven, the president, or the assassination plot, we would end up in a much less comfortable cell for a very, very long time. We were also informed that we would be monitored indefinitely, electronically and otherwise, to ensure our compliance. Eric started to object, but Liu said if Eric was unhappy with the terms, it wasn't too late to file those other charges he'd mentioned. After that, all three of us signed the agreements and handed them back.

"Good," Liu declared, taking the agreements and tucking them into his file folder. "Any questions so far?"

Tentatively, I raised my hand. "Can I ask what happened to Dr. Rodwell?"

"Dr. Rodwell will not be returning to work," Liu said brusquely. "The hospital has been told he's taking personal leave indefinitely. That's all I'm at liberty to say."

Although I would have preferred to hear he was in a jail cell somewhere, it still gave me a huge sense of relief to know Rodwell wouldn't be there when I returned to work.

"What about Brickhaven?" Con demanded. "They've already tried to lock up Miss Keane and throw away the key, and we suspect they wiped her email accounts. Christ knows what else they have up their sleeves."

"Indeed." Liu's sober acknowledgment sent my brief

moment of relief fluttering away like a cloud of starlings. "That brings me to the other issue we need to discuss today. We believe we've already neutralized the specific threats to Miss Keane—to all three of you," he continued. "While it's our expectation that you'll have no more trouble from Brickhaven, it'll take us some time to wrap things up completely. Until we give you the all clear, we ask that you remain alert. If anything unusual happens—calls from unknown numbers, phishing emails, suspected credit card fraud, even a feeling that you're being watched or followed—call Agent Banai immediately so we can look into it." He nodded to Agent Banai, who slid three business cards across the table.

"It'll take some time?" Eric took one of the cards and examined it. "Any idea how much?"

"It's hard to say," Liu replied. "It could be weeks, months—possibly longer."

Con frowned as he looked over at Eric, then at me. "Forgive my curiosity," he asked Liu, sounding anything but contrite, "but I'm wondering why you're thinking it'll take so long. It seems to me that Neve served the bastards to you on a silver platter."

Con appeared calm, but I sensed an intense energy building inside him. I took his hand under the table, half afraid he'd jump over it and strangle someone if they told him something he didn't want to hear.

"It's complicated," Liu said. "Brickhaven is a highly influential organization with well-respected members in high places. So far, their known activities have been perfectly legitimate, at least by Washington standards. The list of names Miss Keane gave us is only a small fraction of the larger organization. What the significance of this list is, we have yet to determine. It could mean nothing in terms of additional threats. Rodwell and a few of his colleagues may have simply gone rogue. However, this list could also represent a splinter group with its own agenda. Therefore, it'll take some time to complete our investigation."

"So it's not over." I only realized I'd said the words aloud when everyone turned to look at me. A flush of heat bloomed across my cheeks. "Sorry, I was just looking forward to getting back to normal. You know, feeling… safe." I swallowed so hard I was sure the whole room heard me.

Con leaned over and slid his arm around my shoulders. My body remained tense, but his closeness helped me take deeper breaths.

"Fear not, Miss Keane." Clearly Liu had no idea he was talking to an Olympic-class worrier. "If we didn't have a high level of confidence that you're safe for now, we wouldn't be releasing you. Our next steps are simply about mopping up and ensuring no future threats emerge. Just stay alert and let us know if anything concerning happens."

"What if we need to leave town?"

I had no idea why Con asked that question, but I

hoped it was because he knew of a remote private island where we could crash for a few years.

"No problem," Agent Banai said. "Just let us know beforehand so we can monitor any changes in threat levels and contact you if needed."

"Threat level changes, great." Eric's voice wobbled. "Anything else?"

The two agents and Liu looked at one another, some unspoken communication passing between them. "That's all for now," Liu announced. "We'll let you know if there are any developments."

"Right, so." Con tucked Agent Banai's business card into his shirt pocket. "Thank you for clarifying our situation. We'll let you know if we see anything amiss, will we not?" he asked, glancing at Eric and me.

"Yes, of course," I squeaked out.

"Yeah," Eric muttered. "Will do."

"Perfect." Liu stood. "We are at your disposal. The president extends his sincere gratitude for your service. What you did here will not be forgotten. Now, though, I'm sure you'd like to get home. You're free to go." Liu gave us one final nod, then turned on his heel and left the room.

The agents produced two black plastic bags and emptied them on the table. Con's keys, the USB half of my necklace, and both of our IDs were in one bag. The other held Eric's cell phone, laptop, wallet, and keys. Con pressed both buttons on his key fob, but nothing happened. Apparently they had erased the recording. I snapped what I assumed to be a now-empty flash drive back onto my necklace. Eric started to ask if his phone or laptop had been tampered with, but a raised eyebrow from Agent Banai made him think better of it.

"If you'll please follow me, I'll take you to your vehicles," the other agent said.

On the way to the parking garage, Eric explained that the day before, when we never emerged, he couldn't stay out of it knowing he might be able to help us. After all, he was the only one who could answer some of the tech questions he knew would come up, especially about the sound recording. After calling his lawyer, he contacted the White House and told them he had information that was relevant to our situation. He said they not so politely invited him to turn himself in.

"You didn't have to do that." I already felt guilty enough about getting Con involved, but I at least thought we had kept Eric out of the fray.

"Yeah, that wasn't the plan," Con added.

Eric threw his hands up. "C'mon, guys, don't take my hero moment away from me!"

"Sorry, Eric! Scratch that. I meant to say thank you." I threw my arms around him and squeezed.

Once we reached our cars, we decided to go back to my place to debrief. Con and I spent the short ride comparing notes on what happened to us after we were detained. It seemed our experiences had been more or less identical. I forced a laugh later when he caught me checking the mirrors to see if anyone was following us. I hadn't even realized I was doing it. Clearly Liu's words of caution had already seeped into my subconscious.

When we reached my apartment, exhaustion caught up with us, and we all collapsed in the living room. I was glad neither of them seemed in a hurry to leave. We needed to process what had happened. Plus, they both looked as tired as I felt, and the catch in Con's gait had become more pronounced, though he was doing his best to hide it.

I allowed myself to completely relax for a few minutes, long enough to get my second wind. Then, rejecting their offers of help, I left Con and Eric in the living room while I brewed a fresh pot of coffee, scrambled some eggs, and laid out fresh fruit.

Once breakfast was ready, we gathered around the kitchen table. Finally I got to ask the question that had been dogging me ever since the dramatic scene in the Roosevelt Room. "Okay, somebody has to tell me, how did you get that recording of my conversation with Dr. Rodwell from Seclusion Room 3? They asked me about it, and I couldn't tell them anything. How did it end up on Con's key fob?"

After exchanging a knowing look with Con, Eric began. "Do you remember the uproar over those personal assistant devices people bought for their homes? The ones we found out were recording and listening to our conversations without us knowing?"

"Yeah, I think I read something about that."

"It wasn't just personal assistant devices. I follow these kinds of stories because, well, *hacker*. Anyway, they recently discovered that a lot of other types of voice-activated wireless systems do the same thing—passively record stuff. Some of the newer versions of nurses' call handsets do it, too. There's a huge lawsuit about it right now because of patient privacy violations. Anyway, from the way you described the handset they gave you on Unit 4, it sounded like Capitol Hill General might have one of these newer systems, so I looked into it."

"You hacked into our hospital?" Somehow, that felt like a sacred violation to me.

"He did what he believed needed to be done," Con said, "just like you did, Miss Breaking and Entering."

Since I couldn't exactly argue with that, I just shook my head.

"Anyway," Eric said, "I confirmed that the nurses' handsets at your hospital are the type that use a passive-recording system. But I still had to try to find the specific recording from the exact time and place where you were being held, which was a whole other problem."

"One which you solved, evidently," I pointed out. "That's amazing, Eric. Genius, even."

"Aw, thanks, Neve." Eric smiled modestly. "I can't take all the credit, though. I mean, it was Con's idea to put the recording on his key fob."

"Oh, really?" I pressed my lips together to keep from smiling. Con wasn't exactly the king of tech.

"Hey," Con objected, "I might not be a computer whiz, but if they can put devices that record and play your voice into a teddy bear's paw, I figured we should be able to slip one into my key fob."

Eric squinted at him. "You didn't tell me about the talking teddy bears."

"The kids in pediatrics get them sometimes," he muttered. "Turns out it wasn't a crazy idea, and Eric found a way to make it work."

"Only with a lot of help from Shane, and not until the wee hours of Saturday morning." Eric rubbed his eyes. "It was touch and go for a while there."

"Well, as far as I'm concerned, that recording saved the day, and that's not an overstatement." I gave Eric a grateful smile, then shot Con a questioning look. "But why didn't you tell me that was in the works?"

"Eric wanted to," Con admitted, "but we couldn't be sure it would work."

"Like I said, we put it together at the last minute," Eric added. "We didn't have time to test it thoroughly. Con might have pushed those buttons, and poof— nothing happened."

Con nodded at me. "You already had enough to deal with, executing the main plan, without having to worry about that as well. The recording was only meant to be a backup, in any case. I decided it was best not to burden you with additional distractions."

"Distractions?" I asked, incredulous. "I'm not a gold-fish, you know! I can hold multiple things in my head at one time."

Eric jumped in. "Not to go off topic, but just FYI, goldfish can remember stuff for weeks." In response to my scowl, he held his hands up. "It's been proven!"

Con rubbed his hand slowly over his jaw. "Neve, no one's calling you a… goldfish? Not that it would neces-sarily be an insult," he said with a nod to Eric. "But you were exhausted, traumatized, and sleep-deprived. In my medical judgment, you'd already reached the limit of what you could handle both cognitively and emotionally. And that's not a criticism of your capabili-ties. I would have made the same call about anyone in your situation."

"But that wasn't your call to make," I said, trying to temper my exasperation. "I'm not your patient, Con. You can't just go around using your medical judgment to decide what you think I can and can't handle."

Con squinted in confusion. "What judgment would you prefer I use?"

Eric snorted with laughter. Then he saw the look on my face and tried to pretend he'd only been coughing.

"Oh for God's sake," I muttered. Was this a preview of what life with a doctor might be like? I already had to deal with Rosanna watching me like a hawk and asking to check my vital signs every time I sneezed. I pressed my palm against my forehead, trying to push away the beginnings of a headache. "I'd hoped you of all people would see me as something other than fragile and weak, and have faith that even after the attack, I can still handle things."

"Jaysus, Neve, what are you on about?" Con exclaimed. "You're the strongest, most resilient person I know. That's the point I was coming to. Even after everything you'd been through, including Rodwell's surprise appearance, when the crucial moment arrived, you were incredible. You did a brilliant job of presenting yourself and your case to the president so that when I did manage to play the recording, it was used to best effect."

Con appeared completely oblivious to the reasons for my annoyance. "I'm guessing that either you have no idea how patronizing that sounds, or you don't give a damn."

He confirmed it was the latter by dryly stating, "One of those, yes."

Eric pushed his chair away from the table. "Wait, hang on, you guys. I want to videotape this for posterity. I need to find my phone."

As he began patting down his pockets, Con and I looked on in confusion.

"Videotape what?" I asked.

Grinning, Eric paused his search. "I've always wondered who would win in a fight: Shadow Keane or Conman the Barbarian!" Leaning toward me, he whispered conspiratorially, "My money's on you, by the way."

"All the smart money would be, in fairness," Con acknowledged, comically somber.

"Good grief." I couldn't help smiling in spite of my unresolved irritation. "What am I going to do with you two?"

Eyebrow arched, Con said, "Well, while it lacks the drama of fighting, we could always celebrate."

"Awesome idea!" Eric pumped his fist into the air. "Man, I would have loved to see their faces when you played that recording. Twenty bucks says they're going to add electronic key fobs to the White House's 'prohibited items' list now," he said, absurdly proud.

"Aren't you're playing a bit fast and loose with that joint bank account?" Con quipped.

"Okay, ten bucks." Looking apologetic, Eric turned to me. "Seriously, though, Neve, I'm sorry if we messed up by not telling you about the recording. But overall, I don't think things could have gone any better, do you? I mean, of course, like you guys, I wasn't thrilled to hear that Brickhaven might still come after us."

"Understatement of the century," I muttered. Con reached over and gave my hand a squeeze.

"But we probably saved the president's life. How many people get to say that? And besides, I even like the guy. As a politician, I mean," Eric said a bit sadly. "Unlike you, I didn't actually get to meet him."

"He seemed sound," Con said, which I knew was high praise in his book.

"I was impressed, too." Maybe they were right, and we should take time to celebrate how well things had gone. After all, I could always argue with Con later.

All at once, it hit me on a visceral level. *Our plan worked. We saved the president. We're even still alive. And on top of that, there's Con and me.* Even when he was infuriating, having Con near me was still the best thing I'd ever experienced. My heart felt floaty, like it was filled with helium, and a warm sense of well-being permeated me.

Con stroked the back of my hand with his thumb. "Happy now, love?"

I nodded as my heart swayed. Not only did his touch make my breath catch, but he'd never called me "love" before. As a nickname, it definitely beat "Shadow Keane." I was both happy and in love. He'd nailed it in one.

28

CORNELIUS

One of the things Con loved most about Neve was her integrity, including the fact that she always did her best to keep her promises. However, he really wished she'd made a onetime exception in Stephan's case.

Con crouched over a tiny table in the corner of the Dupont Circle coffee shop, watching Neve and her ex sitting on the other side of the café. He hoped his flimsy folding chair would hold him for as long as it took Neve to crush Stephan's hopes for a reconciliation. He sipped the black coffee, which matched his mood, and consoled himself with the thought that if things went as he hoped they would, Con would be the only man on the receiving end of Neve's romantic promises from now on.

They'd only been released from the White House a few hours ago, and they had a full day planned. But Neve wouldn't be swayed from making this stop first, insisting she had promised both to call Stephan when they were released and to talk to him about their relationship that weekend. Stephan had tried to convince her to come over to his place to talk. Fortunately, Neve had suggested they meet at the coffee shop instead, saving Con the trouble of objecting.

Initially, Neve hadn't wanted Con to accompany her to the meeting, but it had taken very little effort to convince her that it was better she not go alone. That was all the proof he needed that, in spite of her strength, she didn't feel safe around that mealy-mouthed shitehawk.

In addition to that, while he'd never let on to Neve, Con was on edge ever since their final meeting at the White House. While Liu had expressed confidence that they were safe for the moment, he'd also said that could change. And instructions to stay alert and report anything unusual—Con knew those could throw Neve into an anxiety spiral, given half a chance. He was determined to stay by her side every second he could and try to keep her relaxed, distracted, and as happy as possible until they got the all clear from Liu—no matter how long that took. The trick would be finding a way to keep a close eye on her without scaring her even more. Fortunately, their new relationship should provide ample cover.

However, Stephan definitely did not fit in with that plan. While Con had talked her into letting him come along, Neve wanted time and space to handle things with her ex. They'd agreed that Con would sit as far away as possible, and that if Stephan recognized him at any point, they would pretend Con's presence was a coincidence.

Stephan walked in looking exhausted and relieved, a sign that he might be unlikely to make any real trouble. Con relaxed a bit and checked his email on his mobile while keeping one eye on Neve. While he had yet to receive a full assessment, some test results for his brother's fiancée, Ciara, had begun to trickle in from her doctors in Ireland. They had completed neurological exams, a comprehensive metabolic panel, toxicology screens, and an MRI of the head—all of which made him even more curious about what the presenting problem was. The test results had come back normal so far, and he was heartened by the fact that he knew one of her doctors, a neurologist who was top-notch. Con would have to find out more about Ciara's symptoms and what exactly her doctors were looking for, however, before he could offer Eamonn any useful insights. He would give his brother a call tomorrow.

After ten minutes or so, Con noticed that Neve began to look pained. He put away his mobile, ready for action. Stephan turned ashen, sitting back at first, then leaning forward and pleading with quiet intensity. Con could tell that even after all Stephan had put her through, it hurt Neve to give him the bad news. But he also knew she had a spine of steel, and her determination didn't appear to be flagging.

Con could tell the exact moment when Stephan realized he'd lost Neve for good, because his expression shifted from pitiful sorrow to cold ire. It took every bit of self-control Con could muster to keep from going over there when Stephan began spewing what were obviously angry and hurtful words. Seeing Neve's reaction tore at him. She didn't try to defend herself or stop Stephan's tirade. She simply looked down at her hands, carefully folded in her lap.

When had his radiant, valiant Neve perfected the art of pulling herself into a mental bomb shelter like that? How many times had she had to cope with this bastard's Jekyll and Hyde act?

The more disconnected Neve became, the louder Stephan's voice grew. Con held back in spite of his growing rage, reminding himself that it was her situation to handle as she saw fit. When she'd had enough, Neve shook her head, said a few final words, then grabbed her bag and coat. She walked out the front door without looking back, even as Stephan stood up abruptly and continued to hurl abuses after her.

Con left through the side door and met Neve at his car parked around the corner, as they'd planned. She was leaning against the door, her whole body shaking. He stepped in close to her, positioning himself like a shield protecting her from the world. He ducked his head down so he could see her eyes. They were full of fire.

She held her hand out and watched it tremble. "Don't worry," she said. "It's anger, not fear. Well, mostly."

Each time Con thought his admiration for Neve couldn't be any more profound, she surprised him. "Well done," he said. "All right, then. Let's get out of here."

He unlocked the car and helped her in. "Oh, bollocks," he said, feigning frustration. "I left my coat. Be right back."

"Okay," she said with a forced smile he knew was meant to reassure him that she was all right. He handed her the keys and went back to the coffee shop, this time through the front door.

Stephan was sitting at the same table, looking distressed and telling his woes to the unfortunate barista who had no doubt come over only to see if he needed a refill.

Con approached, catching Stephan's eye just as he reached the table. "Stephan."

Stephan blinked in surprise. "Yeah. Con, isn't it?"

Con was surprised Stephan remembered his name, given that they'd only met a couple times. "That's right. I didn't want to interrupt, but I was sitting across the room there, and I saw you with Neve."

"Oh yeah," Stephan muttered. "She just left. I have no idea where she went."

"You misunderstand. I'm not looking for her."

Stephan's face pinched in confusion. "You're not? Uh, what can I do for you, then?"

Con's deep voice rumbled. "You can tell me you're never going to bother her again."

More confusion on Stephan's face, followed by indignation, then outrage. Con watched him struggle through the procession of emotions. Finally Stephan straightened in his chair. "Oh, I get it! She hopped from my bed to yours, didn't she? Well, that was quick! And you poisoned her against me? It's all starting to make sense now!"

The fact that Stephan was behaving so predictably made it easier for Con to keep his anger under control. "You've got it wrong," he said in a low growl. "I'm just a concerned friend who knows what you did to her."

"Uh-huh." Stephan rolled his eyes dramatically. "Well, whatever story she told you, it isn't true. But I don't owe you an explanation, or anything else for that matter. What I do with Neve is not for you to say, asshole!"

Con rested his fisted knuckles on the table and leaned closer to Stephan, shooting him a lethal look. "If that's the case, then what I do with you if you ever bother Neve again is not for *you* to say." With a menacing wink, he added, "Arsehole, is it?"

Stephan's mouth opened and closed a few times. Con could almost read his thoughts. Had Con really just threatened him, and if so, was he serious?

In truth, the only thing that was keeping him from pummeling Stephan into the ground was the thought of how pissed off Neve would be if he got forcibly detained twice in twenty-four hours. Even at that, it was requiring colossal effort for Con to restrain himself, so he was pretty sure violent intent was rolling off him in waves so powerful that not even a gormless maggot like Stephan could miss them.

Indeed, the smug expression slid off Stephan's face as he copped on to the possibility of impending danger. Con waited a few more beats before asking, "Do we have an understanding?"

Stephan coughed and tossed his ridiculous hair as though trying to shake off the encounter. "I don't want anything more to do with that... that... woman." He spat out the last word as though he'd wanted to use a less polite term but had thought better of it.

Con's glare was as hard and sharp as a cut diamond. "Grand. I won't be seeing you, then."

As he turned to leave, Con heard Stephan whisper to someone, "Did you hear that guy just threaten me?"

Good, Con thought with some satisfaction. He'd made himself understood. Now Neve's future would be that much more peaceful.

She must have twigged that something was up, because when he got back to the car, she looked suspicious. "Where's your coat?"

"Oh, I forgot. I didn't bring one."

She gave him a wary side-eye. "Please tell me you didn't go all Neanderthal."

"I swear to you," Con said, holding out his hands to show his unbruised knuckles, "I didn't lay a hand on the man."

Although she still appeared somewhat skeptical, Neve said, "Okay, then."

He wasn't bothered that she hadn't entirely bought his innocent act. After all, he was sitting in the car next to the woman he loved, and she was safe and headed for as happy a life as he could give her.

As long as he had Neve, Con doubted anything would ever truly bother him again.

29

NEVE

THE BLUR OF PASSING TREES, STILL HANGING ON TO their colorful leaves, and the soft *clu-clunk, clu-clunk* sound as we drove over the seams in the highway soothed me. Eventually I stopped shaking. I was glad for the hour it took us to get to Baltimore. I needed that time to close my eyes and meditate on the fact that I was finally free of Stephan. I hoped that was the end of it, although I knew there might be a few more emotional voice mails and maybe even a drunken late-night visit before he gave up entirely. I also knew his emotional reaction to our breakup didn't have anything to do with me. He was simply unable to accept that anyone could ever reject what he had to offer. Well, there was nothing I could do about that. I set myself a new goal to try to think about Stephan as little as possible.

Con and I were glad to see Amos's comfortable

new setup in the research hospital where he was under the care of Faraz's colleague. He had a spacious private room with cheerful décor and bright windows, and they'd outfitted him with a laptop and a gaming headset. Amos was happy to see us, but he didn't appear surprised. He said his angel had told him to expect us.

We let Amos know that while we weren't able to give him any details, we *could* tell him that it was safe to stop worrying about the apocalypse.

With a wide grin, he said, "I know."

Con and I exchanged a glance. "How?" I asked.

"It wasn't the angel this time," Amos said, holding up a newspaper. "Today's edition."

We looked at the paper. Across the top of the front page, the headline read "President Duran to Host Middle East Leaders for Peace Talks at Camp David."

"I cut out a couple other articles for you, too," Amos said, grinning as he handed us two newspaper clippings. One headline announced "Primehook Security Head Faces Murder Charges." A photo of a man in a suit trying to duck cameras as he entered a courthouse was labeled "Riggs Sanderson, CEO of Primehook Security."

The second clipping read "Attorney General Taul Steps Down Due to Health Concerns." According to the article, Taul had tendered his resignation for unspecified medical reasons. President Duran announced the news during a press conference in which he praised Taul and thanked him for his long years of service.

"Good man," Con said, giving Amos's shoulder a squeeze. "I've never liked loose ends."

"I knew you could do it," Amos said, getting out of bed and embracing us both. "Thank you. I'm sorry if it turned out to be… hard."

"Don't worry about us," Con said. "You focus on getting better." He ordered Amos back into bed, and I promised him we'd keep checking in to see how things were going.

As I leaned down to hug him goodbye, Amos whispered, "You believe me now, don't you? About the angel, I mean?"

The part of me that was tempted to believe battled the skeptical part of my brain as I decided how to answer. "I believe in *you*, Amos, just like I always have."

"That's cool. Thanks, Neviah," he said, smiling contentedly.

Amos's new doctor took us aside to tell us that they found traces of SGLT-2 inhibitors in his tissues. Con blanched, explaining to me that SGLT-2 inhibitors were a class of medications that should never be given to a hypoglycemic patient, as they could induce a coma, or even cause death. According to Con, such medications had never been prescribed to Amos during his hospital stay. The new doctor couldn't imagine how the medication had gotten into Amos's system in that case, but Con and I had a fairly good idea.

We discussed it as we drove west to my parents' house for Sunday dinner. Rodwell had been on the unit when Amos had his hypoglycemic episode. He could easily have entered Amos's room without anyone raising an eyebrow and administered the medication. Con called and left Faraz a message, asking him to check the hospital's inventory of SGLT-2 inhibitors. It was a longshot, since Rodwell could have brought the medication in from outside, but Con thought it would be worth checking out. Perhaps they would find evidence that could put a nail in Rodwell's legal coffin.

It was chilling to realize that Rodwell's murderous intentions might well have extended beyond political assassinations to killing anyone who got in his way. The thought made me shudder.

"You all right?" Con asked.

I stared out the window as we turned off the expressway, leaving behind the heights and curves of the city's architecture. "Yeah, it's just… what happened to Amos. It's terrifying, sickening. To think, Rodwell was capable…. And Amos was so helpless…."

"Amos is fine." With one hand on the wheel, he rested the other on my leg and squeezed gently. "And so are you. Neve, I'm so sorry."

"No, I'm fine. It was just a bad moment."

"No, I mean I'm sorry I couldn't keep Rodwell from getting his hands on you." He gripped the steering wheel with both hands again, so hard that his knuckles turned white.

I turned to face him. "What? How…? Con, you had no idea what was even going on! And the second you found out, you straight up rescued me. Why would you apologize?"

His expression turned into a topographical map of grimness. "It won't make sense to you."

"Try me."

Shooting me an exasperated glance, he said, "After you were attacked, I was by your bed in the ER waiting for you to wake up. Seeing you like that, it put the heart crossways in me. I made a promise to myself that I wasn't going to let anything else happen to you. But it did." He cleared the catch from his throat. "I don't like to break promises."

At his words, a deep knowing settled over me, warm and blissfully inescapable: Orion had finally delivered the man of my dreams. My heart swelled, expanding until it felt like it was filling every inch of me.

My emotions were so intense, I couldn't speak. Instead, I sat back in my seat and leaned sideways toward Con, tucking my hand into the crook of his elbow and brushing a soft kiss over his shirt sleeve before resting my cheek against his arm. I could feel his gaze on the top of my head. It felt like the sun.

We were halfway to my childhood home in Mount Airy when Rosanna called Con's cell phone. We put her on speaker, and she reported that the word had come down: Rodwell was out on personal leave indefinitely due to a "family emergency."

"That was us, wasn't it?" she asked.

"Indeed it was, Lolly," Con confirmed.

Cheerfully, she declared, "I knew it."

Unfortunately, when I asked if that meant I could come back to work on Monday, the news wasn't good. Rosanna said hospital administration had launched an internal investigation into my involuntary hospitalization by Rodwell, and Risk Management was insisting I stay home on paid leave until it was complete. The investigation was projected to take a month at least, maybe longer.

When I objected, both Con and Rosanna came down on me mercilessly, pointing out that most employees would be grateful for a month of paid leave and urging me to take some time for myself "for once." Rosanna put forward her "adopt an alpaca" suggestion again, and I teased Con by revisiting the idea of the full-sleeve tattoo. Eventually I gave up complaining. It wasn't going to get me anywhere with those two.

When I asked if she knew how the apocalypse patients were doing since their discharge, she said they'd followed up with everyone, and all reported they were doing just fine—and still sticking to their "amnesia" stories. I was relieved to hear that their involvement in Amos's plan hadn't led to any negative aftereffects.

After we said goodbye to Rosanna, we drove on in silence for a while, lost in our own thoughts. My mind kept drifting back to Amos's question: Did I believe him about the angel? Given everything that had happened over the past week, I felt like everything I thought I knew had been tossed in the air like a handful of Pick-up sticks, and I had no idea how they would eventually land.

I wondered what Con's take was on the metaphysical aspect of the whole drama. Since we were still a few minutes away from my parents' house, I ventured, "What do you think about Amos's whole 'angel' thing?"

Con stared hard at the road in front of us, contemplating. "Well, I'll tell you," he said. "One thing I know for certain is that there is a God."

My eyes widened. That was unexpected. "You do?"

"Yes." He nodded solemnly. "But not because of Amos or his alleged angel. It's because you're here—here on Earth, in existence, I mean. And here with me. Only a generous deity could be behind that."

Unable to keep from smiling, I poked his shoulder. I suspected Con didn't believe a word of the angel stuff, and I wanted to know just how simpleminded he thought I was for being open to the possibility. "Hey, I'm being serious. I really want to know what you think."

Con's expression betrayed nothing in the long pause before he spoke. "Well, visual and auditory hallucinations would be consistent with the progression of Amos's illness," he said, his tone measured. "He's also a hacker with a gift for convincing other people to do his bidding. As resourceful as he his, he could have recruited an accomplice on hospital staff, bugged your office, put eavesdropping malware on your phone—who knows what. Putting all that together...."

When he shrugged, my heart sank like a river rock. He wasn't wrong. There were alternative explanations for how Amos knew what he knew that I hadn't fully explored. Then again, I hadn't told Con everything that had happened during my unauthorized visit to Amos's hospital room. Even if there were no angels involved, some of the things that had transpired simply defied reason. Someday, when we had time, I'd give Con the blow-by-blow. Until then, I figured he'd be wondering how gullible I was. "Putting all that together, you must think I'm a complete idiot for believing Amos to the extent that I broke into Rodwell's office."

"Hey." Con reached over and gently squeezed my arm. "You wanted my opinion on Amos, so I gave it to you. Don't use that to put words in my mouth—especially not ugly ones."

"What else *could* you think, though? Turn here."

Con pulled the car into my parents' driveway. "I think you experienced something powerful, something you didn't know how to explain." He parked, turned off the ignition, and turned to face me. "You'd been through hell. Then something extraordinary happened. You didn't even have time to process it before Rodwell slapped restraints on you. Since then, you've been going full tilt, trying to save the president's life and stay out of harm's way. Maybe you believed something that I don't, but for Christ's sake, I think you're completely *brilliant*. How could you believe I'd think you an idiot?"

"Because part of me still believes Amos really might have been talking to an angel," I confessed to both Con and myself. "And my rational mind despises me for that."

"Well, tell your rational mind it can feck off, then." He raked his hand through his hair. "You can't blame yourself for not having the answers to questions people have been wrestling with for thousands of years. Even I've seen things that seemed miraculous, things I can't explain. It's sheer arrogance for any of us to claim we know everything there is to know. I may have lost my faith, but that doesn't mean I look down on people who haven't."

I was relieved to hear that Con was so broad-minded about the issue, but I wasn't surprised. After all, it was consistent with the rest of his character.

Before I could tell him so, however, we heard the slap of the screen door closing.

"Hey, you two!" my mother called cheerfully as she and my dad stepped out onto the front porch.

I wasn't prepared for the rush of relief I felt when I saw their faces. I knew Con had been trying to distract me from my anxiety about the potential of future threats from Brickhaven, and he'd been doing a pretty good job. But when we climbed the porch steps of my parents' sprawling farmhouse, that cocoon of safety contrasted so sharply with the week we'd had, it brought stinging tears to my eyes.

I embraced my parents, overwhelmed by the love I felt for them, and by regret that there was so much I couldn't share with them. As we stood making small talk, Con must have sensed that I was in need of support. He placed his hand on the small of my back, and his touch steadied me.

My parents' delight at Con's presence was amplified when they picked up that romance was in the air. Neither Con nor I said anything, but we must have been transmitting subtle cues. At one point, Con brushed a stray lock of hair out of my eyes, and my mother practically swooned. My parents didn't even ask about Stephan, which confirmed what I'd always suspected: they'd supported my former relationship only because they supported me, not because they liked my ex.

While I was helping my mother set the table, Con got a phone call. He said it was his brother, Eamonn, and stepped into the living room to answer it. I couldn't make out what he was saying, but there was a note of concern in his voice. When he rejoined us, he explained that Eamonn's fiancée, Ciara, had been suffering from health issues recently. Earlier in the week, Eamonn had asked him to consult on the case. Con had only seen a few tests results so far and didn't have the full picture yet. Eamonn had just called to let him know that Ciara's doctors couldn't find anything physically wrong with her, so they had moved on to evaluating her for mental health issues.

Pushing aside my surprise that he hadn't mentioned the situation before, I offered to help if I could. Con said Ciara's treatment team would be sending over more records, so he would ask Eamonn if I could look them over as well, given my area of expertise.

I could tell that Con remained troubled by the phone call throughout dinner, although he did a good job of hiding it from my parents. He asked them to share their wildest tales of teaching college. My dad told us that one day, the class clown came in with a "pet" cockroach tied to a leash made of thread, sending half the students screaming and running. Dad's response had been to explain that they had a "no pets" policy in the classroom, which resolved the problem without leaving any room for the student to object—or hurting the cockroach's feelings. When our laughter died down, Con quipped that he could see now where I'd learned my creative problem-solving skills.

After several more stories like that, my parents had our sides aching from laughter. Then Con wanted to hear stories about me as a girl. Mercifully, my parents didn't share any really embarrassing ones, although my mother did tell him about my unique relationship with the constellation Orion and how I used to plead with it to bring me the man of my dreams. I was mortified, but Con said the story was charming.

The dinner itself was a culinary work of art. My mother had gone all out, making a four-course meal that combined her favorite Southern cooking recipes with French and Italian touches. Meanwhile, Con complimented her cooking with every other bite he took. By the end of the evening, I was certain my parents thought he walked on water.

When the time came, we said our goodbyes and walked out to his car, putting it between us and the house to shield us from prying eyes as we stood admiring the clear, mild night. Con peered up at the sky and asked me to point out Orion. When I did so, he had a stern word with the mythical hunter, mock-threatening to destroy him should anyone in the Milky Way try to push Con aside and send a different man into my life.

The sweet moment didn't last long, however. Soon, a troubled look returned to Con's face. As we leaned back against the car and continued to stare into the sky, I asked why he hadn't told me earlier about his concerns for Ciara.

"You've had a few other things on your plate." Other than a quick wink, his expression remained somber. "I'm more worried about Eamonn than I am about Ciara, in truth. I know one of her doctors, and I'm confident she's in good hands. But my brother always says I'm the only doctor he really trusts. Talking to him just now… well, he sounded a bit shook. He would never come right out and ask me to come to Cork, but I think he could use some boots-on-the-ground support. I haven't been home in over five years, so I'm a bit overdue for a visit anyway."

I knew Con hadn't been to Ireland since we'd met, but I didn't realize it had been that long. He rarely volunteered any information about his family, and the few times I'd asked about them, he'd deflected with humor or given only brief answers. For reasons he kept to himself, his family had never been a topic he wanted to discuss.

I didn't allow myself to indulge in any selfish thoughts about how desperately I would miss him if he went to Ireland. Of course, it made sense for him to go. I knew how hard it would be for him to leave his patients, though, so I decided to give him a little encouragement. "You and Faraz cover for each other all the time, right? I'm sure he'd be happy to look after your caseload."

"You think I should go, then?"

"Well, it sounds like your family needs you, and five years *is* a long time. Plus, you've never taken a vacation that I know of."

He peered down at me. "You're one to talk, Miss 'Please don't make me take time off work, oh please, please, Lolly, have mercy on my soul.'"

I grinned. "You're the only one who calls her Lolly. But yes, I think you should go if you want to, if Eamonn needs you."

"Hmm." He rubbed his chin. "Well, thanks to

modern electronic devices, I suppose I can leave the office without really leaving. I would plan for it to be a bit of a working vacation." With a solemn look, Con reached out to take my hands. "You'll have to come with me, though."

A kaleidoscope of butterflies fluttered through my stomach. "What?"

"I won't leave you here on your own. You can't go back to work for a month at least, am I right?"

My breath caught in my throat. "You're really worried, aren't you? You're worried *they* might do something."

"Ah, stop." He stepped close enough to me that I could feel the warmth of his body. "Liu said we're safe, and he doesn't seem like a man to mince words."

"That's true, I guess." I'd been half afraid to ask Con whether he believed Liu's assurances about our safety. It was a profound relief to hear he did.

Con put his hands on my shoulders and began to massage gently. Heat spiraled down into my arms and through my torso. "What I'm *worried* about is that left home alone, you'd go mad with boredom. Every gorgeous inch of you could be covered in tattoos by the time I get back," he said, eyes roaming my body for effect. "I do realize it's more of an extended holiday than a date, but assuming you'll get approval to travel after your scan tomorrow—"

"Wait, what scan?" I bounced from excitement to

confusion. "You mean for my tumor? I haven't scheduled one yet."

Con waved his hand dismissively. "I'll set it up. If Dr. Mohinder says you can go, we could leave within days."

He would set it up? All I wanted was to forget about the damn tumor, but of course Con would put my medical issues before romance. Even worse, he was probably right. I should get it checked out. I had promised Rosanna, after all. And it wouldn't do to get a bout of encephalitis while vacationing abroad.

The thrill I felt at the idea of going with him was undeniable, but it was tempered by a dose of nerves. Taking an extended trip together would be intense, especially given the serious family circumstances.

On the other hand, we already knew each other better than many long-established couples. Plus, I hated the idea of being away from him even for a few days, let alone weeks. And the prospect of going away with Con, meeting his family, spending time with him in his home country…. It was all so romantic, and far too tempting to even consider turning down. Remembering that I might actually be able to help Con with his brother's fiancée's case gave me the final push I needed.

"It would be one hell of a first date," I said, smiling up at him. "I'd love to go."

Con's face glowed in the starlight. I slid closer, surrendering to the urge to lean against him. I wanted to feel his presence in every sense, just to be sure he was really there and that we were actually embarking on this dizzying affair.

"Brilliant!" Looking exultant, he ducked his head down and placed his lips close to my ear. "Since you're coming home with me, would you like to learn a little Irish?"

The heat of his breath on my ear. The vibration of his deep voice against my skin. I shivered with pleasure. "Sure."

Con released my hands and laid his on my shoulders. Then he dipped his fingers inside the collar of my coat, touching the bare skin of my collarbone and tracing a slow, sizzling trail upward until two of his fingers rested against the soft hollow of my neck. I could feel my pulse beating against his touch.

"Repeat after me," he murmured. "*A chuisle mo chroí.*"

I had never been good with foreign language pronunciation, but I cleared my throat and did my best. "*A chuisle mo chroí.*"

Our eyes met like waves crashing. "Well done. You're a natural."

"Thanks for lying," I said. "What does it mean?"

"It means 'the pulse of my heart.'" Con moved his hands up to cradle my chin. "That's what you are to me, you know."

I wanted to reply, but the emotion in Con's eyes pushed every word from my mind.

"Well, that's one oversight corrected. I've asked you on a proper date." He lowered his eyes to study my lips. "But there was another one you mentioned, back at the safe house. Remember?"

My legs quivered. I remembered perfectly. It was the thing I'd been dreaming about every day since the first day we'd met, the day he'd blown into hospital rounds, inserting himself into my fantasies and storming his way into my heart.

My mouth began to water. I swallowed, searching for my voice. "Mm-hmm."

His eyes traveled back up to meet mine. "Well, I'd say it's wrong to let that oversight stand. Wouldn't you agree?"

Con's breathing was ragged. In his eyes was a combination of raw hunger and a determination so strong that I knew beyond a doubt the kiss I'd been pining for was about to happen.

The second I managed a nod, Con's mouth was on mine. I inhaled sharply at the rough warmth of his lips. At first he was gentle, as though searching for some kind of answer. All at once, everything that had passed between us over two years rose inside me like a flash flood—the friendship, the suppressed attraction, the longing, the danger we'd gone through, the trust we'd built. My mouth responded to his like a flame finding oxygen, giving Con the answer he was seeking. His kiss transformed from questioning to adamant.

In reaction, a frenzied desire tore through me. *What*

is happening? I wondered, shocked by my sudden and acute hunger. I'd kissed men before, of course, but this was something else—something far beyond just a kiss. I needed his lips on mine as desperately as I needed air.

Con's mouth continued to devour mine as he pushed open my coat and grasped me around the waist, lifting me until I stood with my toes on top of his shoes. Then, with one step, he rotated us, resting me against the car. The hard, unyielding metal behind me and Con's warm hands holding me in place seemed to flip a switch inside me. My body put me on notice: it was going to do whatever it wanted to from there on in, whether or not I approved. As though possessed, I flung my arms around his neck and arched my back, desperate to be closer to him, ever closer.

Con moved his hands up to cradle the back of my head and slid his fingers into my hair. As I squirmed, my chest rubbed against his, and a cry of longing parted my lips. He deepened our kiss once again, swallowing each sound I made. His tongue lit a fire that seared my blood and sensitized my skin. It seemed as though our kiss was drawing down the heat of every star in the sky.

When it felt as though my very bones might melt, I pulled my mouth away from his in a brief surge of panic. We both gasped. Our eyes locked, and I knew from his expression that my gaze mirrored the combination of awe and ravenous desire I saw in his.

Con's voice was thick. "You all right?"

"Yeah, I just—" But before I could continue, an urgent longing surged painfully through my body, demanding that my mouth find Con's again immediately. "Kiss me," I whispered, tightening my arms around his neck. "Kiss me and don't stop."

To my torment, he resisted the pull of my arms, holding himself back. For a few beats, he looked into my eyes, searching. His gaze held the potent force of a vow, wordlessly pressing home the seriousness of his intent. I sensed that if Con had his way, he would be the only man I kissed from that moment until one of us took our last breath. Finally, he leaned down and claimed my mouth once again, as though he wanted the whole universe to be our witness.

Suddenly there was no more Con, no more me. There was only our kiss, a blazing inferno.

A wisp of fear curled through my mind like smoke. *What if it's all too intense? What if the fire consumes us completely?*

But as the heat forged us together, my fear left as quickly as it came. No matter what happened, we had become one. Even if we were devoured by a fiery incandescence, we would simply rise up into the night sky, forming a new constellation, an eternal kiss. And eternity might just be long enough.

———

Thank you so much for reading *Dead Sound*! I certainly

hope you enjoyed it. If you'd like to help spread the word, please consider telling a friend, or taking a few minutes to leave a review on your favorite book website. Reviews really do help readers discover new books they'll love. Thanks again for your support. It is deeply appreciated!

Sign up for my newsletter, read about my work, and more on my website:
https://AniseEden.com

ABOUT THE AUTHOR

Anise Eden writes suspense novels with thriller, romance, and paranormal elements. She is the author of the multi-award-winning Healing Edge Series. Originally from the US, Anise lives in Ireland with her husband and her canine writing companion.

facebook.com/authoraniseeden
twitter.com/aniseeden
bookbub.com/profile/anise-eden

ACKNOWLEDGMENTS

First and foremost, I would like to express my gratitude to my wonderful readers. It is you who breathe life into these characters and stories, and who inspire me to keep writing.

I would like to extend my heartfelt thanks to my fabulous editor Kristin Scearce, Rebecca Johnson, and the rest of the extraordinary team at Tangled Tree. I'm so grateful for your tremendous support, your enthusiasm for *Dead Sound,* and the warmth with which you have welcomed me into your publishing family!

Special thanks to Rosanna Leo and Shannon Rowan, not only for your feedback on those painful early drafts, but also for your unwavering support, encouragement, and friendship.

Many thanks to the following:

To the wonderful members of the Mallow Writer's Group for making me feel at home in my new home, and for lending me your kind and patient ears as I shared the same (slightly edited) passages of *Dead Sound* over and over again. Extra-special thanks to the Suspicious of Scones Sisterhood.

To Andrea Hurst for your editorial feedback, wise advice, and kind encouragement.

To the Paw Paw Book Club for your warm hospitality, enthusiasm, and support.

To wonderful *anam cara* Dr. Jean Ayers, for teaching me so much about my own mental health, and to the excellent Dr. Craig Haber for inspiring me to write an endocrinologist hero.

To my amazing friends for your enthusiasm, support, encouragement, and love. No matter how far apart we are or how long it's been since we've seen one another, I hope you know how dear you are to me, and that I hold you in my heart.

As always, my deepest gratitude goes out to my beloved parents and family for your unconditional love, support, and belief in me. Every day in big and small ways, you truly keep me going, and you mean more to me than words could possibly express.

And finally, to my husband (and expert plot doctor) —you are my inspiration, my reason, and my heart's safekeeping. Thank you for being you, for keeping me laughing (even in lockdown!), for loving without ceasing, and for never letting go.

facebook.com/tangledtreepublishing

twitter.com/ttpubs

instagram.com/hottreepublishing